THE ART OF REDEMPTION

THE ART OF REDEMPTION

S. B. Bell

ISBN: 1505589223
ISBN 13: 9781505589221
Library of Congress Control Number: 2014922379
CreateSpace Independent Publishing Platform
North Charleston, South Carolina

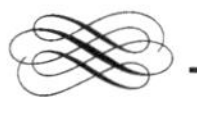

PART I

The quality of life is in the mind, not in the material.

Malcolm S. Forbes

On May 15th, my life changed. I changed and the world around me changed. The birth of all things, both good and evil, begins with the common element of change. I have often wondered if the evolution of man's life and mankind, both significant and small, are shaped by man's deeds or a divine, intelligent plan?

As I sit on the precipice of my own life, I look to the horizon of existence for the answer. Was it will or fate that changed my life that day?

Written by Bryce Elliott two months before his death.

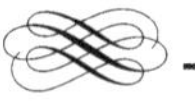

Prologue

Berkeley, California, 1960. The birth of Bryce Elliott.

THE NEW DOCTOR, a young, hopeful resident, closed his eyes and listened for the familiar pitter-patter of a budding life, but instead heard only a faint, barely audible, throbbing. He turned to the doctor entering the room. "The heartbeat—it's very weak."

"Have you attended a cesarean section before?" the doctor asked.

"Yes, several. None with complications though."

"Okay, well, let's see that this is like the others." The doctor approached the anguished mother. "Elizabeth, we've detected that the baby is in distress, so we are going to perform a cesarean section. Do you understand?"

"Please, please don't let anything happen to the baby!" the mother pleaded, tears welling in her eyes and spilling down the sides of her face. "Please, I beg you." She extended her arm out to touch the doctor. "And don't put me to sleep. I want to be awake when my baby is born and—"

"Don't worry, you're both going to be fine." He turned away from her and addressed the resident. "Okay, sedate her with paraldehyde."

As Elizabeth Elliott was being sedated, the nurse prepped the bulging abdomen, and the medical team waited for the drug to take effect.

"Okay, doctor. Patient's ready," the resident declared.

"As soon as I make the final cut through the uterus, you're going to have to get that baby out."

"Right, doctor," the resident replied. He watched him cut a long incision beginning at the navel and extending twelve inches down the protruding stomach.

"Follow me; I'm just about to clear through the uterus," he instructed the resident. "When I say go, gently reach in from the bottom and pull the baby out. If there's no cord around the baby, pull in one long, continuous, smooth movement while supporting the back and head."

The resident nodded. He was so nervous that he could actually hear his own heart pounding in his ears. He'd delivered two difficult vaginal births, but nothing had prepared him to reach through a surgical incision and pull out a distressed baby.

He glanced at a mirror that reflected the mother's face behind the surgical curtain. It was a landscape of emotion. Hope and hopelessness, excitement and terror, promise and despair. When the word "go" sliced though the room, he reached his gloved hands in and pulled. The head emerged face down and there was no sign of a wrapped cord, so he continued in one unbroken movement, just as the doctor had instructed.

Elizabeth looked into a mirror that reflected the delivery and saw the lifeless, blue baby enter the world. She let out a primal cry that seared the room. "Oh please, God, noooo!" she wailed. Not *my* gift, from God!"

"Doctor, there's a knot in the umbilical cord!" the resident said in a low hushed voice. His mind stumbled on the thought, *stillbirth is the most heartless blunder of fate.*

"I see it. I see it!" The doctor's face twisted in alarm as he cut the cord and gazed at the blue baby. "Quick over there!" he called out and motioned for the resident to carry the baby—a boy—to a side table.

For a moment, only Elizabeth's muffled sobs and prayers broke the room's silence. "Divine God of life, do not let this baby die!" She chanted over and over, the tone of her voice shifting from pleading to commanding. Several nurses quickly encircled her in an effort to shield her from witnessing the effort to resuscitate the blue baby boy with crimson lips.

The suctioning did nothing. "Okay, I'm going for an intubation," the doctor said, shoving a tube down the baby's throat. He began pumping a bag connected to the tube. "Breathe please, baby, breathe," he whispered. The baby remained lifeless. "Shit. What next? Electroshock or tracheotomy?" he muttered.

"I don't know," the resident managed to mumble. He was sinking into the realization that the baby was dead.

From outside the OR, the medical team could hear Elizabeth's friends and husband join in her chant. "Divine God of life, do not let this baby die! Divine God of life, do not let this baby die!"

"How about hundred-volt paddles to the chest?" the resident suggested, figuring there was no point in cutting up the dead baby with a tracheotomy.

The doctor shouted, "*Clear*!" and pressed the paddles to the baby's chest. The little infant's body arched up and slammed, with surprising force, back down on the table. "Forgive me. Forgive us," the doctor silently said to himself.

Elizabeth seemed to still herself as a sudden, strange gust of wind enveloped the entire windowless room. Like a whirling mass of energy, the wind seemed to draw everything toward the lifeless baby.

"Where in the hell did that come from?" someone asked.

"*Kamikaze*, the wind is divine!" Elizabeth murmured.

Suddenly, a faint cry of new life pierced the sorrowful room. In stunned amazement, the team watched as the baby's pallid color slowly transformed into healthy pink and his cries grew stronger. The doctor's eyes filled with amazement. He walked the squirming boy over to Elizabeth. As he handed her the baby, he whispered, "Your gift from God."

ONE

New York City, 1998

"Ah, today is a good day, a very good day!" Bryce Elliott thought while lowering the ramp on his treadmill and increasing the pace from a jog to a run. The floor-to-ceiling windows in his Trump Tower condo provided an unobstructed view of Fifth Avenue and Central Park from his private gym. In a couple hours, he would be halfway toward achieving one of his life goals: appointment to chairman of Mortimer & Weintraub. Today he and hundreds of friends, family, clients, and colleagues would be bidding old man Solomon Weintraub *bon voyage* and sailing him off into the sea of retirement.

"Bryce, are you about finished working out? We need to go in forty-five minutes. You know how Mummy and Daddy get so bent out of shape when we're late," Lydia Mortimer Elliott chimed from the doorway.

Bryce glanced at Lydia, successfully hiding his disdain for his wife of ten years. Although she was thirty-eight, the extra fifteen pounds on her 5'4" frame and her overly-done, shoulder-length blond tresses added years to her appearance.

"Don't worry, dear," Bryce responded, looking at his wife in the mirrored wall.

"Do you think I should wear my grey Prada suit or the new Chanel dress?" she asked, walking across the room to face her husband.

"Either one; you look smashing in both," he lied with a friendly wink.

Despite all her shortcomings, and there were many, Bryce knew that Lydia Mortimer—the only child of Abraham Mortimer—was the woman for him the day he'd met her at the Harvard Law School summer alumni party; the annual event was hosted by her parents at their summer estate in the Hamptons.

"Oh, please pick one," she pleaded in a little girl's voice, dangling both choices in front of him.

Bryce's eyes panned to a bronze plaque he'd commissioned when he was a freshman at Yale. Its simple inscription, "100 by 40," provided the motivation and reason behind just about everything Bryce did. The plaque hadn't been cheap, but even though he was on a scholarship and money was tight, it had been worth every penny.

During his college days, Bryce had no qualms about sharing his iron-clad goal: to make one hundred million dollars by the time he was forty. He believed money alone could emancipate a man from the shackles of a powerless, meaningless life. He wasn't going to be a do-gooder like his father had been—always out to save the world and every stray soul that crossed his path. No, Bryce's path was different.

Eight months from now, Abraham would follow Solomon down the yellow brick road to retirement, and he, Bryce Elliott, would take his place as the wizard of the most prominent mergers and acquisition law firm in the world. With that, he'd be awarded 30 percent interest in the firm's partnership—putting him at one hundred million dollars a few months shy of his fortieth birthday.

"*Ahem*, earth to Bryce!" Lydia snapped her fingers in front of Bryce, breaking his reverie. "What should I wear?" she asked.

He looked away from the plaque and back at Lydia, and with a big-picture mindset, he decided, as he always did, that she did not look so bad after all.

"I think you'd look great in the Prada," he managed between gasps for air. By the last five minutes of his rigorous, hour-long workout, his entire body was drenched in sweat.

"Thanks," Lydia responded with the hazy smile that seemed to be perpetually etched on her face. "Now get off that thing before you have a heart attack!"

Bryce responded with a tight grin and lowered the speed back down to a slow jog for his cool-down period. *Not to worry, dear Lydia*, he thought to himself as she left the gym to get dressed. *There's not a chance in hell I'm going to bite the dust before I reach the pinnacle of my life.*

Forty-five minutes later, the Elliotts, radiating self-importance, made their way to their car, which had been pulled around for them by a valet in their building. They were so impervious to the world around them, that they both came close to tripping over a homeless man taking a late afternoon siesta on the sidewalk between their building and their car. Lydia stopped herself and walked around the small blight, while Bryce made a point to step over the neglected and lost soul. The man's plight was downright inexcusable. Bryce thought to himself, *Every man has choices in life and this guy, plain and simple, has fucked up.*

"God, that pisses me off!" Bryce said to no one in particular. "I shouldn't have to put up with that shit after shelling out over a million bucks in taxes last year and fifteen grand a month in condo fees! Even Fifth Avenue is beginning to resemble a human billboard of economic diversity."

Just as Bryce passed over the man, he felt a shock course through his entire body. Every muscle in his body locked up and he collapsed.

"My God, oh, Bryce!" Lydia dropped to his side and grabbed his hand.

The doorman rushed over. "Mr. Elliott, sir, are you alright?"

Bryce glanced at both of them with a look that demanded they get him up. After they helped him to his feet, he ran his hand over his four-thousand dollar Brioni suit to straighten it out.

"Are you okay? I hope—" Lydia asked.

"Yes. Let's go," Bryce interrupted, even though his head was buzzing.

Once in the sanctity of the car, Bryce quickly locked the doors in an effort to escape the crowd that had loosely formed around the scene. Thankfully, it was a Saturday morning, and the streets of midtown were empty of anyone who mattered.

"Bryce, what happened?"

"Just forget about it, Lydia. Let's enjoy our drive up to your parents."

"Okay, darling. It's been ages since we've had a whole hour to ourselves. You look wonderful in your new suit!" she added and pecked the side of her husband's face with a kiss. His penetrating blue eyes, raven black hair, and sharp features made him look more like a leading man, as opposed to an obsessively driven one.

From most peoples' perspective, when Bryce and Lydia announced their engagement, it had been hinted that Lydia Mortimer had hit the jackpot in the husband department. Bryce's competitive nature, chameleon charm, and superior intellectual prowess had secured him a top spot at whatever he set his sights on. He'd graduated *summa cum laude* in his class at Yale and won a Rhodes scholarship to Oxford. His experience in England helped him cultivate and refine his social skills and prepared him for Harvard Law School, where he took advantage of every precious second, graduating again at the top of his class and networking his way through the entire institution. When he finished law school, every firm in the country was vying for him, but he only had eyes for Mortimer & Weintraub, rainmakers of the business and legal world—the *crème de la crème*.

Bryce turned on the ignition and listened intently to the idling sound of his three-month-old Porsche. *Whir-ummm ...whir-ummm...whir-ummm.* "Listen to that!"

"What?"

"The timing's off! I should have gone with a Ferrari!" He slammed his hand on the steering wheel and then zoomed away from the curb, narrowly missing a pedestrian in the crosswalk.

Lydia slipped a random CD into the player. Bryce shook his head and had to give his wife credit. As little as she understood about him, she had learned that music took the edge off. The autumn canopy of trees lining the banks of the river glowed with October hues of red, brown, and gold. By the time they hit the traffic coming off the George Washington Bridge, Bryce had forgotten the events of the morning and was fervently singing along with Jim Morrison. "Come on baby light my fire, try to set the night on *fire*!"

For the next half-hour Bryce zoomed along the Henry Hudson Parkway, singing along with *The Best of the Doors* at the top of his lungs. His enjoyment was so infectious that Lydia joined in on "Break on Through

(To the Other Side)" and "Riders on the Storm." Like Sonny and Cher, the Elliotts bayed at passing cars. Bryce knew every single lyric, hit every note, and his body swayed in unison with the rhythm. Lydia, who was more than slightly tone-deaf, did the best she could.

When the music stopped, Bryce was uneasy about letting this side of him show in front of Lydia. It was rare for him to do that, but some music—particularly his parents' favorite raunchy rock and roll from the seventies—had a visceral effect on him.

Before he was born, his parents had formed a commune with a group of eight friends, and they had collectively purchased a large, run-down, Julia Morgan Craftsman house in Berkeley, California. The members of the Hearst Street Commune had been altruistic, liberal intellectuals. His mother, Elizabeth, was a deeply spiritual, mystical woman, who believed that all religions had merit; she pulled freely from many of them, easily interchanging the Hail Mary with a Tibetan mantra. His father, Joseph, a tall man with shoulder-length black hair and blue eyes like his son's, had worked as an associate professor of philosophy at Berkeley. He'd won many prestigious writing awards but, like other writers, had made little money from it.

"That was so much fun!" Lydia gushed. "Where in the world did this come from?" she asked, holding up the Doors' CD cover.

Bryce tightened his grip on the steering wheel. He silently admonished himself, *Shit, that was careless.* Now he'd have to come up with a reason for why the CD they'd just listened to was in his car. He was normally very careful to keep his love of the sixties and seventies music private. He thought of the Rolling Stones CDs hidden away in the trunk.

"Must have been left by George," he mumbled.

"Who's George?"

"Just a guy who used to work for Virgin Records. I use him from time to time as a consultant on some of our entertainment deals. He's a real throwback to the sixties: beard, jeans, Buddhist—the works."

"Single?" Lydia asked.

"Divorced, I think."

"Why not introduce him to your mother? Sounds like a perfect match," Lydia chirped.

"So, what would you like to listen to next?" Bryce clinched his teeth, and pointed toward a mix of more sedate CDs.

"You," Lydia cooed. "Tell me what you've been up to. Tell me what's been spinning in that brilliant mind of yours."

"Only business that can't be talked about until it's concluded."

"Okay then. How 'bout a deal that's already closed?" She ran her hand along Bryce's thigh, causing him to inwardly cringe.

"Tell me about your trip to Paris with the girls for the fashion shows. All I've seen are the bills," he countered with a chuckle, hoping she'd launch into one of her monologues and he could tune her out and tune in to Wagner's *Der Ring des Nibelungen*.

Over the years, Bryce had become fond of the classical operas that fused religion with tragic human tales. He was an eternity away from being a religious man and had even converted to Judaism with no hesitation to ensure he'd fit the perfect son-in-law profile before marrying Lydia, but this interest in artistic religious expression was an anomaly in his typically agnostic outlook. There was no denying that.

Lydia responded with a squeal of delight, "Do you really want to hear all about it?"

"Every last detail, my dear," he replied and flipped in the Wagner CD.

By the time they pulled up to the enormous cast iron gates of her parents' estate in Bedford, Bryce was half-listening to her incessant babbling about women, like herself, who had too much money and little gratitude for all they had. Smiling and nodding, all he could think was, *Show dogs. They're like little show dogs. Born with platinum spoons in their mouths. God help them if they ever have to hunt for their own meal.*

The private drive meandered around a small lake filled with swans and through a thicket of neatly trimmed, fiery orange maple trees before reaching the grassy knoll that displayed the enormous chateau-style mansion. Bryce swung the car around the circular stone drive and up to the waiting valet. Putting on his best manners, he jumped out of the car and rushed over to open his wife's door, gallantly extending his hand to help her out.

"Thank you, dear," she said, accepting his hand. As they headed for the front door, Bryce heightened the display of affection by wrapping his arm around Lydia's shoulders. As far as the world could tell, Bryce was crazy about his wife.

The butler opened the door and greeted them, "Good evening, Mr. and Mrs. Elliott. Mr. and Mrs. Mortimer are in the library. May I escort you?"

"No, thanks," Bryce replied as they made their way through the enormous foyer and down a gallery-sized hallway to the library. Magnificent paintings covered the walls. There were more than a few masterpieces by Rubens, Monet, Rembrandt, Picasso, Miró, and Dalí. Despite being deeply moved by these beautiful works of art, Bryce couldn't fathom why anyone would pay so much money for them, especially modern paintings that displayed dripping clocks or swaths of color haphazardly brushed across a canvas. He paused at the Monet, cracked a cynical smile, and thought to himself, *The universal truth about art is that it changes ownership, but it always follows the money*. Despite his surface cynicism, he was in awe of the magnificent brush stokes and details in the Ruben masterwork next to the Monet.

"Hello, darling." Rachel Mortimer, who bore an uncanny resemblance to Eleanor Roosevelt, reached out to embrace her daughter.

"Hello, Abraham," Bryce greeted his physically, intellectually, and financially larger-than-life father-in-law with a firm handshake and pat to the back. At 6' 2", Abraham was approximately the same height as Bryce, and he had light brown hair that was streaked with gray and thinning, but his steel-blue eyes had the sharpness of a man many years younger.

Before Abraham could return the greeting, Bryce turned to Abraham's partner. "Big day, Solomon. Lydia and I wish you the best." He reached into his pocket and pulled out a plain white envelope and handed it to the balding, stout Solomon Weintraub. "This is for you and Sarah."

"Perhaps more for Sarah," Lydia added excitedly, clapping her hands and holding them together to her face.

Solomon opened the envelope and scanned the travel itinerary. "Holy moly," he exclaimed, "ten days on the Lady Jenn, a 150-foot yacht in the Bahamas! This is really too much!"

"It's the least we could do, sir. You have been wonderful to me at the firm and like a second father to Lydia."

The women began laughing with glee. For as long as they could remember, Sarah had been dreaming of a voyage on a private yacht with her husband of forty years, but despite his considerable wealth, Solomon couldn't bring himself to shell out the hundred thousand plus for the trip.

Abraham pulled his son-in-law to the side. "That was damn nice of you, Bryce! Very thoughtful."

Bryce smiled in acknowledgement and mused to himself, *Money well spent.* Although he knew he was destined to take over the firm, a little overkill never hurt.

Unlike most business partnerships, Abraham and Solomon's personal relationship had deepened over the years, and each man was like a brother to the other. However, within the firm, they had a reputation for being ruthlessly demanding, with zero tolerance for screw-ups and an unspoken law that one's personal life be devoid of scandal or serious personal problems such as adultery, alcoholism, or drug use.

"How about breaking open a bottle of champagne before the others arrive?" Abraham suggested in his trademark deep baritone voice, with the cork already halfway out of the bottle.

Within an hour of the Elliotts' arrival, the party was in full swing. Hundreds of exquisitely dressed guests spilled out of the chateau and into the gardens and tented verandahs, where no expense had been spared and the weather, fortunately, had cooperated. The day was glorious—a perfect fall day for an outdoor event. A legion of uniformed servants offered hors d'oeuvres on antique silver trays and poured French champagne into stems of fine crystal glasses.

Bryce, the tireless networker who collected contacts like the devil collected souls, had already chatted with the chairman of the Federal Reserve, the chairman of Citicorp, and his sometimes golf partner and failed Republican presidential candidate, Steve Forbes. He also spoke briefly to Ted Perkins, whose partner, Art Payne, had recently died in a sailing accident with his twenty-two-year-old son.

Abraham had limited contact with Payne & Perkins—champions of leveraged buyouts—and he'd never been able to woo them away from the California-based law firm, Morrison & Foerster, where Art Payne's cousin was a senior managing partner of the firm. One of the first thoughts Bryce had when he heard the news about Art and his son was that perhaps he could now manage to do what Abraham couldn't. He exercised restraint while offering his condolences to Ted.

There really was no need for him to mingle over cocktails with any other investment bankers—the firm's lifeblood—because he'd made sure that the key players were all seated at his "A" table. After finishing up with Ted Perkins, Bryce's eyes panned the party, calculating which junior partners and associates were dutifully cultivating business with existing and potential clients, and more importantly, which ones were not.

His eye caught Bill Holt conversing with his stunningly beautiful physician wife, who had a smoky and sexy Elizabeth Taylor aura about her, and Spencer Livingston, another senior associate. Bryce despised Bill, who'd been brought up in a privileged environment. He thought rich kids like Bill were naïve and arrogant. During Bryce's studies at Yale, Oxford, and Harvard, they'd surrounded Bryce—men and women progenies of the lucky sperm club. Just like Lydia, most of them would be mediocre and middle class, at best, if the world were a level playing field.

Bryce walked up to the group. "Enjoying the party?" he asked acerbically. He focused on Bill Holt, whose hazel eyes, thick mane of strawberry-blond hair, sharp Irish features, and classic, expensive suit—all pulled together with a bright red Hermès tie—formed the ultimate New England preppy look.

"Very much, thank you," Bill Holt responded curtly. Among the firm's associates, he was undeniably the biggest producer, billing as many as eighty hours per week, and the brightest, most talented and well liked associate in the firm.

For a brief moment, Bryce eyed Holt's wife with hidden envy and wondered what it would be like to make love to such a beautiful and educated woman. But then, he consoled himself, Bill Holt would never be at the helm of the firm. Power and fortune came with a price, and the price Bryce paid was Lydia.

"And is this a private soirée?" Bryce asked with barbed sarcasm.

"We couldn't ask for a nicer day, setting, or company," Bill Holt replied with a tilt of his glass.

Bryce didn't appreciate his cheeky response. Just because Holt had worked for the past three months on a deal that netted the firm a cool eighteen million, there was no excuse for forgetting his place. Bryce sized him up. "I'm sure some of the firm's clients—especially the ones that just paid a king's ransom for the network deal—would like to shake your hand," Bryce pushed.

"I'm sure they would, and they shall. Just not right this minute," Bill responded, taking a long sip of his gin and tonic.

"The clock's ticking. Never forget you're only as good as your last deal. *Tick, tick, tick*," Bryce pushed in his didactic, deliberate voice.

"Look, we'll be here all afternoon." It was clear Bill was trying to end the discussion and get back to the nice day, setting, and company.

But Bryce refused to let it go and whispered, "Tell me Richie Rich, what's it like to have everything handed to you on a silver platter?"

"I wouldn't know! But perhaps you could tell me what it's like to marry the boss's daughter and get the managing partnership interest handed to you on a platinum platter. You must be licking your chops over this party," Bill replied in a calm, modulated tone.

"Not to worry, pal, while I'm licking my chops, you'll be licking your frickin' wounds." Bryce slapped his hand on Bill Holt's shoulder and cast a hateful look at him before hastily retreating.

When he was about thirty feet away, Bryce turned back and, with a grin, thundered, "Enjoy the party! And if I were you, Spencer," he turned his focus to the hard working associate and affable corporate climber, "I'd keep better company."

When Bryce was out of earshot, Spencer turned and stared bug-eyed at his close friend. "Jesus, Bill, what in the hell were you thinking?"

"I'm not about to put up with his crap after closing the network deal . . . certainly not after reeling in ALPS," Bill snarled, using the code name for a huge deal involving a Swiss pharmaceutical's bid for the largest biotech company in the United States.

"Yeah, but—" Spencer tried to counter.

"I don't give a rat's ass about his veiled threats. What's he going to do? Block me from making partner this year?"

"Yeah, but.... Okay, okay, I know not even Bryce could pull that off, even if he wanted to." It was widely accepted throughout the firm that Bill Holt would top the list of new partners.

"So, let's stop talking about it and enjoy the party." He gave his wife, Liane, a tight squeeze around her small waist. "Heard any good lawyer jokes lately?" he asked Spencer.

"Not lately," Spencer responded flatly. "Look Bill, friend-to-friend, I wouldn't make a hobby of screwing with Bryce. The guy takes no hostages. It's just plain stupid to fuck with him. No doubt you'll make partnership, but that SOB could make your life miserable. Now, if you'll excuse me, I need to go freshen my drink." Spencer tilted his head toward a Goldman associate, who was still standing alone at the bar.

"Come on, you've got to be joking."

"Look, Bill, I'm one of those guys who go to bed every night and pray that I make partner. You, on the other hand, are about as guaranteed to make partner as Mother Teresa is to go to heaven. See ya later. Liane, it was great to see you. Please excuse me."

Spencer walked away, turning back to wave good-bye. As he did so, Bill loosely closed his fingers into an open circle and jerked his forearm up and down.

"Very funny!" Spencer called back.

It was nearing eleven when the last of the guests cleared out of the Mortimer's house, and the Elliotts, the Weintraubs, and the Mortimers made their retreat to an informal sitting room. After the butler served coffee, tea, and cognac, Solomon Weintraub kicked off his trademark sale-bought shoes and propped his feet up on an ottoman.

"Boy, are these puppies tired. Wonderful party, Rachel and Abe, thank you very much. Guess it'll be our turn to reciprocate before we know it," he commented, alluding to Abraham's impending retirement.

"Hard to believe, isn't it?" Abraham remarked, rubbing his hand across his wrinkled face. "Where has the time gone? Are we really seventy?"

"Mentally, no; physically, yes." Solomon responded, with a hint of an Austrian accent that emerged when he was tired. It had taken Bryce years to piece together that, during the war, Solomon's family had been wiped out in the early phases of the Holocaust. They had been in the wrong place at the wrong time—Berlin, at the opening of a new synagogue.

Solomon's father, a wealthy Austrian industrialist and orthodox Jew, had wanted to demonstrate his support for Jews who were feeling the sting of persecution emerging in Germany. He'd erroneously thought his famous name would keep him and his family safe.

Solomon's entire family disappeared in the middle of the night, and they were never heard from again. It happened while Solomon was a freshman at Harvard. The experience left him in an eternal spiritual debate. He and Sarah never had children because he never wanted to risk the pain of losing one.

Religion for Bryce amounted to an untenable leap of faith, best left to the old and infirm who had nothing else to hang their hats on. Bryce steadied himself when it became apparent that the two old men were about to try, once again, to tackle the issue of mortality. Six months ago, Solomon had been diagnosed with a non-aggressive form of prostate cancer. The doctors claimed, given his age, something else would kill him before the cancer. Still, Solomon remained concerned.

"Abraham, of all the paintings in your house, why do you keep that one here, where you spend the most time?" Solomon asked, pointing to Il Baciccio's fifteenth century painting, *Abraham's Sacrifice of Isaac*. It was an enormous oil that depicted the Hebrew prophet, Abraham, preparing to sacrifice his only son, who is saved at the last moment when an angel descends from heaven. Grand and illusionistic, it looked like it belonged in an Italian church.

"I like the name of the guy in the picture," Abraham jested.

"Seriously," Sol pressed for an answer from his friend, who had an unwavering belief in God.

Bryce tried to suppress a yawn and thought to himself, *Oh, Christ! Here we go again.*

"Look at his face, Sol," Abe began. "Abraham's looking up to the heavens. Here's a man, a noble leader of his people, looking up to God for guidance. It reminds me that no matter how important I feel, there's something bigger and more significant."

What a major crock of shit! Bryce thought to himself with a silent snort of disgust. Abraham was one of the most controlling, hard-assed people he'd ever met in his life, and he'd surely never seen the guy drop a nickel in a beggar's hat.

"So, what do you think is on the other side of this life?" Sol asked Abe, with a look of fright in his eye.

Bryce thought, *The question of a man, in the twilight of his life, looking for answers where there are none.* He swirled the cognac in his snifter and answered to himself, *How about nothing? No light, no thought—only silence and solitude. So just let go – this is it and there ain't anymore. You got your brass ring. In the lottery of life, you won big, living a rich, powerful, and fairly long life. Christ, you could have been born one-legged and blind in New Delhi.*

Abe replied, "Oh, my dear friend, Sol, come with us to the synagogue sometime. The rabbis have a leg up on answering questions like that."

Bryce saw a window of opportunity to change the subject. "Is anyone in the mood for shop talk?" Bryce asked, his eyes dancing with delight.

"You bet!" Solomon chimed in. His drawn face began to relax visibly. "After all, I'm still on the board."

"Actually, I've been meaning to ask you about ALPS. How's it going?" Abraham interjected.

"It's going to be a ball buster, for sure," Bryce responded.

"Didn't Holt bring in that deal?" Abraham asked, leaning forward in his chair.

"Not exactly; his brother's an associate with Goldman in Zurich and tipped him off that something was brewing." Bryce glanced over to the far corner of the room to make sure the very confidential discussion was out of the range of the wives. "But, I caught wind of it when I was in London months ago, and I kept in very tight contact with the executive managing director over there. The guy was a very tough sell and even wanted to try to cap the legal fees on the deal. Can you imagine? I'll give him credit for trying—like I said, a ball buster"

"Cap the legal fees?" Abraham broke out in a deep throaty laughter. "Right, just like they're going cap their fees on the deal. So what'd you say?"

"Nothing. I told them I'd think about it, and then..." Bryce began with a devious look on his face, "I went straight to Vevey Pharmaceuticals and got the engagement directly from them! An old acquaintance from Oxford had just been promoted to chief financial officer."

"Brazen. Brazen and brilliant, Bryce," Abraham praised his son-in-law.

Bryce sat back in the overstuffed sofa, soaking up the compliment.

Leaning forward, Solomon caught Bryce's eye. "Just be careful, Bryce, and play by all the rules. The SEC is going to be all over this."

"Of course." Bryce responded, trying to hide his irritation. Everybody and their brother in the M & A business was acutely aware that prior screw-ups and improprieties by the Japanese had caused the SEC to closely scrutinize all major cross-border transactions. At four-and-a-half billion dollars, this was a big deal.

Sol got up from his chair and stretched his arms. "Great, great evening. Thank you so much." He walked over to Abraham and gave him a hug, patting him gently on the back.

Everyone rose and exchanged good-byes. As they were waiting for their cars to be brought to the front door, Solomon took Bryce's hands and looked him directly in the eye. "Take good care of our firm."

TWO

As THE BLUE-CHIP players of the ALPS deal filed into the conference room of Mortimer & Weintraub, a surge of adrenaline rushed through Bryce. The expensively decorated, cherry-paneled room underscored power and money, and its perch on the eighty-second floor of the World Trade Center made Bryce feel as if he were seated at the left hand of God.

Hans Bauer, Bryce's friend from Oxford and now CFO of Vevey Pharmaceuticals, strutted into the room. An Italian double-breasted suit hung from his tall, thin body, and his head was capped with a mass of curly blond hair. *Not bad for a Swiss guy*, Bryce mused and got up to greet the man who helped him to circumvent the fee-cappers at Goldman Sachs.

"When did you get in from Geneva?" Bryce asked as he reached out for a handshake.

"Last night." He leaned into Bryce and whispered, "Came in on the corporate jet. Sure beats commercial. Who'd ever have thought, back at Oxford, we'd be here today?" he asked with amusement.

"We did!" Bryce answered resolutely. "And unlike some others in this room," Bryce glared over at Bill Holt, "we had to work our asses off to get here." Like Bryce, Hans came from a modest background—a small Swiss dairy farm—and this was a key bond they'd shared at Oxford.

As their eyes connected, Bryce could detect his colleague's appreciation for the astonishing success they'd both achieved at such early ages. His attention was diverted when the three Goldman Sachs BSDs entered the room with an air of omnipotence.

BSD, short for big swinging dick, was an acronym Bryce relished using when referring to a senior managing partner of an investment bank.

"Shall we?" Bryce motioned for Hans to join him in receiving the trio of men. He could think of no better coup than welcoming the BSDs with their prized client at his side. As they walked across the room, Bryce made a point to carry on a warm, physically demonstrative conversation with Hans, laughing and slapping his shoulder. Anyone observing the duo would assume they were as close as brothers.

"Hello, gentlemen," Bryce pleasantly greeted the three men. "Good to see you, George. How'd your son do in his early matches?"

"Like a champ. It looks like he's set to play the number one singles position for Stanford this season.

"That's terrific," Bryce began, shifting his glance to the next BSD. "And when are you and I getting together for that long overdue round of golf in Florida?"

"How about the minute our client goes back to Switzerland with BioMolecular on their balance sheet at a winning price?" The group let out a congenial, but nervous laugh.

Just as Bryce had predicted, the deal was full of nail-biting problems. BioMolecular, the largest, most innovative and successful biotech company in the world, was starting to resist the terms of the deal. Now, two weeks before Thanksgiving, the last thing anyone wanted, least of all the client, was for the deal to turn into a hostile takeover.

For the past six weeks, all sides had been walking on eggshells. The longer it dragged, the greater the risk of a leak, which could create a lethal rise in the stock price or—even worse—put the company in play.

"You're on!" Bryce responded enthusiastically, and he made his play for the third and most senior partner, whom he suspected did not care much for him, especially after he'd gone directly to Hans.

"Good morning, Drew," Bryce greeted the man with a firm handshake. "Listen, I forgot to mention last week that Abraham asked me to invite you to a dinner he's hosting on the eighteenth for Henry Kissinger." Bryce had done his research. International politics was one of the great passions of Drew Williams.

Predictably, Drew's dour face began to glow with excitement. "Henry Kissinger? Really? Well…thank you."

Bryce was so deft at the art of stealthy manipulation that even masters of manipulation, like Drew, rarely knew when they had been taken. Abraham hadn't mentioned inviting Drew Williams to the dinner, but Bryce was sure he wouldn't mind the last minute invitation. After all, the entire purpose of the staged event was to solidify relationships with the firm's iffy clients. At a cost of a hundred grand for Kissinger alone, Bryce hoped his father-in-law's over-the-top idea would pay off.

Bryce turned a cool eye to a junior associate from Arthur Andersen, who arrived late and hurried in the door with reams of papers spilling from his arms. He then encouraged everyone to take a seat at a round mahogany table that filled the center of the room.

Several months earlier, after observing that seat selection occasionally turned ugly—with mammoth egos jockeying for positions they believed to be the most prominent—he'd recommended replacing the rectangular conference table with a round one. With a round table there were no seating issues, which put everyone more at ease.

For seven tense hours, a team of five attorneys, three investment bankers, five pampered clients, and two accountants hashed out how to respond to BioMolecular's unreasonable demands and potential deal breakers. The chairman was insisting that his board of directors would not approve the sale for less than $52 per share. The Goldman bankers crunched the valuation out at $44, tops, due in part to the fact that the stock was trading on NASDAQ at $32.50 a share. The difference between the bid and offer was a whopping $750 million. "A rat-fuck situation," one investment banker declared, causing a Swiss executive to howl in amusement and another's jaw to drop in shock.

There was also the issue of a pending patent lawsuit involving the company's most lucrative product, which had been uncovered during the due diligence. When the group began to talk in circles, Drew suggested that they adjourn for a three-hour breather and meet again at eight thirty that evening. All agreed.

As the group began to shuffle out the door, Bryce approached a fatigued-looking Hans and patted him on the shoulder. "Don't worry. It's all going to work out."

"Oh, I'm sure it is. Look, I'm really jet-lagged. I need to go back to my hotel for a quick nap and let my savagely high-priced advisors come up with some clever options."

"Sounds like a sensible plan. Do you have a car?"

"How could I possibly afford one after paying all you guys?" The CFO half-heartedly jested.

"Ha! No problem, the firm's cars will take you and your colleagues back to the Regent."

"Hope the cars don't bill out at eight hundred dollars an hour," Hans chortled.

"It's on the house," Bryce smiled. "I'll have my secretary make the arrangements for the drivers to meet you in the reception area in three minutes."

"Three minutes and not four?" Han laughed. "Still the same old Bryce, manic about time."

"The Japanese love it," Bryce chuckled, and he led the entourage to the reception area.

When the others were out the door, Bryce instructed two Mortimer & Weintraub attorneys to look into the patent issue, another to go over a comparatively benign tax issue, and he told Bill Holt to "suit up" for a pow-wow on the StairMasters.

In the private bathroom connected to his office, Bryce changed into shorts and a t-shirt, and then he headed for the firm's workout room, rushing down a spiral staircase that connected the eighty-first and eighty-second floors. Before entering the gym, he slid a bar on the door to change the color from green to red. The color change indicated that a private and confidential discussion was taking place and no one was to enter unless he or she was more senior than the parties inside. In Bryce's case, there was only one other person who was more senior than him, and there wasn't a snowball's chance in hell that his father-in-law would be looking to use the gym.

Bill Holt knocked on the door before opening it.

"Come on in!" Bryce greeted him with a broad smile as he pounded the StairMaster.

Bill's face twisted with befuddlement. Bryce loved to fuck with people who had fucked with him and saw he was off to a good start. His overly friendly greeting and special workout music selection *Jumping Jack Flash* by Bill Holt's favorite group, the Rolling Stones threw Holt for a loop.

"Hey, did you know the door's red?" Bill asked, pausing warily at the entrance.

"Of course, what do you think we're going to talk about? Our mothers' favorite recipes?" Bryce snapped.

He watched Bill struggle to hold his tongue as he stepped on the StairMaster that faced his. For two long minutes, Bryce said nothing. He knew, when dished out appropriately, silence could be very unsettling.

Finally Bryce huffed out a question with an expressionless face. "Any thoughts on the patent or price issue? I've never seen Drew, Jack, or George sweat like that before. They seem completely confounded."

Bryce was also hitting a brick wall, and it was driving him crazy. He was a firm believer that all problems had solutions and that only the stupid and indolent were incapable of finding solutions.

Bryce studied Bill and could sense he was taken back by the question. Bryce rarely solicited opinions on important issues, and he knew, as much as Bill despised him, he admired Bryce's knack for resurrecting and saving deals. "Well?"

"Um, sorry, my mind just began to wander back through some details."

Bryce did not like Bill's suspicious look. "It's a straight-forward question, Bill. Do you have any thoughts on the patent or price issue?"

"Actually, Bryce, I have more than thoughts; I have solutions," Bill replied slowly and deliberately.

Bryce responded with a calculated silence and a skeptically raised eyebrow.

"The patent issue is a really a no-brainer," Bill finally panted, while toweling the beads of sweat that blanketed his face. "Genticore," he began, referring to the company that had initiated a licensing lawsuit against

BioMolecular, "is just a little thorn in the giant's foot. I calculate the company's worth thirty-five to forty million tops. They've had a shitty year and, except for the patent they licensed to BioMolecular, there doesn't seem to be much in the pipeline. These guys are courting extinction, and no white knights are going to appear while they're in litigation with their only cash-cow."

"You think it's thirty-five to forty," Bryce asked, creating the illusion that he'd already given thought to the same matter, "with the losses over the last five quarters?"

In reality, Bryce had little doubt that Holt's numbers were right on the mark. The guy had a JD and MBA from Harvard, and he was instinctively better than the bankers at valuing a company.

"Trust me; I went through piles of analyst information. I'm convinced forty is the absolute ceiling."

"What's Genticore currently trading at?" Bryce asked.

"Seven and an eighth; it's down over 55 percent since the IPO, and still diving. It's not great."

"Except for our client!" Bryce exclaimed, carefully concealing his jubilation. "What's the ownership structure?"

"It is about 70 percent corporate, 20 percent officers and employees, and 10 percent widows and orphans who were bamboozled by greedy brokers, selling off the second layer of the IPO."

"What does forty mil translate to?" Bryce asked.

"It's roughly nine and a quarter a share. Thirty percent windfall wouldn't be bad for an equity that could wind up papering the bathroom walls one day."

"All things considered, Vevey Pharmaceuticals should go in at thirty-five. Given Genticore's circumstances, they lack the leverage to hold out for more money." Bryce remarked, his face devoid of perspiration.

"I totally agree," Bill replied, toweling his sweaty face again.

"The board can't convince the shareholders otherwise; all they've done is screw up so far. And this patent lawsuit with BioMolecular probably sent the corporate investors over the edge."

There was a startled look on Bill's face. Bryce wasn't expecting a reaction from Bill, especially not at this point in the conversation. He waited for a response, and after a few awkward moments, he resumed.

"So, this price gap of 750 million really is, to quote the BSDs, 'a ratfuck situation,'" Bryce cracked with a grinning ferocity. "How do your numbers pan out against the guys at Goldman?"

"Almost match up perfectly. They're right on the money," Bill replied and then closed up again.

With a degree of irritation, Bryce wondered if Bill was testing to see if he had a solution to the problem. "It's goddamn irregular for a board to turn down an offer that's at a 35 percent premium. Genticore's chairman and CFO counter at 60 percent over current trading price is ludicrous."

"Unless they have something hot in the pipeline that's going to make the company's stock skyrocket. Those things don't always turn up in due diligence."

"They don't have anything in the pipeline," Bryce answered assuredly.

"How do you know?" Bill queried, with a curious look.

"Seek and ye shall find."

"Come on, Bryce, how do you know?"

"Someone in-the-know owed me a favor. As it turns out, despite being a scientific genius, Genticore's CTO doesn't seem to have much knack for business. Apparently, the guy was on the brink of bankruptcy and about to lose his house. How people get themselves into such a bind always beats the shit out of me," Bryce added as a side comment. "Anyway, he spilled the beans. There's nothing in the pipeline."

"Wait, how do you know?" Bill blurted out in astonishment.

Realizing he shouldn't have mentioned it, Bryce could tell that Bill assumed he'd obtained insider information illegally. "Not me! What do you think I am? Stupid? Like I said, someone volunteered the information and passed it on. Besides, the CTO's a Pakistani, and those characters play by different rules and morals. Hard to know what to believe when it comes out of one of those rug merchant's mouths."

"Then why would you believe his claim that no new products are in the pipeline?" Bill inquired in voice barely above a whisper.

Bryce finally broke a sweat. "Aah, guess a man just has to make a leap of faith now and then."

"Right." Bill replied neutrally and took several deep breaths.

Aced him! Bryce congratulated himself. *Guy's in a quandary – if he mentions the conversation to anyone else, and I'm telling the truth, then he'd be fucked for crossing me. If he says nothing, and I lied, then he could be in just as much trouble for not coming forward with the information. Nothing's better than pitching an adversary into a fucked-if-you-do, and fucked-if-you-don't situation.*

"Look we're a little side-tracked here," Bryce said in an amicable tone, determined to figure out how to move the deal to close. "Getting back on the issue of BioMolecular's valuation, how do you explain the insane gap between our very generous offer of forty-four, and the CFO and chairman's counter of fifty-two? We all know no one's going to top us, even if they put the company in play."

"Because they've been caught off guard. The CFO and chairman aren't giving the board of directors at BioMolecular the whole story because neither have a golden parachute. If the company gets sold before they can rectify that situation, they're screwed—out of a job without a parachute. Best these guys could do at this point is one and a half to two million—not nearly as satisfying as the five to twenty mil most guys walk away with from a company that size."

Bryce was infuriated at himself for not having put together the obvious. But that only lasted a second when he realized he now had the solutions.

"Glad to see you're reading the fine print in the 10-K," Bryce responded with a smile. "Once we finish up here, I'll put my solutions down on paper."

"Perhaps it'd be best if I outline and refine our discussion. After all I've given it a lot of thought," Bill tersely replied.

Bryce could tell that Bill was furious. "No I'll do it," Bryce snapped. He did not like Holt's defiance. "Granted, we both kind of worked out these solutions together, but let's face it, associates don't fine tune points, the, partners do, especially senior managing partners."

"Look, Bryce, you and I both know where the idea came from. I'm willing to share credit but not give it away entirely!"

"Give it away! Give it away?" Bryce hissed. "You think you came up with the answers? The whole conversation was academic, just a test to make absolutely sure you're partner material."

"You and I and everyone else in this firm know I'm partner material. You're doing what you do best, Bryce—manipulating and using other people to serve your own interests. You didn't have any solutions. If you had done any meaningful research on Vevey Pharmaceuticals buying out Genticore, then you'd know the shareholders aren't upset about the lawsuit. If anything, the corporate investors probably applauded the move. The entire reason for suing BioMolecular was so they could also license the technology to BioMolecular's competitors. If successful, Genticore's predicament would shift from the brink of oblivion to an astounding financial turnaround. It was basically the company's only hope for salvation.

"And furthermore," Bill bellowed "for your information, the details about the parachutes were vague in the 10-K. I dug it up. You think you're the only guy with sources?"

At least the stupid little prick laid all his cards on the table and now I have the information I need, Bryce seethed as he pounded out his rage on the StairMaster. He heard a buzzing, like the circuitry was surging in the machine. Within five revolutions of the pedals, Bryce was thinking something was wrong—maybe electrically—with the StairMaster. And suddenly, Bryce's body seized. His right foot slid out from under him. He went flying off the machine and crashed onto the floor. Dazed a bit, Bryce glared up at Bill and could tell he was amused.

"Too bad for you I didn't kill myself," he hissed at Bill as he limped back toward the machine.

"Need me to lick any wounds?" Bill asked with unbridled sarcasm, paraphrasing the veiled threat that Bryce had hurled at him during Solomon's retirement party.

During a steaming shower, Bryce managed to clear his mind soothe his rage, and concoct a scheme that would punish Holt and reward himself.

He put on a fresh shirt, tie, and suit, combed his hair straight back, and checked out his reflection before going into his adjoining office. In the nighttime quiet, he sat down at his computer and began to put together solutions to bring this mega-deal to the finish line.

He heard Abraham's familiar, heavy gait moving toward his office. There was the predictable double knock, followed by a silhouette of Abraham's imposing frame in his doorway.

"Hello, Bryce, I thought I'd stop by to see how things are going," Abraham announced in his deep voice, which resonated off the walls of the office. Without pausing, he headed straight for a bookcase that hid a fully stocked, Prohibition-style bar. He poured himself a tumbler of Scotch and water and proceeded to sit in a green leather wingchair that faced Bryce's desk. Raising the fine crystal glass, Abraham said, "Cheers! At seven forty-five in the evening, and at my stage in life, I'm perfectly entitled. Wouldn't you agree?"

"Of course, Abraham. Please go ahead; I just have a few touches to put on this summary," Bryce replied and continued to type on his computer.

When he was done, Bryce glanced up from his screen, leaned back in his chair, and stretched out his arms, settling his palms on the back of his head. "Boy oh boy, Abraham, this has been a taxing deal."

"So, do I have to beg for the details?"

"Of course not, and as a matter of fact, I wanted to run this by you. Is this a good time?" Bryce asked the man who was going to make all his dreams come true.

"Shoot," Abraham replied and took a long sip of Scotch.

For the next twenty minutes, Bryce reviewed everything that had transpired during the meeting and, of course, his solutions.

Pouring his second drink, Abraham blurted out, "Just what do those investment bankers get paid for? It should be their job, not ours, to come up with the solutions. I think I've seen it all now! How much are those overpaid prep-school boys getting for this again?"

"The bankers are going to clear forty on the transaction, while we stand to make a measly ten mil in legal fees." And with a devilish look in his eye, Bryce added, "So I had this little idea."

"And that is?"

"When we reconvene, I'm going to press Drew Williams and his team for tenable solutions for both the patent and pricing issues. Based on their grim faces and sweaty palms when we adjourned at five-thirty, I seriously doubt they have any. Then I'll pull Drew into a side room to have a little private chat. I'll inform him we've come up with the answers that'll save the deal and that we're willing to share—provided they sign this." Bryce pulled a single page document from his printer and handed it to Abe.

Abe slipped on his bifocals, and after reading the short agreement, looked approvingly up at his son-in-law. "It's a novel and very clever idea. Any conflict of interest issues in this?"

"Nope," Bryce answered quickly and confidently.

"Well then, go for it, but be careful. It's going to make Drew so fucking mad that he just might try to push you through the window," Abe commented with a deep throaty laugh as he rose from his seat and began to head for the door.

"Hey listen, Abe, there's one other thing we need to talk about," Bryce called out in a serious tone. "Could you please come back? It's important."

"Sure," Abe replied and sat back down with a look of concern. "What's on your mind?"

"Umm, I don't quite know how to broach the subject."

"Just hit it square-on like you do everything else. What's the matter?"

"It's about Bill Holt," Bryce dropped his eyes to dramatize the gravity of what he was about to say.

"What about him? He's one of the best associates this firm has ever had, except you."

"He's got a serious amphetamine problem, Abe. I guess it was something that started out innocently: an ambitious associate trying to bill more hours than there are in a day, and a physician wife who was able to supply him with the pills. Anyway, I think it's getting out of control."

"How so?" Abraham asked, peering over his glasses.

"Plain and simple, he's losing it. I asked him to join me in the gym after the meeting today because he was so wired. I thought a workout might help calm him down. Then, when we began to discuss the deal, he had trouble finishing one thought before moving on to the next. As we were about to leave the gym for the showers, something really odd and disconcerting happened. He started to mumble something about how his sources had uncovered the parachute idea and how lucky I was that he had come up with the idea for Vevey Pharmaceuticals to buy Genticore."

"How strange. What did you do?"

"I just thanked him for his great ideas. I didn't see any point in upsetting him."

"Strange, he seems so, well, perfectly fine to me," Abe said with a puzzled look. "Are you sure?"

"I think so. While he was in the shower, I found these in his desk." Bryce pulled out a handful of blue capsules that were Bryce's own leftover antibiotics from a throat infection.

"Whoa! Bryce, how do you know they're amphetamines?"

"It looks like stuff I saw in college, plus the rumors."

"What rumors?" Abe asked.

"A mutual friend vaguely mentioned something while we were playing golf a couple months ago."

"These are very serious allegations, Bryce."

Bryce lowered his head and shook it slowly side to side. "I know, I know. But, Abe, what if we announce his partnership and it's true? Should I have these pills checked out?"

Abraham sat back and looked at Bryce, who could hear the buzz of the desk lamp's light bulb through the room's profound silence.

Bryce rubbed his face with his hands and sighed, feeling the need to continue. "You know, another thing I've noticed is that he sometimes withdraws himself from what's going on. Did you see how he and his wife kept mostly to themselves at Sol's retirement party?" Bryce knew that Abe's keen eye would certainly have noticed.

"Yeah, as a matter of fact I did. I remember he wasn't circulating much at the party. It was odd behavior for a star associate," Abe mouthed the stem of his bifocals, clearly digesting this new perspective on Bill.

Bryce glanced down at his watch. "We're reconvening in twenty minutes. Listen, Abe, I need your help. Now that we're in the final stretch of the ALPS deal, I can't risk having Bill around. Are you still meeting with the Morris Stokes people tonight?" he asked, referring to a major cable network based in North Carolina.

"Yeah, at the Peninsula at quarter of nine," Abe responded with a questioning glance.

"Stokes isn't going to be there, right? Just some of his lieutenants?"

"That's right."

"Would you consider taking Bill along? Tell him since he was a major player on our last network deal, you want him to come along to meet the Stokes people. Given the short time frame here, it's the only way to quietly resolve this problem this evening."

Abe looked intently at his son-in-law. "Are you sure this is necessary?"

"Unfortunately, yes."

"Okay then. Is he in his office?"

"I'm sure. Here, why don't you call him now from here and have him go to the garage and meet your driver right away." Without waiting for a response, Bryce punched in Bill's extension and handed Abraham the phone.

After Abraham hung up and left to meet the driver, Bill came flying into Bryce's office. Bryce looked up and flipped on a tape recorder that was hidden in his pocket. *Maybe I'll get lucky*, he mused.

"You fuck! You rotten, stinking bastard!" Bill raged.

"Please, Bill, try to calm down. The clients are going to be coming down the hall any minute." Bryce said in a soothing, patronizing tone.

"I don't give a flying fuck!"

"Please, Bill, at least shut the door."

"What the fuck is going on? Why the hell does the old man want me to meet the Stokes people? Are you pulling me off this deal?"

"Calm down. What's the matter? You should be honored. Abraham asked me if he could take you along. He thought that your work on the network deal was outstanding, and he wanted you to help pitch the Stokes people. You know any deal with them could be twice as big."

"Since when does Abraham Mortimer need a lowly associate along to help him sign a client?" Bill asked. His face was completely red. "You fucking set this up, Bryce, and we both know why!"

"Don't you want to have as much exposure as possible? Did you ever stop to consider that you could be one of the lead attorneys for Stokes if we get the business?"

"*If* we get the business," Bill hissed. "You know as well as I do that they have a reputation for favoring good ol' southern Christian firms. I don't think Mortimer & Weintraub is exactly what you'd call a perfect fit."

"Listen, I need to go. I really didn't have a choice. If Abraham says he needs you, then he needs you, and far be it from me to override Mr. Mortimer," Bryce said in a good-natured tone, juxtaposed with a look of pure hatred in his eyes. He walked toward his door, signaling that the discussion was over.

"Fuck you! Go to hell, you cock-sucking bastard!" Bill fumed.

In a calculated move, Bryce slammed the door to his office shut and turned off the recorder. He didn't want Abraham to hear the rest of what Bill had to say.

"You're not going to get away with this. There is no way in hell I'm going to sit back and let you take credit for my ideas. No way!" Bill opened the door and stormed out of the room.

"If I were you, I wouldn't keep Abraham waiting," Bryce sang out after him.

By eight forty-five all the players, except Bill Holt, were seated at the round table and ready to move on. Bryce had shown up at the last minute, a carefully orchestrated move so he wouldn't have to talk to the bankers before the meeting.

Without missing a beat, Bryce looked directly across the table at Drew Williams. "Our team has worked out all the legal and tax matters, which for all practical purposes are basically irrelevant until we reach resolutions to the valuation and patent issues, so why don't you take the lead, Drew."

"Thank you, Bryce," he responded with a nervous smile and fumbled to put on his bifocals. Then he glanced down at his notes. "As we all know, these are very complex issues." For the next ten minutes, he muddled his way through a non-conclusive, almost incomprehensible monologue. When it became painfully apparent to all that they had zilch, Bryce moved in.

"Excuse me for interrupting, Drew, but something you just said made me think of a matter I'd like to discuss privately with you.

A puzzled-looking Drew peered across the table. "Of course, provided our client doesn't have any objections," he replied with some relief in his voice.

Bryce looked directly over at Hans. "I think it'll be to everyone's benefit. I just need about ten minutes."

Hans exchanged glances with his colleagues and gave a nod of approval. Bryce immediately picked up his file and motioned for Drew to follow him out of the room and down the hall and into the first empty office.

"What's this about?" Drew asked in a perplexed, jittery voice.

"Relax, it's about saving your ass, saving face, *and* saving the deal." Bryce sauntered over to the floor-to-ceiling window and stared out at a glittering Manhattan.

"And?"

"And I have the solutions to keep this deal from imploding." Bryce replied, his back still turned.

"It was very considerate of you to confer with me before crossing into our field," Drew responded, his voice unable to hide his elation.

"Well, it was necessary, really, but before I give away the farm..." Bryce turned around, walked toward Drew—who was seated in a side chair—and tossed a manila file at him. "I'll need your signature on this." He then leaned against a high-back chair that faced Drew to wait for a reaction. This was the best part of having people by the balls—watching their faces at the very moment they realize they're not in control of their own destinies.

After a few minutes and what must have been several reads, Drew ripped his glasses from his flabbergasted face and looked at Bryce. "You can't be serious. This is outrageous."

"I am. And it is."

"You want half our fees and a guarantee that you'll be legal counsel for all our M & A deals for the next twelve months?" the whipsawed banker asked in an incredulous tone.

"Yep," Bryce answered, picking at his cuticles.

"Well you can just fuck off, and it's going to be a cold day in hell before we use Mortimer & Weintraub again."

"Okay, okay, Drew. You win," Bryce responded with his hands and arms thrown up in surrender. "After all, you're in the driver's seat." Bryce plucked the document from Drew's hand and casually strolled back over to the window. "So what now? Go back into the room and babble on and on about nothing? How long do you think it'll be before they withdraw the mandate? A day? A week?"

The room filled with a deafening silence, and Bryce just looked out the window and waited.

"How do I know you really have the solution to closing this deal?"

"Ask and ye shall receive."

"Okay I'm asking," Drew responded evenly.

Bryce nodded toward the document in front of Drew.

"I need to make a call."

"I'll be back in five." Bryce exited the office, firmly shutting the door behind him.

Precisely five minutes later, Bryce knocked twice on the door and entered. Drew swiveled the chair around so his back was turned to Bryce and cupped his hand over the phone. Bryce studied Drew's hunched posture and guessed that he was getting a berating over the phone. He reckoned that Drew must be talking to the big, big cheese at Goldman, who had a reputation for being unforgiving in all things.

After several more minutes, Drew swiveled around to face Bryce. He looked a good five years older than he'd looked earlier that day. "Mind if I put John Schornstein on speaker?"

Bryce was right. The chairman of the firm was on the phone. "No problem. Hello, John! Mind if I tape record the conversation since it's two against one?" Bryce chirped.

"I guess it's okay, provided you turn it on now," a firm, low voice answered from the speaker box. "Is it on?"

Bryce pulled a small recorder from his pocket and flipped it on. "It's on."

"Before we move on, I want to know if Abraham is aware of this arrangement?" John inquired formally. "As you can appreciate, this is highly unusual, and to say the least, I am not happy. We've given Mortimer & Weintraub a lot of business over the years."

Bryce shoved his hands in his trousers and leaned into the speaker box. "He knows. And for the record, we've helped Goldman close a lot of deals over the years, not to mention tipping you off on a deal or two. You guys usually gross four times in transaction fees over our legal fees. On this deal you stand to make forty million against our ten million. And given that we're doing fifty percent of your job on this one, I thought a more equitable fee arrangement was in order."

"We want to counter your fee proposal from twenty to ten million, so our fees will be reduced to thirty million and you will double your fees from ten to twenty million dollars. We will also agree to use you again, with the caveat that you never, ever push us on a fee issue again. Plus, when you go back into that meeting, we want the client to be left with the impression that the ideas were hatched by both parties."

Bryce paused to think for a moment. He decided it would be best if he left John with the impression that he had won the negotiations, so he decided to agree to the ten million dollars without a counter and to share credit for the idea with the client. It would be a terrific way to make sure Bill Holt would look like a real nut case if he tried to claim any credit. Three partners and another associate from the firm were just about to witness the presentation of the joint idea to the client; an idea that was concocted while Bill was not even present. "Okay, we'll accept your counter and call it a day. I'll revise the agreement to reflect the changes so Drew can sign."

"Whoa. Not so fast. I want the solutions before I'll authorize Drew to sign the paper," John's voice growled out from the box.

Satisfied that the taped verbal agreement was binding, Bryce went over the solutions with John and Drew, who seemed in agreement, although Bryce was sure that John would have a word or two with Drew for not coming up with the ideas himself.

Thirty minutes later, the executives from Vevey Pharmaceuticals filed into the boardroom. Bryce and Drew greeted their Swiss clients with smiles that radiated confidence.

"Now gentlemen, thank you for your patience. If everyone can be seated, we'd like to outline our solution," Bryce said.

For the next two hours, Bryce and Drew explained the solutions, in great detail, that would resolve the issues threatening to crater the deal. The Swiss executives were ecstatic, and everyone left with a great sense of relief that evening.

It was nearing midnight by the time Bryce pulled his car up to Trump Tower. He had to toot the horn several times before the doorman came out. Bryce tossed him the keys and told him to park his car, reminding him to be extra careful with it. Then he hurried through a side door of his building, stepped onto the elevator, and glided up to the twentieth floor. He entered his decadent flat and took the curved staircase up three steps at a time.

The instant he walked into the bedroom, Lydia sat up and turned on her bedside light. Bryce guessed she had all the night creams ever invented slathered over her face. *Oh God, she couldn't possibly want to make love tonight*, he thought in horror. It would be a dreadful way to finish an otherwise perfect day.

"Bryce, your mother has been calling all day long and said she urgently needs to speak with you. I think she also called your office several times. Did your secretary tell you?"

"When will she learn I don't take personal calls at the office?" Bryce half growled. "Can't she get it through her hippie brain that time is money?"

"Does she call you often?" Lydia asked, her face glowing like Three Mile Island.

"No, this is the first time in a while. But I've made it very clear that she's not to call me at the office." Bryce unknotted his tie and began to undress, carefully hanging his clothes on the wood valet.

"It sounded like an emergency. Maybe something happened to your brother or sister. She was really upset. She wanted you to call the minute you got in, regardless of the hour."

"Why didn't she tell you anything?" Bryce asked, slipping into his luxurious silk robe with an understated paisley print.

"Because Millie," Lydia said, referring to their full-time housekeeper, "was the one who took the calls. I never actually spoke with her."

"So, if you thought it sounded like an emergency, why didn't you call her back?" Bryce asked in an irritated tone.

" Umm, I guess I thought it'd be better if you spoke with her directly. Knowing your mother, I'm sure that's what she'd prefer." The women were galaxies apart and had never really had a conversation beyond simple pleasantries.

Bryce picked up the bedroom phone. "What's her number?"

Lydia looked up the number in a bedside address book. "5-1-1, 2-8-4, 5-4-1-1."

Bryce dialed the number.

"Hello?" His mother's choked-up voice answered.

"Mom, this is Bryce. Lydia told me you needed to speak with me."

"That's right, dear Bryce. Thank you so much for calling," her voice began to choke and crackle. "I have sad news. Your uncle Frank died today while rescuing two children from a burning car." Frank was his mother's youngest and only brother. The two were extremely close.

"I'm sorry to hear that, Mother."

"He died a real hero, honey. He saved two toddlers' precious little lives before he was killed when the gas tank blew up." His mother began to sob.

"Oh, Mother. . ." The master of legal and business oratory stumbled to find words of comfort, so he drew on an appropriate cliché for the situation. "He's in God's hands now." He figured that would calm down his deeply spiritual mother.

Bryce guessed his mother was shocked at his comment, and he hoped her grief was momentarily broken. He usually used the word "God" in the context of goddamn this and goddamn that.

"Thank you. Honey, the funeral is next Thursday, and it would mean the world to all of us if you could come."

"Mom, I'm in the middle of something really important at the office and it is impossible for me to get to California before next Saturday. I'm sorry." Bryce made a note on a pad next to the bed to have Lydia send flowers to his aunt and mother and a spray to the church.

Bryce hated funerals. Burn and urn 'em made infinitely more sense to him. But no, the Elliotts and Franklins, his mother's side of the family, always had to go the whole nine yards.

"I see. Well then, I'll talk to your Aunt Paula. Perhaps we can put it off until Saturday. As I said, we need the whole family here now, and that includes you. Since he died in the line of duty, it's going to be a full-fledged fireman's funeral."

Trapped! "Very well then, Mother. Please call Lydia back tomorrow and let her know if you're able to change the arrangements. Take care and good night."

"Good night, Bryce. And thanks again for making the effort to come home. I know it's not easy with your busy schedule. I love you."

After Bryce heard the line click, he wondered how truly benevolent people, like his mother, could still exist after thousands of years of evolution The last thought he had before falling into a deep sleep was an image of his mother cradling the homeless man he had stepped over—the one passed out on the sidewalk almost a month ago.

THREE

"THAT BE SEVEN dollars twenty-five pleazze," the cab driver announced as he pulled up in front of a SoHo loft on Greene. His passenger handed him ten dollars and quickly hurried into the building. He pressed the button several times, anxious for the freight elevator to open. When it finally arrived, he stepped in, and it seemed like an eternity for it to lumber to the second floor.

He opened the door to his loft and the scent of turpentine and linseed oil roused his desire—his need, really—to paint. The loft rose twenty feet in height and had an enormous steel and paned glass wall that faced the street; the remaining walls were exposed old brick. The furniture was sparse and modern and very contemporary. Light fixtures dangled at different heights and angles throughout the loft to provide just the right amount of light for his work.

He went into a small side bedroom and quickly changed out of his suit and into a pair of jeans and a white Oxford shirt. He then went into the well-appointed modern kitchen and pulled two bottles of water from his refrigerator. He opened one bottle and sat down on his couch and waited for Becca Wilhelm to arrive.

He'd been working with Becca for a long time. Initially, it had been very difficult to get her to come see his work. As a consultant, Becca was highly selective in her clients. When she was younger, she received a full scholarship to the Oslo National Academy of Arts and then went on to do her postgraduate work at the Royal Academy in London. She was currently the deputy director and chief curator of the Solomon R. Guggenheim Museum, and she had a sideline advising a few carefully chosen artists, whom she felt had great potential. He had sent her pictures of his paintings, and after five months, she'd finally agreed to come and examine them. She agreed to take him on as a client and had been helpful to him, though he couldn't explain how exactly.

The entrance buzzer announced her arrival. He hurried to the door, and the sound of his shoes hitting the polished concrete floors echoed across the open room. He buzzed her in. Three minutes later there was a trebled knock on the industrial steel door.

He opened the door and an attractive woman in her thirties, who looked like a ballerina with her strawberry blond hair pulled back in a twist, entered his flat. She was wearing a long, oversized sweater and jeans. She gave him a slight embrace. "Good evening, Calvin."

"Please have a seat." He motioned for her to sit on the couch. "May I offer you something to drink?"

"No thank you." She sat down, looked directly at him, and placed her hand on his shoulder. "Have you made any progress?"

Becca's eyes surveyed the many unfinished paintings around the room. They were exquisite and seemed as if they'd come out of the sixteenth-century, High Renaissance period in Italy. It was a time when Masters' insatiable curiosity and deep insight into the soul of mankind created paintings that transcended time. Men like Michelangelo, Titian, Leonardo, and Giorgione.

She hoped that somehow she could help Calvin complete his extraordinary paintings. he were at odds with himself. It didn't help that he shared very little information about his life. She often referred to an ancient book, *Art and Artists*, for wisdom and guidance on how to help Calvin finish his paintings. The book was one of a kind. It had been a gift from the Keeper of the Royal Academy in London. He'd given her the book two days before he died, saying it was her mission to find the right person to pass it on to. When she asked questions about the book and how she'd know who the next owner should be, he simply offered four key truths about the book. He told her the book had been in existence for hundreds of years, its contents inexplicably changed from time to time, the ownership was provisional, and her ancestor had been in possession of the book at one time. She tried to ask again for some specifics on whom to look for, but the Keeper put his fingers to her lips and whispered in her ear, "The end will be where the beginning is." It had been the strangest, most defining moment of her life.

After many minutes of silence, Calvin finally answered her question, "*The Drowning of Noah* is almost done." He got up, walked across the room and slowly lifted the cloth he'd draped over the canvas. Becca watched as he stood nervously to the side while she began to study his work. *Is he afraid? Of what?* she wondered.

"People live with contradiction in their souls all the time, Calvin, but your work actually puts me in a very disturbing and dislocated state." Her eyes shifted back and forth between Calvin and his painting. "I don't know how to better articulate it. It—"

"It's what?"

"Technically, it's brilliant. You have an extraordinary gift. But a picture of an angelic looking little boy taunting another panic-stricken little boy, who is obviously drowning, with a rope is . . . well . . . God . . . how do I put it? So evil. And to title it *The Drowning of Noah* seems blasphemous, and I don't even know if I believe in God!"

Becca could not take her eyes off the picture. Even though the subject was disturbing, the technique and quality of the painting was like nothing she'd seen before, except for museum masterpieces. There was a sense of movement and countermovement, and the strong contrast of light and dark coupled with the religious theme made the painting reminiscent of the Baroque period. Set against a majestic landscape, the pond was a crystal clear blue color that mirrored a snow-capped mountain, lush trees, and birds that flew unwittingly above the chaos. The pond also reflected the horror on a young boy's face, as he was about to go under the water for what seemed like a final time. The anguish on the drowning boy's face was juxtaposed against the peaceful look on the other boy's face. The sunlight was partially blocked by a dark cloud, and brilliantly hidden in the scenery was what appeared to be fallen wings capped by a halo.

Calvin looked into Becca's eyes. "How many famous artists, including Rembrandt, painted Abraham's willingness to sacrifice his son Isaac? A father willing to kill his son. Is that not evil? Didn't churches, for hundred of years, use art to scare people into believing in eternal hell?"

"Where did this come from?" she asked with urgency in her voice as she tried to grasp his hand so he would look at her.

He said nothing but his thoughts went back to an incidence that happened in his childhood many years ago.

He could actually feel his mother's joy penetrate him as he jubilantly danced by himself to Sly & the Family Stone's "Dance to the Music" under her protective eye. Intuitively, he knew he was a paradox to all but his mother. People wondered how he could be the product of such loving and creative parents when he was so cold and distant.

At age nine, he had an IQ of 192 and was reading every book he could get his hands on. He had a keen interest in science and math, and he listened with unusual intensity to the intellectual conversations in the commune. His mother tried to get him to paint or listen to music with her whenever possible; these activities opened a small path into his spirit—a connection they could share.

"Life is precious and fragile," she told him. "Realize that regardless of how random events appear to be, there is a pattern. Study the patterns and the infinite wisdom of the ages will gradually and incrementally come to you."

Some days, it felt to the boy as if his mother was the only person who believed there was a special plan or place for him. She spoke of the day he was born as if a resurrection had occurred, which he never believed. She said it as if she wanted to make sure his destiny was realized.

"Come on, join the circle," his mother cried out above the music. The boy looked over at his mother forming a dancing circle with his younger brother and sister and members of the commune. They were at a local music festival in Berkeley. Everyone was happy.

"Please come," she encouraged him with open arms. Standing with her back to the sun, she looked like one of the angels she always talked about. Her long, wavy hair, crowned with a wreath of flowers, shimmered in the light, and her white peasant dress draped gracefully from her tall, slender body.

When he was within four feet of his mother, she rushed to him, swooped him off his feet, and twirled him around and around in the middle of the circle that the family had formed around them. She focused all her attention on her son, blocking out the family and everyone else. She began singing "I Want To Take You Higher" in a clear, choir voice that was a stark contrast to Sly's ear-shattering performance.

The boy innately knew that her rendition had spiritual overtones, and he settled his head on her shoulder and listened to her sing. For the moment, his restless spirit was at peace. When the song ended she whispered, "Everything that rises must converge," quoting the title of her favorite Flannery O'Connor book. She kissed him on the cheek and set him down, and he ran off to join the other children for an afternoon swim.

The boy, like his father, was tall and dark-haired. An exceptionally fast runner, he quickly caught up with the other children at the large pond. He slipped off his leather headband, tie-dye t-shirt, and jeans, and jumped, butt-naked, into the cool water. When he was in the middle of the pond, he heard someone shouting his name.

"Hey, come over here," one of his commune brothers motioned for him to swim toward him.

"What do you want, Noah?" he yelled back.

"We're going to make a rope swing and need your help."

He swam over and surveyed the area. "Limb's too high and the water's too shallow," he quickly concluded.

"Come on! Why do ya always spoil the fun?" Fawn, a commune sister two years his senior, moaned.

"I guess if the rope's long enough, it'll be okay," he reconsidered. "Let me see it," he asked as he climbed out of the water. He examined the rope, and after satisfying himself that it would work, he tried to fling it over the branch. After three unsuccessful attempts, a naked couple came over.

"Need some help?" a young bearded man offered.

"Sure." The boy handed him the rope and watched his fruitless attempts to anchor the line. By his ninth try, the boy grew impatient and figured the glossy-eyed man was strung out on drugs.

"Just wait here, you guys," he instructed Noah and the other children, before heading back to the area where his mother and other parents were splashing in the water with the younger children.

As he swam across the pond, he could hear a stream of announcements coming from the stage. "The brown acid that is circulating is not cool. Stay away from it, man. We need all of the stage electricians to meet immediately at the left stage."

"Mother!" the boy called out.

Topless from the waist up, his mother was holding his brother and sister in each arm and bouncing them up and down in the water. "What is it?"

"I need some help with a rope swing. Do you know where Dad is?"

"No, I haven't seen him for hours. Just a minute," she turned around and talked to Jermaine, a commune member who was sitting on a small knoll above them. "Jermaine is coming to help," she called back. Jermaine got up, ran his fingers through his thick Afro, and pulled on a Nigerian shirt.

Jermaine waved and began walking toward the other side of the pond while the boy swam back. As he neared the tree, he sensed that something was wrong. The stoned, bearded man was diving down in the water toward the end of the waggling rope that was now suspended from the tree. His girlfriend shrieked, "Oh fuck! Oh fuck!"

"What's the matter?" the boy hollered out to Fawn, who was frozen with fear.

"Nooahhh! Noah got caught in the rope. He's stuck under the water!" Fawn screamed.

The boy swam calmly toward the scene, plunged down in the murky water, and could see nothing. As he struggled to blindly probe around under the water, one of his mother's Taoist chants suddenly burst into his head: *muddy water let stand will clear*.

He popped back up to the surface. "Stop moving!" He ordered the frantic man. Just before he dove into the water, he was struck by his reflection of indifference when he saw Noah's frantic hand reach above the water. As the silt cleared, he could see Noah's foot caught in the line that had become anchored somehow to debris in the water.

Just as he was able to free Noah's foot, Jermaine jumped in the water and carried Noah's limp body to shore. He began to pump his chest which caused water to come gushing from his mouth. Noah coughed and came to.

The family members drew around the boy and deluged him with praise. But he felt outside it all. He didn't share the others' emotions or relief that Noah would be okay. The whole experience was almost comical to him—the supreme irony of a guy named Noah drowning. He knew this was wrong, but he couldn't force himself to feel what he knew others expected him to feel. His own detachment bewildered him.

The boy's mother came to the scene, and he reached for the security of her hand.

"What's the matter?" she asked.

The boy glanced away from his mother. "Do you think I'm evil?" he asked pensively.

His mother dropped to her knees, faced him, and brushed his shoulder length hair out of his face. She studied her son's anguished eyes in search of the right words. His mother cradled him in her arms and wept. "Dear, precious son, locked inside of each and every one of us is the love of God," she murmured in his ear.

Calvin was lost in his thoughts, and Becca asked again, "Where did this come from?" she tried to make eye contact with him.

"It wasn't what I intended. I started out painting a scene with two young boys on a rope swing over the pond, but it never materialized. The painting just took on a life of its own." Calvin could sense she was attempting to get a read on him. His old self took control and his face remained expressionless. He was steadfast in his decision not give away any information about who he was. He pulled out a five-by-four foot painting that was leaning against a wall and draped in a white cloth. He was haunted by his inability to finish it—one of the first paintings he had started—but it had worked to redirect Becca's attention.

She walked toward the painting to get a closer look. "I haven't seen this one before. Why?"

Calvin shrugged his shoulders and watched as she quietly studied every inch of the painting for a long time.

"There's a, how to put it, a quiet beauty in this scene. Your unique combination of precision and mellowness is just superb, and the textures and colors are ingenious. But—"

"I know.... But when am I going to finish it?" He had asked himself that same question over and over again. His eyes focused on the picture of a woman who was standing next to the ocean in a long, black dress. A silver dolphin pendant hung from a sparkling chain. The scene was painted so precisely that it could have passed for a photograph. The only details missing were her face and hair.

"Well?" she pressed.

"When her face comes to me."

"I see. What will the expression of that face be, when it comes?"

By the unsettled expression on her face, he could tell she was hoping it wouldn't be something gruesome and numbing juxtaposed against the serene setting. He folded his arms, locked his eyes on the painting, and waited for the answer to come to him. Before now, he hadn't thought about the expression of the face, the focal point—the essence of the painting.

Becca sat in a chair and patiently waited for him to reply.

"Someone who's discovered a profound truth, an infinite existential truth," he finally answered.

"What will that truth be?"

"I don't know," he solemnly replied. He wanted to close the subject on his paintings. "Can we take a break? Maybe have a glass of wine?"

"Okay, a small glass." She smiled. Maybe she understood.

Calvin walked across the room to the refrigerator, pulled out a bottle of wine, and poured two generous glasses. He'd had a long day. He sat down on the sofa and Becca sat in a chair across from him.

For a few minutes they said nothing. Then Calvin decided to ask Becca a question that had been gnawing at him for a long time. "Do you ever wonder how different your life might have been if you still had any of *his* paintings?"

Becca didn't answer; she seemed startled by his question. He'd uncovered what just a few people in the art world knew about her family background. Her great-great-grandfather had been Claude Monet. His son, Michel, had an affair that produced an illegitimate daughter in 1940, who was Becca's mother. Michel kept the daughter a secret, but he'd provided for her. However when he died in a car accident in 1966, the world thought he was heirless, and he bequeathed his estate to the Academie des Beaux-Arts and his entire collection of his father's work to the Musee Marmottan Monet.

"Come on, you must have thought about it!" Calvin pushed.

"Well . . .my life would have been different. I would have had my great-great-grandfather's beautiful works of art to love and cherish."

"I mean financially. Just a few months ago, I saw in the *Times* that one of his paintings sold for a hundred million dollars at auction! Wouldn't your life be different if you had a hundred million dollars?"

"It might be different, but not better," Becca replied. She pulled out the book *Art and Artists* from her Guggenheim Museum tote bag and read aloud. "'Aristotle understood the essence of art when he wrote, 'The aim of art is to represent not the outward appearance of things, but their inward significance.' Now my question for you is why do you paint?"

Calvin took a long sip of wine. Becca was changing the subject, but she asked a question he'd been unable to answer for most of his life. "Obviously it's not for money," he scoffed.

"Again, Calvin, why do you paint?"

Becca had once told him she'd never seen anyone paint with his same fervor. She'd watched him whirl oils around on his palette with paintbrushes and paint with unrestrained passion, spending hours on one cloud or painting a detailed image to perfection in twenty minutes.

"Perhaps the answer's in your little book," he quipped.

FOUR

"You'd think a president had died," Bryce whispered in Lydia's ear as a horse-drawn carriage pulled Frank Franklin's casket through the cemetery gate.

"How long does the interment take?" Lydia asked, eyeing the dark gray clouds that were swirling overhead. "I'll just die if it starts to rain. It'll ruin my new Carolina Herrera suit."

"I told you not to wear that! Christ, Lydia, these people would all fall into their family plots, here and now, if they knew you had four thousand dollars worth of rags on your back."

"I don't think they'd be nearly as shocked over my suit as they were over the two incoming calls on your cell during the service!" Lydia snapped back.

Bryce and Lydia fell back into a respectable silence when the family and a battalion of uniformed fireman neared the plot. After the pastor finished the brief graveside service with the Lord's Prayer, Bryce's mother and brother stepped forward. Elizabeth Elliott, dressed in an African caftan, blew a note into a pitch pipe and Jeff strummed a few bars on his guitar. Elizabeth glanced at Jeff and then dropped her eyes to her brother's casket and began to sing, "Turn, turn, turn...."

Even before her sweet soprano voice began the second song, Bryce knew it would be "Amazing Grace." He looked to the east, in the direction of his father's grave and blinked several times, trying to redirect the emotions that threatened to overcome his composure.

Bryce was trying to block out the memory of his mother singing the same songs at his father's graveside almost twenty-two years ago, but it was hard. She hadn't changed much in all that time. At almost sixty, Elizabeth's hair was still a golden brown. Few wrinkles lined her face and her green-blue eyes were still clear and focused.

When the song came to a close, Bryce's attention shifted to the graveside. He was riveted by the coffin that stood on steel runners above the plot and the mound of dirt that was covered by a carpet of ghoulishly green artificial grass. The pastor nodded his head, giving the mortician the signal that it was time to lower the casket.

The steel casket pitched back and grated against the cement casing as it descended into the plot, causing Bryce to shudder. Once it was down, the mourners began to file out of the graveyard, headed for the reception at his aunt's house.

Bryce was unable to shake the macabre image of the casket going, down, down, down into the ground, and he stood frozen by the graveside. He didn't like the anonymous fellowship of death. He could not fathom rotting away six feet under. Images of what his uncle would look like in a week, a month, a year began to play in his mind, as his eyes maniacally darted back and forth between the hole in the ground and the mound of freshly dug dirt. The more he thought about it, the more he wondered, *Is the only difference between Frank and me—a small matter of time?*

A few droplets of rain began to fall from the sky, interrupting his thoughts and prompting Lydia's tug on his arm. "Come on, it's about to pour."

"Ride back with my sister. I'll meet you at the house," Bryce said, his eyes were still locked on the hole in the ground.

"Are you alright?"

"I'm fine. Go catch Kate before she leaves. And tell my mother I'm fine and just need to run an errand before the reception." Bryce waved at his mother who kept looking back at him as she escorted her bereaved sister-in-law to the waiting limousine.

"You don't have an umbrella or anything. Are you sure?" Lydia asked.

"Yes. Please go." Bryce watched Lydia wobble-run in her high heels after his mother and sister. When they were out of sight, he shifted his attention back to the graveside workers and watched them struggle with the heavy cement lid. After a few minutes, it dropped with a horrifying finality on top of the cement casing.

So that's it, he thought to himself. He looked across the graveyard in the direction of his father's grave. He'd never returned to visit or seen the headstone, but he knew exactly where the grave was. He hesitated for a brief moment and then walked the hundred or so yards to his father's grave. The scent of rain filled the air. On the gravesite was a large angel on her knees. Her wings spanned from the top of her head to the ground. On top of a stone altar, her head was bowed down and nestled in a bent arm. Another arm lay over the altar holding a wreath. She was draped in a Roman gown and she was weeping. The stone altar read

Joseph Elliott	Elizabeth Elliott
1937–1977	1939–
Beloved husband and father	Beloved wife and mother

He studied the headstone for a few moments and wondered how in hell his mother could have afforded such an expensive altar. *The less money people, have the more irresponsible they are with it*, he reasoned as his thoughts drifted back to his father.

While other fathers and sons were bonding at the Scout-O-Rama, tossing baseballs and fishing, Bryce was preparing signs for an anti-war demonstration that his dad was organizing with the president of Berkeley's student union.

"So, who's going to be there?" Bryce asked as Crosby, Stills, Nash and Young boomed out from a pair of massive speakers in the living room. "*Find the cost of freedom, buried in the sand . . .*"

"We thought it'd be good if Angela Davis kicks it off because Friday marks the fourth anniversary of Martin Luther King Jr.'s death. Can you believe it's been four years?"

Bryce shrugged his shoulders but didn't respond. The only thing he recalled from the event, besides his parents anguish, was that he'd had to wear a black armband for the next month to his third grade class.

"Nice touch," Joseph said, pointing to Bryce's painting of a dove flying out of a peace symbol.

Bryce smiled. "Umm, who else is going to be there?"

"There's going to be a vet—a Berkeley grad—who was forced to go to Nam by his CIA dad. Poor guy wound up losing half his face, left arm, and the lower half of his leg. Both he and his father are going to get up together and denounce the war. A career CIA guy, getting up and publicly condemning U.S. foreign policy. It's going to be very powerful."

"What's the man going to do when the CIA fires him?" Bryce asked. "How's he going to support himself and his son?"

"What value does a man's life have if it lacks a moral base?" Joseph retorted.

"What value does a man's life have if he gives up everything he's worked a lifetime for?"

"Immeasurable value. Think, Bryce. The very thing he devoted a lifetime to brought great harm to his son! Unfortunately, enlightenment for many men is spawned by tragedy. At least now he'll be able to give his son infinite love and support." Joseph continued to trace out the words *Give Peace a Chance* on the enormous banner.

Bryce clutched the African prayer beads that hung from his neck and wondered how two people who looked so much alike and shared the same blood could think so differently. For his birthday, he'd wanted one of the new electronic calculators, but was instead given the prayer beads that matched the set his father wore around his neck. Did his Stanford-educated father think praying would be more helpful than a calculator in aiding his seventh-grader through an advanced algebra class for tenth graders? Bryce wondered.

Joseph stood back, folded his arms over his bare chest, and examined the sketch. "It needs something else," he observed, while pulling his hair into ponytail. "Come look, Bryce. You have a good eye for these things." He tugged at the bell-bottom jeans that hung loosely around his narrow hips.

Bryce got up and eyed the banner. "How about a peace symbol superimposed on top of Viet Cong and American flags?" he quickly suggested.

He wanted to speed things up so he could join some boys from his school in an afternoon bike ride before the three commune bikes were claimed by one of the other seven kids.

"Great idea!" Joseph said enthusiastically, hugging his son. Bryce surprised him with a little hug back. Unlike the rest of the members of the family, Bryce didn't like physical contact.

Over the years, he became further distanced from his father. And he always felt thwarted in his attempts to achieve and enjoy success. When his parents vetoed a trip during his senior year in high school, Bryce was unable to contain his disappointment. "You mean to tell me you're not going to let me go?" he asked from the far end of a long harvest table that was in the Hearst Street Commune's dining room.

"No, dear, we're telling you that we cannot afford it," his mother replied.

"You can afford to save the entire world and hand out a sandwich to every homeless person on Telegraph Avenue, but you can't spare four-hundred dollars for the trip?"

"It's just not possible on my salary, Bryce," his dad said.

"What about the commune funds? You put fifty percent of your salary into the fund. Last year, everyone agreed to put up seven hundred dollars to send Lark to Guatemala. So why can't they put up a four hundred dollar matching fund to send me to Washington? I worked so hard to earn the other four hundred!"

Elizabeth got up and sat next to Bryce. "Honey, Lark was going on a Peace Corps mission for a year. It's not the same thing as going to the east coast for a week to participate in a debate contest."

"It's not just a debate contest. Berkeley High is ranked third in the nation. We have a real shot at coming out number one in the finals, and I'm the team captain."

"Honey we're very proud of what you've accomplished, but it just doesn't fit," Elizabeth said, brushing her hand across Bryce's face.

"Doesn't fit what, the peace and love rhetoric? Winning the national debate championships would just about ensure me a scholarship to any of the top schools in the country. Track and academics alone aren't guaranteed to cut it."

"Bryce, you're not going to need a scholarship," his mother countered. "You'll be able to go to Berkeley for virtually nothing when your father becomes a professor. And besides, the money from his book will be more than enough to contribute our fifty percent share to the commune and put all of you children through college." Both his parents firmly believed that a full-fledged professorship was right around the corner and that Joseph's book, which he'd been working on for twelve years, would be picked up by a publisher any day. "Honey, listen to a poem that your father wrote about a young man coming of age. It'll help to put your mind at ease."

Bryce shook his head and buried his face in his hands. "Please, not now." The only thing that kept him from lashing out at his parents was a calming Mozart sonata that breezed over from a neighboring house. To think that Mozart lacked any formal training but soared above his circumstances—just as Bryce so desperately struggled to do.

"So, does that help?" Elizabeth asked after she finished reciting the poem.

Bryce had not heard a word but had a response. "Only if it was published and he made some money from it." In a split-second, his mother's joyful face clouded with despair. When tears began to flow down her cheeks, Bryce was sorry he hadn't kept his thoughts to himself.

"Son, money is not important," his father said, wrapping his arm around his wife to calm her.

"Without it, how could we eat?" Bryce asked.

"I'll concede that for the basics it's important, but beyond that it's not. As Gyatso so eloquently noted, as a man's wealth increases, so does his discontent. Millions of people have died in warfare as a result of humankind's collective discontent. Without contentment we are spiritually impoverished even if we possess a great amount of wealth."

"So can you honestly say you're perfectly content?" Bryce asked.

"We strive to be and make practicing contentment a priority in our lives," his dad answered.

"Hmm, why not try to strike a balance between a little financial security and contentment. Half the people in the commune these days aren't working anymore. If they were, there'd be more money in the commune funds. It doesn't seem fair."

"Son, it's our moral responsibility to take care of one another. Some of our family members are just down on their luck right now. Our purpose in life is to learn to love and give unconditionally," his mother said.

"But to everyone who comes to the door?" Bryce asked. His parents had a reputation for never turning down anyone who asked them for help. Over the years, the steady stream of needy souls filtering in and out of the house began to wear on some of the other commune members and, despite their admiration for Elizabeth and Joseph, they began to move out, placing a heavier financial strain on the remaining members.

"Well, now *I* am at your door asking for help."

His mother reached for his hands and looked over at his father. "I guess we could try to tackle the roof repair on our own. It'd save the co-op about five hundred dollars," his mother said. His father smiled and nodded his agreement.

"Really?" Bryce asked.

"Really," Joseph replied. "I just have one request. Over the next couple of months, I want you to ask yourself where you are headed in life and why. I want you to strive to elevate the ordinary to the extraordinary and never lose sight of the truth that lives in the hearts of all of us."

As his father's words echoed from the grave, Bryce turned on his heals and fled from the land of the dead.

Bryce peeled his rented Porsche out of the cemetery gates and headed up Claremont Avenue, but instead of going to his aunt's, he turned on College, which led to U.C. Berkeley, then up Dwight and onto Piedmont. Shortly after passing Memorial Stadium, the drizzle stopped and he turned off his windshield wipers. He turned onto Hearst Avenue and parked across the street from his old home.

The place that had once housed the utopian dreams of a commune was now a fraternity. The place where Bryce had always felt like an outsider was now teeming with preppy, all-American looking Bryce wannabes. Bryce was struck, but unmoved, by the irony and began to laugh. The more he thought about it, the more he laughed and laughed. His out of control laughter began to catch the attention of some of the fraternity brothers. They began to point and stare at Bryce, who responded with a smile and wave, thinking that they were admiring him and his to-die-for car.

His eye caught the western gable of the roof. For several minutes, he studied it. It was no accident, he reaffirmed to himself for the hundredth time. Several days before his father fell from the roof, doing the repairs so Bryce could go to the debate in Washington, DC, his father had received devastating news. He'd been passed over for full professorship—again.

He'd been a dreamer and unable to comprehend that the Board of Regents would never forgive his disruptive anti-war activities. And every single publisher and agent had summarily rejected his manuscript, calling it "a philosophical tome with no commercial value." The do-gooder who set out to save the world left it at forty, leaving behind a devastated and destitute family.

"*One hundred by forty*," Bryce screamed out at the house and his past. The frat boys quickly went inside as Bryce revved the car's engine. By the time he fishtailed into the rain-slicked Telegraph Avenue, the rain had started again and he was singing "Forever Young" with Bob Dylan on the radio.

Three songs later, Bryce pulled into the driveway of his aunt's modest, but immaculate stucco home, which gave rise to a mix of emotions. His aunt and uncle had opened their home to his mother and siblings after his father's death—the only people willing to help. And for the next nine months, before leaving for Yale, Bryce lived in the 1,300 square foot Oakland Hills home, sharing three-bedrooms and one bathroom with three adults and six kids.

He stepped out of the car and Lydia came running out to greet him. "Are you okay? Where'd you go?"

"I'm fine. Come on, let's get out of the rain." Bryce motioned for her to go back inside.

Just as they reached the porch, Lydia turned back and asked, "How are they going to fit everyone in your aunt's home? There must have been at least 250 people at your uncle's funeral."

"California ingenuity: neighbors are also going to open up their houses, so it'll be like a block party," Bryce answered, wondering if Lydia knew what a block party was.

"Why didn't they just reserve a reception area?" Lydia asked

"Brace yourself, honey," Bryce began with his eyes popped wide open in mock surprise. "They couldn't afford it!"

Lydia let out an embarrassed laugh. "Well, why didn't you just offer to pay for it?"

"Pride. I'm already the black sheep of the family."

"Whose pride?" Lydia asked, genuinely confused. Then, without waiting for an answer, she honed in on Bryce's declaration. "How can you say you're the black sheep when your mother loves you so much?"

"My mother loves everybody. I swear, she'd let Saddam Hussein spend the night if he had nowhere else to go."

Bryce took a breath before stepping into the house and readied himself for the family he'd been able to avoid so far by arriving at the funeral at the last minute.

He opened the front door and stepped directly into a packed living room. Lydia pulled him to the side. "Darling, take a look at this. How sad," she said, handing him a card that had been placed next to a Tupperware bowl.

Bryce took the card and read it:

"We are taking up a collection for Frank's headstone. In honor of our heroic husband, father, brother, and friend, we thought it would be fitting to have a special tombstone made with two angels, symbolizing the two precious lives he saved while giving his own. Any amount you can spare would be greatly appreciated. Thank you from the bottom of our hearts for the contribution."

Bryce shook his head: it was more pathetic than sad to live a hand-to-mouth existence your whole life and not even have enough money for a decent headstone. He tossed eight one hundred dollar bills in the plastic tub and shook his head again, more steadfast than ever in his commitment to never, ever be placed in the humiliating situations his family seemed unable to escape.

"Bryce!" his sister, Kate, called out from the kitchen. "Mom said you were coming, but I wasn't about to believe it until I saw you with my own eyes. My God, it's so good to see you! I swear it's been three years!" She wrapped her arms around his neck and gave him a warm and friendly hug. After releasing him, she gave Lydia a small hug. "It's nice to see you too, Lydia. Thanks for coming. Means a lot to the family."

Lydia pulled back a little. Bryce knew she felt out of place in the touchy-feely world of the California Elliott clan. They were such a stark contrast to Bryce, who only hugged her on very rare occasions.

"We wouldn't have missed it for the world," Lydia lied, with one of those plastic socialite grins. In reality, she had told Bryce how irked she was about missing a dinner Linda Berglund was hosting at that very minute.

"Let me just finish setting up the buffet table in the kitchen and I'll be right back," Kate called out.

"Lydia, how wonderful to see you," Elizabeth Elliott's soothing voice greeted her daughter-in-law with genuine affection. "I only wish it were under happier circumstances."

Lydia gave, her a short, side-to-side hug, then flashed a sympathetic glance as she grabbed both of her hands. "I'm so sorry about your brother, such an untimely death. Why in the world would such a good man die so young?"

Elizabeth locked her eyes on Lydia's. "If we had the answer, then perhaps it would take life's journey away." She gave Lydia another hug before wrapping her arms around Bryce. "I knew you'd come," she whispered, trying to choke back a stream of tears. "It's been a long time."

The scent of his mother's patchouli oil brought back memories of a childhood he'd long ago rejected, believing it would weaken and keep him from achieving his goals.

"How long are you going to stay? Can you stay a few more days and celebrate Thanksgiving with us?" she asked.

"We've got a ten o'clock flight this evening."

"Oh, I see," his mother replied with a smile that didn't mask her disappointment.

"Unfortunately I need to get back." Bryce eyed the potluck buffet that was growing with each person who entered the house. He loathed the world of plastic tablecloths, organic mystery food, Rice Crispy treats, Jell-O molds, and boxed wine.

"I see; excuse me, I need to say hello to someone," Elizabeth replied and darted away from her son to avoid showing him how let down she was.

"Yo, Bryce!" his brother, Jeff, called out from a brown, La-Z-Boy recliner. "If ya don't have anything nice to say about anyone, come sit next to me!" he chuckled. "Besides this place is filling up fast, so it's now or never."

Bryce walked across a multicolor braided rug his mother had made years ago and sank down on the plaid couch that had been in the home for as long as he could remember. He glanced over at Lydia. She was trying desperately to keep up a polite conversation with several women circled around her asking about life in the big city.

Lydia shot a pleading look for him to come and save her, which he ignored. She was a fish out of water in the house that was as small as the little teardown beach bungalow they'd recently bought in the Hamptons. She'd fought the purchase, saying it was ridiculous to buy such a stupid little shack when they could stay at her parents' estate anytime they wanted. But for some inexplicable reason, Bryce was drawn to the cottage and offered full asking price the day he saw it.

"So, how's my favorite, big-shot brother doing these days? Still gonna make your hundred million by forty?" Jeff asked in a jovial, brotherly tone adding, "Man plans, God laughs."

Before Bryce could answer, his sister sat down next to him. "Here," she said, handing him a paper cup. "Someone brought some wine that was not in a gallon jug or box, so I poured a glass for Lydia, you, and *moi*."

"Thanks, Kate. So, did you pick up the French on your last jaunt through the bowels of Africa?" Much to Bryce's dismay, Kate, who'd graduated top of her class at the University of Chicago's Medical School, and completed her residency at Stanford, seemed to be devoting herself to the four corners of the diseased, poverty-stricken world.

"No, but I picked up a whopper of an intestinal infection. It had me down for a month in a hospital in Kenya. I almost died." Kate, like her mother, looked like a perfect throwback to the sixties. African beaded earrings dangled from her ears and Birkenstock shoes capped her feet. But unlike her mother, she had long, wavy, black hair.

"Good God, Kate. Why not focus your attention on people here in the United States? The conditions are more sanitary, and I'm sure you could still find an abundance of downtrodden people to help. You've done your bit for global humanity," Bryce said.

Kate just smiled, shrugged her shoulders, and took a sip from her Dixie cup. Jeff leaned forward from the recliner and toward his brother. "I have a question for you, Bryce. Tell me, when are you going to do your bit for humanity, rather than tearing it apart deal by deal?"

Bryce could feel his blood began to boil. "Jeff, you don't know what in the fuck you're talking about."

"All your mergers, acquisitions, leveraged buy-outs, or whatever you call them are putting folks out of work. Shit, look around—twenty thousand jobs lost in the Chase and Chemical bank merger; IBM spins off something and a hundred twenty thousand go on unemployment. General Motors—seventy-four thousand. Sears—fifty thousand. Where does it stop? If you ask me, the only purpose of these huge deals is to enrich a few at the top and impoverish the rest at the bottom. I don't know how you sleep at night."

"Businessmen call it free enterprise; scientists call it Darwinism. It's just part of the natural order of things."

"Natural order of things? Think about the faces behind the numbers! A father goes home to tell his family he's been laid off from the only job he's ever known. A single mom is downsized and goes to bed in tears every night, praying she'll find a job and that she doesn't get sick and bankrupt the family. The dedicated company man is two years away from retirement and gets zapped by *right sizing*? The guy didn't see it coming, and his twilight years are turned from peaceful serenity to a frickin' *Twilight Zone*!"

"Oh yeah? What about the scenario where cuts are not made and companies fail to remain competitive in the global marketplace? Instead of 10 percent of the employees losing their jobs, 100 percent do," Bryce argued.

"That's a bunch of crap, Bryce. If they needed to cut costs so badly then why don't any firms start with the employees at the top? The SOB heading AT&T takes home eighteen million dollars a year and lays-off sixty thousand workers without a second thought. Nobody—and I mean nobody—does work that deserves that salary! How do you justify some fat cat taking home fifteen million a year and then saying, in the name of survival, that he's forced to cut two hundred and fifty poor bastards making thirty grand a year? Why doesn't he just take a fifty percent cut? Can't get by on a measly seven million?" Jeff added acerbically.

"Listen carefully, little brother, in today's world, there's no such thing as job security—even for CEOs—and people need to get a firm grasp of that fact. Those who do will survive, and those who don't will not. Why do you think I've worked my ass off all my life, because I wanted to study and work after school instead of screwing around smoking pot with friends?" Bryce leaned forward and gave his younger brother a cold icy stare and poked him in the chest. "*No*! It's because I wanted to be in control of my destiny *always*. I am not going to be on a roof, feeling I have to end it all, broke at forty, because my unrealistic dreams didn't pan out. Plus, I wanted to make sure that I didn't have to drink cheap wine out of a fucking Dixie cup the rest of my life!"

"You are a miserable son-of-a-bitch, Bryce. I still can't believe Mom has not seen the light about you. She still believes in her heart-of-hearts that God has a special plan, mission, or whatever she calls it, for you just because you almost died at birth. Your life is nothing but a mission of greed. And because of you, and nothing else, our father is dead, so you could go with your debate team to Washington," Jeff snapped back.

Bryce sat back and shot a haughty look at his younger brother. "Listen, pal, we were both given the same opportunity in life. I grabbed the brass ring and got it. You aimed for nothing and got it. Nothing! Tell me, how's the life of a pseudo poet and Xerox service technician? How you support two kids and a wife beats the shit out of me."

"I'm happy with my life and at peace with myself, which is more than I suspect you are," Jeff snapped back.

The chatter of the surrounding crowd had quieted a bit, and heads had turned toward the couch where the three siblings were seated.

"Stop it!" Kate interjected, and physically placed herself between the modern version of Cain and Abel. "Please, out of respect for Uncle Frank, please for Mom's sake, just drop it. Okay? Please, not here, not now!"

Bryce exercised restraint. He had a strange premonition this would be the last time he'd be in the home at 201 Stantonville Drive, and it made him a little melancholy. The perplexing emotion took him by surprise because he'd never cared for the place and rarely had premonitions about anything except business.

As he and Lydia got ready to leave for the airport, Elizabeth thanked Lydia again and tightly wrapped her arms around Bryce. "Have a safe and peaceful journey, son, and if you ever lose your way, just look for the light."

Bryce kissed her on the cheek. Her religious metaphors made Bryce, the agnostic, uncomfortable. He turned and headed out the door into the gloomy November night.

FIVE

The forty-nine senior associates eyed one another nervously as they sat together in a reception hall at the Plaza Hotel. For as long as the firm had been in existence, it had been a tradition at Mortimer & Weintraub to publicly announce the new partners the second Friday in January and then follow up with a dinner-dance celebration in the Oak Room. As it neared six o'clock, the room filled up with thirty-eight partners and one hundred twenty-three associates who hadn't been around long enough to be in the partnership pipeline.

Spencer Livingston sat three rows back, anxiously wringing his hands. Bill Holt, who was seated to his right, bumped his thigh against Spencer's. "Hey, Spence, calm down. Everything's going to be fine," he whispered in his friend's ear.

Spencer cracked a weak smile.

"Oh, come on, Spencer! I honestly think you've got a very good shot at making it. And if for some crazy reason you don't, you'll certainly make it next year," Bill said. He glanced at his old friend, whose horned-rimmed glasses, bow tie, French cuff shirt, and whimsical cufflinks gave him a distinctive flare. His olive skin and strongly defined nose further distinguished him.

"Yeah right; it's all or nothing. Either I make it this year or wind up a partner at some Podunk practice, but thanks for the encouragement."

As Bryce Elliott approached the podium, there was a low rumble of sighs and shuffling about the room. Bryce had offended, humiliated, or brushed off most of the people in the room at one time or another.

He stepped up to the microphone and tapped on it to make sure it was working. He cast his penetrating blue eyes over the audience with an unnatural intensity before he fixed a large, welcoming smile on his face and placed his hands on the sides of the podium. "In keeping with tradition, it's time, once again, to make our partnership announcements. But before we begin, I want to say, to underscore, really, what a difficult job it was to select so few when we had so many first-rate candidates this year. I can remember, not too long ago, sitting in the same place as all of you." Bryce expansively waved his hand across the group of associates who had their fingers, toes and anything else that would cross, crossed. "And I can empathize that it's not an easy place to be," he concluded in his deliberate and authoritative voice.

Bill overheard a barbed comment shot from someone behind them. "Elliott's about as empathic as a black widow spider spinning her web."

"I can remember," Bryce continued, "all the long hours and sacrifices I made as an associate and my deep anxiety as the time to announce the new partners drew near. Each and every one of you is a winner and talented lawyer. Now, it's time for me to step aside so Abraham can announce this year's partners." Bryce sat down and a soft applause filled the room.

Bill Holt limply clapped his hands together, leaned into Spencer, and snickered, "His cup runneth over with shit."

Spencer responded with an approving chuckle, and then fixed his eyes on Abraham as he walked up to the podium.

"Prior to making the announcements, I want to reiterate Bryce's comments regarding our decision-making process this year. It truly was exceedingly difficult. You are positively the most outstanding class of associates this firm has ever seen."

Abe reached into his breast pocket, pulled out his glasses, and slipped them on. He then smoothed open a piece of paper on the podium and cleared his throat. "As I read the names, I'd like the newly appointed partners to stand and remain standing until I've announced all the new partners."

"Hey, good luck, Spencer."

"Thanks. You too. Winning isn't everything," Spencer paused, "but losing sucks."

Bill laughed.

"The names will be called out at random, so there's no need to twist your brilliant minds trying to figure out who's next. Okay then, let's begin."

The room hummed with the sound of forty-nine senior associates shifting nervously in their seats. "The first associate is about as versatile as they come. He was able to quickly master all areas of the M & A business in a very short time, and his ability to speak fluent German, French, Spanish, Dutch, and Japanese has been immensely helpful in keeping existing foreign clients happy and bringing new ones in. Please join me in welcoming Mike Myers."

Myers stood up to a round of applause. He tried, but failed to keep his exploding jubilation to himself, and cried out, "*Wow*!"

"Congratulations, Mike," Abraham smiled. "Our next associate is a mastermind in both the domestic and international tax arenas. We have never seen a mind that is so knowledgeable, creative, and clever. He truly never ceases to amaze me. Please join me in welcoming Pat Dahlgaard."

Again the room exploded with applause, as the reserved and dignified associate stood up and graciously acknowledged the recognition with several nods and a smile. "Well done, Pat," Abraham congratulated him.

"Our next associate has an uncanny knack for bringing in business and has billed more hours than there are in a day. On top of that, he's an extremely competent attorney, and unlike the rest of us, he's pleasant to be around." Howls of laughter echoed around the room.

In anticipation of Bill's name being called, Spencer slapped his hand against Bill's shoulder. "Way to go, guy!"

"Please join me in welcoming Doug Kari." Doug stood up and graciously smiled and mouthed *thank you*.

"Old Abe must have mixed up the introduction cards," Spencer said wryly to an unfazed Bill.

"Our next associate—" Abe began.

"He didn't say 'final' so there must be five!" Spencer whispered excitedly to Bill.

"Is one of the hardest working souls I have ever come across. For some, life comes very easily; then there are the others who must work extremely hard for every extraordinary stride they make, day in and day out. This hard worker's rise to the top is the result of drive, ambition, and leaping over setbacks with a positive attitude. It is my great pleasure to welcome Spencer Livingston." Spencer was so stunned that he remained glued to his seat.

"Hey, pal, time to rise and shine!" Bill excitedly nudged his friend.

Spencer shot a dazed look at Bill, and rose out of his seat like a zombie. His look of utter shock slowly transformed into a smile, and he turned three hundred and sixty degrees around to acknowledge the applause.

When the cheers died down, the forty-five remaining senior associates sat in agonizing anticipation for the next announcement. Those who were grounded in reality knew the next name out of the hat would be Bill Holt's. Those who were not imagined their own name ringing out of the speakers and filling the room.

When the grand hall quieted down Abraham took back control. "Congratulations to you, Spencer. It appears that your peers and colleagues unanimously back our decision regarding you. Moving on, we have a unique situation that has arisen this year. Due to the large number of outstanding candidates, we have elected to break with tradition and are pleased to announce that six people will be named partners this year. Our fifth partner knows more about the SEC than the SEC itself, just as much or more about the business side of M & A deals than most of the investment bankers, and is one of the toughest negotiators in the business. Please join me in welcoming Suzanne Cole."

A tall, attractive blond with an athletic build and chiseled Nordic features stood up and waved. The remaining women associates in the crowd had trouble hiding their deep disappointment. Everybody knew the female quota had just been filled.

"Now moving on to our final partner announcement," Abraham cleared his throat and took a sip of water. "He is a true Renaissance man. He is a man of great intellect, great insight, and has an insatiable curiosity about everything that surrounds him. Along with being a superb lawyer, he is by far one of the most interesting people I have met in my life."

Spencer started to shift nervously back and forth on his feet and glanced down at Bill who seemed just as perplexed as he. 'A Renaissance man with insatiable curiosity' was not a very good description of Bill Holt.

"Please join me in welcoming Barry Brandeis!" Abraham announced earnestly.

The room once again broke out in polite applause, while the forty-three senior associates whose names had not been called tried to keep a stiff upper lip. Spencer looked down in stunned disbelief at Bill, who sat expressionless in his chair, and his disbelief was shared by all of the other associates, who were seated around them. No one could believe that Bill Holt had not made the cut.

"Congratulations to you, Barry. Now without further ado, let the celebration begin!" Abraham declared with zeal. "I believe all of our spouses and significant others are eagerly waiting for all of us in the Oak Room." Abraham walked down the stairs and began to shake hands and work the crowd.

After the room had cleared, Bill Holt buried his face in his hands, slumped over, and shook his head back and forth in disbelief. Spencer sat down next to his friend and said nothing. After three long minutes Spencer spoke. "What in the fuck happened, Bill?"

"Elliott somehow got to Abraham and the other senior partners and screwed me," Bill muttered, his face still submerged in his hands.

"Shit, I told you to never underestimate him, Bill."

Bill slowly sat upright and blankly stared at the deserted room. He said nothing, struggling to regain his physical and mental strength and control. Then his mind went into high gear and he began to think, analyzing questions on how and why this had happened, and what to do next. Bill glanced at Spencer with the familiar look of determination and an enigmatic smile on his face. "This time, my friend, it is Bryce who has underestimated me. Now, let's go enjoy the party."

"Enjoy the party?" Spencer asked with a puzzled look on his face. "Umm, what about Liane?"

"She'll be fine. Trust me. I have a plan, and part of that plan includes marching into that party with a positive attitude."

"What's the plan?" Spencer asked.

"I'll tell you if you want, but before you answer, give it some serious thought. I'm going to have to do this on Bryce's level."

"Bill, you've always been there for me, so if you need me, I'm—"

"Still think about it. And just in case you decide to go along with me, it's best if you distance yourself from me during the party. Circulate, suck up, and play the role of a guy who just made partner to the hilt. Act and be happy."

"Shit," Spencer said, shaking his head.

"Don't worry, just trust me. Bryce won this battle, but I'm going to win the war. Now hurry up. I need to talk to Liane. I'll follow you in a few minutes."

By the time Bill made it upstairs to the lobby of the hotel, Liane had been standing outside the entrance to the Oak Room for forty-five minutes waiting for her husband. Her face was a kaleidoscope of worry and concern.

"God, Honey, what happened? Spencer just told me the news!"

"Bryce screwed me big time."

"That malevolent asshole. How?"

Bill wrapped his arm around his wife and walked slowly away from the Oak Room and toward the legendary Palm Court. "I don't know but I'll find out. He's gotten away with so much shit, he thinks he can do anything to anyone. He's convinced he's indestructible." Bill paused and continued to walk. "But ya know what?"

Liane shrugged and opened her hands.

"I think I know how to take him down," Bill replied, a sharp confident look in his eye. "Let's get quick drink in the Oyster Bar and then go to the party. This'll make more sense when you hear what I'm thinking."

Bill and Liane Holt entered the grand Oak Room with their heads high and warm smiles on their faces. It was loud—the twenty-five-foot ceilings and sable, oak-paneled walls crafted the acoustics of the room such that groups of people needed to speak loudly to be heard. They accepted glasses of wine from a server, and the first person they ran into was Mike Myers. Bill extended his hand, "Congratulations, Mike," he said, shaking his hand, "your appointment was well deserved."

Mike cast a dismayed look at Bill before leaning in to whisper in his ear, "We're all dumbfounded. What in the hell happened?"

"Don't worry about me; I'm a big boy and I'll be fine." Bill felt no need to whisper. "If I don't make the cut next year, I think I'll become a house-husband and just let Liane bring home the bacon," he jested loudly, and slipped his arm around Liane's waist. "Good thing I married a doctor!" Mike laughed and Bill led Liane to a circle of people. Bill was glad he put Mike at ease. Mike had done the same for Bill. His colleagues seemed to think that there had been a miscarriage of justice. It would help with his plan.

Just as dinner was announced, Bill was in the midst of offering his congratulations to the last of the six new partners, Doug Kari. Doug was extremely upset about Bill's fate. When they were both neophytes at the firm, they had shared an apartment for a couple of years before Doug got married. Over the years, a strong friendship had formed between the Holts and the Karis.

"But why?" Doug pressed for the hundredth time.

"Look, it's just one of those things, Doug," Bill answered shrugging his shoulders. "Don't worry. I'm sure by this time next year, I'll be partner."

"Did he have anything to do with this?" Doug asked, nodding his head over in the direction of Bryce.

"Who knows. Let's just drop it and enjoy this nice party. Do you mind if Liane and I join you?"

"I'd be honored," Doug replied sincerely and slapped his arm around Bill. As the two walked toward their table, Bill glanced around the room and his eyes finally captured Bryce's. He shot him a warm, friendly smile and thought, *You're not as untouchable as you think.*

By nine thirty that evening, Bill had made four calls from a pay phone at the hotel: one to Air France to book the first flight to Paris in the morning; and three calls to offshore bankers.

By eleven o'clock, the party was breaking up and the esteemed partners and associates from Mortimer & Weintraub began to slowly file into the lobby and out the elaborate front entrance of the Plaza, where a light snow dusted the trees surrounding the fountain. Bryce was by the door to bid farewell to everyone.

Bill waited patiently in the suck-up line to make sure that he, too, got his chance to tender his *adieux* to dear old Bryce. Bryce was noticeably surprised when Bill and Liane presented themselves. Bill took it upon himself to extend his hand. "Liane and I just wanted to personally thank you for including us in this dazzling and most enlightening event."

"Bill and I hope we have the opportunity to reciprocate your hospitality," Liane added with a gaze that lit up her blue-violet eyes. She looked over at Bill, "Don't we, dear?"

"Yes, of course," Bill answered, trying to hold back a snicker that would expose him.

"That would be very kind, thank you," Bryce responded, working to free his hand from Bill's firm grip. Bill delighted in Bryce's cocky smile that said it all; Bill could see that Bryce thought he'd successfully brought the associate to his knees.

Fifteen minutes later, the taxi dropped Bill and Liane off at their co-op on East 69th between Lexington and Park. Bill had asked Spencer to stop by after the party, and it wasn't long before the intercom buzzer rang and the doorman announced Spencer's arrival.

"Everyone in that room wanted to know what the hell happened!" Spencer declared as soon as he'd shut the apartment door.

"Bill, Spencer, I'm going to say goodnight. I had rounds early this morning, and this has been a very long evening. I'm exhausted. I trust you won't mind."

Bill smiled at his wife—he'd already discussed his plan with her and knew she supported him.

Spencer's eyes met hers. "Goodnight, Liane."

As soon as she'd gone down the hallway toward the bedroom, Bill looked at Spencer. "Bryce screwed me. I still don't know how."

"That's the thing though. As tough as Abraham is, he's always been fair. Bryce can't override Abraham, can he?"

"I think it goes back to the ALPS deal when the negotiations seemed to hit the wall." And Bill recounted how Bryce had used his information and pushed him out.

"You know, I heard from another Mortimer guy in the room that Bryce and a senior Goldman guy left the meeting to pow-wow," Spencer began. "When they came back a half an hour later, they had solutions to the problems holding up the deal. Bryce is just like a frickin' cat that routinely and meticulously covers his shit *and* the tracks leading to it."

"Listen, the solutions for the ALPS deal were my ideas. Bryce took full credit for them."

"Typical."

"I've got a hunch he said something to Abraham that I had some type of substance-abuse problem. And you know how Abe and Sol feel about that type of stuff."

"That's absurd. Everyone in the firm knows you're a lightweight."

"Abraham made a comment in the car on the way to meet the Stokes people. I was so pissed after Bryce booted me out of the deal. I was sweating, wringing my hands—the works. Abraham specifically asked me if I was on any drugs that made me," Bill paused to recall Abraham's exact words, "edgy or restless."

"Hmm, how'd you answer that?" Spencer asked.

"I told him of course not. I was actually thinking *hell, no,* but I didn't say it."

"So what's the plan, Bill?"

"Basically, it involves insider trading, the type that gets guys in big, big trouble. I'm gonna buy options for BioMolecular and trace the account back to Bryce."

Spencer raised his eyebrows and looked down at his hands folded in his lap. Bill could tell he was thinking about the logistics.

Bill pushed Spencer's feet aside so he could sit on the ottoman. "You see, my granddaddy Holt," Bill began, referring to his famous grandfather, who'd made hundreds of millions of dollars in the oil business, "got a little eccentric in his old age."

Spencer smiled. It was well known that in the last decade of his life, John D. Holt was loonier than a fruit bat. "I'm beginning to wonder if those crazy genes are beginning to surface in one of his descendants," Spencer chortled.

Bill's eyes shifted. The whole plan violated his principles, but he was determined not to let Bryce get away with this. "Anyway, granddaddy Holt was convinced that liberal U.S. politicians were on a mission to re-distribute the wealth, and he didn't want his hard-earned money being taken away. Whenever the topic of the IRS or government came up, he'd get red in the face and yell, 'Already gave those sons-of-bitches a fortune in taxes and they're not gettin' any more.' To make a very long, complicated story short, he stashed away money for each of the grandchildren in secret numbered accounts in Switzerland. Until the day he died, he drilled into us two rules that we were to abide by regarding the accounts. One, we were never to discuss them with anyone under any circumstances. And two, we were not to touch the money in our account unless we needed it to survive. Up until today, I've made good on both of Granddaddy's requests, even Liane didn't know about the Swiss account until tonight."

"Wow, that's totally nuts. So what are you going to do?" Spencer asked.

"Basically, I plan to use some of the money in my secret account to purchase BioMolecular options in accounts linked to Bryce through an offshore bank that has an office in Switzerland."

"When?"

"I leave for Europe first thing tomorrow morning."

"And then…?"

"After the Vevey-Bio acquisition closes, I'm going to place an anonymous phone call to the SEC."

Spencer sat back and rubbed his face with his hands. "God, Bill is it worth it? It sounds really risky to me. If you're caught, you could lose everything and wind up in the slammer. Your flight is a traceable event. When you tip off the SEC, there's going to be a major investigation, and

Bryce will not go down without a battle that will rival Jericho, it could all point back to you. Picture this: Bill Holt happens to take a weekend jaunt to Europe, the very same day the shares are bought . . . mere coincidence?"

"Your point about the flight is good and it's a risk I have to take. But the records won't show the options being purchased tomorrow. I'm going to have them sync with the dates when Bryce took trips to Geneva for the ALPS deal."

"Huh? Are you going to have David Copperfield book the trades?" Spencer asked skeptically.

"Funny. No. I'm going to tie the purchases to BioMolecular options that expired on those dates. The Goldman guys kept a day-to-day record of trades related to the target company. And I'm still authorized to tap into the system on the ALPS deal. I checked it out as soon as I got home; so I've got the dates."

"Okay, but how do you buy expired options? And, assuming you could, who's going to execute backdated trades?"

"Shady off-shore bankers can set up the paperwork. They'll buy the options at today's price, so they won't actually be buying expired options. I'm lucky that it's traded within a band of a buck, plus or minus, since the deal has been underway, Bill replied.

"And you know who these guys are?"

"I've got the names of three pros that were involved in the Drexel mess. They're still open for business."

"And they're going to be waiting for you tomorrow—on Saturday? What are—"

"Trust me, these guys are not Swiss; they just base themselves in Switzerland. Most of them work at home with their colleagues, Mr. Telex, Mr. Fax, and Mr. World Wide Web. I contacted them and told them that I needed to meet with them tomorrow, and I guaranteed a twenty-grand payment just for the pleasure of their company. They'll be there."

"Another traceable event," Spencer countered.

"All the calls were made from pay phones at the Plaza. Plus, I only left my middle name—David."

"Okay, so what are you going to do about the flights and entering the country? Someone's gonna have to stamp your passport."

"I've thought about the flight record. Here's my plan. Liane's thirty-fifth birthday is Sunday, so I'm going to," he raised both hands and made the quote-on-quote sign with his fingers, "surprise her with last minute trip to Paris for the weekend. We'll fly into De Gaulle and then I'll train it to Geneva, take care of business and then return to Paris to spend the night."

Spencer sat back in the chair and studied Bill's face. "You're serious, aren't you?"

"I am," Bill replied evenly.

"Bill . . . you're a guy who never breaks the rules and goes out of his way to help others. Think about it, in the end, who really gets hurt by revenge? The old law of an eye for an eye leaves everybody blind. I'm thinking you should just walk away."

"I can't; if Elliott's not taken down, he'll continue to hurt countless others. He is a blight who will never do anything but bring pain and misery to everyone who crosses his path. I cannot live with that.

"Why not just go to Abraham on Monday and tell him your side of the story?"

"Because, I'm at a huge disadvantage. I don't know the whole story. God only knows what lies Bryce told him about me. I need a catalyst to bring Bryce to justice."

Bill looked down at the floor and pondered his predicament. He'd never been vengeful. It went against the essence of who he was. *This isn't revenge; it's justice, and it's for others who could fall prey to Bryce,* he quietly struggled to convince himself.

SIX

Bryce picked up the latest issue of *Forbes* magazine and smiled. The high-priced publicist he'd hired six months earlier was finally earning her keep. Bryce's eyes rested on the caption: "Mortimer & Weintraub Capture an Astonishing Seventy Percent of M & A Deals. How Do They Do It? A Discussion with Bryce Elliott, Ace Lawyer and Consummate Dealmaker."

The cover shot of him was the perfect picture of power. The gray, double-breasted Armani suit accentuated his athletic physique and added an aura of worldliness and sophistication. The photographer had posed him leaning against his English partner's desk, which had been the Duke of Windsor's, and captured the impressive view of Manhattan filling the background.

Adding to Bryce's elation was an article in the far right hand corner of the morning's *Wall Street Journal*: "U.S. Biotech Giant, BioMolecular, Acquired by Vevey Pharmaceuticals. Swiss continue their buying spree of U.S. biotechnology industry." Bryce scanned the article and saw that while he and Drew Williams had been quoted throughout the piece, Bryce's name was used far more often.

Bryce blithely twirled his chair around, plopped his feet atop his credenza, and looked out over the resplendent view of Manhattan and the Hudson River. It was the end of January; a covering of snow glistened in the sunlight. He felt like a king surveying his realm, intoxicated with power. He was a man in control, not one of the poor fuckers who spent a lifetime kowtowing to a chain of morons —themselves powerless peons. It had been two weeks since the new partners were announced, and Bryce was feeling like there was no limit to what Mortimer & Weintraub could accomplish with him at the helm.

Bryce knew that some people, his brother for instance, thought he was narcissistic and heartless—a man who'd do anything to get to the top. But if one really took a cold, hard, objective look at the world they lived in, they would realize humanity as a whole was not very humane.

Over the years, Bryce had concluded that people from all walks of life subordinated others: rich and poor, the powerful and the powerless. It was the natural order of things. And he had a theory that the lower people were on the socio-economic totem pole, the more cruelly they treated others.

Mercy, benevolence, and truly charitable deeds were about as rare as the Hope Diamond, and they sure as hell didn't pay off. His parents were testaments to that. He was a winner in the game of life because, unlike the masses, he understood what life was about: money and power.

Bryce whirled his chair back around and faced the computer on his desk. In a span of twelve hours, he'd received eighty e-mails. Most were from partners and associates who'd become hostages to his goals. Some messages were congratulatory notes on closing the BioMolecular deal; half were about deals in progress; and the remainder concerned potential deals. He noted an interesting idea about merging two technology giants and e-mailed the sender a message to be in his office at eleven fifteen that morning. Then he buzzed his secretary.

"Good morning, Mr. Elliott," a pleasant voice answered.

Bryce was taken aback by the unfamiliar voice.

"Good morning, Mr. Elliott. What can I do for you, sir?" The voice inquired for a second time.

"Who is this?" he asked tersely.

"Audrey, Mr. Ryan's administrative assistant. I am filling in for Mimi, she's unable to come in today."

Bryce cut her off. "Not coming in today?" he asked in an annoyed voice. "She sure picked the mother of all days not to come in. I'm booked solid until eight o'clock tonight."

"Yes, sir, I am aware of that. When Mimi called in this morning, she made sure that I was up to speed on everything. She's already given me a run-down on what's in progress and where everything is."

Bryce was fuming. He was working on a highly confidential matter that required transcribing some extremely sensitive information. "So, do we know why Mimi's not coming in today?" Bryce inquired caustically.

"Oh, I'm sorry, sir. She got word late last night that her best friend's husband died, and she flew down to Atlanta to attend the funeral. The family's Orthodox so they needed to bury him before sundown today."

"Attending the funeral is not going to bring him back," Bryce snapped and flipped off the intercom line.

Suddenly and unexpectedly, Abraham appeared at the door, catching him by surprise. Bryce had not heard Abraham's familiar heavy step, which usually gave him advance warning.

Bryce folded his hands on his desk, like an obedient schoolboy, and smiled. "Good morning, Abraham." He greeted him cordially and motioned for him to have seat in the green leather chair that faced his desk. He then rose from his desk and walked toward the tea tray that had been wheeled into his office minutes before. "Can I get you anything?"

"A cup of coffee," Abraham responded before plunking himself down in the chair.

Bryce handed him the cup of coffee and sat in the twin chair that faced his father-in-law. "So, what brings you down here so early?" he asked amicably.

"That," Abe responded flatly, pointing to the *Forbes* magazine. He paused and took several sips from his coffee before continuing.

Although Bryce had mentioned there was going to be an article, he downplayed it because he hadn't wanted Abraham to poke around, adding his two cents here and there.

After a few seconds, Abraham cleared his throat. "Attending *whose* funeral is not going to bring *who* back?" he asked with disapproving curiosity.

"Oh, the husband of one of Mimi's friends," Bryce replied evenly, hoping that Abraham would not delve any further into his caustic remark. When Abraham did not like something, he had a habit of drilling down and down until the object of his displeasure was reduced to pulp. Bryce was in no mood to have Abraham break the spell of this special day.

"I see," he huffed.

"Great news! Payday for BioMolecular happened yesterday. At three p.m., twenty two-million was wired into our corporate account." Bryce reversed the negative tide of the conversation. "And, just as you requested, I followed up with the Stokes people. Good news, Abe. Morris Stokes is flying up from North Carolina tomorrow, and I've set up a meeting with the legal and financial folks at CBS. Plus, Morris has accepted our offer for dinner tomorrow evening. This deal could be big, Abe, really big."

Abraham's eyes widened with delight. "How big?"

"Twenty-two billion dollars big!"

"Incredible. I'm confident you'll make it happen. Just remember in the future I don't want anymore surprises on the press front." He tapped the Forbes magazine. "How about if you and Lydia join Rachel and me for dinner at Palio's this evening? It's been a while since we've all gotten together."

"That would be great, Abe, but I'm booked solid until eight."

"Fine, I'll have reservations made for eight forty-five. My secretary will call the girls. Okay?"

"I look forward to it," Bryce lied. Recently, every time the four of them got together, Lydia and her mother ganged up on him and started pushing the baby issue. Bryce couldn't bear the thought of Lydia mothering his children. Each year he used the excuse that he just needed a little more time before being ready for fatherhood. He figured if he was able to delay it long enough, her biological clock would finally stop ticking, and the issue would become irrelevant. But, to his horror, Lydia had announced the night before that she had tossed out her birth control pills and declared that it was time to make a baby, "No ifs, ands, or buts."

Bryce knew, sooner or later, even Abraham—who was dying to have grandchildren—would join the fray. *Time for the old snip-snip*, he thought.

With an ache in his groin, he jotted a note on his calendar to make an appointment for a vasectomy. *Procreation is out of the question*, he silently decreed.

Abraham picked up the *Wall Street Journal*, slipped on his bifocals, and began to read the article on the Vevey-BioMolecular deal. After a few minutes, he folded the paper and patted it on Bryce's knee. "Great deal, Bryce. I'm extremely pleased with how brilliantly this deal was handled. In celebration, I'm picking up the tab, so order champagne from the right-hand side tonight!"

Two blocks away, Bill Holt sat in a small, nondescript deli in the shadows of the Twin Towers. Like Bryce and Abraham, he too was celebrating the closing of the deal, but for very different reasons. His eyes fanned over the *Wall Street Journal* article for the hundredth and last time. *With any luck, it won't be long before Bryce makes the headlines again*, he mused.

"You want anythin' else, hun?" a middle-aged waitress with a beehive hairdo asked in a strong Queens accent.

"Just the check, please," Bill responded politely. While he was waiting, he debated whether or not he should make the call from the pay phone by the men's room here at Nathan's Deli, or go back up to Midtown and make the call from the hospital where Liane could keep an eye out for anyone who might overhear.

But the hospital might not be a good place if the call were traced; there was always the chance he could be linked to it through his wife. Plus, what if one of her colleagues at Mount Sinai noticed him and questioned why he wasn't at work?

Bill barely noticed as the server placed the bill for his tea and toast on the corner of the pea-green Formica table. He sat still and worked on getting up the nerve to place the call that would land someone behind bars. He just hoped it'd be Bryce and not him.

He'd been very careful in his preparation, planning, and set-up; he'd arranged for confirmations of the backdated trades to be planted in a bureau in the private dressing room adjoining Bryce's office. Spencer had skillfully executed the risky deed about a week before when Bryce had invited all the new partners to his office for drinks before taking them out to dinner. Just as they were about to leave, and after everyone was sufficiently loosened up by a drink or two, Spencer asked if he could make a quick stop in Bryce's private bathroom.

"Be my guest," Bryce graciously replied. He even allowed several other new partners to use the bathroom, which they secretly dubbed Las Vegas on Steroids because of its gaudy gold fixtures, excessive marble, and view of the Hudson River. *What will Bryce do when forced to use a steel, lidless can in the slammer?* Bill wondered as he mustered the courage to make the call. He paid the $5.98 tab, added a 15 percent tip, and headed toward the men's room. At 9:38 a.m., the coffee shop had just about emptied out, leaving him, the staff, and an elderly couple.

Bill entered an alcove by the restrooms in the far left hand corner of the restaurant and looked around to make sure he was out of earshot. He picked up the receiver, dropped in two dimes, and whispered, "Showtime, you bastard," before carefully punching in the telephone number for the SEC. When he heard the line ring, his heart began to thunder in his chest, and for a fleeting moment, he felt like slamming the receiver down and calling it quits.

"U.S. Security and Exchange Commission. How may I direct your call?"

"The director of compliance," Bill replied, his voice hoarse with fear.

The line began going through a series of clicks, and any person placing an ordinary call would think little of it. But for Bill, paranoia overtook his normal sensibilities, and he began to imagine a gigantic monitoring room in the SEC where incoming calls were traced. He pictured a wall-sized electronic map of the city with red lights blinking like crazy at the corner of West Broadway and Barclay Street, pinpointing his precise location.

"Mr. Starr's office," a bureaucratic voice answered.

"May I please speak with him?" Bill asked, his voice growing more hoarse by the minute.

"Who's calling please?"

"I prefer to remain anonymous."

"I'm sorry; he's in a meeting right now. May I take a message so he can call you back?"

Bill breathed deeply before responding. "I'm sorry, ma'am, but as I mentioned, this is an anonymous call, and it's rather important," he said in a direct, but exceedingly polite tone.

"I see. Well, perhaps you could call back."

"Is his second-in-command available?" Bill pressed, wanting to get the whole ordeal over with.

"That would be Mr. Mori. Let me transfer you. The phone rang several times.

"Jim Mori speaking."

"Yes, Mr. Mori, I'd like to place an anonymous tip. Are you the correct person to speak with?"

"Depends. What is it regarding?"

"Insider trading."

"Yes."

Bill paused and took several deep breaths. "Well then, are you prepared to take notes?"

"It'd be better if you could come down."

"I'm sorry, that will not be possible."

"Okay then, shoot."

"Before I begin I have two questions. First, I'd like to know if this call is being traced? And, second, I'd like to know if it is being taped?"

"In answer to you first question, no, it's not being traced. In response to the second question, with your permission, I'd like to record the call."

"I don't want this call recorded," Bill said sternly, and did not get into threatening legalese that could give away the fact that he was an attorney. He knew without his approval, the call couldn't be recorded and if it were, it couldn't be used in any legal proceedings against himself or Bryce. "After you confirm that the call won't be recorded, we can move on."

"Not recording the call. I'm ready when you are."

"This information is tied to the Vevey Pharmaceuticals acquisition of BioMolecular. In a nutshell, the lead counsel representing Vevey purchased options of BioMolecular during the course of the deal. I don't know the exact amount, but I'm assuming it must've been quite a bit to make it worthwhile." Bill started to sweat. Of course he knew exactly how many options had been bought, down to the last dollar, and how much profit had been made—a million options, yielding a net profit of twelve million dollars. "The individual in question is Bryce Elliott, partner of Mortimer & Weintraub." Bill heard an audible gasp whisk across the line.

"Bryce Elliott?" the SEC man asked, unable to hide the astonishment in his voice.

"Yes, Bryce Elliott. I believe the trades were executed offshore."

"Where offshore?"

"No idea, but I believe somewhere in Europe," Bill responded and thought to himself, *Unless this guy is a complete idiot, he'll narrow it down to Belgium, Switzerland, or Ireland.*

"What else?"

"That's all I know.

"Are you sure you don't want to come forward? I assure you we'll protect you and your identity."

In Bill's mind, he thought, *Yeah, right up until you subpoena me to testify before the Grand Jury.* But he answered politely, "I'm sorry, no," and hung up. He leaned against the wall and caught his breath. By the end of the conversation, his heart was pounding so hard it was ringing in his ears. He went into the bathroom and looked in the mirror. *Fuck, I hope this doesn't blow up on me,* he thought and splashed some cold water over his sweaty face.

Just as he was toweling off, the pay phone began to ring and ring. He raced to it, overcome by a sense of dread and thinking, *What should I do? What should I do?* On the fifth ring, he picked up the line and said nothing.

"Please deposit an additional seventy cents," a computer-synthesized voice repeated. Bill let out an enormous sigh of relief, dropped the money into the slot, and left the receiver off the hook just in case the SEC tried to call back. He caught his breath, combed his hair, smoothed out his shirt and tie, and walked through the deli, opening the door onto a shadowed, early winter sidewalk.

He entered the lobby of the World Trade Center, waved his ID in front of an inattentive security guard, and headed for the massive bank of elevators. He followed several people into the car and pressed the button for floor eighty-one. *If Bryce Elliott had never been born, I'd be headed to eighty-two, the partners' offices*, he thought bitterly.

The elevator ascended at ear-popping speed before stopping at eighty-one. He stepped out and quickly tried to blend into the pack of hurried-looking people who were rushing about. He'd left his coat and suit jacket in his office, hoping no one would notice he'd been gone for an hour. He turned right, headed down the hall that lead to his office, and ran smack into his secretary.

"Bill, where've you been?" she asked with a look of panic on her face. "I've been looking all over."

"I had to look up a few things in the library, and then I went down to the pharmacy to pick up some medicine. Trying to fight a cold I feel coming on. Why?" he asked in a nonchalant manner that masked the alarm that exploded inside him.

"A half hour ago, Abraham invited everyone up to the boardroom for coffee and pastries to congratulate the Vevey-BioMolecular team."

Bill's stomach cramped and his mind swirled with a thousand incriminating thoughts. *God, now the whole firm knows I couldn't be found at the precise moment that the call was made to the SEC. Oh God, I'm screwed!*

"Bill, are you okay?" his secretary asked, her tone laced with concern.

"This cold may worse than I thought. I feel terrible," Bill responded, using the illness as an excuse for the look of death that probably swept over his face. "I think I'll be okay once I sit down."

"Is there anything I can get you?"

"A glass of water would be great," Bill answered, already making a hasty retreat to his office.

Two weeks later, SEC officials Mark Starr and Jim Mori sat in a small conference room pouring over the past four months of trading activity for both Vevey Pharmaceuticals and BioMolecular stock for the zillionth time.

"This has got to be it," Mori declared, pointing to a single page wedged among reams of computer paper. "These blocks of options were all purchased in the last couple of months, and then cashed in just as the deal was closing. See?" he said, shoving the paper toward his boss.

"Yeah, and look, whoever set it up knew what they were doing. The shares were cashed out at the same time BioMolecular shares were transferred to Vevey Pharmaceuticals. Very clever. If we hadn't had the tip-off, I doubt our auditors would've noticed these million shares. Only someone very sophisticated and close to the deal could have pulled it off," Mark Starr concluded.

"Too sophisticated!" Mori huffed. "Unfortunately the trail ends with a transfer to an offshore account in the Netherlands Antilles." Under a treaty between the U.S. and Switzerland that covered insider trading, the SEC had been able to secure limited cooperation from the Swiss authorities, but there was no such treaty between the U.S. and the Netherlands Antilles. "It'll be impossible to get the boys in the Netherlands to release any info on the account. And if they do, I'll bet it's going to be a secret numbered account. I'm almost sure of it."

"Have we been able to trace any unusual movements of money in or out of Elliott's accounts?"

"Hard to say. The guy spends buckets, and his wife's share of the spending rivals an Arab sheikh's. Listen to this." Mori slid on his horn-rimmed glasses and read from a computer-generated report. "This is what our guys have summed up for the past four months: sixty-two grand for his mortgage payments to Chase; thirty-grand in condo fees; over a hundred grand on credit card expenses; and one hundred and twenty grand on a private yacht lease."

"Did he take the trip to Europe?" Starr asked hopefully.

"Don't know; we're checking on it right now. You want me to continue?"

"Yes."

"Okay let's see," Mori traced his finger back to where he left off. "Wife spent about thirty grand on clothes and beauty salons, and another twelve on a bunch of miscellaneous stuff. And they bought a property in the Hamptons for six-hundred and sixty-eight thousand."

"Six hundred and sixty in the Hamptons? Must have been a real dump," Starr said, half jokingly.

"Yeah, six-hundred grand—a teardown, no doubt."

"Life's tough!" Starr said sarcastically. "How old is this guy anyway?"

"Thirty-eight."

"Any red flags in his history?"

"Nope. Guy seems to be a driven little bugger and has worked his butt off to get where he is," Mori answered. "But on the other hand, he's no saint. Apparently he can be a tyrant to work with. Here's the most interesting tidbit of all. During our background check, the clear motivating force behind this guy is money. All the way back to his days at Yale, he's been vowing to make one hundred million by the time he turns forty."

Mark Starr's eyes lit up and he leaned across the small conference table. "So what do we put his net worth at today?"

"Well, we've got forty-eight million on the low side and sixty-five at the high. There's no way of telling for sure at this point," Jim Mori answered. "But he's more than a tad off from the hundred million goal."

"So, when's our friend turning forty?" Mark asked.

"Not until April of 2000."

"Hmm, he's only got fourteen months. What do his tax records show?"

"He's only making a measly six mil a year," Jim answered in mock sympathy.

"Tisk, tisk." Mark said, shaking his head. "And what about his passport record?"

"Let me call Liz O'Neill. She was supposed to have it to us this morning." Jim dialed the number of the international investigator.

"O'Neill speaking," the voice rumbled out of the speaker box.

"Hey Liz, it's Jim. Any word from the State Department on Elliott's travel schedule?"

"It's your lucky day. Came through the fax five minutes ago. Want me to walk it up?" the investigator asked.

"In a while. For now, can you just read off the dates and locations?"

"Sure. Commencing when?" Liz asked.

"Five months ago—so starting in September please," Jim answered.

"Okay, let's see here." Jim and Mark could hear papers shuffling. "In September, a three-day trip to London. In October, a trip to Geneva and Frankfurt—"

"What were the dates in Geneva?" Jim interrupted.

"Ah, let's see. That would be the tenth and eleventh." Liz responded.

Jim pointed his finger at Mark, and mouthed "bingo."

"And in December," Liz's voice went on, "there was another trip to Geneva on the sixth and seventh, and London on the eight through ninth. Then in January, he was in Geneva on...."

Jim flashed a piece of paper at Mark with *3 & 4* scribbled on it.

"The third and fourth," Liz said matter-of-factly, oblivious to the elation on the other end of the line.

Mark responded to Jim's option trade dates with a thumbs-up sign.

"That's it, guys. No more traveling from that point on."

"Thanks a lot, Liz. When you have a chance, can you get a copy to me?" Jim asked.

"You bet. Catch you later." Liz signed off, and Jim and Mark just stared at each other for a few moments before either spoke.

"Okay, we know he did it, but how do we prove it?" Mark asked and downed the remnants of his morning coffee, now cold and bitter, causing his lips to pucker.

"I guess we dig around and try to find any accounts that have gone down about a million and a half over the period when the options were purchased. It's not easy to move that kind of money out of the country, ten grand at a time."

"We can try, but you know how these guys operate. He's too smart to move any amount that would force a bank to throw up any flags. Or leave any trail."

"Probably. Can we get any more out of the Swiss?" Jim asked.

"They claim they've provided all they've got."

"What about asking them for the name of the broker or brokers who handled the transactions?"

"We can try," Mark said, reaching for the phone.

SEVEN

THREE OF THE nine passengers riding the elevator to the eighty-second floor of the World Trade Center wore leather holsters concealing semi-automatic pistols beneath their suit jackets. One carried a court order and search warrant, another clutched a metal briefcase that was filled with evidence collection paraphernalia, and another carried a large legal briefcase that was empty in preparation to be filled with the State's evidence. The three remaining men were armed only with their SEC identification.

Mark Starr and Jim Mori exchanged glances. They'd done a tactical dry run earlier that morning, but they knew their asses were on the line. If they failed to find anything, Mortimer & Weintraub would go after them, the SEC, and the courts with the equivalent of a nuclear arsenal. They'd run out of options though. They were so close and so sure, but they lacked additional evidence needed to guarantee a conviction against Bryce Elliott.

The elevator opened to the cherry-paneled reception lobby of Mortimer & Weintraub, and the men quickly filed out. No one said a word. By the look in the receptionist's eyes, Jim Mori could tell she immediately sensed something was wrong. Mark Starr and an FBI man walked up to the young woman, whose dark eyes had grown to the size of saucers. She was just transferring a call when another line began to ring.

"Don't answer it," the FBI man said in a stern commanding voice.

"Excuse me, sir?"

"Please don't answer the phone. FBI." The man flashed his badge. "We want you to take us directly to Bryce Elliott's office."

"Is he expecting you," she asked.

"No," the FBI man responded.

"Well then I need to call him. I'm sorry, sir, but I'm not authorized to let anyone pass until I have clearance from the person they're meeting."

"We have a court order." A man from the back stepped forward and handed her the search document.

The receptionist noticed the agent's gun holster, and she accepted the document with a trembling hand. "I'm sorry, but I'll need to call my supervisor or Mr. Elliott. I'm not in a position to let you in on the basis of a piece of paper."

In a rush, two FBI men walked around to the receptionist and each gently reached for her arms. "Now, if you'll please lead us directly down to Mr. Elliott's office."

The woman stood up, and had a terrified look on her face. "Who are you?" she cried out. "Oh, please, don't hurt anybody!" The terrorist bomb that had exploded in the garage of the World Trade Center several years before left most people with a heightened sense of fear and vulnerability.

"We assure you we are with the FBI and are not going to hurt anyone. Now please, take us to Mr. Elliott's office."

A team of two agents and one SEC official swung their dark blue sedan into a yellow loading zone on Fifth Avenue and parked directly across from Trump Tower. In a rush, they crossed against the red light, entered the building, hurried past the upscale shops, and headed directly to the rear of the opulent lobby. An FBI agent approached the uniformed doorman.

"Good morning," she greeted him in a voice slightly above a whisper. "We're with the FBI, and have a search warrant for unit #58JKL." She displayed her badge and handed him the court paper.

"Mr. and Mrs. Elliott's apartment?" he asked with a raised eyebrow.

"That is correct," the woman answered.

"Just a moment, please, and I'll call up to the unit," the doorman replied.

"Actually, we'd prefer you didn't."

"Okay then, but I'll need to call our security and have them escort you up."

"We need to go right now."

"I'll have security here in a minute."

Bryce was sitting behind his massive desk, holding court with two lawyers and three tobacco executives. They were discussing several target companies for the executives to consider. Tobacco companies were Bryce's favorite clients because they never complained about the high legal fees and were always extremely eager to diversify into other areas.

"It's all about seeing a window of opportunity and going for it. And this is a terrific opportunity," Bryce said with conviction. He reached into his breast pocket for the obligatory cigarette he always smoked with his tobacco clients, and he insisted that the other attorneys on the team do the same.

"I still don't know, Bryce," the CEO hesitated. "If you ask me, a Virginia tobacco company buying a life insurance company could get some pretty bad press."

"Political *kamikaze*," the head of the acquisitions division interjected. "No, thank you," he responded to Bryce's offer of a cigarette. As Bryce sat back down, he caught a glimpse of his reflection in an antique framed mirror on the wall. He brushed back a wisp of hair that was out of place.

"Yes and no," Bryce replied to the executive's rebuttal, and lit his cigarette with an expensive gold lighter. "It all boils down to how you spin it in the end. I was thinking—"

The double doors to his office popped open and nine people, whom Bryce had never seen before, burst into his office. Bryce was furious and ready to kill Mimi, who trailed behind the group.

"I'm terribly sorry, Mr. Elliott," she said in a pleading voice.

Acutely aware that his clients were present, Bryce resisted the urge to scream out, *Get the fuck out of my office*! Instead, he took his anger out of the freshly lit cigarette, crushing it into the ashtray. He walked calmly toward the group. "Excuse me, gentlemen, there seems to be some mistake. Now if you'd be so kind as to leave my office, my secretary will be happy to help you find whoever or whatever you're looking for," he said while arrogantly looking several of the agents up and down. Most of the men looked nothing like the well-heeled CFOs, CEOs, and chairmen of major corporations that typically graced the eighty-second floor. Surely, this group was supposed to be meeting with some associates on the floor below. Bryce turned to go back and join his clients when he felt a firm grip on his shoulder. He slowly turned around and his entire face was twisted with rage.

"We're in the right place," Mark Starr evenly responded, tightening his grip on Bryce's shoulder. He flashed his SEC card, and the head FBI man stepped forward and presented his ID.

"Call security this instant!" Bryce commanded his secretary.

"Who are these other people?" the FBI man quietly inquired, tilting his head in the direction of the tobacco clients and attorneys.

"None of your fucking business," Bryce hissed back in his face.

"Last chance, Mr. Elliott. Who are these people?" Mark Starr asked.

Deciding it would be in his best interest to be more cordial, Bryce responded, "They are other attorneys in the firm and executives from U.S. Tobacco."

"I'd suggest, for your own benefit, you end this meeting now and ask these gentlemen to leave immediately," the FBI man said.

"End the meeting?" Bryce asked incredulously. "These men have flown up from Virginia to meet with me. I'm not ending this meeting."

"No, the meeting ends here and now. Either you do it your way, or we will," the FBI man said as he held up the search warrant for Bryce to see.

Bryce said nothing as he scanned the document. Blinded by shock, he could barely make out the words on the page. He walked to his clients and colleagues, all of whom looked at Bryce expectantly, like he'd have an explanation that made all of this make sense. "I'm terribly sorry, but something of extreme urgency has come up. Mike, please take our clients down to the boardroom and continue without me. I'll join you as soon as I take care of this."

"Is everything all right?" John Minor, the CEO of the tobacco company asked in a tone more prying than concerned.

"Just fine, John. I'll join you as soon as I can. Please accept my apology for the interruption. And thank you for your patience."

John Minor nodded as Mike rose from his chair and motioned for the clients to follow him.

As soon as they were out the door, one of the FBI agents shut Bryce's door. "Mr. Elliott, we have a court order and search warrant authorizing us to search your office and your home," the agent informed Bryce.

"My office and my home? Why on earth . . . ? What the hell is going on?"

Another FBI agent stepped forward. "You have the right to remain silent. Anything you say can and will be used against you. You have the right to an attorney, and if you cannot afford one, one will be provided by the courts. Do you understand your rights Mr. Elliott?"

"Am I being arrested?"

"That depends on what we find. Now if you'll please have a seat on the couch with Agent Hutch."

"Someone's at my home?" Bryce asked, trying to mask his irritation. Someone had made a mistake, a horrible mistake, and when he found out who, he would crush them. His mind started to work on who or what might have caused this.

"Yes, two agents and a representative from the SEC have been dispatched to your home," the FBI agent responded.

Bryce's anger turned to fury. He tried to keep calm because he knew it would be to his benefit. "What is this all regarding? I have a right to know."

"Technically, you do not have a right to know unless we press charges against you, Mr. Elliott. Perhaps you'd better call an attorney who can advise you."

Bryce thought, *Better call an attorney who can advise me?* He was struck by the irony. Here he was, grand Wizard presiding over 212 of the brightest legal minds in the country, and none could do the job. Outside of the firm, no one's name came immediately to mind. *Perhaps I should call Abraham*, but then he thought better of it. Abraham was meeting with some of the firm's most important clients. He needed to consult his personal list of contacts. "I need access to my computer. All the attorneys I know are in my directory."

"I'm sorry, you can't have access. If you give us the name of the file and the person, we can look up the number for you," the FBI agent answered while opening a drawer in Bryce's desk.

Bryce did everything he could to keep from exploding. He knew the warrant gave the agent the right to search, but in Bryce's world, no one but Bryce had access to that desk. He closed his eyes and tried to think. "I honestly don't know offhand. I need to look through my directory." Several of the authorities raised an eyebrow to his reply. Although Bryce had nothing to hide, raw fear and anger surged through his body. It was interfering with his ability to think.

"I'm sorry. That's not possible," the agent replied.

Millie Smith, Lydia Elliott's housekeeper was beside herself with worry. For ten minutes, she'd been trying to call Mrs. Elliott. The agents instructed her to stay in the foyer and not to move unless told otherwise. So she sat, perched like an obedient dog, on the bottom stair of the main staircase, nervously tapping her foot on the marble floor. She clutched the portable phone and kept praying it would ring. It was Tuesday. Herbal wrap day. Millie had left three messages already.

"Where is Mr. Elliott's office?" one of the agents asked.

"Downtown, in the World Trade Center. He is a very important person. You know he's going to be very mad when he finds out you've been here. I hope he's not—"

"No, his office here at home. Where is it?" the agent huffed.

"No one's allowed in there. You cannot go in. Even I'm not allowed to clean in there unless Mr. Elliott is home. He keeps it locked," the uniformed maid chirped, almost in victory.

"Where is it?" the agent asked sternly.

"Second door on the left down that hallway." She pointed to the corridor that banked the left side of the foyer.

The agents marched quickly to Bryce's office, picked the lock on the solid mahogany door, and disappeared inside.

It took fifteen minutes, but the name of a Securities Law attorney finally came to him. "Jack Thomas, that's it!" The guy had tried hundreds of SEC cases and won more than 80 percent of them. He approached the head FBI official. "Could you please look up the number for Jack Thomas of Thomas, Martin & Perry?"

"Sure," the man replied, and directed the agent who was obviously the computer whiz to do so. Several minutes later, the man wrote down the number and handed it to Bryce.

"I'd like the call to be private. Surely I have that right," Bryce said.

"Yes, you do, Mr. Elliott. One of our agents will escort you to a conference room. We'd prefer glass, otherwise the agent will have to go in the room with you."

He wanted to shove the guy out of his office and make the fucking phone call, but he restrained himself. There were other ways, later on.

Bryce stood and grabbed a yellow legal pad from a side table and went for the door, thinking, *Fuck them—whoever is assigned to be my hall monitor will have to catch up.*

On opening the door, Bryce was startled to see a group of about fifteen people milling around his secretary's desk, watching the firm's head security man arguing with a female FBI agent while a guy from the SEC looked through files on Mimi's computer. The desk looked like it had been ransacked. Everyone turned to look at Bryce.

He looked down at the number written on the paper in his hand. Trying to think quickly, he asked, "Don't you all have work to attend to? Mimi, write down the names of all these people who have nothing better to do than stand around other people's desks."

"Yes, sir," Mimi replied hesitantly.

"And as soon as Mr. Mortimer finishes up with his clients, please ask him to come down to my office." Before heading down the hall, he shot a long hard stare at the flock of people who knew that there'd be hell to pay.

Bill Holt was just finishing up a conference call with some German bankers when an associate tapped on his open door that was slightly ajar. Bill motioned for the guy, who had a look of urgency on his face, to come into his office and have a seat. The instant Bill hung up the phone, Al's mouth opened. "Did you hear what's going on?"

"No, what?"

Al's eyes looked like they were going to pop out of his head. "No one knows for sure, but something's coming down. The FBI and SEC are tearing the office apart," he replied, short of breath.

"Tearing the office apart?" Bill asked evenly. Inside, his heart was pounding. *Day of reckoning*, he thought, surprised at how quickly the SEC had acted. It had been almost a month since he placed the call—but he'd called about Bryce, not the firm. "What do you mean tearing the office apart?"

"Well, not exactly the whole office. Apparently they're concentrating on Bryce's office and Mimi's desk."

Bill let out an internal sigh of relief. "Does anybody know why?"

"Nope. Apparently Bryce went ape shit when he saw some people hanging outside his door, so the word's out to stay clear."

"Well, I guess all we can do is wait. Now if you'll excuse me, I need to make another call," Bill said with a smile. "And please close the door to my office on the way out."

"Sure."

Bill got up from his desk, walked to the window, and looked at the world before him. He pumped his fist in the air and knowing no one could hear, he whispered, "You'll never hurt anyone again. The gig is up, you bastard." As he turned, he caught his reflection in the window and wished he hadn't. A man with a guilt-ridden face stood paralyzed in the moment. In his entire life he had never intentionally harmed anyone. He tried to reassure himself that this was justice, not revenge. "Justice, *not* revenge," he whispered to his conscience.

Abraham was in the midst of an intense conversation with some of his favorite clients—executives from the largest food conglomerate in the world, who had a seemingly insatiable appetite for buying companies—when his secretary knocked on the door and handed him a note. As she walked out, Abraham finished talking and discretely flipped on his bifocals to read the typed note.

"*Your daughter is holding on line four. She said it is an emergency and must speak with you right away.*"

Abe was unnerved by the message and feared something dreadful had happened to his wife, who had a heart condition. "Could you please excuse me for a moment? I need to respond to an urgent message." Abraham masked the dread that gripped him as he looked up from the note.

"Of course, perhaps this would be a good time for a short break to stretch our legs," the senior executive replied.

"Thank you very much. I'm sure I'll just be a few moments," Abe said as he cordially walked his clients to the door. "If you need anything please don't hesitate to ask my secretary, Miss Miller."

His secretary ushered them into a conference room across the hall, asking if she could bring them any refreshments. Abraham shut the door to his office and rushed to take the call. "Lydia, darling, what is it?"

"Daddy, I just got off the phone with Millie, and she said the FBI and some other officials are ransacking our house!" Lydia began in a hysterical tone.

"Slow down, honey. Where are you?" Abe asked.

"At the spa. I'm getting dressed and going home right now, but I wanted to talk with you or Bryce first. What should I do?" She was frantic.

"Where's Bryce? Have you spoken with him?"

"I tried, Daddy, but his private line kept ringing and ringing, then it goes over to the reception desk or his voicemail. What's going on? That's never happened before!"

"I have no idea." Abe answered just as his secretary entered his office again and passed a second typed note to him.

"*Mr. Elliott would like to see you in his office as soon as you are finished with your client meeting. Extremely important and urgent. 10:45 a.m.*"

"Listen, honey, I just got a note that Bryce wants to see me. I'll check with him and call you back. In the meantime, get to your apartment as soon as possible to observe what's going on. When you get there, don't say a word, and *do not* answer any questions. Just wait until Bryce or I arrive.

Okay, honey? And please, remember under no circumstances are you to say anything."

"Okay, Daddy. Why in the world would anyone be searching our home?" Lydia asked with whining concern.

"I honestly have no idea, dear. Try not to worry. I'm going to try to get a friend of mine, William Cella, a top attorney, over there post-haste. His office is just blocks from your place. If he comes, you can talk to him, but not in front of the officials."

"Daddy, what's going on?" Lydia asked, sounding like she did when she was eight years old.

"Honey, just let me get off the phone so I can find out." After he hung up the phone, he raced to Bryce's office at the opposite end of the hall. He saw a man and woman going through Bryce's secretary's desk. "Who the hell are you?"

"SEC and FBI," the woman answered and shoved her badge in Abraham's face.

Wasting no time, he turned toward Bryce's door.

"I'm sorry, no one may go in there unescorted."

"Then escort me the hell in there. You better have an airtight court order and search warrant. I want to speak to Mr. Elliott and whoever is in charge here," Abraham thundered.

"Mr. Franklin is the head FBI agent and Mr. Starr is the head SEC officer. Now if you'll please follow me."

Abraham followed the woman into the office and his jaw dropped to the floor. Files sat in small piles on chairs, tables, the floor—it was impossible to walk around in the customarily immaculate office. "I demand to know what's going on in here!"

Mark Starr stepped toward Abraham and extended his hand. "My name is Mark Starr and I'm the director of compliance with the SEC. And you are…?"

"I am Abraham Mortimer, chairman of this firm," Abraham replied with a less than enthusiastic handshake. "What you are doing and where is Mr. Elliott?" His voice was in full authoritative throttle.

"Mr. Elliott is trying to reach his attorney in a conference room. For now I would prefer not to discuss the purpose of our search."

"Excuse me?" Abraham's voice boomed. "I believe you must, if asked, declare the purpose of your search."

"Not in this case. Now if you'll please excuse me." The SEC director turned and resumed his searching of the place.

Abraham was stupefied. *Why is Bryce calling an attorney?* he wondered as his mind raced through many possibilities. Bryce suddenly emerged through his double office doors, escorted by a young agent. He had a dazed and bothered look about him. For some reason, at that moment, Abraham thought of Sol and wished he were here. "Bryce?"

Bryce looked up with searching eyes. "Abraham! Abraham, do you know anything about this?"

Abraham led Bryce to the far corner of his office, as far away from the ears of the watchful agent. "No, I haven't the slightest idea. Do you?" Abraham asked, searching Bryce's eyes for an answer.

"God no!" Bryce replied in panicked voice. "How can we end this search? Is it legal?"

"If they have a bona fide search warrant, it's legal. I seriously doubt we can put an end to it. The agent said you were calling your attorney. Who?" Abraham asked.

"I tried to reach Jack Thomas, a classmate from law school."

"Why him?" Abraham fired back. Everyone knew Jack Thomas as a top criminal lawyer who'd handled, and won, most of the high profile SEC cases.

Bryce immediately went on the defensive. "Because without warning, the SEC rushed into my office this morning with a search warrant. What would you have done?" Abraham could see Bryce struggling to keep it together and hoping to get some sign of agreement from his father-in-law.

"How about try to call me immediately," Abraham answered tersely. "Whatever this is, it's big. Did you know they're also at your home?"

"Yes."

"Before we get counsel over here, I am going to ask you one last time, and then I will not ask you again. Do you have any inkling, whatsoever, about what's going on?"

"Absolutely not. You have my word, Abe."

"Okay then, let's get to my office." Abraham patted Bryce's shoulder, and the two began to walk toward the door. "So have you spoken to Thomas?" Abe inquired in a low whisper.

"He was on the phone. I told his secretary it was urgent, so I expect he'll call back any minute."

"I was thinking that William Cella could also be of help. Perhaps we could ask Thomas to come here and have Cella go to the apartment. Lydia called me. She's on her way there now," Abraham said, as Bryce opened the door for him.

"Excuse me, gentlemen, where are you going?" Agent Franklin asked, after being alerted by his subordinate that Abe and Bryce were leaving.

"To my office," Abraham answered indignantly.

"Someone will have to escort Mr. Elliott."

"Under what authority? He's not under arrest, is he?" Abraham asked, his voice thundering across the room.

"No, Mr. Mortimer, he is not under arrest. However, under the terms of the search warrant, we are authorized to keep an eye on him until our search is completed."

"I see," Abraham flatly responded, reining in his anger. "Well then, escort us! We are leaving now." Abraham declared and motioned for Bryce to go out the door first. The pair walked down the hall, eyes straight ahead, without saying a word. No one dared to look at Bryce or Abraham as they passed by. There wasn't a soul in the firm who wasn't aware of what was happening. The two men entered Abe's office and were trailed by a young FBI agent. Abraham turned to him. "Excuse me, but you are not invited. This call is private. I know we've a right to that."

"That is correct, Mr. Mortimer, however, under the terms of the court order, I'm authorized to keep a constant eye on Mr. Elliott."

"Just stand at the door and watch," Abraham said.

"I'll go along with that, provided you don't log onto your computer or put any documents or papers on your person."

"'Documents or papers on my person?' Where did you learn English?" Abraham asked in a nasty, condescending tone.

"In this country, sir. I went to Yale, same place as your son-in-law. I'm an '88 man, six years behind Mr. Elliott."

Abraham knew now they'd done their due diligence. The agent pulled a side chair from Miss Miller's desk and sat down at the threshold of the door.

"Oh damn, what am I going to do about the Foodsource America people?" Abraham half mumbled to himself and looked at the FBI agent who was planted at his door. "I can't just leave them waiting."

"How about if John Pipia takes them to lunch," Bryce suggested, referring to a senior partner, whose cousin happened to be the chairman of Foodsource.

Abraham glanced down at his watch. "Eleven forty-five. I guess we really don't have much of a choice. I'm going to personally obliterate whoever is responsible for this fiasco!" Abraham looked at Bryce, shook his head, and with a measured degree of irritation, said, "I'd better track down my clients so they don't stumble on a goddamn G-man at my door. You get a hold of Cella and Thomas. Send Cella to your place and get Thomas here." Abraham walked up to the agent at the door, expecting him to move out of the way. When the man stayed in place, Abraham grew fierce but composed himself with a deep breath and a few steps around the man in the chair.

Bryce sat down at Abraham's desk to make the calls.

Forty-five minutes later, William Cella arrived at the Elliotts' apartment and Jack Thomas stepped out of the elevator doors onto the eighty-second floor of the World Trade Center, where he was met by Miss Miller, who briskly walked him down the hall to Abraham's office. After offering to take his coat and asking if anyone wanted anything to drink, she departed, firmly shutting the door behind her.

Jack extended his hand to introduce himself to Abraham. "Hello, I'm—"

The door to Abraham's office swung wide open, and the young FBI agent resumed his watch at the door. Abraham glanced over at him with fury in his eyes, but said nothing.

"I'm Jack Thomas," he finished without much more than a glance behind him at the young agent in the doorway.

"Pleased to meet you," Abraham replied.

"Hello, Jack. Thank you for coming on such short notice," Bryce said and extended his hand. "Shall we?" Bryce motioned for Jack to move to the corner farthest away from their FBI spectator. As the trio sat around a small English antique table, Bryce looked out the window. Clouds had moved in from the south, and the sunny March morning had suddenly turned gray and gloomy. Bryce tried to think if he'd seen any clouds in the sky earlier that day.

"So gentlemen, how about a quick run down on what's going on? Who is at the door?" Thomas asked as he pulled a yellow notepad from his briefcase.

"He's an FBI agent. The terms of the search warrant provided them with the authority to keep an eye on me," Bryce replied.

Thomas raised a questioning eyebrow. "May I see it?" he asked.

Abraham looked expectantly over at Bryce. "I don't have a copy," Bryce replied.

"You don't?" Abraham asked.

"They didn't give me one. I glanced at it when they presented it though. There is a clause in it that states they have the authority to keep watch over me during the search," Bryce replied.

Abraham's eyes bore into Bryce. "You mean to tell me that you allowed these assholes to plow through our firm after *glancing* at the warrant?"

"I looked at it, Abe, and I read the court order. They have the right to search my office and home. I'll get a copy from our *friend* at the door."

Bryce walked across the office, requested and received a copy of the warrant from the agent, and then proceeded back to the corner table and handed it to Jack.

After reviewing the document for several minutes, Jack looked up. "Bryce is right; they have the authority to conduct the search at both his office and home and to keep an eye on him." Jack rubbed his eyes. "The thing I don't understand is why they're focusing on just Bryce and not the firm. Are you sure you have no idea what they're after?" he asked Bryce.

"Absolutely not. I—!"

"Which brings up another question," Abraham interrupted. "Can't we demand an explanation, at the very least, as to what this is all about?"

"They haven't told you?" Jack asked, both surprised and concerned.

"They've said in this case they don't have to," Bryce responded. "Is that unusual?"

Pulling his phone from his breast pocket, Jack answered, "It is. Let me try my contacts at the SEC and see if I can get some information."

Bryce and Abraham looked at each other and then at the agent at the door.

Speaking into his phone, Jack regained their attention. "Yes, this is Jack Thomas, of Thomas, Martin, and Perry. I'd like to speak with Mr. Baxter please." The lawyer's eyes caught Abraham's and Bryce's eyes and then shifted back down to his legal pad where he started to doodle. After a few moments, he spoke again. "Hello, Vince, thank you for taking my call."

Bryce was sufficiently impressed, and he could tell Abraham was too. Their counsel was on the line with the head of the SEC. "I'm with a client, Bryce Elliott, right now and I have a few questions." Abraham and Bryce, listened intently as Jack recapped the situation before beginning to quiz Baxter.

After a few minutes, it was clear by the look on Jack's face that he was not getting very far. "Sure, sure, I understand. If the situation changes, I'd appreciate it if you could give me a call."

Bryce nervously tapped his foot on the floor.

"Yeah, you bet," Jack continued to talk into his phone. "I'm looking forward to teeing off with you on Sunday. Fingers crossed for good weather. Okay then, thanks."

He clipped his phone shut and glanced up at Abraham and Bryce. "He wouldn't budge. We have no choice but to wait and see. Given what you've told me, Bryce, there seems to be some terrible mistake or misunderstanding. From time to time, the SEC gets a bad tip and overreacts. So, since there have been no improprieties that both of you are aware of, and they seem to just be focusing on Bryce, they'll probably wrap it and leave in a couple of hours. At this point, it would be my recommendation for you to just sit it out."

"That's it?" Abraham asked.

"At this point, it seems so. Given the circumstances, I see no need for me to hang around. You could just call me when they finish up. In the unlikely event something comes up, I'll be back over in a flash. Believe me, I wouldn't lose any sleep over this."

"Perhaps you wouldn't, Mr. Thomas, but I sure as hell will!" Abraham said abrasively. "I had to brush off some of the firm's top clients this morning, and by now the rumor mill is probably spinning out of control. I want you to go back to your office and think about what recourse we have against these assholes."

"I'll give it some thought, but I don't think there's much that can be done. Just be thankful that it's a mix-up. I assure you Mr. Mortimer, after years of trying these cases, the last thing a top-notch firm like yours needs is to be associated with anything that even remotely reeks of an SEC violation. My advice would be just to drop it and move on." The lawyer opened his briefcase, slipped his notes inside, and rose from his seat.

Bryce piped in. "Do you think there'd be any benefit to giving William Cella a call before you leave? He's at the apartment now, overseeing things."

"Sure. To make sure it's smooth sailing. Good idea."

Bryce hit the speed dial on Abraham's phone that was marked 'Lydia,' and flipped on the conference box. After two rings there was a pick-up. "Good afternoon, Elliott residence."

"Millie, this is Mr. Elliott. Could you please put Mrs. Elliott on the phone?"

"Certainly, just a moment, sir."

"Bryce!" Lydia exclaimed, obviously relieved to hear her husband's voice. "Did Daddy tell you what's going on?"

"Yes, dear. Is William Cella with you?"

"Yes, he's in your study."

His inner sanctum. He shuddered and asked, "May I speak with him please?"

"Is everything all right, darling? What's going on?" Lydia asked.

"Everything's under control, honey. As a matter of fact your father is here with me right now."

"Daddy?" Lydia called out.

"Yes, dear, I'm here. Now please put William on the phone," Abraham said.

"William Cella speaking," a clear, controlled voice bounced out of the box.

"Hi, William, it's Abe. We've got Jack Thomas here at the office, and decided to give you a call before he heads out. How are things going?"

"Hello, Abraham. Hello, Jack. Is Bryce there?"

"Yes, hello, William. I'm here," Bryce replied.

"Hi, Bryce. Have you been able to determine the cause of the search? The officials here refuse to talk. The only thing I've been able to get out of them is a copy of the court order and search warrant."

"We're in the same boat down here," Jack Thomas replied.

"Strange. So no charges have been pressed against Bryce?" William asked.

"That's right," Jack answered.

"Damn curious. I've been keeping a close eye on them and have inventoried the items that they've collected," William said.

"They're collecting evidence?" Abraham asked with a startled look on his face. "What type of evidence?"

"So far a personal calendar and passport."

"Hmm, maybe I'd better go back to Bryce's office," Jack mumbled.

"Might not be a bad idea," William replied. "Unless there's anything else, I'd like to go back to keeping an eye on these guys. Abe, I'll call you and Bryce straight away if anything else comes up."

"Thanks, William. We'll speak later then," Bryce replied, looking at Abraham, who was nodding his head, and disconnected the line.

"In light of William's information, I'd like to go to Bryce's office for a while to observe." Jack got up from his chair.

"Should I join you?" Bryce asked.

"No, I think for now it's better if you stay out of the picture."

"What would they want a personal calendar and passport for?" Abraham asked. By the look in his eye, it was clear to Bryce that Abe wondered why he hadn't asked the question.

"Information on someone's comings and goings. Beyond that I don't know." Jack headed for the door. "If it looks like there's no need for me to stick around, I'll stop by and let you know before I leave." Jack glanced at Bryce. His face betrayed him, showing fear and anguish, a contrast from his typical aura of impervious omnipotence. "Hey, you've done nothing wrong, so there's nothing to worry about."

As Jack walked out, Abraham looked Bryce straight in the eye. "Nothing to worry about, right?"

"Nothing to worry about," Bryce answered resolutely.

"In that case, I'm going to reconnect with the Foodsource people. They're probably just starting lunch." Abraham stood up. "I'm going to bury the bastard who's responsible for this!" He walked past the agent seated at the door, this time without waiting for him to move.

As Bryce's eyes roamed the immense room, a peculiar sense of not belonging began to grip him. He hadn't felt this way since he was a child. It was a feeling foreign to him in his adult life. Not only did he always belong, he wrote the rules of membership.

Bryce was not going to let these insignificant government peons get the better of him. With the FBI escort on his heals, he marched back down to his office. Like it or not, they'd just have to work around him! He swung his office door wide open in a dramatic and challenging announcement of his arrival and was greeted by a round of astonished stares. Agent Franklin walked rapidly toward Bryce with a look that was so intense and purposeful, Bryce unconsciously took a step back. When he was face-to-face with Bryce, he pulled a small laminated card from his breast pocket and began to read him his Miranda rights for a second time that day.

"You have the right to remain silent. Anything you say can and will be used against you. You have the right to call an attorney...."

Bryce shot a look at Jack, thinking, "Why are you just sitting there? Do something!"

"Do you understand your rights?" Franklin asked him.

Bryce said nothing and kept his eyes locked on Jack.

"You need to answer the question, Bryce," Jack said.

Bryce's lock on Jack broke and his eyes slowly panned to the man standing two feet in front of him.

"Do you understand your rights?" Franklin asked for a second time.

"Yes," Bryce answered flatly, and his eyes shifted back to his lawyer.

"You are being charged with conspiracy to commit fraud under United States Code: Title 18,1348," the FBI man stated evenly and motioned for a subordinate to come to him. When the man arrived, Franklin said, "Cuff him."

Speechless, Bryce felt his arms being drawn behind him. "Damn it, Jack, do something!" he called out to his attorney.

"Len, please don't cuff him. Walking out of his office in handcuffs could do irreparable harm to my client's reputation."

"Sorry, rules are rules."

"You and I both know it's not necessary."

"I can meet you halfway; we'll cuff him with his hands in the front and allow him to drape his coat over them."

"Goddamn it!" Bryce bellowed. "Just hold everything. I'd like to confer with my attorney, privately, for just one minute."

"You can go to the corner and talk privately, but we can't leave you alone in the room," the agent responded.

Jack wrapped his arm around Bryce. "Listen very carefully. Things are serious, very, very serious, Bryce. About a half an hour before I came down here, the agents found a series of options that were purchased on BioMolecular."

"What?" Bryce asked, utterly confused.

"Not the actual options, just confirmations. Either way, it's just as bad," he said in a voice slightly above a whisper.

"Well, I sure as hell don't have anything to do with them! How stupid do they think I am? If I were involved in any illegal trading activity, which I am not," Bryce stressed, "the last fucking place I'd leave evidence would be my goddamn office. Think about this, Jack. It's preposterous!"

"Bryce, I know you're anxious to talk. But this is not the place. Just go with them without making a scene, and I'll follow. We can talk later."

"Where the hell are they taking me?" Bryce asked in a voice somewhere between angry and scared.

"I presume the FBI headquarters in Manhattan. I'll confirm and be there before you. I promise."

"Okay, but I refuse to let them handcuff me. You tell them I refuse to walk out of my office in handcuffs," Bryce said.

"It's better if you cooperate," Jack advised.

"I don't give a shit. I haven't done anything wrong and you just tell them it'll be a cold day in hell before I waltz by everyone in this firm in handcuffs."

"I'll do it, but it's against my better judgment," Jack replied and walked over to Agent Franklin.

After a few minutes of an intense conversation, he returned. "Okay he'll do it, but here's the deal. You will be escorted out of the office with a man in the front, rear and either side. Once we're in the elevator the cuffs go on."

"That's the best you can do?"

"It's really better if you cooperate. I know you understand this. You don't have to walk by everyone on the floor, but once you're in the elevator, it's different," Jack replied. He then announced to the investigative team, "Gentlemen, we're ready."

The group quickly gathered up what they had come for and headed toward the door. As Bryce and his unwanted entourage spilled out into the corridor, people—partners and mail clerks alike—cast a cautious look as they passed by. There was not a doubt in anyone's mind that something was wrong, very wrong.

The young agent nervously punched at the elevator button, while the anxious group stood impatiently around the door. A bell and red light above the door signaled the arrival of an elevator on the eighty-second floor. Before the door was fully opened, the group began to file into the elevator, and the young agent eagerly punched the *close* button. The door snapped shut, and an agent ordered Bryce to put his wrists together and in front of him. Then without saying another word, he slapped on the handcuffs.

Bryce was overcome with an overwhelming feeling of claustrophobia. He wondered if the handcuffs alone evoked that type of reaction, what would happen if they locked him in a holding cell? Every pore in his body began to break out in a cold sweat. He knew he had to get a grip, get control. Bryce closed his eyes, took several deep breaths, and succeeded in pulling himself together. However, his regained composure was short-lived when the doors opened to the gigantic lobby of the World Trade Center.

"We're getting out here and not the garage?" Bryce's lawyer asked.

"That's correct," the head agent responded. "Mr. Elliott, please proceed." His hand motioned for Bryce to step off the elevator.

Bryce's knees locked and he turned back and looked at his lawyer in disbelief. "In the lobby? We're going to pass by at least a hundred people! They've got to be kidding," Bryce said in a modulated, arrogant tone that implied there was no way in hell he was going to get off the elevator."

"Time to get off the elevator now, Mr. Elliott," agent Franklin sternly directed him.

"Come on Bryce, it's not going to be to anyone's benefit, least of all yours, to get into a pissing match on the elevator. I agree that the garage would have been preferable, but...." The lawyer eyed the crowd that was impatiently milling around the lobby waiting to board the elevator.

"Hey, Mister Rogers," a bicycle courier yelled out to the agent—a spitting image of Mr. Rogers—holding the door. "Some of us haven't got all day, so do us all a favor and get off the elevator and go back to your neighborhood." Much of the crowd let out an approving laugh.

Jack draped his coat over Bryce's cuffed wrists. "Come on Bryce, the sooner we get out of here, the better."

Bryce reluctantly stepped into the lobby. The unconventional tightness of the group walking across the expansive lobby attracted curious glances. As the group exited the building, Abraham's Town Car pulled up, and he emerged from the car with the Foodsource clients. Taking a deep breath, Bryce stepped out onto the sidewalk, glanced at Abraham—who had thankfully not noticed him—and then back over at what looked like the FBI's cars. He calculated there was a fifty-fifty chance he'd be able to slip into the car without Abraham seeing him. Innocent or not, Abraham would go berserk if his most important clients witnessed Bryce being led away in handcuffs by an army of Feds. He was perhaps thirty feet from the car when the coat draped over his arms slipped down between his legs, causing him to trip and crash to the pavement. He couldn't break the fall with his handcuffed hands, and his face hit the ground with an audible crack. Bryce's lawyer and several of the agents dropped down to the ground to determine if Bryce, now sprawled face down on the ground, had been seriously injured in the fall. One agent yelled for a first aid kit. The commotion drew the attention of many people, including Abraham and his clients, who stopped to see what was happening.

Abraham watched, in shocked disbelief, as Jack helped Bryce up to a sitting position. Bryce's face, shirt, and tie were splattered with blood, and the right sleeve of his suit had a large rip.

"What the devil is going on over there?" a curious Foodsource executive inquired.

"You know New York, never a dull moment," Abraham flippantly replied and steered the group toward the revolving door of the lobby. Once his clients were safely inside the lobby, Abraham snapped his fingers. "Damn, I left something in the car. John," he said, turning to his colleague, "there's no need to hold everyone up. Why don't you take our clients to my office and I'll be up in a flash."

"You bet," John replied, ushering the unsuspecting clients toward the elevator.

Bryce's head was throbbing and he felt a stream of warm blood gushing down his face. He burrowed his face into his upper arm and tried to wipe away the blood, which was not an easy task with his wrists locked in handcuffs.

One of the agents wiped away the blood with a cotton pad and examined the cut on his forehead. "Doesn't look like anything serious. Worst case, he might need a few stitches." Two agents moved to either side of Bryce and helped him to his feet. He staggered to the car, leaning on one of the agents for support.

"Please get into the car, Mr. Elliott." An agent gently maneuvered his head so it would clear the frame.

The official's words barely registered. Bryce could just make out the sound of his lawyer's voice demanding that they remove the handcuffs, and then he saw Abraham's blurred face appear in front of him before everything went black.

EIGHT

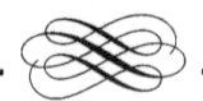

"Here you go, Mr. Elliott," Millie said cheerfully as she placed a bran muffin and slice of melon in front of Bryce. "Some coffee this morning?" she asked, reaching for a silver pot that was placed on a priceless antique buffet table.

"Please," Bryce responded without looking up. He was too preoccupied reading a stack of financial newspapers and praying that his name and the name of the firm would survive another day without hitting the headlines. For the past three weeks, they'd been lucky.

After pouring Bryce's coffee, Millie drew open a row of cream-colored Roman shades that covered a wall of floor-to-ceiling windows in the formal dining room. A flood of early spring sunlight washed over the room. Bryce looked up to see rays of light illuminate the Baccarat chandelier; the two thousand pieces of cut crystal produced a spectacular show of prism lights that danced around the room. The dazzling display was a welcomed contrast to the gloom that had hung over the Elliott residence for the past two weeks.

"Good morning, Mrs. Elliott," she greeted Lydia emerging from the kitchen door. "What would you like for breakfast, ma'am?"

"Just some fruit and yogurt," Lydia answered and placed herself at the opposite end of the fourteen-foot-long dining room table.

"Yes, ma'am," Millie answered.

Bryce set his papers aside, glanced over at his wife and then down at his food. Much had changed in the last few weeks—including where Lydia chose to sit. She'd always sat near him at the head of the table, not fourteen feet away. The thought of the nine o'clock meeting with Abraham and his lawyers took away his appetite, and the one o'clock appointment with the SEC made him physically sick to his stomach. He had a dark feeling. The hypnotic display of lights filtering through the chandelier diverted him momentarily, and he imagined himself embraced and comforted by a gentle sea breeze. *Everything's going to be all right*, a voice inside told him.

Oh God, I'm really losing it now, he thought to himself. *Things could not be worse, you stupid asshole*, he admonished himself. There was no doubt that someone was behind the systematic destruction of his life, but who? He wondered if he'd be able to find out in time. So far the detective he hired had come up with interesting speculations, but nothing tangible. He looked across the long table at Lydia, who was thumbing through a tabloid magazine. He knew he needed her support. He got up from his seat, picked up his cup of coffee, and walked toward her; then he sat down in a chair that was adjacent to her and smiled.

"It was getting pretty lonely down there," he said and affectionately pushed a lock of hair from her face.

She responded with an icy stare and said nothing.

"Darling, during this trying time, you alone have been my rock."

She remained silent as her eyes bore into him.

"Lydia someone did this to me. Someone framed me! I swear to you. You must believe me!" he implored. "Why in the world would I risk everything for a measly twelve million dollars?"

"Why in the world would you get a vasectomy without consulting me?" she asked, tears welling in her eyes. "Don't talk to me about risk. You're a fucking bastard, Bryce. You've ruined everything!" Lydia buried her face in her hands and began to sob uncontrollably.

Bryce stared at her in shocked silence, and his mind began to spiral into a free fall of disturbing thoughts—*How did she find out about the vasectomy? If she knows, then who else knows? Abraham must know! But how?* Then, as if the answer were dancing in the lights above him, he realized Old Abraham must have sicced the FBI-trained private investigator, whom the firm used for background checks, on him! That explained why the PI had been so standoffish when Bryce had called to hire him to find his mysterious adversary. What to do next? He needed Lydia on his side. Perhaps he could soothe her physically. No matter how mad Lydia was, she never turned down the opportunity to have sex with him. He got up and stood behind her. He wrapped his arms protectively around her quivering shoulders and began to lightly kiss the back of her neck, and then he slowly guided her face to his. After gently wiping the tears from her drenched face, he slipped his tongue in her accepting mouth and began to kiss her deeply. For the first time since they had been married, he actually wanted, needed, to have sex with Lydia.

Without saying a word, he gently pulled her up from the chair, wrapped his arm around her, and led her up the grand staircase to their bedroom. He shut the door and made love to Lydia like never before, making sure he sent her to the moon and back. When they were done, Bryce pulled Lydia close to him.

"Dear Lydia, I will never be able to repay you enough," he cooed in her ear and brushed her tousled hair from her face. "Thank you for believing in me. I knew I could count on you."

He turned her head to kiss her cheek and was met by a renewed flood of tears streaming down her face.

"Honey?"

"Bryce, my whole life—our whole life—is ruined, scandalized. Why?" she asked through tears of rage. "Because I made a vow to love, honor, and cherish a cold-hearted, opportunistic bastard!" She rolled over and kneed him as hard as she could in the groin. Bryce howled and pulled himself into the fetal position. She got out of the bed and threw on her silk robe.

Bryce looked up at her like a wounded animal, but was in too much pain to say anything.

"How does it feel, Bryce?" she asked with a hard, callous look. She drew the back of her hand across her face to wipe her runny nose. "I know you'll never have the heart to feel gut-wrenching pain that comes from betrayal and deception, but maybe physical pain where it counts will come close, you son of a bitch!"

Bryce's dazed eyes studied his wife as electrifying pain continued to override his ability to speak, to think. Hatred, sadness, and despair and heartache all played across her face.

"You know, for what it's worth, I actually loved you." She wept, her moist eyes fixed on Bryce. "You've betrayed all of us, and I hope you go to fucking hell!" she cried out before running to the bathroom. A ripple of goosebumps broke out on his arms—tiny bumps, like beads of cold sweat. Her words seared into him. For the first time in his life, he actually felt her pain —someone else's pain —and it was an uncomfortable and alien sensation. No words or logic could describe the confusing and disturbing emotion . . . maybe the painkillers he'd been taking after splitting his head on the pavement were playing tricks on his mind. He glanced over at the bedside clock—7:13—and panicked! He needed to get ready for his meeting.

Bryce stepped into the lobby of his attorney's office. His Savile Row suit was cut from the finest English cloth, and his sky-blue tie complimented his eyes. "Bryce Elliott to see Jack Thomas," he announced with the voice and confidence of a network news anchor.

"Yes, Mr. Elliott, please follow me."

With the posture of a general in wartime, he followed the receptionist down a gallery-sized corridor of the firm. They arrived at a set of double doors that blended with the Asian motif of the office.

When the door opened enough to provide a clear view, Bryce took in a very different scene from what he was expecting. The four lawyers who were working on his case were deep in conversation with Abraham. Half-eaten pastries and empty coffee cups were telling signs that they'd been in conference since early that morning. Bryce looked down at his watch. He glanced at a clock on the wall. Both read eight fifty. He took a breath to try to quell the fury he felt rising up as he realized they'd started the meeting long ago—without him.

"Hello, Abraham, Jack," he tersely greeted them with a slight nod. "I see there's been a mix-up on the starting time," he said. "I was under the impression that the meeting was to begin at nine,"

"Your impression was correct," Abraham said. "For *you*," he paused to emphasize the word, "the meeting was scheduled to begin at nine. You're early." Abraham rolled his fountain pen in his hands and looked back down at a piece of paper he was studying.

Bryce quietly took a seat at the conference table. After patiently waiting for a few moments, he spoke. "Would it be possible for me to see a copy of the document you all have in front of you?"

The lead attorney looked to Abraham for direction. Abraham gave his nod of approval, and the lawyer slid a copy down the table at Bryce. The draft document was entitled "Securities and Exchange Commission vs. Mortimer & Weintraub. Terms of Agreement."

Bryce scanned through the fifteen-page document. It was a negotiated settlement. He had been involved in creating many, many of these during his time at Mortimer & Weintraub. But what made this one unlike all of the ones he'd worked on was that, in the document before him, Bryce was in the lead role of sacrificial lamb.

His head clouded over with terrible thoughts and images. He was struck by a clear image of the painting that hung in the Mortimers' informal sitting room—*Abraham's Sacrifice of Isaac*. He envisioned himself as Isaac, the innocent, only son of Abraham, turning away just as Abraham is preparing to fatally plunge the knife into his heart. *For Christ's sake, snap out of it or you're going to walk out of here a dead man*, Bryce internally reprimanded himself. *There are no such things as angels that descend from heaven to save a man.*

Bryce cleared his throat and regained his composure. "Abraham, would it be possible for us to have a word alone?" he asked politely.

Abraham nodded. "Gentlemen, a few minutes please."

As they got up to leave, Bryce moved from his seat at the end of the conference table to one that was directly facing Abraham. When they shut the door behind them, Bryce looked Abraham squarely in the eye. "This," he began, holding the document up in his hand, "is completely unacceptable. I swear to you, I have done nothing wrong. Please Abraham, believe me—someone is trying to frame me, to destroy me."

Abraham got up from his seat and began to pace back and forth with his hands clasped behind his back. "What goes around, comes around. This is a fact in life, like a boomerang, Bryce—what you hurl into this world comes back in the same form. You know, you really had me—had all of us—going. Had I known your true colors, I would've been glad to bring you down personally. But, because there's justice in this world, you took care of it yourself. At this point, I really couldn't give a shit if you were framed. But with all the evidence stacked against you, I hardly believe that is the case."

"Listen, I admit I've done things others think of as wrong, and I've perhaps hurt a few people, but nothing that merits this level of retaliation!"

"Oh I see. So, who do you think might have framed you?"

"Well, actually several people could have. Peter Hancock," Bryce began, naming the son of a famous senator who'd wanted to become an associate with the firm. Bryce had turned him down gracelessly. "Or Mike Clayton," he said, referring to an investment banker whom he'd publicly chastised and humiliated over a failed deal. "Or what about Bill Holt? He was none too pleased about not making partner. Who knows what all those drugs have done to his mind," Bryce said flippantly.

"Bill Holt? You think?" Abraham asked and thoughtfully rubbed his chin.

Bryce's eyes lit up. "Actually, I think he's the top suspect," Bryce said soberly, thinking, *Yes, now we're on a roll.*

Abraham's face grew red and the veins on his temples started to pulse so hard they looked like they might burst out of his head. "Who could blame him, just a boomerang returning to its thrower?" Abraham growled.

Bryce kept a straight poker face and did not respond.

"Don't act like you don't know what I'm talking about. When you set him up, perhaps you were unaware that Holt's father and I are on the board of directors of two companies together.

"When the shit hit the fan on this insider trading, I started to do a little poking around myself. Last week, George Holt took me out for a drink after a board meeting at Manhattan International Bank and began to grill me on why his son had not made partner. To make a long story short, I told him about your discovery and subsequent confirmation of

Bill's amphetamine abuse. The very next day, Bryce, he had a documented printout sent to me of every prescription his daughter-in-law had written for the past year. And guess what?" he hissed. "Not one—I repeat—not one of the 957 prescriptions was for amphetamines.

"Moreover, he had the hospital where his daughter-in-law works issue a statement that the hospital pharmacy was able to fully account for the amphetamine drugs in their inventory. Plus, thirty minutes after we spoke, Bill Holt voluntarily rushed to a clinic and had a drug test. And you want to know the results Bryce?" Abraham queried rhetorically. "There were no traces of amphetamines in his blood or hair sample, which typically carry traces for up to two months! Oh by the way, while we're on the subject of Bill Holt, I'd love it if you could recap for me, just one more time, how you brilliantly saved the Vevey Pharmaceuticals deal. Also, I'd love to hear the truth, and really nothing but the truth, on what was going through your mind when you had that surgery a couple of weeks ago."

Abraham's words and accusations landed like punches, stinging uppercuts, short jabs, one blow after another. His head was pounding.

Bryce sat motionless. His eyes stared blankly at nothing. But he was thinking. He was thinking of ways to turn the situation around and regain Abraham's trust. *All problems have solutions. All problems have solutions. All problems have solutions*, he chanted over and over again in his mind.

After several moments of silence, he got up and walked over to the wall-to-wall window that had a commanding view of Wall Street. He shoved his hands in his trouser pockets and gazed down at the New York Stock Exchange. *Only the strong survive*, he reminded himself quietly. He was strong. He was clever. He would survive. And he would kill whoever put him in this position.

He turned around and faced Abraham with eyes that were filled with simulated sadness. "I'm so very remorseful and sorry for having had the vasectomy without discussing it with Lydia. You see, six months ago, a cousin of mine had a pair of severely mentally disabled twins with horrible deformities. It broke my heart, Abraham." Bryce lied with a pained look in his face. In reality, he hadn't seen his cousin in years and didn't really give a shit about the poor little twins or what was going on in his cousin's life. "I just didn't have the guts to tell Lydia."

Bryce looked over at Abraham, and was unable to read whether he was getting any mileage out of the story, so he decided the situation called for drastic measures. He willed himself to cry. As far as he could remember, he hadn't cried since he was a child. In a few seconds, his anguished face was made believable by the tears welling in his eyes. Bryce was pleased to see a look of shock spill across Abraham's face. He had captured his attention and now it was time to go in for the kill.

"When Lydia threw away her birth control pills," Bryce began in voice choked with emotion, "I panicked, knowing how deeply she is opposed to abortions. I didn't want to risk impregnating her with a baby that would know nothing but pain and suffering all its life." Bryce buried his face in his hands and began to sob. The ache in his head spread through his body. Strange pulses of pain made it difficult to control his muscles, taking Bryce by surprise. He now had to struggle to control both his physical and emotional reactions.

"This is the truth?" Abraham said.

"Yes."

"Did you ever plan on telling the truth to Lydia?"

"I don't know. I think the truth would have been too painful."

"Then what did you plan to do, Bryce? For as long as I have known you, you have never been without a plan," Abraham asked, walking closer to Bryce so he could look him in the eye. Abraham had said on many occasions that he believed a man's eyes were the gateway to his soul.

"I did think about this. You're right. I planned on saying that my sperm count was too low to father a child and that we should opt for artificial insemination. Just because I had a problem did not mean that Lydia couldn't have a baby. We both want children very much."

Abraham said nothing and studied Bryce's eyes. Bryce knew that Abraham was judging him and that his torment had better be genuine, so he thought back to the horrible day in May of 1978 when he was not chosen to be the valedictorian for his high school graduation. Pain overtook his entire body.

After several minutes, Abraham broke his icy stare and settled back in his chair. "Bryce, in my experience, and I've lived a long life, one lie generates more and more lies, because it is impossible for one lie to hold its own against the truth. I have many faults, Bryce, and have done things in my life that I am not proud of, but I have never, ever told a lie."

Bryce thought to himself that was the biggest crock of shit he'd heard in a long time. Abraham wrote the goddamn book on how to manipulate the truth. The line between manipulating the truth and telling a lie was insignificant as far as Bryce was concerned, but he sure as hell wasn't going to challenge Abraham now. He waited for the next dreaded topic to come up.

Abraham took off his glasses, jabbed the stem into his mouth and thought for a few moments. "What about this Bill Holt matter? How do you explain it, Bryce?" he finally asked.

"Fifty-fifty at fault. I came up with the solutions on the deal. Holt came up with the notion that a few of his insights somehow saved the whole deal. He made it clear that he intended to go back into the meeting and seize control, pure unadulterated insubordination, not to mention foolish. He didn't have the experience or tools to do either."

"And for that, you falsely accused him of using drugs?" Abraham evenly asked.

"No!" Bryce answered emphatically. "I found the drugs in his drawer, sent them to a lab, and had them analyzed. I still have the report in my office." Bryce had been smart enough to cover his tracks, and had in fact sent some amphetamines to a lab for analysis.

"Then how do you explain these?" Abraham asked, pulling a handful of blue capsules out of his pocket. They were the same as the ones Bryce had claimed were the drugs in Bill Holt's desk. "During the search of your office, the FBI found these in your private bathroom and had them analyzed. Their lab identified the drug as Ceclor, an antibiotic."

Bryce carefully masked the shock that rocked through him. "Of course those are my antibiotics, but I fail to see what they have to do with the amphetamines in Bill's desk?" Bryce responded in a calm polite tone.

"Everything!" Abraham shot back. "These are the pills you showed me that day. I remember thinking how much they looked like the pills I'd taken for bronchitis. To make sure my recollection was correct, I called my doctor two days ago to find out what he'd prescribed. Guess what?" Abraham angrily poked Bryce in the shoulder. "Ceclor!"

Deny, divert! Bryce's mind barked out the next order of tactical survival. Just as he was about to respond, there was a tap on the door and Solomon Weintraub entered the office. He looked exhausted. He nodded first at Abraham and then at Bryce, and he plopped down in a chair. Bryce wanted to ask why Sol was here but knew that he was in no position to demand answers from either Abe or Sol.

The silent room was like a tinderbox. Bryce knew he had to choose his next words and move very carefully. Should he get back into the amphetamine thing and deny it or move on to the crux of the entire situation—the illicit options? *Better to go for the options*, he reasoned. At least in fighting that charge he would be telling the truth. "Abraham, can we discuss the insider trading accusation—the heart of this entire matter? Then I'd be happy to discuss any other issues that are outstanding or unsettled in your mind."

Abraham looked over at Sol and then back at Bryce. "We're all ears," he responded in his gravelly baritone voice.

"Thank you," Bryce, politely replied. It wasn't easy—he was desperate for relief from the pulsing pain in his body. He cleared his throat and looked Abraham squarely in the eye. "I swear, in the name of God, that I did not purchase those options," Bryce began and was interrupted by a look of pure disdain that swept across Abraham's face.

"For a man who doesn't believe in God, those are empty words, Bryce!" Abraham burst out.

"Abraham, Sol, you have my word. I did not purchase those options. Why would I risk everything I've worked my entire life for, for twelve million dollars? At the time of this alleged act, I knew I was within five months of having this firm entrusted to me. And if I had done it—which I absolutely did not—why in the world would I keep the evidence in my office? Even a moron wouldn't do that. And where's the missing million-plus dollars that was used to purchase these options? If you look at all these things separately and together, it does not add up." Thinking that the short, simple approach would be best with Abe and Sol, he crossed his arms over his chest and waited for a response.

Abraham's face tightened with anger. "Greed often defies logic, Bryce. But if you want to take the logical approach to analyzing this situation, I have a simple question for you. As you know, all the physical evidence points to you. The options were purchased on dates that coincide with when you were in Switzerland. All the options were sold at a time that only an insider on the deal would know when to sell—the date that Vevey took ownership of BioMolecular. The confirmation for the options was found in your office, along with a piece of paper that had the number of the offshore account in the Netherlands Antilles where the proceeds were sent. Now, I have one simple question. Who would want to set you up bad enough that they would simply piss away almost a million dollars? That, Bryce, defies logic,"

Bryce's argument had blown up in his face. But he was innocent! He had to fight back, but how? "I'll tell you who: Bill Holt. He has the financial wherewithal and access to information to pull this off."

"Knowing that that would be your answer," Abraham snapped back, "I asked the investigators to check all his accounts. Clean—all of them."

Bryce could no longer hold back his emotions. "My accounts are clean too!" Bryce said pounding his hand on the conference table.

Abraham stood up. "ENOUGH!" he shouted. "I've had enough of your lies and deceptions. It's over Bryce. Some missteps can be forgiven, but not this, Bryce! NOT THIS!" he bellowed, and abruptly turned on his heels and headed for the door. Before exiting, he turned back for one final word. "I will send the lawyers in so they can explain to you the next order of business." Abraham paused to catch his breath and wipe the beads of sweat that rimmed his thick brows. He looked fiercely at Bryce. "I never, ever want to see you again!" Abraham slammed the door behind him.

Bryce was stunned. He gazed over at Solomon, who refused to look in his direction. He wanted to say something to Sol, but he was in such shock, no words would come out. The pain overtook him. His whole body began to convulse uncontrollably, and his head pounded so violently he thought he might vomit. Solomon, obviously alarmed by what seemed like a seizure, rushed over to Bryce and grabbed his wrists. Bryce was surprised at the strength of Sol's hands.

"Stop, Bryce! Get control. You mustn't let the lawyers see you like this."

Bryce looked hopefully at Solomon. "You understand?" he asked with pleading eyes. "Oh, Solomon, tell me you believe me," he begged in a queer, childlike voice.

"Nothing's inarguable, Bryce," he neutrally responded. "Now sit down, and I'll get you a glass of water." Solomon walked to a side table, poured some water in the glass, and handed it to Bryce before quietly exiting the room and leaving Bryce to recover on his own.

Shortly after Sol closed the door, the team of lawyers descended on the room, their arms laden with stacks of paper.

Without the usual round of small talk and niceties, the lawyers somberly sat down at the conference table. Only Jack Thomas, his old classmate from law school, glanced over at him, but it was impossible to read anything from his face. One of the associates placed a neat stack of documents in front of Bryce and sat back down. Stymied by fear, Bryce did not look at or touch the documents.

Jack broke the silence. "Bryce, before you are three sets of documents we need to discuss." He rolled his Mont Blanc pen in the palms of his hands. "The first is the Securities and Exchange Commission vs. Mortimer & Weintraub Terms of Agreement. It is an agreement that we hope will keep you out of jail and prevent any formal charges being filed against Mortimer & Weintraub. The second document, Severance Agreement between Bryce Elliott and Mortimer & Weintraub, outlines the terms of your departure and also includes a letter of resignation you will be required to sign. The third group of documents are, well, more personal. Your wife is suing you for divorce. This package includes a petition for legal separation, proposed settlement of assets, and signed indemnity from you to your wife that protects her from any further lawsuits or judgments that may arise against you. With regard to the first two items, I am willing to act on your behalf, if you would like to have me represent you. For the divorce, I advise you to seek counsel that specializes in that area."

Bryce sat stone-faced. The documents before him represented a devastating and total loss. "Where's the document that allows me to select the method of execution?" Bryce asked caustically.

"Bryce, there's no time to fuck around. We need to discuss these documents prior to the meeting at the SEC," Jack said with an impatient edge.

"There's nothing to negotiate or discuss. I didn't do it!" Bryce said emphatically. He slapped his hands on the desk and stood up. "Now if you gentlemen will excuse me." Bryce cast a disdainful look at the attorneys, buttoned his suit jacket, and headed for the door.

"Bryce," Jack warned, "if you walk out of this room, you will be tried, convicted, and sent to prison for a long, long time. We have worked out a preliminary settlement with the SEC that avoids all that. It's the absolute best that can be done."

Bryce turned around and did not know what to do. His eyes drifted around the table at the team of lawyers, who were indisputably the best for a situation like his. The gravity of the situation washed over him. His worst nightmare was coming true; he was being thrown off the roof and falling into an abyss of a powerless, meaningless life. He, Bryce Elliott, had lost control of his destiny Bryce's eyes focused on Jack. "As my attorney, is it your professional opinion that these settlements are in my best interest?"

"Unfortunately, yes."

"I see," Bryce said with a dazed look. He walked a few steps before freezing in the middle of the room. For the first time in his life he didn't have clue what his next move would be. After a few awkward moments,

Jack got up from his seat and guided the shell-shocked Bryce back to the table.

For the next two hours, the lawyers walked Bryce through the terms of the settlement with the SEC and Mortimer & Weintraub. The clever team of attorneys had managed to dig up a few esoteric failings on the part of the SEC during the investigation that would ensure a long, drawn-out case—the type that the SEC director hated. They had also pointed out that without Bryce's cooperation it would be next to impossible for the authorities to get their hands on the twelve million dollars sitting in the offshore account

The lawyers explained to Bryce that in exchange for his signed confession and for signing over the twelve million dollars, the Feds would not prosecute him or the firm, and they had agreed to sign a confidentiality agreement that would permanently seal the case, thereby keeping it out of the press. The agreement also had a provision that banned Bryce from ever practicing law again or working in any securities-related business.

The severance agreement with Mortimer & Weintraub was short and to the point. Bryce would resign by midnight, never come within a thousand feet of the firm or its principal partners, and he would forfeit his right to severance pay, his interest in the firm, and any other accrued compensation.

Jack nervously eyed his watch. "Do you have any questions, Bryce?"

Bryce slowly lifted his face, which was buried in his hands, and his glazed eyes wandered around the room, unable to focus on anything or anyone.

"Bryce, I know this is all very difficult, but you must make a decision. Our appointment with the SEC is in forty-five minutes. If we fail to provide a signed agreement at the onset of the meeting, our negotiating position could be substantially weakened. As your attorney, I'm advising you that it's in your best interest."

Bryce remained mute and continued to blankly stare at nothing.

Jack got up and put his hand on Bryce's shoulder. "Bryce, do you understand?"

Without looking up, Bryce could feel the penetrating gazes of the lawyers covering him, suffocating him. "Perhaps not every problem has a solution after all," he said as he reached into his breast pocket and pulled out his Cartier gold pen that had signed one huge deal after another, personal checks for astonishing amounts of money, and letters to movers and shakers around the world. In his thumb and forefinger, he held the pen about a foot from his face and studied it. How ironic that the same pen would now sign away everything he'd worked for. He pulled the documents in front of him and signed each one.

NINE

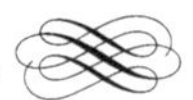

THE MEETING WITH the SEC was shorter than Jack had expected. Everything went as planned, and from Jack's standpoint, it was a complete and total success—the SEC had agreed to countersign the document without changing a word. Bryce was silent in the taxi back to the office. Jack knew Bryce would need time to recover, so he just remained silent too.

When they arrived at Thomas, Martin & Perry, Jack invited Bryce into his office.

"Let's have a seat over here." Jack motioned to a small seating area in the far corner of the room.

Bryce walked over sluggishly and sat down on a contemporary gray sofa.

"Can I offer you something to drink?" Jack asked.

The polished, weary looking Bryce just shook his head no.

Jack sat down on an identical sofa on the other side of a glass coffee table and looked over at Bryce slumped in the corner of the couch. "Bryce," he began in a low sympathetic voice. "Unfortunately you still need to address the divorce papers. This morning, I glanced over them, and they do not look good. Did you have a chance to look at them?"

Bryce remained mute and shook his head no.

"If I were you, I'd get a divorce attorney on it right away. Do you know any good ones?"

Bryce slowly shook his head no.

"There is an attorney, Colleen Mihelitch, one of the best, in my opinion. Would you like me to call her?"

Bryce shrugged his shoulders.

Jack leaned forward. "Look, Bryce, you need to get on this. Financially speaking, this divorce settlement is very important. It's your fucking lifeline. As of two hours ago, you're no longer allowed to practice law or work in the securities business. It could take a long time before you get back on your feet. You're going to need the money."

Bryce looked Jack straight in the eye. "Do you think I did it?" he asked, his voice full of lament.

"No," Jack lied. In truth, he'd never seen so much incriminating evidence stacked against a client before, and it had been the first time he'd advised a client to settle without a fight. Like Abraham, he couldn't logically explain how anyone would piss away a million bucks just to frame Bryce. It made no sense. Moreover, if someone were out to frame Bryce, buying illegal options would not be the smartest move, because it could have easily backfired and put the perpetrator in jail. "Bryce–" Jack, was interrupted by a buzz on his intercom. "Yes, Suzanne," he responded, pushing his secretary's line.

"Sorry to interrupt, Mr. Thomas, two boxes just arrived for Mr. Elliott. Shall I sign for them?"

"Who are they from?" Jack asked.

"Mortimer & Weintraub."

"Are you expecting anything, Bryce?" Jack asked.

"No," Bryce replied.

"Go ahead, sign, and have them delivered to conference room three. Oh, and please lock the door and post a note stating that no one is to use the conference room," Jack directed.

"Yes, sir." The line clicked off.

"Bryce, getting back to the divorce, it's my sense you need to have an attorney on it immediately. If you don't have any objections, I'd like to call Colleen and see if she's available, and if she's not, then to move on with someone recommended by her."

"Sounds like I don't have much of a choice," Bryce muttered.

Jack picked up his line and called the lawyer. After a brief conversation, she agreed to meet with Bryce and to review the divorce documents as soon as Jack sent them over to her office. Jack hung up the phone.

"Okay, Bryce, it's all set. Colleen will be here around five thirty. In the meantime, would you like to wait in the conference room? It's two doors down and on the right. Perhaps you could look through those boxes that were sent to you." Jack was hoping he'd accept. It had been a long day, and there was other business he needed to attend to.

"Right," Bryce said and got up to head for the door.

"I'll come down and introduce you to Colleen when she arrives," Jack assured Bryce as he shuffled toward the door. Never in a million years did Jack think he'd live to see the day when he felt sorry for Bryce Elliott. But the man had just taken one of the biggest falls he'd ever witnessed.

At precisely five thirty, Jack's secretary buzzed his intercom. "Mr. Thomas, Ms. Mihelitch is here to see you."

"Thank you, please show her in." Moments later, a deceptively sweet looking woman in her early forties—who'd earned the moniker of Tiger Lady—stepped into his office. Jack stood up. "Hello, Colleen, please have a seat." His hand motioned in the direction of a small table in the corner of the room.

"Thank you."

"Coffee?" Jack asked.

"That'd be great. After reading those divorce documents, I have a hunch it's going to be a long evening." She sat down in the chair, plunked her briefcase on the table, pulled her blond hair into a ponytail, and looked questioningly at Jack. "So what gives? My God, Jack, these are by far the most one-sided agreements I've ever seen. Out of a sixty plus million dollar estate, he gets ten grand, and she gets to keep the rest? What did he do, kill her favorite hair dresser?"

Jack reviewed Bryce's situation with Colleen, and she sat back in her chair and shook her head in disbelief. "Wow, this guy is knee-deep in shit! Does he know the proposed terms of the settlement?"

"No."

"How do you think he's going to react?" she asked.

Jack paused for a minute before speaking. "Knowing Bryce, I wouldn't put suicide out of the range of possibilities," he said in a dead serious tone. "So what are the chances of him walking away with more than ten grand?"

"Slim to none. The fraud complaint against him is airtight. Essentially the signed confession with the SEC is indisputable proof that he pulled one million out of the estate, without his wife's consent, and used it for fraudulent purposes. Unfortunately it also provides a fairly compelling argument in support of her damages claim, and claims under similar circumstances usually run ten times the amount of the fraud. So, net-net if you take ten million restitution to settle the fraud complaint, you're left with roughly fifty mil. Under community property laws, each party would be entitled to half, but this case is different. There's about a 99 percent chance that she and Mortimer & Weintrab could further sue him for damages, leaving him with two hundred fifty thousand dollars, before shelling out another two hundred grand plus in legal fees—assuming this goes to trial."

"Are you sure?" Jack asked.

"I didn't build my reputation on conjecture or speculation, Jack," she answered impatiently. "I'm sure the scenario I just outlined will be the outcome. So my recommendation to the client will be to settle outside of court and avoid the costly trial. It sounds like he's going to need every last cent."

"Might as well go break the news to Bryce then," Jack sighed.

Jack knocked several times on the conference room door. When there was no response, he became concerned. "Bryce, you in here?" he asked in a loud voice as he opened the door. The attorney's eyes scanned the empty conference table before dropping to the far corner of the room, where Bryce was sitting on the floor with organized piles of stuff circled around him.

As the attorneys walked toward Bryce, they began to make out the objects. There were framed pictures of Bryce in happier times, stacks of law books, piles of Lucite tombstones from mega deals he'd worked on, pads of yellow legal paper, a box of Cuban cigars, several briefcases, coffee mugs, a calculator, at least fifty commemorative signing pens from deals he'd worked on, and a box of Kleenex.

Bryce sat dead center in the middle of his possessions, with his legs crossed like an Indian. His clothes and hair were a mess, and his face was pale and expressionless with dark circles under his eyes. In a catatonic stupor, he stared down at the issue of *Forbes* that had the picture of him—"The Ace Lawyer and Consummate Deal Maker"—on the cover. His Tiffany-framed degrees from Yale, Oxford, and Harvard were oddly placed around the magazine.

"Bryce, Colleen Mihelitch, is here to see you. She's reviewed the divorce papers," Jack said, lightly tapping Bryce's shoulder.

Bryce's crimson-rimmed eyes looked up at Jack, but he did not say a word.

"Do you think we should wait? It doesn't appear he's in the best frame of mind to discuss the divorce right now," Colleen whispered in Jack's ear. Jack nodded his agreement.

"Bryce, are you all right?" Jack asked, kneeling down so he could be face-to-face with him.

Bryce's eyes dropped back down on the floor.

"Bryce, perhaps it'd be best if we delay this meeting. Maybe a doctor could help," Jack gently suggested.

"The last thing I need is a fucking shrink!" Bryce yelled, causing a startled Jack to jump to his feet. "I'm sorry. I didn't mean to scare you." Bryce said, retreating into an odd little boy's voice and wrapping his arms around his knees, now drawn up to his chest.

"Bryce, I really think it'd be in your best interest if we put this meeting on hold," Jack said.

"No, I want to get it over with," Bryce said. He slowly rose to his feet and shuffled over to the conference table. The tail of his wrinkled dress shirt hung out over his pants, and his tie hung loosely around his neck. He sat down, folded his hands on the table, and looked expectantly at the divorce lawyer.

Colleen handed him a manila folder with "Client's Copy" typed neatly on the tab. "Before we begin, would you like to have a quick read through of the documents?" she asked Bryce.

"No, my lawyering days are over," he said dejectedly.

"Okay," she stole a look at Jack, "I'll summarize the situation."

Bryce nodded and looked out the window at a large system of storm clouds swallowing up the twilight.

Colleen began with a short overview of the documents that had been submitted by Lydia's lawyers, and she quickly outlined Bryce's options. Bryce showed no signs of emotion.

Jack knew that Bryce understood the importance of what was being discussed, yet he appeared unable to focus. Bryce kept staring out the window and seemed only to hear the rumble of thunder in the distance instead of the words spilling out of Colleen's mouth at a rate of five dollars per word. He didn't flinch when she advised him that his best bet was to walk away with two hundred fifty thousand dollars.

Jack had seen this before in other clients—a coping mechanism maybe. It was as if Bryce's detachment from his own life was increasing with each sheet of rain that collided against the large windowpane. An awesome streak of lightning illuminated the dark sky with brilliant flash of light. It was closely followed by a sudden, violent, deafening crack of thunder that caused the huge, glass panes to rattle. The sight was so spectacular that Colleen stopped talking mid-sentence.

"Wow, I've never seen anything like that!" Jack exclaimed.

"That was amazing," Colleen agreed, and she looked over at Bryce, who appeared unmoved by the spectacle.

Sensing that Colleen was just about to wrap up, Jack decided that the break would be a good time to try to pull Bryce into the conversation. "So Bryce, what are you thinking at this point?"

"I want the cottage in Southampton," he mumbled in a soft, garbled voice.

"Sorry, Bryce, I didn't understand what you said," Colleen remarked.

"I want the place in the Hamptons, payment for attorney services, and fifteen-hundred dollars."

Jack had to pause and think before responding. "Why?"

"The why doesn't matter. That's what I want."

Jack thought the notion seemed to come to Bryce out of thin air, like the bolt of lightning and thunder that had rattled the room.

Jack watched Colleen flip through the papers from Lydia's attorneys. "Ah, here it is, the Southampton house. Valued at $668,000." She looked back over at Bryce. "The house is worth $418,000 more than what we think we can settle for without a fight. If you want to move to the Hamptons, perhaps you'd be better off taking the cash settlement for two hundred fifty and renting. From a realistic standpoint, it might take you a while to find a job, and fifteen hundred bucks won't provide much security."

Bryce's mind was a galaxy away from logical, pragmatic reasoning. "Get me the house. Make it work. I don't care about the details, just get me that house."

"But, Bryce, it's not rational, not in your best interest. Why don't you sleep on it?" Jack tried to reason.

"There's nothing to sleep on. I want that house." Then he added, "I want everything settled by tomorrow, no later than noon. This should be very straightforward. She's getting over 99 percent of the assets in a community property state. I don't have the money or time for a long, protracted divorce."

"Bryce, that's just not going to happen; it's just not that simple. At best, it'll take weeks of negotiation," Colleen responded.

"Well, I don't have that kind of time."

"You're asking for $418,000 above the quick settlement number. Besides, Bryce, you're the one in the tight spot, not your wife. She really has no incentive to rush this," Colleen answered and turned her head around in a circular motion as if to get rid of stiffness in her neck. "The harsh reality is that she has all to gain and nothing to lose, and you have all to lose and nothing to gain."

A sudden spark of the old Bryce's ignited. "You want incentive, I'll give her incentive. "My wife doesn't like the house and she has no attachment to it. If she is unwilling, tell my father-in-law that if this thing is not settled by noon tomorrow, I'll go to the press and drag Mortimer & Weintraub down to the gates of hell with me. After all, I have all to lose and nothing to gain."

"Bryce you signed documents prohibiting you from privately or publically disclosing anything about the settlement with the SEC," Jack warned.

"So what are they going to do? Throw me in jail? At least I'd have a place to sleep," Bryce quipped.

"Please be reasonable, Bryce. At the very least, I'll get you the two hundred fifty thousand dollars," Colleen said.

"All I want is the house, payment for attorney fees, and fifteen hundred dollars. Just get it any way you can." His eyes stared blankly at nothing and he sat dead still. It was clear he had nothing more to say.

Colleen stood up and placed her hand on his shoulder. "I will do my best, Bryce. I better get back to my office and start working on the counterproposal." She collected her papers and placed them in her briefcase.

Bryce's eyes floated towards her. "Thank you."

Jack had never heard Bryce thank anyone in a genuine way. It was hard to imagine, but he couldn't help but wonder what lay ahead for Bryce.

As the two attorneys packed up, they hastily conferred with one another on some final points. Neither of them noticed Bryce as he got up and walked over to the corner of the room. He got down on all fours and began to place all that was left of his career in two moving boxes.

"Bryce," Colleen turned to the place where he had been sitting

"Yes?" an anemic voice responded from the corner.

Colleen and Jack looked over at the sight of Bryce crawling from object to object in the corner of the room.

"Never mind," Colleen answered. With her briefcase packed, she turned to Jack and shook his hand. "Where can I reach Bryce tomorrow?"

"Ahh, good question." Jack looked at Bryce and thought better of asking him. "Just give me a call in the morning," Jack answered.

"You bet. We'll talk tomorrow."

As soon as Colleen was out the door, Jack walked over to Bryce. "How 'bout a hand?" he asked in a low voice.

Bryce's dim eyes looked up at him. "No thanks, I'm almost done," he answered as he picked up the items one by one.

Jack shoved his hands in his trouser pockets and looked away from the pathetic scene. "Listen, Bryce, I need to get back to my office," he said, glancing out the window. "I'm ordering some Chinese food for dinner. Would you like some?"

Bryce shook his head no.

"Sure? I'm starving. Neither of us had lunch today."

"I'm sure," Bryce muttered.

"Okay then. Just in case you change your mind, I'll order some extra. I'll be in my office." Jack slowly turned around and walked to the door while Bryce continued to crawl around, collecting his possessions.

At ten o'clock, Jack decided it was time to stop for the day and flipped off his desk light. He briskly walked down the darkened corridor to the conference room where he'd left Bryce and tapped twice before opening the door. He saw Bryce sitting on the floor mesmerized by the sheets of rain blowing horizontally into the pane. His back was propped against the boxes that contained the vestiges of his life.

"Bryce." Bryce did not move. "Bryce, I need to lock up the office and go home now."

Bryce slowly rose from the floor and tried to pick up his two large boxes, which was an impossible task.

"Here let me help you," Jack offered and leaned down to pick up a box. "Ready to go?"

Bryce nodded yes and followed Jack down the hall.

Jack hit the elevator button and turned to Bryce. "Can I give you a lift?"

"I'll just grab a cab," Bryce answered as the elevator door opened.

"I don't think you'll have much luck getting a cab down here at this time of night and in this rain. Listen, I'm on the Upper West Side, so it's no problem." Given Bryce's state of mind, Jack was reluctant to leave him in the deserted financial district. The elevator doors opened to the garage and Jack stepped out. Bryce remained in the corner.

"Come on, Bryce, get off the elevator before the door closes." As much as Jack felt sorry for him, he was growing impatient with Bryce and wanted to get home. Juggling his briefcase and the box wasn't easy. Plus it had been a long, hard day and he was dog-tired. "Come on," he urged him again, and Bryce finally stepped out of the elevator. "This way." Jack led him to his olive green Range Rover, snapped opened the back door to his trunk, and hastily shoved the box inside. Bryce, on the other hand, carefully and methodically set the box he was carrying in the car.

After he finally got it in, Jack, who was now annoyed with Bryce's tortoise pace, slammed the rear door shut. The two men got into the car and Jack sped out of the garage and onto Pine Street. In autopilot mode, Jack started to head for the West Side Highway before suddenly stopping and looking over at Bryce. "Where to?"

"Greene and Spring."

"The SoHo flat you were renting?"

Bryce looked at him, with a shocked expression. "Yes, how did you know?"

Jack pulled over to the side of the street. "Sorry, I guess Colleen didn't tell you."

"Tell me what?" Bryce asked.

"During a forensic asset review, your wife's attorneys uncovered the rental payment. They claimed it was misappropriations of your community assets so they stopped payment on your check. They shut the place down."

"Oh my God!" Bryce shrieked.

"Bryce it's not that big of a deal. You can stay in a hotel."

"What about my things?"

"What things?" Jack asked.

"Things that I had in the apartment?"

"I'm sure they had the manager pack them up. It would be illegal for anyone, even Lydia, to take anything."

"But it's not an apartment. It's a privately owned loft I'm renting," Bryce responded in a panicky voice.

"Was there anything illegal in the place?" Jack asked.

"God, no! They were...well...personal."

"Don't worry. One way or another, the owner is legally obligated to store your personal belongings for at least sixty days."

Jack looked over at Bryce, who was clearly in distress. "Listen, Bryce, you've got a lot more important things to worry about than some stuff in an apartment. First thing tomorrow morning, my office manager will arrange to have your things packed and forwarded wherever you want them sent. Okay?"

Bryce nodded.

"So where would you like me to drop you off?"

By the look of despair on Bryce's face, Jack could tell that he had suddenly came to the grim realization that he had nowhere to go. He could not go to his office, because he no longer worked for Mortimer & Weintraub. And he could not go back to his condo, because the terms of the separation agreement prohibited him from coming within a hundred yards of Lydia.

"Grand Central Station," Bryce answered.

"Are you going to leave the city?" Jack asked, pulling away from the curb and turning his windshield wipers up to the maximum speed so he could see through the blinding rain.

"Yeah, I thought I'd go and stay with my brother in Westchester county," Bryce said. Jack hadn't remembered that Bryce had a brother, but he actually knew very little about Bryce's personal life.

"Are the trains still running?" Jack asked.

"Hopefully, if not I'll just stay at the Grand Hyatt."

"Okay," said Jack. For the next fifteen minutes the two men rode in silence. "Here we are," Jack announced, pulling up to the main entrance of the station.

"Can you pop the trunk open so I can get my boxes?" Bryce asked.

"If you'd like, I can keep them here in the trunk overnight and give them to you when you come to my office in the morning. It might be a bit much to handle them in this downpour."

Bryce turned around in his seat and gazed at his boxes.

"I'll take very good care of them, Bryce. I know how much they mean to you."

Bryce continued to stare at the boxes as Jack's patience wore ever thin. "That's okay, I don't need the things in the boxes anymore. They no longer have any meaning."

Jack thought Bryce was growing more bizarre by the minute. "I'll return them to you in the morning. So what time are you planning to come to my office tomorrow?"

"A little before noon, so I can sign the final papers."

"Perhaps you should come earlier, just in case Colleen hits some glitches. Remember, she thought the noon deadline might be really tough."

"I'm confident she'll come up with something. If I can, I'll come earlier." Bryce stepped out of the car and into the pouring rain.

"Would you like to borrow my umbrella?" Jack offered, extending his umbrella to Bryce.

"Thanks." Bryce accepted it.

"Is there a number where I can reach you at?"

"Nope. I'll see you tomorrow." Bryce shut the car door and disappeared down East 42nd Street.

After being out in the chilly rain for more than an hour, Bryce realized he was not going to find a cheap hotel. Two seedy hotels in the area were full, a third was reserved exclusively for hookers and their clients, and the entrances to the rest appeared to be locked up for the night. As Bryce crossed the squalid sidewalks, he paid little attention to the nomads that roamed the streets of New York City at night. A gust of wind caused his umbrella to blow out. Bryce made a mad dash for the alcove of a condemned building and tripped over a man who'd made it his home for the evening.

The raggedy-looking man bolted up from his grimy sleeping bag, and howled. "Yo, you motha fuckin' son of a whore! Get the fuck outta here fo I bash yo fuckin' monkey brains outta yo head." The bearded man reached for a crow bar and began to poke it at Bryce in a threatening manner. Bryce didn't react. His senses were so dulled that he felt no anger or fear and just retreated into the rain with his crumpled umbrella. He didn't know where to go. Soaked and exhausted, he decided to walk the three blocks back to the Hyatt.

The night doorman at the hotel gave the wet, disheveled Bryce a suspicious glance as he entered through the revolving door. Several patrons at the bar overlooking the dimly lit lobby of the hotel did the same. Bryce, usually keen on impressing others, didn't even notice he was the center of disapproving attention. In a dreamlike daze, he walked up to the check-in counter.

"Yes, sir?" the front desk clerk stiffly asked.

"What's the cheapest room you have available for this evening."

"That would be the standard single, at a rate of $185, excluding tax.

Bryce was relieved that at least it was under $200. "I'd like a room please."

The clerk peered over his bifocals and readied himself at the computer. "Name?"

"Bryce Elliott."

"Home address?"

"Trump Tower," Bryce answered.

"Fancy," the clerk responded with a touch of cynicism. Trump Tower gents didn't get wet in the rain. They rode around in the backseats of their hired Town Cars.

"Credit card?"

Bryce handed him his platinum American Express card and did not even notice the clerk's surprised look. The clerk slid the card through the authorization machine and waited. He sighed and passed the card through a second time and then handed it back to Bryce. "I'm sorry, sir, but this card has been canceled."

"Canceled?" Bryce flatly asked.

"Yes, sir."

Bryce placidly handed him his Diner's Card and the same thing happened to it, and his Gold Visa and MasterCard. Normally, Bryce would have gone ballistic over such a humiliating situation, but he just stood there unfazed. *Lydia and Abraham must have canceled my cards*, he thought passively. He fumbled through his wallet and counted out a hundred and sixty dollars in wet bills. "Any chance you might have anything available for less?" he asked.

"Sorry, sir, $185 is our lowest rate."

Bryce left his voided credit cards on the counter and drifted toward the lobby and out the door. The first thing that caught his eye, once he was back on the street, was Grand Central Station, and he entered through the Park Street entrance to get out of the downpour. It had been a lifetime since he'd been in a train station. He was trying to remember how long exactly, but he gave up as he walked down the long corridor that led to the massive center of the grand station. Bryce marveled at the magnificent architecture. At the far end of the enormous hall was an elegant double marble staircase that flowed down to the lobby, and a beautiful depiction of the Northern constellations graced the ceiling. As his eyes explored the station, he noticed a small wood bench hidden under a stairway and walked over to it. He collapsed down on the bench and was so tired he didn't notice the stench of vomit and urine permeating the air around him. Under the watchful eye of Orion, he fell asleep.

"Rise and shine, buddy."

Bryce opened his eyes, and saw an older cop with a red nose standing over him.

"Time to go set the world on fire, pal," he said in a crisp morning voice. Bryce rubbed his eyes and turned on his side. "Come on, fella, one more warning and I'm going to have to arrest you." He poked Bryce with his nightstick.

Bryce blinked a few times, let out a big yawn, and stretched his arms, which brought the police officer's attention to his left wrist. "Where'd you get the watch?" he asked and pointed to Bryce's gold Cartier watch.

"It's a wedding gift from my wife," he answered and glanced at the time. It was five thirty in the morning. His clothes were still damp.

"May I see some identification please?" The police officer asked as the first wave of morning commuters began to pass through the station.

Bryce pulled his wallet from his back pocket and handed it to him.

The cop plucked out his drivers' license and was shocked to see a prestigious Fifth Avenue address. He was even more surprised when one of Bryce's business cards fell out.

"Mr. Elliott, are you all right? Why were you sleeping in the station?"

"Because I couldn't afford the Hyatt and had no other place to go," he answered with the simple honesty of a child.

"Does your wife know where you are?"

"No."

"Perhaps we should call her," the police officer suggested.

"Not necessary. She's divorcing me." Bryce said, as he watched the early bird office workers file past him, wondering which one would catch the worm today.

"Well then, how about your office?"

"They fired me yesterday," Bryce answered matter-of-factly.

The cop raised his eyebrow. "Is there anyone we can call?"

"No one comes to mind," Bryce replied.

The officer studied Bryce and wondered if he might be ill or have been the victim in some sort of crime that left him disoriented. "Would you like to go to the station to freshen up or to the hospital maybe?"

"No, but I'd like to get a cup of coffee." Bryce got up from the bench, grabbed Jack's battered umbrella, and headed to a concession stand.

At ten forty-five, Colleen nervously paced the floor of Jack's office and glanced at her watch for the hundredth time. "Where the hell could he be?"

Jack shrugged. "Who knows. Maybe he was held up getting back to the city from Westchester."

"Do you have any idea where in Westchester he was going?" she asked in an irritated tone.

"No he didn't tell me, but my secretary is looking up every Elliott in Westchester County right now."

"Damn it! It's quarter to eleven. At his goddamn request, his wife's attorneys are expecting me to get back to them by noon."

Jack was almost relieved to hear the buzz on his intercom. "Yes, Suzanne?"

"Mr. Elliott has arrived and is on his way to your office."

"Thank you." Jack clicked off and looked anxiously at the door. Moments later there was a tap. "Come in," Jack responded and the door opened to a dazed, disheveled Bryce. Jack tried to mask his astonishment with a smile and got up from his desk to escort Bryce, who stood like a statue at the door, into the office. "Let's have a seat over here," Jack motioned his hand in the direction of a small round table.

Without making eye contact or saying a word, Bryce walked to the table, filling the office with a faint stench of mildew.

"Good morning, Bryce." Colleen extended her hand and was obviously relieved when he did not accept it. "Bryce, we have a very short time to discuss what we were able to negotiate. Are you ready?"

He nodded.

Colleen handed him a copy of the agreement. "Under the time constraints and circumstances, this is the best I could do."

Bryce didn't bother to look at the document.

"Would you like to have a quick read through before I go into the details?" Colleen asked.

"No. Just tell me what it says." His lusterless eyes gave little clue as to what thoughts lay behind them, but they did reveal one thing—he seemed very much alone.

Colleen slipped on her glasses and consulted her notes. "In brief, you will be allowed to live in the Hamptons home; however, you will not have clear title. A lien will be placed against the house for $398,000, which included ten thousand in legal fees, and you will have five years to pay it off. If, at the end of five years, you are unable to pay the note in full, the house will automatically revert back to Lydia. During this period, you will be responsible for all maintenance and property taxes, and you will not be allowed to sublease or sell the home or take out any loans against the property. Ms. Mortimer has also agreed to give you the fifteen hundred dollars you requested, plus a hundred dollars for, and I quote, 'Services rendered yesterday morning at approximately seven o'clock.'"

Colleen pulled her glasses from her face, leaned into the table, and looked gravely at Bryce. "As your attorney, under these terms, I would advise you to forget about the Hamptons home, and take the $250,000 cash settlement."

Bryce stared at his reflection in the glass window. All sense of purpose drained from his being. He felt a funeral in his brain.

TEN

At three o'clock, Bryce sat on his possessions—two bags of clothes packed and messengered by Millie and the two boxes Jack had kept overnight for him— at 59th and Lexington, waiting for the Hampton Jitney. Against his attorney's advice, he signed the deal for the Hamptons cottage and sixteen hundred dollars in cash. For the next half hour, a small group of upscale New Yorkers began to descend on the spot, anxiously awaiting their spring getaways to the Hamptons.

Ten minutes later, the jitney pulled up, and a preppy looking young woman jumped out. "Hamptons?" she asked with the enthusiasm of a cheerleader. "Please board. Leave your bags on the curb and the driver and I will load them in." After everyone was on the bus, she welcomed the passengers and announced the locations that the bus would be stopping in the Hamptons. She then added, "There've been several accidents today caused by the rain earlier. So we're going to have to backtrack a bit and head out on Fifth. Thank you." She exited the bus.

The bus shifted into gear and made its way to Fifth Avenue, spewing a stream of black diesel fuel in its wake. As it crossed East 57th and bellowed past Trump Tower, Bryce felt no sentiment whatsoever. It was as if he'd never lived there. The only sight that held his attention was a rail-thin, well-dressed woman who was having it out with her uniformed maid on the sidewalk. The maid was trying, but obviously failing, to adequately help her employer empty an uncountable number of designer shopping bags from her shiny Jag. *He who lives in gold towers has hideous distortion of life*, Bryce recalled this Chinese proverb, but he couldn't remember how he knew it. He was still pondering the thought when the bus descended into the Queens Midtown Tunnel, leaving behind one man's failed attempt to frame and control his own destiny.

The bus rumbled along 495, deep into the heart of Queens, before pulling off to pick up more passengers. Bryce read the enormous billboard that loomed above the stop. It read "House Foreclosure? Call BUCCS-4-U." *High finance, Queens style*, Bryce mused and let out a chuckle.

A group of fun-loving, noisy old-timers tottered onto the bus. Their sweet scent, slightly sharper than a baby's, wafted past Bryce as they shuffled down the aisle. As Bryce watched the seniors dodder past him, his thoughts strayed off to the remarkable parallels between those in the dawn of their lives and those at the sunset: Soft skin, innocent faces, sensitive stomachs, and eyes filled with fear, curiosity, and wonderment over the unknown. Was it a mere coincidence? Or was man's existence in some way circular? He gazed into the cataract-impaired eyes of a very old man wobbling down the aisle and wondered if the man was about to embark on the ultimate journey back to where he came from. As the old man passed Bryce caught a glimpse of his own reflection in the bus window and wondered about his own destination. He felt a profound sense of emptiness.

For the next two hours, as the bus traveled east on the Long Island Expressway, Bryce's eyes peered out the window, but he saw and felt nothing. By the time the bus exited the expressway and headed south to Manorville, Bryce was lost in his own space and time. He hardly noticed when the bus began to head east on Sunrise Highway. Forty-five minutes remained in his trip. As the Shinnecock Hills loomed into sight, Bryce caught the briny scent of the Atlantic, which slowly stimulated his dulled senses. The storm that had belted New York City the night before paled in comparison to the deluge now pounding the eastern Atlantic coast. Bryce watched as the rain pelted the windshield of the bus with such force that the driver had no choice but to pull over. Nobody could see anything out there.

After some time, the winds howling along the eastern seaboard died down, allowing the bus driver to drive the final leg into Southampton.

The bus pulled in front of the Omni Health Club, its final stop for the night. Bryce got off the bus and waited patiently as the bags were unloaded.

Because he had been among the first to board, his boxes came off last. He handed the driver his four claim checks and retrieved his two boxes, a garment bag and a suitcase. He watched listlessly as the last taxi disappeared into the inclement night. He decided he had no choice other than to walk four-and-a-half odd miles to the cottage and leave his boxes behind. He swung his garment bag over his shoulder, picked up his suitcase, and ventured out into the rain. He was no more than twenty feet into his trek when the bus driver called out to him, "Sir, you forgot your boxes!"

Bryce kept walking.

"Hey!" The driver shouted above the storm, pulled up the hood to his slicker, and took off after Bryce. Once he caught up to him, he tapped him on his shoulder. "Mister, you forgot your boxes!"

Bryce turned around. "I know. I might come back and get them later."

"If you're not going far, I'd be happy to help you with the boxes."

"Thank you, no. My destination is too far." Bryce turned and continued to press on into the blustery night.

"Poor soul," he mumbled. He picked up his pace and caught up to Bryce. "How about if I give you a lift? I don't need to be back at the stop for thirty more minutes and this rain isn't letting up. How far you going?"

Bryce turned back and gazed at the older black man, who had a graying beard and deep creases in his face. "Why?" Bryce asked with an inquisitive look.

"Because it's the Christian thing to do. How can I enjoy my warm cup of coffee knowing that y'all will be out in the rain, wet to the bone?"

Bryce just stood in the pouring rain and said nothing.

"Now come along and get out of the rain before you catch your death." The driver gently pulled Bryce's suitcase from his hand and started walking toward the bus. "Come on now." He called back to Bryce with a merciful glance and hand signal to move on. Bryce turned and blindly followed. As the driver loaded Bryce's second box into the bus, he said. "What in heaven's name do you have in this box, books?"

Bryce nodded and wiped the moisture from his face.

"What kind of books?" he asked, closing the door to the bus.

"Nothing great."

"In my mind, there's no such a thing as a bad book. The Good Book has given me guidance and peace," he said tapping a worn Bible that was on the dashboard of his bus. "James Cavell, here," he pointed to *Noble House*, "has taken me to places I could never afford to go, like Hong Kong. Maya Angelou's prose has warmed my heart, and Stephen King has scared the bejesus out of me!" He chuckled, and glanced at a somber Bryce in his rear view mirror. "So where you heading?" he asked, cranking up the engine, and placing his hand on the gear knob.

"Meadow Lane," Bryce managed to mutter.

"Just need directions, and we'll be on our way," the driver responded cheerfully.

"Drive down a bit on Montauk and make a right on First Neck Lane until it ends at the dunes and then go west on Meadow Lane."

The driver pulled out from the Omni Club. "Hard to believe it's so cold this time of year," the driver remarked as he carefully drove down the narrow, two-lane road in the pounding rain. "Read in the *Times* this morning that it got down to forty-nine last night in the city. Forty-nine degrees! Paper said, aside from 1933 and 1957, it was a record low for this time of year."

Bryce said nothing and stared straight ahead into the night. He was well aware how cold it had been the night before.

"If this keeps up, I reckon the church elders are going to be rounding us up to help the homeless. Never before, this time of year. It's crazy. I heard this entire year is going to be record cold."

Bryce caught the African-American man's eye in the mirror, and suddenly, like a broken dam, every racial epithet that had ever crossed his mind or flowed out of his mouth flooded into his head—welfare junky, stupid, worthless, genetically inferior, dumb lazy bastards, dangerous, violent, unmotivated. As the slurs and characterizations pulsed through Bryce's psyche, his eyes continued to intensely study the bus driver's reflection in the rear view mirror. None of that fit this man.

Then something very odd happened. Bryce felt the pain of this prejudice hurl back at him, like the driver's reflection in the rearview mirror.

Violent bolts of jagged lightning streaked the sky. A clap of thunder rattled the bus as it turned onto Meadow Lane.

"God Lord! What ever would make God mad enough to launch a storm like this?" the driver said, shaking his head back and forth. "Who knows anymore. I was thinking—"

"Ahh," Bryce interrupted. "The place is about a mile and a quarter down the road, across from the mouth of Heady Creek."

With the wipers on full speed, the driver carefully maneuvered the small bus down the narrow road. When he saw the sign for the creek, he slowed and sighted an unpaved driveway with a mailbox that was blown over by the wind. "Is this the one?" he asked, coming to a full stop in front of the driveway.

"Yes."

"Can the bus make it down?" the driver asked, eyeing the rustic road with streams of water flowing down it.

"There's no place to turn around. I'll walk; it's not far."

The driver opened the door, and a gale force wind whipped into the bus. "Man-o-man, the ocean is behind the house, isn't it? If this storm gets any worse, I might not be making my run back to the city tonight." He picked up one of Bryce's boxes and made his way down the driveway.

"I can come back and get it. No point in both of us getting drenched," Bryce said.

"I won't get wet. This old Army slicker and these boots'll keep me bone dry. How 'bout you? Do you have a coat or heavier shoes?" he asked, eyeing Bryce's soaking wet suit and dress shoes.

"Don't know, but I'm wet already, so it really doesn't matter." Bryce slung his garment bag over his shoulder, picked up his suitcase, and headed down the pitch-black road. Seconds later, a light from the driver's flashlight illuminated his way to the door of the small stone cottage. Bryce stood in front of the weather-worn, double-Dutch door, and realized he didn't have a key. He jiggled the door latch in the hope that the door wasn't locked, but it was. He hadn't been to the place since escrow closed, and now he couldn't remember where he'd put the key.

"No key?" the driver asked.

Bryce fell to his knees, crumpled in defeat, and began to pound his fists against the door. "Mother of fucking God," he cried out.

The bus driver bent down to his level and put his hand on his shoulder. "Listen, man, just come back to town and get a room for the night."

Bryce ignored him and continued to beat the door.

"I'm going to get your other box. Please think about coming back to town. I gotta leave in a few minutes or I'll be late." As the driver jogged back to the bus, ear-splitting cracks of thunder drowned out the sound of the surf behind the house.

When the driver returned, Bryce had stopped banging the door and was sitting on the porch with his face buried in his bloodied hands. "Sure you don't want to ride back with me? I hate to leave you like this."

Bryce just rocked back and forth, broken and done.

"I can send someone down to help, like a locksmith. How's that sound?"

Bryce dropped his hands from his face and glanced up. "No," he replied.

"Sure you'll manage?"

Bryce nodded and waived him on.

"Here keep the flashlight, I've got another in the bus, but do me a favor and shine it on the road so I can see, okay?"

Bryce flipped on the light. Without saying a word, he watched the bus driver race up the driveway until he disappeared into the night. The bus driver was twelve minutes behind schedule. About eleven people were waiting. He hurried out of the bus, apologized for being late, and began loading the passenger's belongings. As a middle-aged woman boarded the bus, he overheard her mutter to her husband: "What is it with blacks? They have no sense of responsibility! So utterly thoughtless to keep us waiting in the freezing rain." The driver turned his head, exposing his other cheek, and continued to load the bags.

Bryce started to shiver uncontrollably. He rummaged through his suitcase and found a warm, dry jacket and pants that he quickly changed into. Then he huddled up on the front porch and listened to the surf pummel the shore only a few hundred feet from the backside of the cottage. He was captivated by the wild streaks of brilliance that illuminated the sky. After an hour or so, there was a break in the clouds and he could see Perseus in the northeastern sky.

He hadn't looked up at the stars in years. When he was a child, his father used to spend hours sharing his astronomy hobby with him and his siblings. By the time Bryce was twelve, he'd learned all the constellations. As he gazed at the stars, he began to picture himself as a minuscule speck on the earth being pitched about by powers beyond his control. Mixed in with the wind, he could clearly hear his father's voice teaching him about the stars. "When you look up, son, be aware that half the stars you can see no longer exist. Long after they've imploded, their images keep traveling millions of light years, just like we do."

PART II

"What happens to a man is less significant than what happens within him."

Louis L. Mann

ELEVEN

Bryce awoke to a brilliant ray of morning light breaking through the gray clouds and touching down on his face. He glanced at his watch and noted it was eleven o'clock, April 22, his birthday. As he braced himself with his hands to get up, his bruised and bloodied hands exploded in pain. He carefully tried the latch on the front door; it wouldn't budge.

The house had been built as a guesthouse in 1885 and was adjacent to the original estate. Unlike all the surrounding properties that were three to ten acres, this cottage was unusually small and on a unique, half-acre parcel, which is why he could pick it up for under a million. The low price was an anomaly for the area where land alone sold for millions, and places rented out for as much as two hundred and fifty thousand dollars for the summer. He tried to pry open a small, leaded-pane window in the front without success, so he moved to the side of the cottage. The two windows, framed in bleached-out green shutters like the rest of the house, also didn't open. He stepped around to the back of the cottage that faced the Atlantic, and jiggled an ancient brass knob on a pair of double French doors. With a little tug and push, the door creaked open. He entered the cottage, and the old hardwood floor moaned under his feet as he set out to explore his new home. When Bryce purchased the cottage, he hadn't bothered to look inside the place. It had been a teardown, after all.

The living room floor was the original pine, and the well-used fireplace, centered between the two double French doors, was made from the same river stone as the house. Two small rattan sofas with worn nautical blue cushions sat on either side of the fireplace, and a small, plain wood table with four chairs was in the corner next to the kitchen door. Indigenous seashells decorated the mantle, and a small glass coffee table was wedged between the sofas.

Bryce walked into the bedroom. It was barely large enough to accommodate the double bed and two nightstands, and like the living room, the bedroom had a view of the ocean. The faded bedspread had a pattern of seagulls, which was accentuated by a pair of wooden seagull lamps on the nightstands. A narrow door led to a minuscule bathroom from another era. Black and white honeycomb tiles covered the floor and walls, and an Imperial porcelain tub with iron legs dominated the room. A brass rod held a moldy shower curtain that was placed over the tub. A small washbasin, in the shape of a shell, was tucked in the corner, and an old toilet with a water tank above it was squeezed in between the sink and tub. Bryce gave the room a nonchalant once-over and left to view the kitchen.

As he meandered back across the living room, he heard a faint dripping sound, and noticed large beads of water dropping from the rafters to the floor. The rain had penetrated the heavy slate roof, but he didn't really care. The kitchen had a wood and gas stove, an old cast iron sink, the original white marble counters, and a comparatively new refrigerator.

Bryce opened the front door and brought in his boxes and two bags. The distant rumble of thunder and a sudden rainsquall rattled the old windows and drew Bryce out of the kitchen and back into the living room. He sat down on one of the small sofas, pulled his long legs to his chest, wrapped his arms around them, and stared out at the storm. The small ray of sunlight that had managed to beam though the clouds earlier was gone, and the sky had become dark and menacing. A chill pulsed through the cottage.

In Bryce's upside-down world, dusk emerged at high noon. The thundering percussion of the rain, the rhythmic pounding of the raging surf, and the scent of the ocean had a hypnotic effect on Bryce. Although he'd only been awake for an hour, he felt himself drifting back to sleep.

Later that evening, Bryce woke up hungry and confused. He untangled his body and looked out the window. He peered at the ocean, which was illuminated by a full moon, and saw nothing. He heard only the sound of the lapping tide against the shore. As he continued to stare out at the vast sea, a brilliant mélange of phosphorescent lights—hundreds of them—appeared from a strange mist and shimmered above the dark gray water. Gradually a purple light became markedly brighter than the other colors, and the sounds of the ocean stilled. From the light, an unfamiliar voice began to whisper his name: "Bryce, Bryce, Bryce," and he began to see hazy vague images appear in the dark cold sky.

He saw his mother, but she was young, very young, perhaps no more than twenty-four years old. She was in a blindingly bright, green-tiled operating room with her arms stretched to the heavens. She was wailing, "Not my gift from God!" The image blurred and in the next flash of light, he saw his father, looking much as he did when he last saw him. He was reading his manuscript. He picked up the pile of rejection letters, tossed them into the fire, and smiled. "Even if they don't want it, I have a beautiful gift to pass onto my children and friends," he murmured. Suddenly his father was on the roof of the Hearst Street House, and Bryce cried out for him to get off, but his father couldn't hear him. Bryce helplessly watched the scene unfold as his father bent down to fix a downspout. After losing his footing on a patch of moss, he tumbled over the edge of the four-story home and fell to earth.

The manifestation abruptly flashed out with a streak of orange light, and Bill Holt appeared. His was in bed with his wife, and instinctively Bryce knew it was the night that they announced the new partners. Bill's wife tenderly cradled his head in her arms as he sobbed inconsolably. A violent flash of blue light blotted out the scene, and an image of Lydia emerged. She was rocking a newborn. With great sorrow and tears in her eyes, she rocked the baby until her arms could no longer hold on, and she reached out to hand the baby to Bryce. As the blue light dimmed, the image of the baby ebbed back out to the sea. Intense and penetrating—Bryce felt he was searing in the collective pain he'd inflicted on others.

When the last light faded into the horizon, Bryce's shame grew into a malignant ache that pierced the core of his soul. There was a final flash of excruciating, intense light and everything went white. Bryce wondered if he was dead. He thought about the irony of dying on his thirty-ninth birthday.

In what seemed like an eternity, Bryce slowly emerged from the white void, uncertain as to whether or not he was glad to be alive.

He was making his way to the bathroom when his head began to gyrate like a top. He began slowly sinking to the floor and groped the doorframe for support. He lowered his head between his legs in an effort to avoid blacking out. After a few minutes, he felt a little better and headed to the sink to splash water on his face. He turned on the faucet and watched a stream of brown water slowly sputter out. As he waited for the water to clear, he pressed his hands on the edge of the sink and leaned into the mirror, barely recognizing the image that stared back at him. His deep blue eyes were dull and rimmed with deep dark circles. His hair was disheveled and dirty. A thick forest of whiskers darkened his face.

When the water cleared, he gingerly cupped his bruised hands under it and splashed his face. He dipped his hands back down into the sink and repeated the pattern. His stomach ached with hunger. Even in his dazed state, he realized he needed to take a shower, change into clean, dry clothes, and get some food. He couldn't remember how long it had been since he'd eaten.

A little after one o'clock, Bryce headed into the foggy afternoon and down Meadow Lane. He took one step at time, moving forward, moving forward, fearful of falling all the way back down into himself. Except for the occasional caretaker, most of the homes on Copper Beach were deserted, which was not uncommon during weekdays. He assumed a small grocery store would be somewhere off of Montauk Highway, and he turned up Halsey Neck Lane in search of one. He walked past his old stomping grounds of grand manor homes gracefully hidden behind tall manicured hedges and gates so high, the day-trippers couldn't see how the other half lived.

A couple blocks down the highway, he stepped into Harbor Point Store, an upscale Southampton version of a 7-11. An old man with a belly protruding out of his cardigan sweater suspiciously eyed Bryce over his bifocals as he entered, setting off twinkling little bells that were attached to the door.

"May I help you?" he asked, his tone implying that he was watching the deranged-looking stranger with suspicion rather than offering assistance.

Bryce nodded yes and lingered at the counter. It had been years since he'd bought groceries, and he couldn't remember where to begin.

The man reached for something under the counter. Bryce, who was unaware of the proprietor's fright or what he was about to pull out from the counter, put his hand in his pants pocket to make sure he had remembered to bring some money. The man screamed out, "FREEZE OR I'LL SHOOT!"

Bryce looked up and saw the barrel of a .38 caliber pistol aimed at his head. His jaw dropped and his weak exhausted body began to tremble, but he was too stunned to say anything.

"Put your hands up in the air, or I'll shoot!" the man commanded, with beads of sweat forming on his forehead.

Bryce raised his hands. The man came around the counter with the gun cocked and pointed at him. The man instructed Bryce to keep his hands up and press himself against the wall. Bryce obliged and the man frisked him. After finding one hundred seventy-two dollars in his pocket and no weapon, the man relaxed.

"You can put your hands down. Who the hell are you, and what do you want?" he asked with a combination of irritation and relief.

"I need some food and personal items. Can you help me? I don't know where to look."

The storeowner gave him a curious look. "So tell me, son, what do you need? Is anyone with you to help?" he asked in a friendly manner, the way one would address a child or an adult with a diminished capacity.

"I just need some food."

"What kind of food?"

"Just the basics. Can you put together a basket for me?"

"Sure. Anything else?"

Bryce's face contorted, and he had the pained look of someone trying to solve a complex mathematical problem. "Umm, other things, you know for cleaning up. Like personal hygiene items and things for the house, the basics." Bryce hung his head and stared at the floor.

"I think I understand. Do you want to follow me around to make sure?"

Bryce shook his head and stared blankly at the floor.

The man brought goods to the counter and rang them up.

"I do have one more question; can you tell me how I can get the electricity turned on in my home?"

"As a matter of fact, I can help with that. Just fill out this form and give me a fifty dollar deposit, and I can pass it on to the electric company."

Bryce paid for his goods, filled out the form, and gave the man the deposit.

An hour later, he was back at the cottage. When he finished putting the food away, he sat down at the table in the living room and hungrily squeezed Cheese Whiz onto some Ritz crackers, ate ravioli out of a can, and drank a Dr. Pepper. With the distracting pangs of hunger gone, he walked to the beach. The sand sifted underneath his feet, and the briny salt air mixed with the scent of decomposing seaweed. He starred out at the vast indomitable sea and felt as if he were drowning in a mire of oblivion.

TWELVE

THE MINUTES BECAME hours, the hours days, and the days passed slowly. The man who'd been on a steadfast mission to govern his own destiny was adrift in a world of stifling solitude. The tiller was broken.

Day in and day out, Bryce's blistered soul sought solace in nothingness and sleep. Aside from occasional trips to the bathroom when necessary and eating when hungry, he did little else. His vacant eyes, peered into an unfathomable emptiness. He had the look of a man who had been in exile from life for a very long time.

A knock on the door echoed throughout the small living room, stirring Bryce from his catatonic state. BANG, BANG, BANG. "Hello, is anyone home? FedEx." BANG, BANG, BANG.

Bryce slowly rose from the couch and made his way to the thundering door.

"Hello, anybody home?"

"Just a minute," Bryce responded, and opened the door. The FedEx deliveryman took one look at Bryce and stepped back.

"Good afternoon. Would you please sign and date this this, sir?" he asked, stretching his hand out as far as he could to hand Bryce the receipt.

Bryce took it and signed. "Can you remind me of the date?"

"May 15, sir."

Bryce dated the slip and handed it back.

"Thank you. Be right back with your delivery." The deliveryman reached for the signed copy and quickly retreated to his truck and brought back twelve packages using a large dolly.

As Bryce began to drag the large boxes into his house, he noted that the return labels were from Thomas, Martin, & Perry. He opened the first box, and it was filled with his clothes, as was the second. When he was halfway through opening the third box, his face exploded with delight. Jack had remembered! The box contained his art supplies from his SoHo studio. He pulled out an unused pure red sable filbert brush, closed his eyes, and outlined his face with its soft bristle. The sensation aroused a deep yearning to paint. Slowly, one by one, he pulled out his tubes of oils, palettes, varnishes, and linseed oil, savoring every cherished item. The scent of the oils permeated the small room.

He quickly moved to open the other boxes that were flat and the size of a large coffee table. *Could it be?* His heart pounded with excitement, and he carefully pulled at the string that opened a seam in the box. *It was!* His unfinished painting of the woman by the sea!

His elation was abruptly broken when a second painting became visible - —*The Drowning of Noah*. He recalled how hard he'd tried to paint a picture of two boys blithely swinging on a rope over a pond, but it never materialized. He continued opening the remaining boxes and they contained all of his paintings that he had never been able to finish.

With startling force, a burst of music vaulted and reverberated against the walls of the small cottage.

"What the hell...?" he mumbled and walked around the room, trying to find the origin. It seemed to come from every angle in the room, but there was no visible source. A strange sensation of the ethereal melody pulsed through his body, and the dark thoughts evoked by the picture of Noah left him. The music was familiar and intoxicating. It was Elton John, one of his parent's favorites. He knew every song and every word.

In a trance-like state, Bryce walked out to the back porch. "Don't Let the Sun Go Down on Me" boomed from the cottage, and the synergy of the ocean and the music stirred the embers of Bryce's childhood memories.

He began to sing along with the song, "I can't fight . . . no more haunted darkness." As the song flowed out of Bryce, a panorama of his life played in his mind. While the past events and people surrounding those encounters were the same, he was not. Instead, he saw and felt images of how his life might have been, if he had not been on a steadfast mission of amassing great wealth. As the vision faded away, he was overcome with the unbearable weight of regret. His deep blue eyes brimmed with tears that coursed down his hollow cheeks. He folded his face into his hands, and wept with inconsolable grief, as the song concluded. " . . . although I've searched myself, there's always someone else I see. . . Don't let the sun go down on me."

"Are you all right?"

Bryce looked up and saw a woman in a fisherman's sweater and jeans walking up from the beach toward him. The sun was behind her and formed a strange aura around her figure. He made an attempt to dry his tears with the back of his hand and shirtsleeve.

"I don't mean to intrude, but I could feel your pain all the way down the beach," she said.

Bryce cast a curious glance in her direction, and then he quickly lowered his eyes to hide that he'd been crying.

"I'm sorry, I mean...umm... I could see that you were in some type of distress. Is there anything I can do?" she asked again.

Bryce positioned his hand like a visor over his eyes to shield them from the light, and he glanced up at the stranger. She was tall and graceful looking. Her chestnut brown hair was pulled straight back into a ponytail, and large pearl earrings adorned her ears. There was a classic elegance to her. Her delicate face had a few wrinkles of wisdom framing her grey-blue eyes.

"I'm all right," Bryce replied.

"Elton John's a master. Such beautiful lyrics and melody."

Bryce nodded his agreement.

"Are you new around here? This is the first time in years I've seen anyone at this cottage."

"Yes and no. This is my first time living here." Bryce stopped short of mentioning his in-laws' estate.

"Are you visiting?"

"No, I just moved here."

"Where are you from?"

Bryce paused for a moment before answering. "Berkeley."

"California?" she asked.

"Yes."

"Oh, my husband went to Berkeley."

"When?" Bryce asked, wondering if he had marched in a peace parade with the woman's husband.

"He graduated in 1970."

She moved closer to him, and Bryce's eyes caught a silver dolphin pendant hanging from a long silver chain around her neck. *The woman by the sea! Had the face for his painting finally come to him? Walked right up from the shore? Oh my God, am I going mad?* he wondered. *Visions of an altered life playing in my mind, voices and images coming from lights in the sea, and now this!*

"I'm very sorry, but I need to go," Bryce said abruptly.

"Oh, okay. You're sure there's nothing I can do?"

"No. No thank you." Bryce nervously got up from the porch.

"I'm Mary Payne. I live about three miles down the beach on Gin Lane." She extended her hand, and instinctively Bryce pulled back his. He couldn't let her touch him. Not now, but he wasn't sure why. He paused for a moment and wondered if he should introduce himself as Calvin Boston or Bryce Elliott. He thought it would be best to introduce himself as Calvin Boston, but....

"I'm Bryce." He finally introduced himself with his hands shoved deep into his pockets. "I don't mean to be rude, but I really must be going."

"Sure, I'm sorry to hold you up. Perhaps we'll meet again. I walk the beach several times a week. Maybe you'll join me sometime. It can be very cleansing for the soul."

"Yeah, maybe."

"Take care," she said as she walked off into the dunes.

Bryce didn't know why, but the emptiness and desolation weighing on him lightened. *Mary Payne, Mary Payne.* Bryce kept rolling the name over in his mind. It had such a familiar ring to it. Finally, he remembered hearing about her and the accident. It was at Solomon's retirement party. He remembered the dinner conversation with Ted Perkins of Payne & Perkins, the undisputed champion of leveraged buyouts.

Ted Perkins had told the story of how his partner, Art Payne, had died in a sailing accident off the Hampton shores a few days before the retirement party. Art and Mary's only son, a twenty-two year old medical student, had also been lost in the accident. At the last minute, Mary had changed her mind and did not sail with them that day. Ted had said that all who knew the Payne family agreed they were very special. They quietly donated millions to many causes but few knew about it because the family wasn't ever featured in the society page pieces about lavish fundraisers. Bryce also shuddered at the thought that the main thing going through his own mind at the time of the conversation was that the accident might've opened the door to wooing Payne & Perkins.

As he headed back inside the cottage, Elton John's "Madman Across The Water" pulsed out of nowhere. "I can see, very well, there's a boat on the reef with a broken mast – and I can see it very well." Bryce softly sang along with the words he knew.

A brilliant sunset poured through the windows and burst into a magnificent array of colors as it traversed through the beveled glass. Bryce sat very still on the sofa and intently studied the spectacular display of light that danced around the room. He began to paint pictures on the canvas of his mind. Rays of yellow light became a meadow of marigolds. Streaks of purples and blues transformed into a peaceful Japanese garden with ponds edged by double Dutch irises. And the orange light morphed into Koi that filled the pond. The hues of green swirled into a glistening emerald sea that opened to a vast world for all to see and explore.

As the sun set into the horizon, it pulled the extraordinary palette of colors in its wake. When the colors were gone, Bryce slowly awakened to a normal stream of consciousness. The quiet peace of early evening hung over the room, and Bryce mounted one of his unfinished pictures on the easel, determined to create a painting that would build a sense of calm in his soul.

He returned to unpacking the boxes of art supplies. When he was just about finished, he discovered a small brown package wrapped in twine. Curious, he reached into the box and pulled it out. There was a note taped to the front of the package.

May 7, 1999
Dear Calvin,
When I was at the Royal Academy in London, The Keeper of the Royal Academy gave me this book two days before he died. He told me it was my destiny to find the right person to pass it on to. When I asked him about the book and how I would know who to pass it onto, he offered me *four key truths about the book. He told me the book had been in existence for hundreds of years; it would inexplicably change from time to time; the ownership was provisional; and my great-great-grandfather had been in possession of the book at one time. When I tried to ask again about finding another owner for the book, he said it's impossible to answer questions when the answers are indefinite and intangible.*

When I came and found strangers packing up your flat, I looked at all of your unfinished paintings, including the picture of the woman by the sea. Then, just like that, your promise echoed in my mind. "She will have the expression of one who has found a profound truth in the infinite horizon of existence" At that point, I just somehow knew you were the person for the book.

I don't know what has happened to you. But if I may offer some parting advice, remember –there's always a way out of the prisons people find themselves trapped in. The end will be where the beginning is.
Fondly,
Becca Wilhelm

With great care, Bryce ran his hand over the soft leather and examined the outside of the old book, but he was unable to make out the worn, engraved titled. Carefully, he pressed the book open with the palm of his hand, and an ancient scent—the type that lingers in medieval churches and castles—filled his nostrils.

In search of the title, he gingerly flipped through the beginning pages until he found a page that read *Art and Artists*. On the next page was a contents page that listed the names of some of the great masters—Van Eyck, Leonard da Vinci, Michelangelo, El Greco, Rubens, Rembrandt, Vermeer,

Monet, Cezanne, Rodin, Renoir, Van Gogh—mixed with names he didn't recognize.

He turned the page to the preface. There was no author name or information regarding the publication. *A peculiar absence*, he thought as he settled back and began to read.

Art, be it written, sculpted, scored as a musical composition or painted, remains one the great miracles wrought by human genius. It is the medium that allows man to traverse the boundaries of time and touch another man in the house of tomorrow. Confucius' words written twenty-five hundred years ago, still provide wisdom today. A musical composition written hundreds of years ago has the power to influence a man's mood and thought long after the composer is gone. What man-be he a non-believer or a child of God-can walk in an ancient cathedral, temple, or mosque and not be deeply moved and humbled by the beauty that surrounds him? And what man can cast his eyes on a great painting and not feel the pull of images before him. Images of a time before him, images that are capable of capturing his heart or bringing out his wrath, images that can seed a spiritual rapture or stir a spiritual crisis. Images that force a man to think about a world that is filled with passion and heartache. Images that tell him that in a world of change, the essence of human nature remains unchanged.

Bryce lingered over the message from the unknown author before reading more. He randomly flipped to a section titled Vincent van Gogh. There on the page was a personal letter.

July 9, 1890

Dear Theo,
My dear brother, why is it that my life has been one of agony and despair? Every morning when I wake, I ask God this question. Every morning I pray for the pain to end. Only my passion for painting and your generous support has kept me going. Is pain and suffering the passage to my salvation, or is it my painting? Are the two intertwined? Such a cruel destiny.

Nevertheless, I know this is my fate because the emotions are sometimes so strong that I work without being aware of working. And the strokes come with a sequence and coherence like words in a speech or a letter. How ironic, brother, that in painting, I aspire to give pleasure and solace to all humankind, yet I am, without a doubt, the loneliest man in the world.

In God's hands,
Vincent

Bryce glanced at a picture of a painting on the page adjacent to the letter. It had what appeared to be Van Gogh's signature and employed the artist's distinctive brush stokes. But Bryce had never seen it before. It was a picture of a man with a tormented look on his face. The right leg, anatomically too short, was stepping down into a freshly dug grave, while his left arm and hand, anatomically too long, reached toward the image of an angel emerging from a glistening sunset. At the bottom of the picture, a handwritten note was difficult to read because of its fancy looping and old-fashioned handwriting. After several attempts, Bryce finally figured out what it said.

The day after my brother wrote the letter and finished this painting (which I subsequently destroyed), he ended his life at the age of thirty-seven. If there is such a thing as God, may he grant him peace.

"How could a painting that had been destroyed appear in the book?" Bryce asked out loud. Then he recalled Becca's quote from the Keeper of the Royal Academy: "It's impossible to answer questions when the answers are indefinite and intangible." Tears welled in Bryce's eyes, and anguish crushed his heart. He thought about Vincent van Gogh's question about his existence. 'Is pain and suffering the passage to my salvation, or is it my painting?' He studied the painting, and wondered: *What has become of me? What will become of me? Is there such thing as fate, or do our deeds shape our final destination?*

Bryce flipped to the back of the book to read a passage from an artist he'd never heard of. He dried his eyes and runny nose with the sleeve of his sweater and continued to read.

All my life, I was blessed with good health, good family, good friends, and good fortune. Although I was never a rich woman, I was never poor. We had all the money we needed to be comfortable and then some. Rarely was there a day that I was not thankful for all I had.

I strongly believe in every person's life there is a turning point, an awakening. For me it happened when the war broke out. I witnessed the best and worst of humankind, ruthless brutality juxtaposed with selfless benevolence, and it left me with several questions. Why is there such a large divide in human nature? How is it that the most ordinary people are capable of committing the most unspeakable crimes? Are people born into this world good or bad or do they build their own paths?

After years of painting, all the while searching for the answers to my questions, I concluded that some souls are born into this world predisposed for either good or bad. Others are born with a little of each trait and ultimately left to find their own ways, and a few are born with traits that are relentlessly at war with their inner psyches.

Of all my subjects, the most inspirational soul was the blind Delhi beggar. Never had I seen a man more destitute then he. Never had I ever met a man who was more at peace. The moment I saw him, I knew I had to paint him, but before I could paint him, I had to meet him, study him, and learn as much as possible about him. The next day I hired a translator and went back to the marketplace in search of him. When I finally spotted him, I sat down on the dirt beside him, introduced myself, and explained how I was drawn to him. He told me of a dream he had about me many years ago and it was our destiny to meet. For hours, I listened in awe to words of wisdom, beauty, and humility that poured from him and felt our spirits connect. Not once did he utter a complaint. When I dared to ask him why he bore no bitterness over his plight, he told me life was about two things–loving and learning–and as long as life provided that, he was content. When the streets became so dark I could no longer see, I invited him back to my hotel to share a meal. He gracefully declined and quietly slipped away into the night.

Out of all my subjects, unquestionably the most pathetic soul was a wealthy woman of forty. She was a spiritless creature, caught in her own vortex of self-imposed isolation. From the moment I entered her world (before painting a subject I insisted on spending one day silently beside them, just observing) it was painfully obvious she took great care to orchestrate and manipulate her sterile existence. Clearly, there was an underlying pathological dread of having to put up with anyone or anything that did not fit her superficial environment of pleasant chit-chat, women's social leagues, private clubs, overdone homes, and neighbours and friends who delighted in their common bond of wealthy sameness. The most puzzling thing, aside from giving off little genuine warmth or emotion, was her seemingly insatiable appetite for material things and complete lack of gratitude for all she possessed. Although she was dripping in jewellery while the world was at war, she was consumed with her next acquisition.

When she invited me to stay on for dinner, I declined, not wanting to be the latest acquisition paraded before her friends, and I slipped into the night thinking of the beggar a half a world away.

To be compassionately inquisitive, open-minded, and passionate about life and one's fellow man is all that's needed to create a beautiful and meaningful life.
Kathe Gutman, London, 1944

The painting of the Delhi beggar, next to the letter, reminded him of something, but he could not recall where or when he'd seen an image like it. His mind had been playing tricks on him lately, and he didn't quite trust his memory to work as it once did. He wondered how these extraordinary images, private letters, and messages came together to create the book. And why? He re-read the message from the Keeper of the Royal Academy in hope an answer might emerge. For hours, he immersed himself in the book.

He rose from the sofa, walked over to his painting of the woman by the sea, and was determined to finish it. The mysterious book had both captured and released something deep inside of him. He picked up a palette and dabbed small mounds of oils on it. Then he began to paint. The strokes came naturally and with great ease, almost as if he and the picture were one. He lost track of time and didn't noticed that a new day had come and gone until it was dark.

He flipped on several lights in the living room and headed for the kitchen to eat something. Soon after eating, his neglected body was overcome with exhaustion, and he decided to take a shower and call it a night. Although he wanted more than anything to keep working on his painting of the woman by the sea, he knew he needed sleep. Naked as the day he was born, Bryce slipped into his bed, tucked himself into a comforting fetal position, and fell into a deep sleep.

Dawn broke, and the new day cast its shadow on yesterday – making it the past, while the very same beams of light concurrently lit the path to the future. Sunrise: yesterday's link with today and today's link with tomorrow. Bryce awoke with half of his face bathed in sunlight, and he could hardly wait to begin working on his painting, which had grown more defined in his dreams. He jumped out of bed, raced to the living room, and began pouring out the vivid image from his mind and onto the canvas.

He worked for hours, oblivious to the world around him, his brush strokes moving swiftly across the canvas and breathing life into his subject. A morning jogger had slowed to a walk and made loud, jeering sounds from the beach, interrupting his intense concentration.

"Hey, you stupid pervert, you'd better put some clothes on before I loop back or I'm calling the police!" he shouted and then took off.

Bryce, who was standing in front of an open door that faced the beach, realized he was stark naked and instinctively covered his genitals. He set his palette and brush down and made a hasty retreat to his bedroom, where he quickly washed up and slipped into a pair of jeans and heavily starched custom monogrammed dress shirt, a remnant from days gone by.

THIRTEEN

On the eve of the second week of working on the woman by the sea, Bryce was interrupted by a sharp knock on his front door. He opened the top half of his Dutch door and was face-to-face with a middle-aged man who looked like he'd stepped right out of the nineteen fifties.

"Are you Bryce Elliott?" He asked in a deep Dragnet-like voice.

"Yes," Bryce answered hesitantly.

"Here." The man shoved a manila envelope in his hand and abruptly turned and walked away.

Bryce opened the letter and a thin piece of paper slipped out of the oversized envelope. He bent over and picked it up from the floor.

May 25, 1999
Dear Mr. Elliott:
Warning. This is your third and final notice. You are delinquent in paying your property taxes. If this office does not receive a certified check for the full amount of $6,250 within a week, we will begin foreclosure proceedings on your property. If you have any questions, please contact the undersigned immediately.
Signed,
Wm. Bottomly, Long Island County Assessor's Office

He held the notice in his shaking hands, reading it repeatedly, while mumbling "six thousand, two hundred and fifty dollars." His whole body began to shake.

"What's the fucking point?" he asked, eyeing a can of lighter fluid on top of the mantle. "WHAT'S THE FUCKING POINT?" He asked again, hurling his words in a voice so thunderous that bolts of lightning seemed certain to accompany them. He walked over to the mantle and picked up the lighter fluid and thought about what it would be like to light himself on fire. Would the agony of the physical pain be worse than the mental? Could it be? With both hands, he raised the can above his head and christened himself with the toxic fluid that broke into several legs and streamed down his face. He then knelt down by the fireplace, pulled a camping match across the stone hearth, and watched the tip ignite with a sudden burst of light. The brightness of the light momentarily blinded him, and from out of nowhere, his mother's parting words echoed across the small cottage. "Have a safe and peaceful journey, son, and if you ever get lost just look for the light." A sudden gust of wind blew the door open and out went the match.

"Why is it that people don't pay attention to the light until there is darkness?" a vaguely familiar voice asked from the darkened doorway. Bryce glanced up, and standing before him was Mary Payne.

"Can I help? What have you spilled all over yourself?" she asked with great concern. She extended her hand. "Here, let me help you up."

Just as Bryce was about to accept her reach, she pulled back and whirled around. "No, no, stay out!" she shouted to her dog.

Bryce watched a large English sheepdog jockeying for a position inside the cottage. "Sorry, he has a tendency to make himself at home just about anywhere." She stepped out on the porch and kissed the whining dog on the nose. "I'll just be a minute," she said to the dog. The dog seemed to accept her promise and lay down.

"What's his name?" Bryce asked trying to divert attention from himself.

"Mr. Wags," she answered.

"Mr. Wags?"

"Yes. I didn't have the heart to have his tail docked when he was a puppy, so my husband named him Mr. Wags." For the first time in months, Bryce let out a hearty laugh from his heart.

"I hope I'm not making a pest of myself, but I noticed that your door was opened and I just wanted to check to make sure you were all right."

"I'm fine, I just knocked this bottle of—" Bryce stopped short. "Actually, I couldn't decide if I should light the fire or myself," he said.

She responded with a knowing look of concern. Bryce remembered the sailing accident. "How about if I help light the fire? It's a bit chilly in here."

Bryce did not want her to come back in the house or for her to see any of his paintings. "Don't worry about the fire; I can get it started." Bryce rubbed his hands together to ward off the damp, cold May afternoon.

"I'd feel a lot better if you let me start the fire. Or if I could stay and make sure that everything is okay. You know, I know several local people who are very handy around the house; perhaps they can help get a heater in here."

"I can't afford a heater, let alone a handyman." Bryce replied matter-of-factly, pausing at his candid response and wondering, have *I just openly admitted to a stranger that I cannot afford a heater?* The admission of any weakness was unthinkable just months ago. And exposing any type of vulnerability was inconceivable.

A mystical twinkle lit up in the woman's face. "I think Plato once wrote that poverty consists not in the decrease of one's possessions, but in the increase in one's greed."

Bryce stood still and silent, frozen by her sharply perceptive words. *Who is this woman?* he wondered. Mr. Wags began to bark, breaking the intense moment.

"Okay, sweetie, I'm coming." She calmed the barking dog. She looked beseechingly at Bryce. "You're not going to do anything rash, are you?"

He shook his head no, while thinking the world would be better without him, and he would be better off without the world.

"Time to go then. Good seeing you again. Next time maybe you'll join Mr. Wags and me for a walk."

"Maybe," Bryce replied, studying every detail of her face.

"Have a nice evening."

Bryce watched her walk along the beach until she disappeared into the dunes. Then he went back into the house. He looked at the lighter fluid, the match, the foreclosure warning and his unfinished painting. He wanted to strike the match and finish the job, but instead he unwittingly picked up his pallet and stepped in front of the painting. Throughout the night, the brush strokes moved freely and skillfully across the 5' by 4' canvas until he was done. When he finished, he stood back.

The painting was a perfect image of Mary Payne standing barefoot in a black dress and facing the sea. Her ears were adorned with pearl earrings and her long, wavy hair blew across part of her face. The silver dolphin pendant at her neck shimmered just like the real one Mary wore.

Although the woman appeared to be the focus at first glance, Bryce had worked to ensure that no part of the canvas was empty of meaning. Like a piece of music, a sense of movement and counter-movement carried the piece. On the shore, the water gently ebbed back to the sea while in the distance great waves in hues of blues and greens and white violently raced toward the shoreline.

One of her hands was placed on the crown of a young boy's head. His face was clouded in darkness, but her hand seemed to channel the rays of light from the sun directly to the boy. His hand clutched a broken shell. Her face was serene and had the expression Bryce had predicted. The woman by the sea seemed to have discovered a profound and mysterious truth. A truth, Bryce sensed, that was somehow tied to him. He titled the painting *Epiphany*, turned it toward the wall, and fell into a deep sleep.

When Bryce awakened, he was consumed by his desire to finish his other paintings that were scattered about his small home. His intense focus made him forget about his pending problem with the property tax bill. But an hour or so into the project, he noticed he was running low on paint. He needed to go into town for more paint and materials. He reeked of lighter fluid and knew he'd attract unwanted attention if he didn't clean up. He went to the bathroom, turned on the shower and waited for the water to heat.

It's not getting warmer, he thought.

He gave up waiting and tried to clean himself with a wet towel and soap. He hoped the strong smell of soap would at least mask the smell of butane. As Bryce began his trek along the beach, a tangy ocean breeze grazed his face. His eyes explored the stretches of endless dunes for an unbroken shell. Minutes into the journey, he began to struggle through the drifts of sand and his legs began to cramp, but his eyes—fast and nimble—continued to comb the shores for the perfect shell.

All he could see, though, were fragments of shells. Bryce bent down, and he picked up the remains of a clamshell. He rolled it around in the palm of his hand and wondered just because a thing wasn't physically whole, did that make it broken? The beach he was standing on consisted of an infinite number of grains of sand—pieces of something else—that, together, formed a majestic shoreline. *Is life so different?* he wondered. He tightened his hand around the broken shell before carefully lowering it in his pocket.

The exhaustion in Bryce's gait was hard to miss as he neared the snack shack at Cooper's Beach. Mrs. B.K., who'd run the concession stand for years, looked at the drawn man as she was sweeping the deck and preparing to close the place. She turned to a friend walking out the door and gestured toward Bryce. "So sad. Probably another victim of AIDS. We've seen so many pass through here, seeking solace from the ocean while death nips at their heels."

The friend nodded in agreement and waved good-bye.

"Can I get you something to eat or drink?" she called out to Bryce.

Bryce, not hearing her above the roar of the ocean, plodded on toward the parking lot that led to Meadow Lane.

Mrs. B.K. dashed out after him and called several times. Bryce, thin and haphazardly clad in expensive, casual clothes, finally turned around.

"Would you like something to eat, to drink?" she asked with a friendly smile.

A faint smile emerged on his face. "Thank you, thank you. That would be very kind," he replied to the portly grandmother figure. He felt a deep sense of compassion emanate from her.

"Please then." She signaled for him to follow her up to the deck of the light blue building with white trim. She held open the screen door for him. "So what can I get you? We're closing up, so unfortunately the menu's limited."

"Whatever's easiest for you."

"How about a tuna sandwich?"

"That'd be great."

"So are you visiting?" She asked in a light, friendly tone as she prepared the food.

"No. Just moved here. I'm on Meadow Lane."

"Oh, where?" she asked.

"Just before Shinnecock Road." Bryce responded, glancing around at the knick-knacks.

"My goodness, that's a long walk!"

"It's not that bad," Bryce lied trying to ignore the stabbing pain in his calf.

"I'm sorry, but I don't have any tables inside," she said, wiping her hands on her apron. "Would you like to eat out on the deck? It's finally starting to warm up around here, just today it seems."

"That'd be fine."

"Okay then." Mrs. B.K. walked out to the porch and placed a tuna sandwich, a bag of chips, an apple, and bottle of Orange Crush on one of the picnic tables overlooking the ocean. "What else would you like? We have cookies or maybe a brownie?"

"No, thank you. How much do I owe you?"

"It's on the house," she replied with a smile.

"Please, I insist."

"Five dollars even then—and no tip!" she chuckled.

"Thank you." Bryce handed her a five-dollar bill and began to eagerly wolf down his food while Mrs. B.K. busied herself with chores. When he finished, Bryce cleared his place and took the plastic sandwich basket back inside. "Thank you, again. It hit the spot," he called out to Mrs. B.K., who was scrubbing down a large commercial grill.

"You're welcome," she answered.

Bryce pushed the door open and headed toward the road. As he turned the bend on Meadow Lane to First Neck Lane, he passed the prestigious Meadow Club. A few years back, he'd had to sell his soul to get into the old mainline club started by grand old families back in 1887. Now he barely noticed it. The Bathing Corporation down the street—where he'd delighted in sipping many a gin and tonic with East Coast bluebloods and captains of Wall Street—also held no interest.

Bryce trudged up First Neck Lane, oblivious to the world around him. As he walked up the gently slopping street, he was jarred out of his thoughts by the toot of a horn. He turned around and saw Mrs. B.K. smiling broadly behind the wheel of her powder blue Plymouth.

"Can I give you a lift?" she asked, leaning over to the passenger side window.

Bryce's mind paused for a moment before his aching body made the decision for him. "Thank you," he replied, and crawled into the front seat next to her.

"So where are you going?"

"To the art store to purchase supplies."

"Goodness gracious! You were going to walk all the way from your place into town? It must be at least a good two-and-a-half to three miles! How in the world were you going to get back with your supplies?"

Bryce shrugged. His planning days were behind him now.

Mrs. B.K. pulled out from the curb and drove along the tree-lined street that had beautifully manicured knolls of grass in front of ten-foot-high, neatly trimmed box hedges. "Besides these are not the easiest streets to walk along," she added as an afterthought.

Bryce surveyed the idyllic street, glancing at Mrs. B.K. and then back at the strips of grass that gently slopped down to the road, which made it very difficult to walk on anything except the narrow street. Subtly missing along the deceptively friendly-looking streets of privilege were sidewalks, a subdued yet effective defense against gawking tourists.

Bryce was amused by the names given to these second and third homes —The Dolphin Barns, Seven Maples, Broad Trees, and Sitting Pretty. *No one in Berkeley named their homes*, he thought. As they drove past Roseland, he imagined someone sneaking out in the night and changing the name on the carved limestone post to "Narcissusville" and then replacing the perfectly trimmed, budding rose trees that lined the long gravel driveway with narcissus plants.

Mrs. B.K. glanced over at him as she swung right on Hill Street, passing the Top of the Hill Chevrolet dealer. "Penny for your thoughts?" she asked.

Bryce told her his idea about changing the names and the plants. She laughed. "Oh dear, could you imagine? You know the funniest thing of all is that half the residents probably wouldn't even notice the name change. In the last fifteen years, I swear, half the places have been bought by foreigners and snooty movie people. Don't know who lives here anymore. So where can I drop you?"

Bryce shrugged his shoulders. "Here's fine."

Mrs. B.K. pulled over to the side of the road, and Bryce got out of the car.

"Thank you again, for everything," he said, shutting the door.

"You bet. See you around." As she drove away, she watched the young man shuffle down the street and said to herself, "I wonder how much longer he has to live. Poor man."

For almost an hour, he aimlessly roamed Southampton's charming commercial district until he spotted the shop he was looking for. He stood across the street from The Morris Studio, trying to place the shop's inexplicable familiarity. Unable to remember, he gave up and crossed the street.

"Welcome," a cheery voice called out called out from the back of the shop as Bryce opened the door. "I'll be with you in a moment—almost done unpacking a small box."

"Sure," Bryce answered, just barely loud enough for the woman to hear. The smell of the oils and mediums was comforting to Bryce. He walked up to a large display of brushes, pulled one out, closed his eyes, and outlined his face with its soft bristle.

"Aw, a man after my own heart. A pure red sable filbert," the shop owner purred with approval as she approached Bryce. "Let me guess, a classical artist who paints with passion in search of . . . ?" She paused to let him finish the sentence.

Bryce opened his eyes to a petite woman in her seventies. Her pure white hair was pulled back in a bun, and her perceptive violet eyes studied him.

Bryce shrugged.

"What do you paint?"

"Nothing in particular," Bryce replied.

"My late husband believed that art helped connect the soul to the man. Tell me, who is your favorite artist?"

Bryce, again, shrugged.

"Oh, surely you must have someone you admire; something must have moved you."

"Perhaps the composer who wrote *Scheherazade*, or Leonardo da Vinci," Bryce muttered the first names that came to him. "What about you?" he asked.

"Ah, Nikolay Rimsky-Korsakov! A brilliant, self-taught man who rarely stopped creating once he had the guts to follow his heart and reject the Naval career his father had arranged for him. What draws you to da Vinci?"

"His genius and curiosity."

"Have you studied his works?"

"No. Just seen them."

"In Milan or Paris or . . . ?"

"In books mostly."

"I see. So how may I help you?"

"Oh, I need some supplies."

"For what kind of paintings?"

"Paintings that will never end."

"Paintings that will never end?" She cast a curious glance at Bryce. "You know, young man, my husband would have loved, and probably even understood, your answer. He was a wonderful portrait artist with a gift for bringing his subjects to life. All sorts of famous people, like President Kennedy, commissioned him. See that over there? That was one of his favorite paintings."

She pointed to an oil painting of a one-legged, blind beggar, the same painting he'd just come across in his book. It came to him; he'd seen the painting before in this very shop a lifetime ago. What struck Bryce more than anything else about the painting was how the serenity on the beggar's face belied the severity of his afflictions.

"My husband met the artist, Kathe Gutman, a German woman, in London during the Second World War, and they fell in love. He said she inspired him to become an artist. The Nazis killed her in France just months before the war ended; she was aiding the underground movement."

Bryce was stunned by the strange coincidence. The shopkeeper just kept talking.

"For years the summering society folks were all after him to sell it, and a couple of summers ago, a famous actor offered two-hundred and fifty thousand dollars! My husband thanked him for his appreciation of the painting, of course, and then turned him down. The painting was a part of him. He couldn't possibly sell it. Then two days later, a lawyer from the city, who'd apparently heard the story at the Meadow Club, swaggered into our store mumbling something about everyone having their price. He offered my husband three hundred and twenty-five thousand dollars for it! Woo-wee!" the woman exclaimed. "In forty-five years I'd never seen Henry so angry. He was hooting and hollering that a man who tries to buy another man has already sold his soul. And then he shooed that man out the door, yelling, 'You have the pissant morals of a jackass—'"

As she talked and talked, Bryce shrank. He was familiar with this story because he'd been the arrogant lawyer who had so angered Mr. Pinkerton.

His attention shifted from her story to the painting. He carefully studied it, noting every brush stroke and detail. The unclipped, twisting toe nails, the deep set pupil-less eyes, the pleading hand holding a tin cup that reached out for mercy, the green oozing infection on the stump of his leg, the soiled orange cloth that was draped around his body and his tough leathery skin. The hardness of the destitute man's existence was starkly juxtaposed to the tranquil expression on his face. Bryce could almost see the man's courage rising above despair.

As the woman continued to talk, one of his father's sayings came to Bryce with incredible clarity, as if he were whispering it in Bryce's ear. "We do not come to grace; grace comes to us."

"I'm sorry. I got a little sidetracked," Mrs. Pinkerton interjected. She must've seen Bryce lost in the painting. "So what supplies do you need?"

"Oils and brushes," Bryce replied. He didn't know what to do with the information about the painting in the book. He knew Mrs. Pinkerton would marvel at the letter—*how inexplicable, all this*.

"Shall we go take a look?"

Bryce nodded yes, and she led him to the back of the shop filled with ready-made canvases and oils. He picked out what he needed and went to the front of the store to get extra brushes.

When they got to the register, she added the brushes to a handwritten invoice. She put on the bifocals dangling from a chain around her neck and proceeded to add the items up on an ancient adding machine. Her arthritic fingers punched in the individual prices, producing a white strip of paper. After several minutes, she peered at the total and announced, "That comes to $120.84, including tax." She paused and smiled. "And, in the spirit of my late husband, I've given you 10 percent off as a good luck token for starting out."

"Thank you," Bryce replied as a look of concern washed over his face.

"Is something wrong?" she asked.

"No. Ah, no," Bryce stammered. "I just realized I don't have enough cash on me. I'll need to run home to get some."

"A credit card or check would be fine." Mrs. Pinkerton suggested.

"I'm sorry, but my money is home."

"You come back in the morning. It's nearing closing time."

"Oh, please!" Bryce pleaded. He hadn't noticed how desperate he was to get back to his painting until tears welled in his eyes. "You see, it's just that I'm hoping to get started right away."

"Where do you live?" she asked.

"Meadow Lane, just past Shinnecock Road."

"Meadow Lane, just past Shinnecock Road! Why that's almost three miles. How in the world are you going to manage? It's nearly six already. It'll be an hour before you get back!"

"I'll manage somehow."

"How about if I call to see if I can get you a taxi? You're going to need one to get all these things home anyway."

"How much will it cost?" Bryce asked nervously.

"I would guess no more than three to five dollars," she answered.

"So, to go home, come back, and go home again would cost nine to fifteen dollars," Bryce calculated aloud.

"Listen, if I can get a hold of a friend of mine who drives for a fee, you don't have to come back. I'll just have him collect the remaining balance from you. Would that be okay?"

"Yes, thank you," Bryce replied with a sigh of relief and watched her place the call.

After a brief conversation, she hung up the phone and smiled. "We're in luck, my friend Fred Williams will be here in five minutes."

"Thanks." Bryce handed her the sixty dollars he had. "So, I believe I owe a balance of sixty dollars and eight-four cents."

"That's correct."

A man who had to be in his early eighties parked in front of the store and emerged out of an old white Ford station wagon with wood side panels. He walked into the shop and planted a big kiss on the side of Mrs. Pinkerton's face. "How's my favorite gal?"

"Couldn't be better, you old flirt," she laughed.

"Any interest in going to the cinema with a dirty old man tonight?"

"As long as you promise not to take me to a dirty movie again. That last one, whatever it was called, nearly gave me a heart attack."

"*Basic Instinct?* Oh, for God's sake, Lillian, this from the most beautiful girl of our day who used to think nothing of skinny dipping in Agawam Lake?"

"Please, Fred!" She grimaced. "Such an imagination. Now if you could please take—" she stopped mid-sentence and glanced over at Bryce. "I'm so sorry, all this time and I never did get your name."

"Bryce."

"If you could please take Bryce home. When you get there, he will pay you the balance he owes me. Okay?"

"Sure, sure. So, are we on for the eight o'clock show?" Fred asked while helping Bryce gather his things.

"Of course," Mrs. Pinkerton replied with a wink.

When they arrived at the cottage, Bryce loaded his arms with his supplies and hopped out of the car. He brought the supplies into his cottage and returned to give Fred the balance he owed plus the fare for the ride.

He put his supplies in order and pulled out the broken shell he'd been carrying in his pocket. He placed it near his supplies.

He turned to a canvas depicting a prosperous family on one side and an impoverished family on the other. He hadn't worked on the painting for some time because he simply had no idea how to finish it. But the vision now came to him. He added some oils to his painter's palette and began to paint a bridge between the families. Slowly and very deliberately his brush strokes created a large stone bridge. His focus was intense and for the moment, there was nothing in the world except him and his painting—The Judgment Bridge.

FOURTEEN

"WHY, BRYCE, WHY?" Mary Payne cried out to the sea and dropped to her knees, soaking her long black dress in the tide as a sudden gust of wind blew her hair across her anguished face.

Bryce awakened from his dream with a start, and despite having had extensive and vivid dreams all night, he could recall none of them.

He was hungry and needed a shower. He slipped out of his clothes and headed for the bathroom. After waiting hopefully for the water to warm, it became apparent that the hot water heater was broken. So he stepped into the stream of cold water and showered as quickly as possible. After dressing, he went into the kitchen for something to eat and found only a few scraps of food. It had been a while since he'd been to the Harbor Point Store.

Also gnawing at him in the fresh light of day was the looming tax bill. He needed to take care of the problem or he wouldn't have a place to live. Worse, he'd have no place to paint. He shoved a hundred dollars in his pocket and headed for town.

After a pleasant walk in the bright June morning, Bryce slipped into a small coffee shop across the street from the Morris Studio. He ordered tea and began scouting through *The Southampton Press* "Help Wanted" section. He thought perhaps he could find a part-time job and negotiate some type of payment schedule with the tax assessor. His eyes zigzagged up and down the columns:

Actress-author needs part-time secretary...Amagansett Estate needs hardworking individual...Cake decorator ...Chauffeur...Collector...Central Station answering service dispatcher...Deli counter:..Oil Burner Service Tech...Tree Trimmers...

Waitperson... Sales at busy upscale china & crystal store... Swimming Pool sales...Stay Home! Make $240 weekly processing gift certificates!

Hoping to avoid contact with other people, Bryce put checks next to the central station answering dispatcher, collector, and the work-at-home jobs.

He calculated that, on the average, the positions would pay a little over seven hundred a month and still leave him with time to paint. It was a long shot, but he would try to negotiate a reduced bill and a workable schedule of payments with the tax assessor. He finished his tea and got up to call the assessor's office from a pay phone in the far corner of the restaurant.

Bryce plunked seventy-five cents into the phone and dialed the number listed on top of the letter. After six or seven rings, there was finally an answer.

"Good afternoon. County assessor's office. How may I direct your call?"

"Mr. Bottomly please."

"Just a moment."

After several clicks and five rings—"Bill Bottomly speaking."

"Uh, Mr. Bottomly?" Bryce asked nervously.

"That's just what I said, didn't I?" a gruff voice snapped back.

"Yes, yes you did. I'm calling about a delinquent tax bill for a property in Southampton."

"Ah, yes. The place on Meadow Lane? Don't get many delinquencies in that neck-of-the-woods. Are you representing the property owner?"

Bryce paused for a moment before answering and listened to the assessor take a long drag on a cigarette. "Actually, I'm the property owner. An attorney's out of my reach at the moment."

"Hee hee!" the assessor giggled, causing Bryce to let out a little sigh of relief. "If those sons-of-guns keep it up, they'll become so expensive that even Bill Clinton will have to stop using them!" The assessor snorted, obviously amused by his own little joke. "So what can I do for you, son?"

"I'm calling to see if I can settle my obligation over time, instead of in one lump sum payment. It's just that I'm somewhat short of cash," Bryce replied.

"That's a bit tricky. Why don't you take a loan out against the property? I see that there's no debt on the place."

"Unfortunately the provisions of a divorce settlement forbid me from doing that," Bryce responded.

"Boy, my heart goes out to you. Goddamn lawyers! I'll bet they took you to the cleaners. But I really can't help. The best I can do is to give you an extra week or two months if you put the place up for sale."

"Can't do that either. Divorce settlement prohibits me from selling the place."

"Holy moly, they really cleaned your clock... Geeezzzzz..." the assessor hissed.

"Listen, Mr. Bottomly, I'm really in a fix. Please, is there anything you can do?"

"Call me back tomorrow; but, I'm cautioning you, don't get your hopes up."

"Okay, will do. And thanks."

"You bet. Take care."

The line clicked off. Bryce leaned against the wall and stared out into space. "Don't get your hopes up," echoed in his ear. Bryce hooked the receiver back on the pay phone, shook his head in defeat, and walked back to his seat at the diner counter. Just to make sure he hadn't missed anything, he picked up the paper to check the help wanted ads one more time.

Just as he was folding the paper back up, the "Articles For Sale" section caught his eye. He glanced at it and then at his eighteen-carat gold Cartier Panther watch; the thing retailed for 16,500 dollars. A small grin broke across his worried face as he thought, *That's it! I can sell my watch. Lydia's wedding present could pay the tax bill, and then some.*

"Excuse me." Bryce caught the attention of the waitress at the counter. "Can you tell me how to get to *The Southampton Press*?"

"Sure, just continue up Main, and when you see Catena's Market, make a left on Jagger Lane. It's at the end of the street."

"Thanks. How much do I owe you?"

"That'll be two and a quarter."

Bryce dropped three dollars on the counter and headed out to place the ad. As he was walking up Main, it occurred to him that he didn't have a phone number. He'd need that and a phone before placing the ad. He slipped into the A & P and made the arrangements for the phone. Then he marched up to the end of Jagger Lane and placed the ad: *10 yr. old; solid 18-carat men's Cartier Panther watch. Perfect condition. Retail $16K will sell for $10k.* 728-3877.

He figured it was a fair price and would give him a much-needed cushion of an extra thirty-seven hundred dollars. Bryce stopped again at the A & P, picked up a few staples, and was eager to get home, as images of his next painting were already forming in his mind.

The more Bryce painted, the more his passion for paintings went beyond obsession. He was possessed by it. The paintings seemed to take over all his senses, both physical and mental. Everyday he would paint until his hand became too weak to hold his paintbrush. He barely noticed as the phone rang four times, stopped, and then rang again. On the third ring, he picked it up, but said nothing. Instead, his eyes and attention remained focused on his painting; he was trying to decide if he should add more detail to the subject's face.

"He-llooo, is anyone there?" an agitated voice inquired.

"Yes." Bryce simply answered.

"I'm calling about the watch."

Ah, the watch. He'd almost forgotten about the watch. No one had called about it since he'd placed the ad a week ago. Mr. Bottomly had called, however, and told him that he needed the full property tax payment or he'd be out by the end of this week. "Yes," Bryce answered his caller.

"Well is it still for sale?" the impatient voice snapped.

"Yes, yes, yes—"

"Do you speak English?" The person interrupted after the third yes. "Listen, I'm a busy person and don't have time for this shit. Either you're selling the watch or not. And if you are, I'd like to see it. I need to head back to the city in forty-five minutes."

"I'm selling the watch."

"Good, where should we meet?"

"How about my place? I don't have a car."

"Where do you live?"

"Meadow Lane. Thirty-five Meadow Lane, just before Shinnecock Road."

"Christ! You live all the way down in east Jesus and you don't have a car? I'll meet you in ten. Just need to finish loading my car."

"Fine." And he hung up.

Time passed and Bryce sat in front of his painting, deliberating over how to improve the pose and harmony of his painting, when a sharp tap on the window broke his concentration. "Listen, buddy, I haven't got all fucking day! I've been knocking on the door!"

Bryce hadn't heard any knocks, but he figured the guy wasn't making it up. He walked over to the door to let him in. He pushed through the door with a chesty gait and condescendingly surveyed the cottage. Bryce figured they were about the same age, give or take a year or two, but Bryce was considerably taller.

"Stew Higgins." The guy shoved his hand into Bryce's. "Do I know you? You look damn familiar!" He rubbed his beard as he peered at Bryce through his glasses.

"I don't think so," Bryce hedged. He knew they'd met before but wasn't sure if it was through business or some party in the Hamptons. He also knew with his weight loss and unshaven face, it was unlikely he'd be recognized.

"Are you sure? Have you been to my place for a party? It's called Sitting Pretty—on First Neck Lane." His face broke into a haughty laugh. "Decided to name the place that after all the great deals I've closed to make it happen," he chortled.

Now it came to Bryce. Stew Higgins, the man with the eyes that laughed at people and not with them, the unbridled arrogance. "Flash and show," that's what Stew and his wife had been dubbed by the Hamptons' old-money families—always buying something bigger, better, and more garish. After one party at their house, Lydia had joked that her three-carat engagement ring looked like a promise ring next to Sandy Higgins' seven-carat Liberaci-esque ring. "No, we've never met," Bryce lied.

"So let's get down to business." Stew rubbed his hands together.

Bryce lifted his watch from the mantle and handed it to his unwelcome guest. He wanted to get back to painting.

"Do you have the box and certificate?" he asked.

"No."

"How do I know it's real?"

"You have my word."

"Oh now that's a good one," he replied, carefully examining the watch. "Listen pal, the higher the risk, the higher the return. Since I have no way of knowing if this is real or not, my risk is higher. Five grand is my top offer."

"Sorry." Bryce reached for his watch, reasoning to himself, *Not enough to take care of my tax problem.*

Stew playfully pulled it away. "Not so fast. Okay whatta ya say to six?"

Bryce reached again for his watch.

"Okay, okay. For an artist-hippie type, you're good. Sixty-five hundred, and that's my top offer."

The unwelcome guest was the first and only person to call on the watch ad, and Bryce only had a few more days to pay the taxman. At least he'd be able to pocket an additional two fifty to add to the money he had left from his settlement with Lydia. "I guess so," Bryce replied.

"I take that as a yes."

Bryce nodded at the man and his vulture grin. But the man pulled out a checkbook and began to write a check.

"Sorry. Cash," Bryce said.

"Yeah, as if I have six grand on me."

"Okay then the price is nine grand. The higher the risk, the higher the price. How do I know your check is any good?" Bryce asked.

"For a stupid-assed hippie-artist, you learn fast. But no way...sixty-five hundred is my offer. You can call my bank."

"You want it for sixty-five hundred, then go to the bank right now and cash your check."

"Sorry, pal, no deal. I've gotta get back to the city."

"Okay then, no deal." Bryce could not let the only asset he had walk out the door. If the check bounced, he'd be on the street. "I'll just have to go into the city and pawn it there. You know I've gotten offers as high as nine," Bryce bluffed and reached for the watch.

"All right, all right, you've got a point; I'll come back with cash. You know you have a knack for making deals. Have you ever thought of doing something, uh, more productive than painting?"

"In another lifetime," Bryce answered with his palm extended.

Stew dropped the watch in his hand. "I'll be back in a flash."

True to his word, Stew returned with the cash, and the exchange was made. "Buy some furniture for this place, buddy. It looks like a fucking Goodwill store in here!" He shoved the watch in his navy blazer breast pocket, dashed out the door, and hopped into his new BMW.

Bryce stood by the window and watched the reflection of his former life whip down the gravel driveway and, mercifully, out of his life.

FIFTEEN

As THE WATER pinged into six buckets scattered about the cottage, Bryce raced to move his paintings and materials out of harm's way. He plucked his treasured book from a side table and was immensely relieved that *Art and Artists* had not been ruined during last night's downpour.

When he was certain everything he cherished would stay dry, he fell to the floor, hot and exhausted. The humidity hung in the air and blanketed the eastern shore. Everyone hoped the rain would not continue and spoil the Fourth of July.

After paying the property taxes and a myriad of other expenses, Bryce was left with just a little more than seven hundred dollars, not much of a safety net, especially after he'd been fired from a part time job as a Central Station answering dispatcher. "Too many unexcused absences," complained his boss. But it was beyond Bryce's control because when he was painting, he lost track of time. And Bryce painted every moment he could.

Bryce got up to make a call to the owner of a local bakery. Mrs. Pinkerton had suggested that Bryce try for a part time job at the bakery. After speaking with the owner, she asked if he knew how to decorate a cake. Two hours later, he produced a cake that took her breath away. Now he hoped she'd have some good news. With a leaking roof and very little money, he had no choice but to find a job he could hold down.

There were two short rings and then "Corti Bakery, Maria speaking."

"Yes, Mrs. Corti, this is Bryce Elliott. I was calling to see if you've had any feedback."

"Yes!" exclaimed the Swiss-accented voice. "Excellent news. I *vas* just about to call you. I have an order already and can pay seventy-five dollars if you can you turn a cake into Cezanne's *Mountains in Provence*."

"Yes!" Bryce answered excitedly.

"Mrs. Brooke Astor herself noticed your version of Van Gogh's *Sunflowers* in *zee* shop *vindow* and came to order a birthday cake for her friend. Can you imagine *zat*? Never in my twenty-nine years in Southampton have I had one of *zee* Grande Dames come into my little store and order a cake! Your idea just might *vork*!"

"I hope so," Bryce needed the money. With ten or so cake jobs, he would be able to patch the roof, and with nine more, he might even be able to get a new furnace before fall.

"*Zee* cake needs to be ready by five o'clock Saturday afternoon. Can you do it?"

"What day is it?" Bryce asked.

"July eight."

"No I mean what day is today?" Without a regular job, television, or newspapers, it was hard for Bryce to keep track of time. His only contact with the outside world was running essential errands and visits from Mary Payne and Mr. Wags when they spotted him from the beach.

Mary hadn't been to see him in a while, and he missed her. He wondered if he'd hurt her feelings when he turned down the homemade bread and turkey soup she brought the last time she dropped by. He felt he had no choice because it was beginning to seem like every time she came, she brought something: her husband's foul weather gear after she caught Bryce in a blinding rainstorm in just a pair of jeans and cotton sweater; her caretaker to help repair Bryce's roof after the last rainstorm, which he refused; and an ax to split the firewood that he collected from the beach. Her gifts, just like her demeanor, were sincere, understated, and heartfelt. Nonetheless, he wanted nothing from her except her company, which he found to be soothing and comforting.

"Bryce, dear, are you still *zere*?" Mrs. Corti asked.

Bryce snapped out of his private musings. He hadn't heard her answer to his question.

"Yes, Mrs. Corti, I am. I'm sorry."

"*Zat's* okay, dear. I said it *vas* July first."

"What?"

"*Zee* day is July first, and I need you to do *zee* cake on July eight. Mrs. Astor is going to have someone bring a picture of *zee* painting in *zee* next couple of days. Is *zis* okay?"

"It'll be fine. Yes, I can do it on the eighth."

"*Zat's vonderful.* I'll pick you up at eight. Do you *zink zis* is enough time to finish by five?"

"Plenty."

"Okay, I'll see you in a *veek*. *Vhen* I pick you up, may I see some of your paintings *vhile* I'm at your house? You know, Bryce, if you paint as *vell* as you decorate cakes, you could sell *zem* in town to *vealthy* people. I could even hang some of your paintings in my shop for, maybe, a 5 percent fee or *vatever*."

"Thank you for the offer," Bryce cut in. "I'm not ready to show my paintings to anyone, let alone part with them."

"I understand, but if you ever change your mind, let me know."

"Sure," Bryce replied. So far, only Becca had seen his work. He was still debating whether he was ready to share the paintings with Mary. Something inside kept urging him to do so, even to show *The Drowning of Noah*.

"Oh, and please be sure to use the name Calvin Boston for the cakes," he added before hanging up.

"No problem. *Zis* is your *nom de plume, no?*"

"I guess you could say that."

"Okay *zen*, I'll see you on *zee* eighth."

Bryce hung up the phone and retreated to his bedroom to get his book *Art and Artists*. The words and images inspired him, offered companionship, and gave him comfort in the knowledge that he was not the only artist who was both tormented by life and fearful of what was on the other side of it.

He took his book to the living room, turned on a fan, and flipped to a passage written by Cezanne.

"Isolation is what I am worthy of. Yet, my solitude always oppresses me a little; but I am old, ill, and have sworn to die painting rather than sink into the nasty corruption that threatens men who allow themselves to be dominated by degrading passions."

He was interrupted by a knock on his door. Gently setting his book on a side table, he stood to answer the door and heard, "Hello, Bryce, I hope I'm not catching you at a bad time."

Bryce squinted his eyes against a brilliant streak of light that silhouetted the figure at the door. When the light evaporated back into the sky, he saw it was Mary! She was clad in a light cotton dress and was holding a Tupperware bowl. After an awkward pause, he finally spoke. "No, no, please come in. Where is Mr. Wags?" He asked peering around the door.

"Sulking at home. For the first time ever, I left him at a kennel while I was away."

"You could have brought him here," Bryce said.

"Perhaps," Mary answered, surveying the buckets of rainwater around the room.

"Haven't had the..." Bryce wanted to say time to get around to fixing the roof, but instead the truth flowed out of him. "Money or time to get the roof fixed."

"Well then how about some nice grilled chicken?" she asked, raising the Tupperware bowl.

"Can you join me?"

"I'm not interrupting anything?"

"No, I was just reading up on Cézanne."

"Are you a fan of his?"

"I was after seeing the exhibition at the Tate Gallery last year."

"You were in London?"

"Yes." Bryce curtly answered and wanted to change the subject. Trips abroad were part of a past he was not ready to share with anyone, not even

Mary. "How about if I warm up the chicken? To tell you the truth, the leaking roof kept me so busy this morning that I forgot to have breakfast. I'm starving."

Mary glanced at her watch. "You must be! It's nearly one thirty. Why don't we make a full meal out of it? I have fresh bread and salad fixings in my car."

Bryce's aching stomach accepted Mary's gift of food. "As long as you don't mind sharing the meal with the elements," Bryce pointed around to the buckets full of water where the rainstorm had come through the house.

"We'll be fine," Mary replied, heading for the car.

"No, let me get it." Bryce intercepted her at the door.

"Thank you. Just bring in the bag that's on the passenger side of the truck."

Bryce put on his shoes and made his way to the car. He was surprised that a woman who appeared to have the means to buy any car she wanted drove an old truck. It was the first time she'd driven to his place; all the other times she'd walked up from the beach. During her absence, Bryce had ventured down to Gin Lane in the hopes of running into her. He remembered she'd mentioned that her husband, Art, had named the house The Love Shack. When he found the home, it was anything but a shack. Two doors down from The Bathing Corporation, the house was on the beach and couldn't have been more than five years old. Just like Mary, it exuded understated beauty and grace. It was a shingled, two-story, Nantucket-style home trimmed in white, with a whimsical wing that looked like a windmill tower.

Bryce pulled the grocery bag from the passenger seat and headed back into the house. Mary already was warming the chicken.

"Oh, great." She smiled and reached for the bag. "How about a glass of wine?" She pulled a bottle of Merlot from the bag.

"If I can find a corkscrew," Bryce replied, shuffling through the kitchen drawers and cabinets.

"While you're looking for the corkscrew, could you also check for a bread knife, vegetable peeler, and colander?"

"What's a colander?"

"You know the bowl used to rinse veggies and stuff," Mary laughed.

Bryce gave her a blank stare.

"The one with the holes in it," she explained.

"Oh, I think I might have seen one around."

Mary chuckled. "How long have you been living here?"

Bryce rolled the question over in his mind. How long had he been there? He really had no idea. Then he remembered the dates on the legal documents that Lydia had signed. Traces of his photographic memory came back to him. April…that was it. "About three months—"

The phone rang, interrupting him.

After the fifth ring, Mary said, "Are you going to answer it? I think you should; I sense it's good news."

Bryce handed her the corkscrew and knife and picked up the receiver. "Hello," he pensively answered.

"Bryce, guess *vat*?" Maria's excited voice quizzed him at rapid-fire speed. "You're never going to believe *zis*. Since I last spoke to you, I got an order for a cake from *zee* mayor. A surprise party for *zee* town historian, Robert Noll, in two *veeks*. Caroline Schlossberg also ordered a cake for an engagement party *zat* she is going to have for a friend next month, and she is having it delivered all *zee* way to *zee* city."

A smile creased Bryce's lips. "Thank you."

"No. Thank you! I'll give you *zee* details *ven* I see you next week. I just wanted to let you know."

"Thank you," Bryce hung up the phone and looked over at Mary finishing preparations for the meal.

"Good news?"

"Yes, something I'm doing to make a little extra money seems to be working out."

"May I ask what?"

Bryce hedged. The cake decorating was something he wanted to do anonymously.

"That's okay." Mary said, "You don't need to tell me."

"No, no, it's okay. I'm decorating cakes."

"Are you the one who did that beautiful Van Gogh? I saw it yesterday when I was in town. It drew quite a crowd around Maria's window!"

"Yes."

"Bryce, it was…."

Bryce swallowed hard.

"It was far too magnificent to eat!" She handed Bryce a glass of wine. "Cheers, here's to your success."

Bryce raised his glass and clinked with hers. "Cheers."

Mary moved to the couch. "So what cake have you been commissioned to do?" She looked around the room. Bryce figured she was wondering about the canvases that were facing the wall or covered.

"The first one is Cézanne's *Mountains in Provence*."

"Ah so that's why you were boning up on Cézanne. That's a magnificent painting. Did you know it's been in the Astor family for a long time? Pity it's privately owned. Things of such beauty should be shared."

""That's who I'm doing the cake for!" Bryce replied with the excitement of a child. "For Brooke. Do you like his work?"

"Cézanne?"

Bryce nodded.

"For abstract expressionism he was the best. There's an extraordinary power in some of his paintings. Pity he spent so much time in isolation. In the end, I believe he even refused to allow anyone to touch him." She paused and looked at him thoughtfully. "Why do you think such a gifted person would choose such a life and avoid the touch of another human being?"

Bryce reflected on the question that seemed to be more aimed at him then Cézanne. Bryce had been careful to avoid Mary's or anyone's touch. He didn't entirely know why—maybe out of fear that his dark side might be exposed. Bryce eyed his latest painting. The back of the canvas faced the room. After a long pause, he answered in a slow, modulated tone. "Perhaps his work provided him a needed solace. In the end, he swore to die painting rather than sink into man's degrading passions. For several days he painted outside in a fierce thunderstorm, and came down with pneumonia. A week later he died of pneumonia."

A look of dread washed over Mary's face, and Bryce wondered what she was thinking about.

"Another glass of wine? And then lunch." Mary suggested.

The smell of the grilled chicken permeated the cottage, and the wine in Bryce's empty stomach had a pleasant, mellowing effect on him.

Mary brought the food into the living room and set it down on the coffee table. Bryce filled Mary's glass and then eagerly pulled a piece of French bread from the loaf on the table. He was about to stuff it into his mouth when Mary lowered her head. "Thank you, God, for all your blessings and the food on this table." She looked up at Bryce and smiled. "*Bon appétit.*"

"Thank you," Bryce said, raising his glass and gazing up to the ceiling.

"Who are you thanking, God or me?" Mary asked.

Bryce paused to consider. He was unsure. God was not something that crossed his mind very often, except in the past month when he was working on his latest painting. "Don't know," he answered with blunt honesty. "But it's nice to have you here. May I ask where you've been?" He took an appreciative bite of the chicken.

"A dear friend's daughter was diagnosed with an aggressive cancer, and she asked if I could come to Boston to help."

"How old is she?" Bryce asked.

"Thirty-two, married, with three-year-old twins, a boy and a girl."

"If there's a God, why would he allow such a thing to happen?"

"We're all born with death on our shoulders."

"But why a young mother, why not . . ." *someone like me*, Bryce thought to himself.

"I wish I knew, but part of the miracle of life is in not knowing. The human spirit is intriguing; our darkest hours trigger our most profound revelations. Those who have had their souls rubbed raw with pain often wind up with a profound understanding and appreciation for life. Much more so than those who have not."

"But what about people, good people, who suffer terrible tragedies and never recover and die bitter and sad? What's the point for them?"

"I believe our spirit takes on a body to experience pain—a cleansing of sorts that allows us to learn and enlighten our souls. Show me a person who's had no adversity in life, or refuses to face it, and I'll show you a soulless creature. And, death is not the end of the journey."

"How can you be so sure?" Bryce asked skeptically.

"Faith, and a belief that all of us, regardless of our transgressions, have a deep-seeded need to seek salvation. Think about it. If there were no life after death, then why would the need for salvation occupy such an eminent place in mankind's psyche?"

"Do you believe what we do in life affects us after we die?" Bryce asked, finishing the rest of his wine.

"What have you done with your life?" Mary asked.

Bryce felt her soft eyes boring into his soul. He asked himself, *What have I done with my life? How can I answer honestly?* Bryce got up and walked over to his three completed paintings facing the wall. His heart began to pound in his chest. He reached for the picture he had just completed, and for a spilt second he hesitated. To answer her question honestly he would also have to show her *The Drowning of Noah*.

He glanced at *Epiphany* and then back at Mary, and something inside told him that now was not the right time to share his picture of the woman by the sea. He pulled out *The Drowning of Noah* and walked back to her. Her serene face looked up expectantly at him.

Bryce slowly turned *The Drowning of Noah* around and placed it on the sofa so it directly faced Mary. Her face tightened and she brought her hands to her face. He watched her eyes as they combed through every detail of the painting depicting an angelic looking little boy taunting another panic stricken little boy, obviously drowning, with a rope. Bryce stood frozen with fear next to his blasphemous creation. Finally, after what seemed like an eternity, Mary spoke.

"How does this relate to your life?"

Bryce shoved his hands in his pockets and felt a lump build up in his throat. He blinked several times in a feeble effort to clear away the tears welling in his eyes.

"Does the painting have a title?"

"*The Drowning of Noah*," he mumbled.

Mary got up from the floor to face him. "Where did this come from? Did you know a child named Noah? Did he drown?"

Tears began to stream down Bryce's cheeks, and he lowered his head staring at the ground. Finally, he had the courage to look her in the eye. "He did not drown. I saved him."

"Then where did this come from?" she asked again in a perplexed tone.

"It just came. I set out to paint a picture of two young boys having a good time swinging over a pond. But this emerged instead." Shame washed over his face. "What would your God think of this?"

Mary studied Bryce's anguished eyes. "The ways to God are infinitely diverse," she said in a voice just above a whisper, and then she looked back at the painting. "Do you follow Tao?" she asked.

"No. Why?"

"I noticed the yin-yang symbol in the water just below the boy's hand, the hand holding the rope."

Bryce glanced at the picture and had to look for several seconds before he could find the subliminal symbol swirled in the corner of the painting. He didn't recall intentionally painting it, but he knew where it came from. His mind drifted back to his mother's explanation of yin-yang, right after he had saved Noah. His mother's words rang in his head. '*Can you see how the black and white are opposite, yet converge into a whole?*'

"Of course you can," Mary chimed in, startling Bryce. It was as if she were reading his thoughts. "People live with contradiction in their souls all the time. That's not all bad. I believe this contradiction helps us understand how life's basic oppositions complement and balance each other, ultimately making everything whole."

"Did you know what I was thinking?" Bryce asked, and without waiting for an answer, he rephrased the question "*How* did you know what I was thinking?"

"I can not read your mind but I can feel your emotions."

"Feel my emotions? You can feel other people's emotions?"

"I can't explain it. How about more chicken?" Mary asked and held her hand out for his plate.

"Thank you." Bryce handed her his empty plate and watched her disappear through the kitchen door.

She returned with a steaming plate. Just as she sat down, a second crack of thunder rolled overhead and the lights flickered and went out for a moment and then came back on. "Quite a storm. I heard on the news the winds could get up to fifty knots later on. I hope the Lombardi brothers are back. I saw them going out this morning."

Bryce tilted his head in a questioning manner.

"They're local fishermen. Very dear to me. May I use your phone to call Sam's wife and make sure they're safe?"

"Sure." Bryce waived his hand in the direction of the phone, and Mary got up to make the call.

"Thank God," she smiled putting the receiver to her ear. "The phones are still working." She had a brief conversation and hung up. "They're fine. Sam's wife said they got in about fifteen minutes ago." Mary sat back down on the floor and poked at her food.

"Have you known them a long time?"

"No, just about nine months, but they're cherished friends. They risked their lives trying to save my son and husband and they were perfect strangers." Mary's lip quivered and her eyes filled with tears.

A strange sadness washed over Bryce, as if he were actually experiencing Mary's pain. As another clap of thunder boomed through the windows, Bryce flashed back to Solomon's retirement party. The thoughts that crossed his mind that day came back to him with painful clarity. *With Art Payne out of the way, he would now be able to woo Payne & Perkins— the crème de la crème of leveraged buyout firms—over to Mortimer & Weintraub.*

Bryce's body pitched forward with a jolt as he reconnected with the side of him that was capable of viewing another man's death, so coldly, so opportunistically. He wondered if it was a mere coincidence that he now grieved with the widow of the dead man or, if there was truth in what his mother said to him at the end of each and every day....

'Life is precious and fragile, my son. Realize that regardless of how random events appear to be, there is a pattern. In your life, study the pattern and the infinite wisdom of the ages will come to you.'

Bryce walked over to Mary, folded her in his arms, and he wept. He wept for her, he wept for himself, and he wept for who he'd been. After there were no more tears, he released her from his embrace. "How does someone survive something so awful?" he finally asked.

"Faith and perseverance. Faith that beyond the darkness there is light. And perseverance to keep putting one foot in front of the other, even in the darkest hours. When Art and Peter died, I couldn't understand why I wasn't on the boat to die with them. They were my life, and without them, my life was over. I wanted nothing more than to crawl into my husband's casket and be cremated with him."

"So was your faith challenged? "Didn't you have doubts about the existence of God?"

"For an entire month my life stopped. I could not see anything beyond my tears. I could not hear anything beyond my wailing, and, I could not smell anything beyond the scents of my husband and son. Their clothes, towels, sheets and other personal items—everything—they all became vessels of my memory. Grief and unbearable pain was my existence, my reality, my life and I asked God, repeatedly, why. Why he did not intervene? Why didn't he allow me to die with my son and husband? Why was I forced to remain and endure the pain?" Mary put her hand on her mouth, closed her eyes, and paused for a moment. "You know, it took me an entire month before I could bring myself to release them and scatter their ashes. But I knew —I knew—I had to free them to free myself. I could no longer allow my grief to hold them back from passing on. I never felt my own mortality the way I felt it the day I scattered their ashes at sea. It was a moment of profound sorrow and grace. It was a moment that, I realized there was a reason why my journey on this earth was not over, and that there was a reason as to why I was left to carry on."

"And what was that reas—" the small candle on the table suddenly went out.

Mary reached for the candle, lit it, and placed it back on the table. "Perhaps to provide you with light," Mary said with a small smile.

Bryce shifted nervously and Mary filled his wine glass. "So what's the first notion of God you remember having?" she asked.

Bryce stared at her for a very long while but said nothing. What was his first notion of God? He struggled to answer. After a few minutes, he got up, pulled his latest painting from the wall and leaned it against a chair directly in front of Mary. Not even Becca had seen this painting. Mary was the first. But he knew this painting was the answer to the question she'd asked.

"Oh, Bryce," she gasped with a look of astonishment.

He knew the details of the painting, in some ways, better than he knew himself. The massive painting was centered on a picture of a tormented man falling from dark sinister clouds filled with demons into the arms of the archangel Gabriel. Encircling the man were angels representing the four graces of Love, Faith, Hope and Charity.

Mary pushed Bryce's bearded chin up, and her eyes captured his. "It's extraordinary, Bryce. What do you call it?" she asked, reaching for his hands.

When their hands connected, he could not help but notice the look of bewilderment that rippled across her face. She tightened her grip and it felt as if she was catching his soul. He tried to shake his hands free from her grasp.

"Please," he pleaded, trying to free his hands. When she finally released his hands, confusion and understanding played across her face, but Bryce was too frightened to ask what she'd felt.

She looked at Bryce. "Do you want to know?"

Bryce took a deep breath and thought, *Do I want to know? How strange to be asked if I want to discover the essence of my own existence*. He nodded yes.

Again, Mary reached for his hands, this time her grasp was soft and gentle. She closed her eyes and lowered her head. "I sense electrifying and confusing signals I can't understand," she began, her voice barely above a whisper. She continued, "I feel a tortured soul tethered to a thread of grace and inspiration."

She reached for his face, held it in her hands, and kissed his forehead. "The painting," she said, "should be titled *The Art of Redemption*."

SIXTEEN

The warmth of the late August breeze felt good against Bryce's face as he neared Main Street on the way to the Corti's bakery. For the past month, he'd rarely ventured out of his cottage. Earlier in the month, he'd a very bad bout of the flu, and a nagging cough still lingered. He rejected Mary's pleas to see a doctor, certain the cough would subside in time. He'd only seen her twice, explaining that he needed to immerse himself in his painting. His only company had been the images that began in his mind and took shape on his canvas. His book, *Art and Artists*, became his closest companion. He knew the cake decorating jobs would dry up after Labor Day weekend, when all the beautiful homes would be closed up for the season and the avaricious owners moved on to their other residences in exotic ski and tropical beach destinations for the winter.

Bryce passed one estate after another on First Neck Lane, and he thought about the irony that the grander the home, the less time the owners seemed to spend in it. He wondered, *was it just human nature to want to improve one's existence through one's possessions? Even at the bottom of the socio-economic ladder, isn't everyone still striving to improve his or her lot with possessions? Was the only difference between the rich and the poor the price tag on those the possessions? Had his goal to make one hundred million dollars by the time he was forty spawn from greed or human nature?*

Lost in his thoughts, he absentmindedly turned right on Hill Street, which in turn became Jobs Lane. Before he knew it, he'd made his way to Main Street, his cough started up again and he was exhausted. He paused to catch his breath before he walked two blocks down the road and into the Corti Bakery. The little Swiss cow bells attached to the door announced his arrival, and the portly Mrs. Corti, adorned in her ever-present white apron, came running out from behind the counter and gave him a big hug.

"*Zere* you are, my boy! I've missed you! It has been *veeks*!" Her eyes lit up with delight. She released her hug and had a long hard look at Bryce. "My dear friend, you've been lost in your painting, I can see." She eyed Bryce, whose beard had grown longer, his raven hair—a curly mass—reached his shoulders, and his blue eyes were rimmed with fatigue.

Bryce had awakened that morning with an odd sense of limbo after finishing a painting. He'd started the work a long time ago in SoHo, but he'd been unable to finish it until yesterday. Several passages from *Art and Artists* had inspired and guided him to do so. The painting had pulled him into a deep, existential abyss, sapping him of all his energy. He looked forward to seeing Mary in the afternoon; there was so much he needed to talk to her about.

"So, my dear boy, are you ready?" she asked, pulling Bryce from his thoughts. "*Zee* last cake of *zee* season—a big one too. *Zank* you for all *zee* attention you have brought to my little shop." She gave Bryce another hug.

"Thank you," Bryce replied with quiet enthusiasm. Today he was going to decorate a cake with *Garcon a la pipe* by Pablo Picasso. The client had ordered the cake to celebrate his purchase of the painting, which he'd just outbid the world to own. Eighty million dollars it had cost him. Bryce went to the back of the shop where Mrs. Corti had an enormous sheet of cake on top of the table. It was the exact size of the painting—39" x 32".

"I have a picture of *zee* painting here for you." Mrs. Corti handed it to him.

Bryce coughed into his sleeve as he studied the painting that depicted a young Parisian man holding a pipe in his left hand and wearing a wreath of flowers on his head, and wondered *what was Picasso thinking when he painted it. What was the message he wanted to convey? Why did the young man look to the side with a quirky smirk on his face? How strange to put a wreath of flowers on a young man's head.* Bryce contemplated these questions while reading letters between the young Picasso and Cèzanne in *Art and Artists*.

My dear Pablo,

Thank you for sharing a drink with an old man last night. I have been thinking back on our conversation, and I advise you to see within nature its geometric

compositions. I myself become more lucid before nature, but the realization of my sensations is always very painful, as I cannot impose the intensity that unfolds onto my canvas. Is God unjust or does he only appear that way?
Yours,
Paul

Dear Paul,
Painting is a moral struggle, is it not? Is it not an expression in which our search for identity is fused with the desire to find the reason for our very existence? What about those before us? What has become of them?
With admiration,
P.P.

My Dear Pablo,
In my opinion one does not replace the past. One creates a new connection to it.
Paul

Bryce glanced back at the picture of *Garcon a la pipe* by Pablo Picasso and wondered about the reason for Picasso's existence. For Mrs. Corti's existence. For his own? What became of all the human beings who no longer exist? Where did they go? As these thoughts penetrated his psyche, he began to mix the colors in the frosting. He wanted this cake to be his best for no other reason than to show gratitude to Mrs. Corti.

Inspired by feelings of appreciation, four hours later the cake was transformed into an incredible replica of *Garcon a la pipe*. Bryce wheeled the cake out to the front of the bakery, and Mrs. Corti's eyes brimmed with tears when she saw it.

"A masterpiece, my dear Bryce. *Vere* does *zis* talent come from?" She held his face in her hands and kissed both his cheeks

The little Swiss bells tinkled on the door, and an elderly woman walked in and embraced Mrs. Corti. "Hello, dear friend, how is life treating you today?"

"*Vonderful*, Lillian! I *vould* like to introduce you to the young man who has been decorating *zese* spectacular cakes for me. Bryce, please meet Lillian Pinkerton."

Bryce immediately recognized the woman with the violet eyes as the owner of the Morris Art Studio.

She extended her hand to Bryce, "Hello, dear, it is nice to see you." A look of vague recognition edged across her wrinkled face.

"Mrs. Pinkerton, it's Bryce. I've come into your store several times to buy art supplies." He gently clasped her boney hand.

For a brief moment, she looked confused. "Bryce? I am sorry I didn't recognize you." Bryce knew his appearance had changed substantially over the months he'd been at the cottage. He hadn't realized he'd become unrecognizable.

"Lillian, you must see *zee* cake Bryce just finished! Come, come see!"

Lillian walked over to view the cake and her eyes moved back and forth from the cake to Bryce. She looked Bryce directly in the eye and asked, "Who are you?"

Bryce caught her gaze and flatly responded, "I don't know." His mind beseeched his soul for an answer.

Mrs. Corti gave him a long hug and then pressed two hundred fifty dollars in Bryce's hand. "Good-bye, dear Bryce. Have a safe journey home."

No voice could come out of Bryce's mouth, and he acknowledged both women with a gentle nod. He exited the bakery and headed home.

Bryce took in the breezy smell of the Atlantic Ocean, trying to force the air into his lungs, as he walked back down First Neck Lane. It was a lovely day, and the road was bordered by towering privet hedges that shrouded the homes of the privileged from the masses. His stomach ached of hunger. He wished he'd stopped at the café for a small bite before starting the walk back.

When he was about half a mile away from Meadow Lane, a classic 1937 forest-green, two-door Roadster MG came up the road in the opposite direction. The car came to an abrupt stop across the street from Bryce.

"Hey, Bryce! Is that you?" a friendly voiced called from the car.

Bryce looked up but said nothing.

"Bryce, it's Gabriel Tuttleman!"

Bryce caught a glimpse of a man about his own age with curly black hair. Wayfarer Ray-Ban sunglasses covered his eyes, and he wore a white polo shirt. "How you doing, buddy? Long time no see!"

Bryce tried to jog his memory as to who Gabriel Tuttleman was exactly. His old life had become a blur, as if it had been someone else's life. *Gabriel Tuttleman, Gabriel Tuttleman, Gabriel Tuttleman*, he rolled the name repeatedly in his mind. Then it came to him; he'd worked with him on the *Harvard Law Review* when he was a student. Blue blood flowed through every vain of Gabriel's blood, but he was different from the other members of the Lucky Sperm Club. He had a very eclectic group of friend and acquaintances and almost went out of his way to avoid the East Coast aristocrats.

"Bryce, how about a little hello to an old friend?"

Bryce walked over to the car. "Hello, Gabe."

Gabriel eyed Bryce. His eyes no longer had the intense killer look to them, his gait no longer had the confident swagger, and his toned athletic body was frail and thin. *Just in time, Gabriel thought to himself.*

"So tell me what you've been up to. I heard a rumor you're no longer at Mortimer & Weintraub."

"That's right," Bryce replied with little emotion. He could tell that Gabe was struggling to have a conversation with him. Bryce decided to help him and asked, "So what've you been up to?"

"Well for a while I worked in a major law firm and wondered what value I was bringing to the world, suing one corporation after another on behalf of my corporate clients. Very nasty business and wasted energy and resources. So one day, I just quit."

"What did you do?"

"I crisscrossed America, from the mountains to the inner cities. There are so many in this country who just need love, basic education, a safe place to sleep, and food on the table. I thought my energy and resources would be best directed to help those who have nothing. There's no greater gift than giving people's spirits love, hope and motivation. With those three things all things are possible, are they not?"

"What are you doing in the Hamptons, Gabriel?"

"I'm back because now that both of my parents are dead, I'm closing down the property and selling the place." Gabriel's father had created the Tuttleman Company; it was one of the most respected engineering, procurement, and construction companies in the world. It was commonly known that Gabriel's parents had played a major role in teaching their son humility and charity. Bryce remembered that Gabriel had lived very modestly in college.

Bryce's memory drifted back to his days at Harvard and his first encounter with Gabriel. Bryce had been elated at the prospect of working on the *Law Review* with the son of one of the wealthiest men in the country. Gabe was meant to be another notch on Bryce's belt, a prize addition to his collection of influential contacts. But Gabriel had always been different and tried to make Bryce see the world beyond his goal of amassing wealth. Bryce recalled the many occasions they were locked in a debate about the importance of money, and Bryce unilaterally rejected all that Gabe had to say. *How could someone who had everything teach someone who had nothing?* he reasoned. Realizing that Gabriel had nothing to offer in terms of helping him accomplish his goal, Bryce had moved on.

Gabriel startled Bryce by pulling his hand. As if in a dream, they were suddenly in a house at a party he'd been to on Great Neck Lane last year. The estate was a replica of the Villa of the Papyri, built by Julius Caesar's father-in-law. The owner, John Berling, had purchased and torn down three estate properties to build it, and he had run into an epic battle with Robert Noll, the town historian, in the process. Berling made his vast fortune in the for-profit, higher education sector, hoodwinking vulnerable people and veterans into taking on student loans they couldn't possibly repay. Word on the street was that he personally pocketed 50 percent of the fees and spent more money on marketing and promotions than educating students.

Bryce saw the party playing out before him, just as it had a year ago. The only difference, however, was that he seemed to be more of an observer than a participant. *How can this be?* Bryce wondered in shocked disbelief. *I was at this party over a year ago.* He looked over at Gabriel for an explanation, and Gabriel just smiled and put his finger to his lips, signaling for Bryce to be quiet and observe. They seemed to float above the party, and Bryce wondered if he was dead. *Had he and Gabriel been hit by a car?* He could see himself below.

They drifted over an open courtyard flanked by ten columns, which supported a roofed portico whose inner walls were embellished with elaborate wall paintings of landscapes and trompe-l'oeil architecture. A swimming bath graced the center of the courtyard.

"Bryce! Hello, my darling," a thin woman in her mid-thirties, with her blond hair sculpted perfectly into a ponytail, came up behind him and wrapped her bony arms around his neck and gave him a quick peck on the cheek. A colossal diamond on her finger dwarfed her entire hand, and a display of gold and diamonds garnished her wrists, neck, and ears. Her head was adorned with an 18-karat golden wreath.

"Hello, Melissa, and happy birthday!" Bryce replied.

Across the courtyard, the middle-aged host of the party and husband of the birthday girl was dressed in a toga that couldn't hide his bulging stomach. He eyed his Girard-Perregaux watch and signaled for his butler, a neat and trim young man, who gave his employer a knowing nod and briskly headed off. Suddenly women with harps appeared at each of the columns and began to play music in preparation for his wife's grand entrance.

As the guests began to gather around the Greek courtyard, one of the women at the party, engrossed in an insipid conversation about her latest purchase, a pied-à-terre in Italy—and speaking too loudly to indicate sobriety—bumped into a waiter carrying a tray of champagne for the guests. It caused the man to fall and all of the crystal flutes to fly through the air, spraying champagne on every person within twelve feet of the spectacle.

After the glasses came crashing to the ground, one of the women wailed, "Look what you've done to my dress!"

The waiter, a black older man, was sprawled out on the intricately tiled mosaic floor that was rumored to have cost more than a million dollars.

Lydia began to squeal, “Oh my God!” She broke down in sobs as she glanced down at her champagne-splattered toga and ran her fingers through her wet hair, disheveling the curls and ribbons her hairdresser had spent three hours on earlier that day. Bryce hurried across the courtyard to his distraught wife.

“Lydia, are you all right?”

“Just look at me. What do you think?” she responded. Her mascara was streaming down her face.

All eyes were on Bryce. He glanced down at the man on the floor, surrounded by broken glass and champagne. The man extended his hand toward him, perhaps hoping for a hand up since the ground around him was covered with broken bits of crystal.

Bryce’s piercing blue eyes bore down on the man. “Excuse me, but I have yet to hear an apology from you. Because of your carelessness, these lovely ladies are a mess and you have ruined the party for them.”

The waiter pulled back his hand and seemed to be looking for a safe way to stand up.

“I’ll have some towels and brooms brought to you so you can clean this mess up as quickly as possible.” Bryce wrapped his arm around Lydia’s waist and walked away from the scene amidst approving glances from the other guests.

The view of the party began to fade into a cloud of grey mist and Bryce looked over at Gabriel. After what seemed like an eternity Gabriel spoke, “This party; how ironic that it was in a Roman home with a Roman theme. As you may know the Republic of Rome died, not because it was inefficient, but because the leaders behind that system had been corrupted and blinded by greed and glory. The very people they were intended to serve were the ones that they exploited and in the end, those people turned against them resulting in the Republic’s ultimate collapse. This should be a very important lesson for anyone about the dangers of greed and excess at the expense of others. Not only did the Roman Empire die, so did the souls of all those men. This party was a microcosm of men of privilege at their worst. Did you know that the man on the floor was the bus driver who helped you the very night that you arrived in the Hamptons? He was filling in for his brother-in-law who was feeling bad after a chemo treatment earlier that week. The pride, envy, gluttony, lust, anger, sloth and greed, where does it come from? Bryce, this was not your fate, this was not your destiny."

His body convulsed with anguish, regret, shame and remorse. Tears poured from his eyes, clouding everything. All at once, he was back in the spot where Gabriel Tuttleman had pulled up to meet him—a half-mile from Meadow Lane. Gabriel and his car were gone, but where? Bryce's mind began to splinter in a thousand directions. The beautiful light of day turned sinister with the revelation that the waiter and the bus driver, who helped him the night he arrived in Southampton, were the same person. He needed to get home. He yearned for forgiveness and redemption, but was sure neither would be forthcoming for someone like him.

When Bryce arrived at the cottage, his mind was reeling in a cacophony of sounds—the harps, the crashing of the champagne flutes, the screeches of the women, and his own words…and deeds. He could almost hear Gabriel's voice—the Gabe he'd worked with on the *Law Review*—asking, "Pride, envy, gluttony, lust, anger, sloth, and greed, where *do* they come from?"

Bryce sat on a chair in the living room, staring at the canvas in the corner of the room, waiting for Mary. It was the fourth painting he'd completed. He had an idea about what he wanted to title the painting, but first he wanted to discuss it with Mary. He picked up an apple that was on the side table and bit into it.

Bryce's thoughts drifted to Auguste Rodin's sketches of his sculpture *The Gates of Hell* and his correspondence with Claude Monet, transcribed in *Art and Artists*. Was it fate or coincidence that these two masters' paths had crossed the eternal spectrum of time?

September 5, 1900
Dear Claude,
I am eternally grateful to you for getting my work into the Paris Exhibition. Although the show was a great success, it has left me with mixed feelings. After working for so long on The Gates of Hell, I was exhausted and in need of money. I often wonder, did I sell those sculptures at the expense of my soul? My notion of hell is that it has three gates: desire, anger, and greed. Who has not lived life and had moments of desire, anger, and greed? Are these human weaknesses, part of my life's journey, going to condemn me to hell, or will moments of grace save me? Am I a man obsessed or possessed? The loss of a soul is truly tragic because it is the loss of life for eternity. I just realized that today marks the twenty-fifth anniversary of your dear beloved Camille's death.
Fondly,
A.

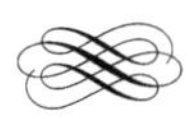

Dear Auguste,
Your questions have forced me to examine issues of my own mortality and conduct in life. Few people know that two years before marrying my beloved Camille, money problems drove me to attempt suicide by throwing myself into the Seine. If this is not greed and anger, than I am at a loss to know what is. What is the difference between me and the 180 lost souls sinking into hell in your sculpture?

Perhaps our destiny might be purgatory? Personally, I view purgatory as a place for contemplation of what's ahead and atonement for what's behind, a place to prepare us for the sight of God. I often wonder if we are predestined from the day we are born to be good or evil.

In two months, my friend, we shall hit a milestone and celebrate our sixtieth birthdays. The fact that we were born the same year and only two days apart is intriguing.
Claude

There were two taps on the door. Bryce set his book down on the table and rushed to the door to greet Mary. A warm evening breeze flowed into the room.

"Bryce, dear friend, it is so good to see you," Mary said as she entered his cottage. Mr. Wags came bouncing through the door.

"You brought him!" Bryce said, petting the dog.

"He brings happiness, doesn't he?" she said with a smile. Her brown hair was casually pulled back into a ponytail. She wore a simple, white cotton dress and a pair of sandals. She had on her ever-present pearl earrings and a gold charm bracelet laden with memories.

Mary gave Bryce a warm embrace. "My dear friend, have you been eating?" She stepped back and took a long hard look at Bryce. His face was sallow, his eyes were rimmed in red, and his hair was a tangled mess of curls that fell to his shoulders. His knit sweater hung from his bony shoulders, and a belt held up his jeans.

"Well, I just ate an apple. I've been so focused on my painting for the past month that I forget to eat some days," he said while suppressing an urge to cough, which he knew would concern Mary.

"Well we will stop at Mrs. B. K.'s for a bite to eat before we take our walk on the beach. It is such a beautiful evening. Are you ready?"

As hungry as Bryce was, he wanted her to see his painting before their walk. "Can I show you my painting first?"

"Of course! How about a glass of wine?"

"That would be nice."

While Mary opened the bottle of wine she'd brought with her, Bryce centered his latest painting in front of the sofa.

Mary returned with two glasses of wine and guided him to the couch. She gently touched his face and was struck at how matted his beautiful hair had become. She pulled a brush from her purse and without saying a word, she began to gently brush his hair. Bryce closed his eyes and his mind cleared. Her brushing gave him peace. Mr. Wags sat below Bryce and put his furry head on his feet.

As she brushed out the mats in his hair, Mary's eyes focused on the painting he had just finished. In the center of the painting was a large, ancient-looking stone bridge. On one side of the bridge was a family who appeared to be prosperous. On the other side of the bridge was a family who appeared to be destitute.

The odd thing was that the scenes surrounding the families seemed to be juxtaposed. The impoverished family was enveloped in a beautiful, lush forest filled with life; they were sitting on a beautiful woven blanket in a meadow.

Although the woman's and girl's clothes were tattered and old, their heads were crowned with brilliant wreaths of flowers, and there was immense joy in their interaction as they sat next to a bubbling stream. The man's hands, which were blistered and dirty from manual labor, reached to a radiant blue sky to celebrate the beautiful doves that flew above the family. His young son, thin with hunger, was feeding a rabbit next to him.

On the other side of the bridge, the prosperous family's surroundings were dark and ominous. The two women, one old and one young, were resplendent in their fine silk dresses. Their hair was soft and flowing and adorned in ribbons. The man and his son were dressed in finely tailored cotton shirts and beautiful wool trousers, silk scarves, and soft leather loafers. The older woman was admiring herself in a hand mirror she held in her bejeweled hand. Through the reflection in the mirror, she cast an envious glance at her youthful and beautiful companion, perhaps the daughter of the older couple or the daughter-in-law.

The young woman's face was twisted in anger and contempt. A chest of gold coins surrounded the older man, and his eyes were lustfully fixated on the maiden's ample bosom. The heavy-set son was eating a large leg of lamb. A golden tray in front of him was overflowing with a gluttonous amount of food. There appeared to be no elements of life surrounding the family of four. The ground was like desert sand, and the few trees dotting the landscape were dead and barren. The sky was grey and filled with ominous clouds.

As Mary continued to brush Bryce's hair, she looked down at him resting serenely. She looked back at the painting.

Bryce opened his eyes and turned to look back at Mary. "What do you think?"

"Let's take our walk; it is such a beautiful evening. We can talk on the beach."

Bryce got up from the couch and followed Mary and Mr. Wags to the door. Mary removed her sandals and knelt down to her dog and rubbed his head. "Be a good boy and stay with us or I will have to put you on a leash," and she held up a leash that was embroidered with nautical flags.

They slowly walked down Copper Beach, which was full of people enjoying the summer evening. The beach strand was broad and long; it seemed to go on for miles. Large beachfront homes were set back behind dunes, and a beautiful blue-green ocean gently broke against the shoreline.

They reached Mrs. B.K.'s concession stand. "I'll get us some food; how about if you keep an eye on Mr. Wags? What would you like to eat?"

"Anything will be fine," Bryce replied and sat down on the beach with his arm around the dog. Mary had stepped onto the porch of Mrs. B.K.'s when Bryce's cough came on strong.

When Mary returned, she was carrying a basket filled with a cheeseburger and fries and another basket with a ham sandwich. She handed Bryce a milkshake and the burger and fries. "This should put some meat on your bones," she said with a smile.

They sat up by the dunes and Mary said nothing as Bryce ate at a painfully slow pace. As hungry as he'd been, he just couldn't get the food down very easily. Mary fed Mr. Wags half of the ham sandwich and ate the other half.

When Bryce finally took the last bite and drained his shake, he turned to Mary with an intense gaze. "So please tell me. What did you think of the painting?"

Mary looked out at the sea and took his hand. "It's magnificent and provocative."

"I titled it *The Judgment Bridge.*"

Mary took a sip of water. "*The Judgment Bridge* ... *The Judgment Bridge*. Where did the idea come from?"

"I don't know. It just came to me in a vision many years ago, but I never could finish it. In my first attempt, the well-to-do family was in the beautiful surroundings and the poor family was in the barren desert. That was my reality, how I viewed things. Beauty was afforded to those who earned it and unsightliness was for those who didn't." Bryce watched the ebb and tide of the ocean.

"And what about now? Why *The Judgment Bridge*?"

"Do you believe that one day we'll all be judged?"

"Yes," Mary replied. "Bryce, very few paintings, especially contemporary ones, have been able to depict the seven deadly sins. But you've done just that. The family on the right side of the bridge is enveloped in all the elements: pride, envy, gluttony, lust, anger, sloth and greed. And they've been judged."

"Do you believe in hell?"

Mary raised her hands to cup Bryce's face so she could look directly at him. "Hell and damnation are difficult notions to get my head around."

Bryce thought about his book *Art and Artists*. Reading the book made him realize he'd placed the families on the wrong sides of the bridge in his first attempt. "From what I've read, it seems that all the major religions of the world believe in a form of hell or a need for atonement. I read a passage written more than nineteen hundred years ago that was discovered in the Holy Land; it helped me finish the painting."

Bryce closed his eyes and a vision of a page from *Art and Artists* came to him. He began to recite the passage. "'There is a bridge that separates the world of the living from the world of the dead, and all souls must cross the bridge upon death. It is the day when each individual will stand before his God and be questioned about his life, how he spent it; his youth, how he utilized it; his wealth, where he earned it and how he spent it; and his knowledge, how he put it to work. On that day while crossing the bridge, one looks to his right and sees nothing but his good deeds, looks to his left and sees nothing but his bad deeds, and looks ahead and sees his eternal fate. Those with a good heart full of good deeds, kindness, and faith will be safe from eternal punishment, and those that commit the seven deadly sins—sins so terrible that they jeopardize the sinner's spiritual salvation—will be damned to a place of eternal suffering.'"

"Do you believe in redemption?" Mary asked.

He opened his eyes, but he did not answer. Not for people like me, he thought to himself.

Mary continued speaking. "I think Thornton Wilder's take on the subject is beautiful. It gave me comfort when I most needed it. The passage was read at Amanda Tuttleman's son's funeral, and I have read it every day since my husband and son died. 'But soon we shall die, and all memory of those who have left earth, and we ourselves shall be loved for a while and forgotten. But the love will have been enough; all those impulses of love return to the love that made them. Even memory is not necessary for love. There is a land of the living and a land of the dead, and the bridge is love. The only survival, the only meaning.'"

Bryce thought for a moment before speaking. "But what about those who commit unspeakable crimes against humanity, is there no accounting for their actions when they die? Is there no judgment or punishment for Emperor Hirohito and the Rape of Nanking, or Josef Stalin who caused millions of people to starve to death, or Adolf Hitler, Pol Pot, Caligula, Kim Il-sung? Is there no judgment for a man who is solely focused on improving his lot in life at the expense of others?" Bryce cast his eyes down and reflected on all the harm and pain he had inflicted on others—

"Dear Bryce, in the history of the world there are good men and evil men. Perhaps hell is a place where there is no love."

"What about those who live in great privilege while the world is filled with people who live in squalor?"

"You know the story of John D. Rockefeller don't you? He was haunted by the Bible verse: 'It is easier for a camel to go through the eye of a needle than it is for a rich man to enter the kingdom of heaven.' He had one of the greatest personal fortunes in history—almost two percent of the economy at one point. But he embarked on a journey of atonement and endowed his foundation with a hundred million dollars 'to promote the well-being of mankind throughout the world.' This wasn't enough for his son, John Jr., who was troubled by the proverb '*to whom much has been given, much shall be required*,' because he realized he'd been given more than anybody else in the world, so he was required to give more than anyone else. The impossible burden left him isolated and discouraged, even though he'd given away over five hundred million dollars by the time he died."

Bryce thought about his painting and his former goal to make one hundred million dollars by the time he was 40, regardless of who he hurt. He had been impervious to the consequences of his actions and indifferent to the catastrophes he left in his wake. He focused on the bridge. "Do you think all rich men are condemned?"

"Not all— perhaps those whose signature sin is greed, which leads to a multitude of other bad actions and deeds. There are also many wealthy people who spend a lifetime giving back. The Tuttleman family was enormously wealthy, but they lived a life full of love, kindness, compassion, and generosity. They created many wonderful jobs for an untold number of people. Gabriel never forgot that his grandparents were immigrants who'd worked as a janitor and housekeeper. After Gabriel's death five years ago, his parents followed his path and traveled throughout the United States and the world seeking out those in need and suffering. Just six months ago, they both succumbed to a terrible virus that they contracted in Africa. At the time of their deaths, over ninety percent of their vast wealth had been given away. You see, Bryce, at the end of the day it all comes down to the human spirit, is it generous and good or greedy and evil? There are wicked people who have wealth beyond imagination, and wicked people who have nothing. And there are good people who have nothing and there are good people who have wealth beyond imagination."

Bryce's mind went into a free fall of thought, *Gabriel Tuttleman? I was just with him. How could he be dead for five years?* Bryce worried he was going insane, but he remained quiet and tuned in to what Mary was saying.

As Mary talked, he worked on another painting in his mind's eye that had eluded completion many years ago. Two questions still weighed on his mind: *Does the arc of a life follow one's deeds or a divine, intelligent plan? And is there forgiveness for those whose words, thoughts and deeds have brought great harm to other?*

Mary reached out to Bryce, grasping both of his hands. His eyes were closed, his chest felt tight, and he was adrift in a universe of his own foreboding thoughts.

SEVENTEEN

THE FIRE IN the fireplace was reduced to embers after hours of burning unattended, and the buckets scattered about Bryce's cottage were filled with rain that had accumulated in the last few days. The warm days of summer ended after Labor Day and quickly turned into a cold September. Bryce stood in the middle of his room, transfixed on the enormous canvas before him. For the past month, he'd lived in virtual isolation and only ate and drank when the pangs of hunger and thirst were too much to bear. Mary had come by to visit several times, bringing food, friendship, and silent comfort.

His belt barely held up his jeans, and his wool pull-over sweater weighed heavily on his bony shoulders, as did anguish, regret, shame and remorse. Nothing he owned fit him anymore. His hair was matted and an untrimmed beard covered his gaunt face. The only perceptible signs of vitality left in Bryce were in his eyes and in the images that emerged on his canvas. He'd studied and worked on his painting for hours, and when he could stand no longer, he sat down in a chair and picked up *Art and Artists*.

Bryce cradled the book against his chest. The words from the artists that flowed from the book provided Bryce with the inspiration to continue. For the past month, his mind and dreams drifted to his past, and the images and dialogues from that time gone by tore at the core of his soul. Trembling from the cold, and tortured from his dreams, he randomly opened his treasured book, seeking solace and comfort. The book opened to an etching by Rembrandt, simply titled "Faust". To the right of the etching there was a letter to Rembrandt's friend, Jan Six.

Beloved Jan,
At dinner last night, you suggested I make some statement for posterity, to preserve in writing what life has taught me because you believe my paintings will survive and be appreciated many years after my death. Given my plight of bankruptcy and personal despair, I cannot share your vision. If I am worthy of regard, why is it there are no more commissions for my work and I am reduced to painting pitiful self-portraits?

My life has been darkened by the deaths of a wife, a beloved son, and three children in infancy. I have had to sell everything I own to pay my debts, and my house has been auctioned. Perhaps the poverty in which I am now living is penance for the opulence of my earlier lifestyle. But what God would take a man's children and wife before him?

Although many of my paintings depict scenes from the Bible, I have no interpretation or message beyond what I put on the canvas. Are they not just stories about the plight of the human condition?

What have I learned in life you ask? Instead I give you Faust: A man so lost in his ambition, that he surrenders his moral integrity and makes a deal with the devil in order to achieve success and power. The eternal question is, is he saved by God's grace in the end or does the devil come and carry him off to hell? Life, my friend, does not provide answers, only more questions.

I wish you all happiness and the blessing of salvation. Amen.
Rembrandt
22 April 1669 Rozengracht

Bryce began to cough uncontrollably. He knew he was sick, but he didn't have the money or desire to go to the doctor. Perhaps the illness would take his shattered soul from this earth. Would he find peace? Would he find forgiveness? Did Faust, he wondered?

He thought about the infinite number of people who had died before him. He had read somewhere that since 10,000 BC over 107 billion people have been born. How could God possibly keep track of all of those people, he pondered.

Bryce was exhausted and spent. He lay down on his tattered sofa and fell into a deep sleep. His dreams slowly began to come to him, bringing his past to the present. He smelled the scent of his mother's patchouli oil, and it brought him some comfort. He saw a vision of his family on a hike in the Berkeley Hills. The sun was bright and the wildflowers had come into full bloom. They sat down on the side of the hill and looked at the beautiful view of the San Francisco Bay and the Golden Gate Bridge. Kate and Jeff were running around, picking the wildflowers. They presented their mother with a beautiful bouquet and placed a flower in the buttonhole of their father's shirt. All the while, Bryce sat off to the side of the family, lost in his own world. The scene began to fade and his eye caught the western gable of the roof of the Hearst Street house where he grew up. He saw his father struggling to keep his balance as his foot began to slip on some moss on the slate roof. In agonizing slow motion, Bryce saw him throw the tools from his hand so he could grasp a rain gutter as he began to slip. There was a sense of surrender to his fall; he stretched his arms out and looked up to the sky. The moment this was happening, Bryce saw himself basking in the glory of winning first prize in the high school debate championships in Washington, DC.

Bryce's father appeared to him in his dream, as he had many times before. His eyes were filled with love as he spoke. "Ask yourself where you are heading in life and why. Strive to elevate the ordinary to extraordinary and never lose sight of the truth that lives in the hearts of all of us." Bryce's mother and sister also appeared in the dream. Their faces were filled with love and joy. They each took his father's hand and the three of them rose together into a bright light.

Bryce awoke from his dream drenched in sweat and wondered why his mother and sister had joined his father, but not him or his brother. His ribs ached from the continuous coughing that plagued him during his sleep. He got up, went into to his kitchen, and found a banana and a roll. He ate and then drank three glasses of water to quench his thirst. Bryce went outside to get some wood so he could lay a fire to warm his chilly cottage. He brought several armfuls of wood into the house, carefully placing the logs in the fireplace so the fire would quickly take hold. He emptied the buckets of water and put them back in their original locations so the water wouldn't come close to his paintings.

Bryce turned his attention back to the painting near completion. The final touches were the most difficult; they had to bring everything together. He picked up his palette and began to paint. For days and nights, he kept adding detail upon detail until his picture mirrored the emotions churning inside of him.

When he was finished with his painting, he was more exhausted than he'd ever been. His illness had worsened; he'd slept and eaten very little. He'd never been able to fix the water heater, so he had to bathe with water heated on the stove.

He quickly dried himself and put on a pair of expensive corduroy pants and a thick cashmere turtleneck sweater, remnants from his former life. He towel dried his hair for a few minutes and then tried to comb out the mats. He looked in the mirror and studied the unrecognizable face peering back at him. Remembering the day he stepped over the homeless man who'd passed out on the sidewalk, Bryce was haunted by the words and deeds from his past. He looked closer at his reflection, and all he could see was the beggar's face looking back at him. He and the beggar were one.

Interrupted by a knock on the door, he closed his eyes and ran his hands over his face. There was another knock, and he heard the door open. "Bryce, it's Mary. Are you home?" Her voice was laced with concern.

Bryce stood frozen in his epiphany. He looked at his own reflection. *Is this what madness looks like?* He heard Mary walking around the cottage calling for him, but he could not speak or answer her.

"Bryce! You scared me!" Mary said as she poked her head into his small bathroom.

Bryce said nothing and continued staring at himself in the mirror. After a brief moment, his eyes moved to catch Mary's reflection in the mirror.

Her normally tranquil face was flush with alarm. She moved in front of Bryce and held his head in her hands and looked into his eyes. His body shook with chills and fever. "Bryce, please speak to me. Are you okay?"

She guided him into the living room. "Have a seat here," she motioned her hand in the direction of a small sofa. Bryce sat down silently. Mary went into the bedroom and came back with a blanket. She placed it on his lap.

"Bryce, it's so cold in here and it's going to rain tonight. I think we should gather your paintings, so they don't get ruined, and take them to my house. Okay?

"Thank you." Bryce said in a whisper.

"I have room for a couple in my SUV. Which ones would you like me to take?"

Bryce pointed to two paintings but said nothing.

Mary went to her car and came back with some blankets. She carefully wrapped the paintings and moved them to her SUV. Bryce sat shivering on the sofa.

"All right, my friend, ready to go?"

"Yes," Bryce said and put his book and the broken shell he'd found on the beach into a leather shoulder sack that was next to the table.

She helped Bryce to his feet and guided him to the car. Seven minutes later they turned off the road down the long gravel driveway that led to Mary's house.

"Okay, we're here," she said as she opened the car door. He grabbed his sack and followed her down a brick walkway to a massive red double door. As she put the key in the lock, Mr. Wags began to bark and run down the hall. She opened the door, and the shaggy dog skidded across the polished wood floors and bumped into Bryce, causing him to fall to the floor. "Oh my, Bryce. Are you okay?"

He smiled for the first time that day, and hugged the dog. "I'll forgive him."

Mary extended her hand and pulled him up. "I'm so sorry." She led him down a wide hallway framed by glossy white wainscoting and a high, coffered ceiling. They turned into a homey family room. Mary pointed to a sizeable sofa filled with decorative pillows. "Please sit. I'm going to pull the car into the garage and bring in the paintings."

"Thank you," Bryce replied. He sat down on the sofa, and Mr. Wags jumped up on his lap.

After Mary brought in the paintings, she asked Bryce, who was very still and lost in his thoughts, "How about if I make some hot chocolate to warm you up?"

"That would be nice," he replied as Mary worked to light a fire in a large fireplace framed by an old stone mantle. Her hair was tied back, and her tall, healthy frame was enveloped in a heavy Fisherman's sweater, jeans, and knee-high boots. She looked a lot like she did on the day he first saw her.

Sometime later, Bryce couldn't tell how long—time seemed to have little meaning to him anymore—Mary emerged from the kitchen with two steaming mugs of hot chocolate and two turkey sandwiches covered with warm gravy. She set the large tray down on the coffee table and handed him the cocoa. "Drink this," she urged Bryce, "it will warm you up." She then took the tray and set the sandwiches and silverware on a table next to the fireplace.

Bryce managed a faint smile and brought the drink to his lips, taking a few appreciative sips and feeling warmer already. For a long time, he said nothing and just stared into the fire. Mary sat next to him in comfortable silence.

She randomly picked up a CD and slipped it into the music player. The music and lyrics of the Beatles began to fill the room. She gently led Bryce to the table. Bryce could tell she wanted him to eat.

After saying grace and watching Bryce eat half of his sandwich, Mary said, "Do you want to talk?"

"After you see my painting." He nodded his head in the direction of the covered canvas in the corner of the room.

Mary looked over. She hadn't looked at the painting when she'd covered it at his cottage. John Lennon's voice sang "In My Life," filling the room with strength somehow.

The song pulsed through Bryce's body and it brought him back to another place and a time. He thought about his father's funeral, his painting, his mother and sister, Mary's loss, and a life filled with transgressions.

Mary shifted her attention and looked out a large bay window as the waves pounded the shore. Bryce wondered why she would still want to be near the sea that had taken her son and husband. He could feel both the pain and love inside her heart. He got up, went to the other side of the table, and offered Mary his hand. She accepted and he led her to the corner where his painting was. He lifted the blanket and watched Mary.

She moved closer to the painting and then further back. She clasped her hands and then brought them to her mouth. In the center of the painting was an angel. The angel was on her knees and her wings reached from the top of her head to the ground. Her head was resting on top of a stone altar, and it was nestled in one arm that was bent at the elbow. Her other arm lay over the altar holding a wreath. She was draped in a Roman gown and she was weeping. A Latin inscription, *Angelus Luctus,* adorned the altar. Scenes depicting the dark side of the human condition surrounded the angel. In the top left corner, there was a battle scene. Floating above the poor men dying in the trenches were wealthy leaders and kings fighting over how to divide a colossal chest of gold coins. In the right top corner, groups of peasants hoarded as much food as possible in their small homes, while a mother and child lay starving on the street. In the bottom right corner, a very old woman lay in a modern hospital room on life support, surrounded by doctors and nurses trying to keep death at bay. In the left bottom corner, a man dressed in fine clothes stepped over a pitiful beggar sprawled out in front of a resplendent door to a lavish home.

"Bryce, this is one of the most spectacular pieces I've ever seen." She could see that Bryce was shivering again, and she led him to the couch in front of the fire. While Mary added some logs to the fire, Bryce reached over and pulled his book, *Art and Artists,* from his shoulder sack.

Mary sat down next to him and her eyes locked on Bryce. "My dear friend, there is so much I do not know about you, but I sense that for you, your paintings are stepping stones to the truth, one brush stroke at a time. How do the subjects come to you?"

Bryce embraced his book with both of his arms and held it close to his chest. "I don't know; they just come."

"What is the name of this painting?"

"*Angel of Grief.*"

"Tell me about the vignettes surrounding the angel. The old dying lady, and the fear of death surrounding her. Why?"

"No one wants to fall into the abyss of the unknown. Her family needs proof that will not come, that there is life after death. So they prolong her life because of their fear of death."

"And this scene, the war scene?"

"Human nature: Man's inhumanity to man. A few men lord over the masses to empower and enrich themselves, more often than not, in the name of religion. If you stop and think of all the wars instigated by religion, you're forced to ask, where's God?"

"In the hearts of those who choose grace over greed."

"And what about the man who steps over another man? What is to become of him and what is to become of the man on the ground?" Bryce asked, eyeing the vignette with fear.

"God extends grace and forgiveness to flawed human beings."

It was easier for Bryce to say nothing than to respond to that, he was beyond flawed, he was broken. He started to cough, a deep, bone-rattling cough. Mary put her hand to his forehead. "Bryce, please lie down." She propped a pillow at the end of the sofa, gently guided him and covered him with a blanket. "I'm going to get some medicine. We need to get your fever and cough under control."

"Thank you," he whispered.

When she returned, Bryce had started to cough again. She gave him some cough syrup and cold medicine. He felt exhausted. When his cough subsided and his chills were gone, he fell asleep. Mary sat in a chair by his side and stared at *The Angel of Grief* until she dozed off too.

Later, when Mr. Wags began to whine and nudge Mary, she woke up with a startle and said, "Oh, sweetie, I am so sorry. You need to go out, don't you?" She looked over at Bryce, who seemed to be sleeping soundly.

When she returned from the walk, the dishes had been cleared and the fire had been stoked. Bryce was sitting up and reading his book. When she walked in, he stopped reading, marked the book's page with a red ribbon, and looked up at Mary.

"Bryce, thank you for tending to the dishes and the fire. I had to walk Mr. Wags, poor guy. Have you been awake long?"

Bryce was deep in thought. "Is anyone sure, really sure, what they're here for?"

"You mean other than walking the dog?" she jokingly asked as she patted Mr. Wags on the head. "Are you?" Mary asked. She took his hand.

"I thought I used to know."

"What about those who've loved you and those you've loved? Is love in and of itself a reason for being here?" Mary asked.

Bryce reflected. He'd been loved, but he hadn't really and truly loved anyone. "But why is there so little evidence of that? Why do humans have a history of bringing misery and destruction to others?"

"Humans have also brought great joy and created beautiful things."

"Why does love matter if in death we all wind up in a place where there are no desires, memories, or hope. A final eternity of silence and solitude."

Mary winced a little. Bryce could tell he was testing her, but she plowed ahead. "I have comfort in my heart, knowing I'll be with my son and husband again."

"How do you know?"

"Because love transcends death. A person who gives and receives love cannot be cast into oblivion."

Bryce was overcome by a profound sense of loss and loneliness. "Where does love come from then?"

"Where grace resides. Grace. It's a gift, Bryce. Accept it."

"What makes you think anyone, much less God, would offer me the gift of grace?"

"For the same reason that he offered me the gift of meeting you. There are no coincidences in life, Bryce."

EIGHTEEN

Bryce stood and looked at the canvas before him. He wasn't used to finishing a painting as quickly as this, but the brush strokes had come almost on their own. His ability to paint was inversely proportional to his deteriorating health. The sicker he was, the faster he seemed to paint. He stepped further back. This one was more abstract than the others.

A gray, ghostly figure emerged from the bottom of the painting, overshadowing a ray of light. It was as if the light, destined and determined to shine, was mired in a blizzard of images that were set in a frightening netherworld. As another grim, foggy figure continued its ascent, five brilliant little flickers of light struggled to penetrate the gray pall. At the top of the canvas, a burst of warm light encompassed an entire spectrum of colors embracing and catching a ghostly, ominous figure with the four angels. The blue ribbons on the angels' gowns were labeled Love, Faith, Hope, and Charity.

His painting seemed to have taken on a life of its own. Wanting to understand what significance it might have, Bryce thumbed through *Art and Artists*, hoping there'd be something in its pages to guide him. Although he felt as if he'd read every page in the book, every time he turned to it, he found something new. It defied logic. In lucid moments, he knew how impossible the notion was that this book would contain answers to such questions, but the book hadn't let him down yet.

He randomly stopped at a painting of a king, a merchant, a beggar, a child, and four skeletons dancing in a dark forest. A skeleton took each mortal's hand, and they formed a circle, holding hands and alternating the dead and the living. There was a Latin inscription at the bottom of the painting, *Quod fuimus, estis; quod sumus, vos eritis*. Bryce thought about the inscription's meaning—What we were, you are; what we are, you will be—and studied the faces of the subjects. The child was content and happy at play; the beggar was amazed at the circumstances; the merchant was searching for an opportunity; and the king was torn between contempt and the fear of having his mortality stripped from him.

Bryce read the letter that was next to the painting:

April 1466
Lübeck, Germany
My Dear Patron Guenther,
I hope that the frieze I have painted has not caused offense. You are a generous benefactor who has not been poisoned by your position or wealth. You are a unique man of grace and have provided love, faith, hope, and charity to so many, even as you were suffering from the burden of losing your family to the Black Death. If I have learned anything from the Hundred Year War and this pestilence, it is that death makes no distinction. I hope my work will remind people of the fragility of their lives and how vain are the glories of earthly life. As Dante wrote, if you reduce salvation to a state of well-being, then heaven is impossible. His notion of heaven was that it is a state of being in which we open ourselves entirely to love. Why is it then that we cannot have heaven on earth? Why is it that man's nature is to avoid love when, at his core, he wants to love and to be loved? Is it the fear that he will not be loved in return?

The greatest poverty of all is the absence of love. Just as food is to the body, love is nourishment for the soul. Without food the body is weak, without love the soul is weak. Love is the only meaning. Unless man is capable of love, man's life will be meaningless.

Faithfully yours,
Bernt Notke

Bryce set the book down on the table and noticed that his frail hands had a tinge of yellow to them. His chills were constant now, and for the past week he hadn't been able to stop coughing. At night he felt he was drowning in his phlegm. He wanted to light a fire, but he was too weak to get up, and his stomach ached with hunger. He remembered Mary coming by to check on him and bringing him food, but he couldn't remember when that had been. She'd been very upset when she found him painting on the porch in a thunderstorm, but he'd told her he needed time alone to finish his painting.

More than anything, now that the painting was finished, he wanted her to come see it. He called it *The Journey of the Soul*. He wondered if the feelings he had for her were signs of love. And, if it was love, he wondered if it was generated from his heart or from fear of a living a life void of love. He lay down on his sofa, looked out to the ocean, and wondered if she loved him. He covered himself in a blanket and fell into a deep sleep.

"Bryce, Bryce, are you all right?"

He felt soft hands caress his face and he slowly opened his eyes and felt blinded by the light filling the room. After a few minutes, his eyes adjusted, and he saw Mary's face overflowing with concern. He tried to speak but could not.

"Dear Bryce, my God, what's happened to you?" Mary left him and went to get a glass of water in the kitchen. She came back to the room and gently put her arm behind his back and raised him slightly. His entire body was drenched in sweat. "Here, please take a few sips of water."

After drinking, Bryce was able to speak. "Thank you." He shivered and his teeth were chattering.

"Bryce, you need to see a doctor. You're not well."

"No, please. I'm fine."

"You are not fine. I wish you'd let me see you." For weeks he'd only talked to her through the door and accepted the food she left on his porch.

As Bryce struggled to sit up, the blanket covering him fell to the floor. Mary gasped when she saw him. He was only wearing his boxers. There was no muscle or mass to his body. Mary could count his ribs and see his pelvis bone. His face was skeletal, and his eyes were hollow and rimmed in red. His hands and feet were noticeably yellow. Mary picked up the blanket off the floor and wrapped it around Bryce.

"Bryce, it is so cold in here. You need to get some clothes on, and we need to get you to a doctor now."

Bryce shook his head, no. "Please, just need to be warm and eat a little." His voice was weak and his breathing was labored.

Mary's eyes scanned him from the top of his heat to his feet. "I'll give it an hour, and if you're not better, we're going straight to the doctor. Here take these." She reached into her purse and pulled out some ibuprofen.

A faint smile crossed Bryce's face. "Okay. Thank you."

"I'll get a fire started to warm this place up, and let's get you into some warm clothes and have dinner. I made soup, fresh bread, and some chicken cacciatore."

"Smells good." Bryce watched Mary get up. She was wearing a camel turtleneck sweater, matching slacks, and a long gold necklace; her ears were adorned with big gold earrings. She turned back and gave him a concerned smile before going outside to gather some wood. A few minutes later, she brought an armful of logs in and quickly lit the fire.

"Okay let's get some warm clothes on you." She steadied Bryce to his feet and led him to his room. "Do you feel well enough for a bath? It might help to warm you up."

Bryce nodded yes.

"Okay, get into bed then, and keep warm while I fill the tub." Mary went into the bathroom to draw a bath for him and after five long minutes, she called out, "Bryce, you have no hot water. How long has it been this way?" She paused and resumed. "I could take you to my house for a bath, but if I'm going to take you anywhere, it'll be to a doctor."

She went into the kitchen and pulled out the largest four pots in the kitchen, filled them with water, and put them on the stove. After placing the chicken and soup in the oven to warm, she returned to his room and went into his small closet for fresh clothes.

"Why in the world does he have such expensive clothes?" she asked herself.

She pulled out a navy blue mock turtleneck sweater and a pair of grey slacks. All the jeans and more casual clothes were crumpled in a box and needed to be washed. At the bottom of a small chest, she found a pair of Hanro boxers that still had a seventy-four-dollar price tag on them.

After waiting for the water to boil, Mary went back to the bathroom, filled the small imperial porcelain tub with some cold water, and then went to the kitchen to fetch the water that was now boiling in the pots. She carefully brought the heavy pots to the bathroom and poured them into the tub, creating a warm bath.

Bryce got out of bed, the blanket still around his waist, and shuffled to the bathroom. Before getting into the tub, he dropped the blanket and his boxers.

Like a mother caring for her child, Mary instinctively reached for a washcloth and a bar of soap. She kneeled down on the black and white honeycomb tile floor and began to wash his arms and back. As he bent down, every vertebra in his spine became visible and his shoulder blades winged out. She gently tilted his head back and used a pot to wet his hair. She cleaned his hair and scalp with shampoo and rinsed his hair. Bryce closed his eyes and Mary continued to bathe him.

When she was done, she handed him a towel, helped him step out of the tub, and quickly dried him. She wrapped him in a blanket, sat him on his bed, brushed his hair until there were no more mats, and cut his beard close to his face. "Bryce, here are some clothes for you. I'll get dinner ready. Are you okay? Can you manage by yourself?"

Bryce nodded yes.

The fire had warmed the cottage, and Mary set the small table in the living room nearest the fire. After a few minutes, Bryce emerged from his room, dressed in the clothes Mary set out for him. Even with his sweater tucked in and a belt, his pants barely stayed above his hips. He walked very slowly toward the table, and by the time he sat down, his breathing was shallow and labored.

Mary cast a look of concern at him as she brought the food to the table. "Here start with this." She placed a steaming bowl of soup and some warm bread in front of Bryce.

Bryce took several spoons of the soup, and a small bite of bread. His hands shook, but he tried very hard to steady his hand and concentrate on getting the soup to his mouth.

He looked up at Mary, "Thank you. It's delicious."

"When was the last time you ate, my friend?" Mary asked.

"Don't know. I've been painting."

"Did you finish it?"

Bryce nodded.

"May I see it after?"

Bryce nodded again and took another spoonful of soup.

When he'd eaten half of his soup, Mary brought out a beautiful plate of chicken cacciatore and placed it in front of him. The smell of the tomatoes, oregano, and garlic enveloped the room. For the next few minutes, he picked at his food in silence.

"Is the food all right? Some spices can be a little too much when you're not feeling well. Do you want some plain chicken instead?"

"It's good, thank you. Just not hungry." He smiled warmly at her.

"Please try to eat, Bryce. It will help. I promised an hour and won't break my promise. You have to eat though, or we're going to a doctor."

Bryce knew that Mary was right, and although he had no appetite, he continued to take small bites of food to please her. Mary watched him silently. Bryce could tell she was concerned, but he just didn't have the breath for a conversation, and he felt his paintings would speak for him. He wondered what Mary would think of the painting he'd just finished.

She got up and put a few more logs on the fireplace. When she sat down again she pleaded, "Try to eat just a little more, Bryce."

"I will." Bryce took her hand. "Why've you been kind to me?"

"Why not? I'm so glad I met you that day I was walking on the beach. You know, all friendships start from a first encounter where two people stumble upon each other. Ours started right out there." She pointed to the porch and smiled.

Bryce pushed his plate forward, unable to put any more food in his mouth, so Mary cleared the plates and returned to the table. When she sat down, Bryce locked his elbow on the table and put his chin in his hand to try to steady his head. He looked intently at Mary. "What does love feel like?"

Mary shifted her gaze to the candle that was flickering on the table. "It feels like a whisper of serenity and tranquility that comes from deep in the soul, and it feels complete when another soul whispers back at you."

"Can love only exist between two people?"

"You want to know what I think?"

Bryce nodded.

"I believe there can be infinite whispers among many souls."

"What about the souls when no soul whispers back?"

"I don't believe that is possible," was Mary's quick reply. She sounded so certain.

"What becomes of a man born without a soul and never hears the whisper?" His voice died in his throat.

"Bryce, we're all born with souls."

Bryce gazed into the light of the candle, his chin resting on his closed fist. He struggled to fight the chill that was overcoming him. Distantly familiar feelings surfaced. He closed his eyes and saw himself as he was before; strong, bold, and in control. He wondered if the fever was causing him to hallucinate or if it was a dream.

He could feel a voice calling out to him. It was distant, but distinct. *What's become of you, Bryce? Where is your greatness? Why have you allowed yourself to be reduced to a frail, powerless, pitiful man? It's your destiny to be the master of your own universe! Not shackled to this powerless, pathetic, and meaningless life! This woman is deceitful. There is no love, no souls that whisper. No God, no heaven, no hell. Just here and now. Death is the end, the last heartbeat and breath, the completion of the life cycle.*

Bryce felt one with the voice and an icy wind that swept through the room. It was the same gust of wind that enveloped the room when he was born. All the candles in the room spluttered and blew in the wind as if the flames were being lifted from the wicks. Bryce slumped in his chair.

"Are you all right?" Mary got up to rush to Bryce's side, and was hit by a turbulent squall that was so forceful she lost her balance and fell to the floor.

He slowly raised himself bracing his arms on the table. A look of shock washed across his hollow eyes, as Mary struggled to reach him. He got up and walked toward her. As he passed the window, he caught his reflection. His hands touched his face to make sure the image he was seeing was his. He cried out, "Who is this pathetic, weak, pitiful man?" Spasms of shaking and coughing caused him to nearly fall.

Mary fought the wind, got up and wrapped her arms around him and held him tight. "Close your eyes, take a deep breath." She rocked Bryce in her arms. As the tension in Bryce's body began to subside, so did the mysterious wind. "You're all right, my dear friend. You are loved." Mary helped him lie down on the couch. "Close your eyes and rest." She wrapped him in a blanket and tucked a pillow under his head.

He felt the whisper of her love, and the serenity in his heart gave way to welcome rest.

Mary sat on the floor in front of the sofa and held his hand. His breathing was shallow but steady. As he slept, she spied his treasured book on the side table. By the flickering glow of the fire, the book looked even more primeval and extraordinary, like a relic from another place and time. In the corner was a painting shrouded in a sheet, but rather than approach it, she knelt down beside Bryce, tucked her head on the side of the couch, and fell asleep.

A few hours later, the rain that began as a light shower intensified into a major hailstorm, waking Mary. She immediately pulled the buckets from the front of the house and placed them in their usual spots. Water rings dotted the floor like placeholders. The volley of hail against the cottage didn't wake Bryce. She sat down next to him and looked at how tranquil his face was. She held her hand to his forehead. His fever had subsided, as had his cough. He awoke with a start. There was a brief smile on his lips, an evanescent flush of contentment.

"What are you thinking?" Mary asked.

"Amid the chaos of good and evil, sometimes you get the best light from a burning bridge."

"What do you mean?" Mary asked as she threw a few logs on the warm embers in the fireplace.

"At the end of dinner last night, I felt a pull. It is —hard to articulate. It felt familiar, yet distant. It was disturbing . . ."

"What was it?"

"A distant and compelling voice beseeching me to be true to myself and return to how I once was. But the voice was weakened by a whisper of love and I drifted into a deep sleep. I had a dream where I floated into my body and saw trillions of cells. In every single cell, I could see thousands of chemical reactions going on every instant, endless chemical reactions. It was turbulence and chaos. And with all of this happening, I could see that the cells lived because in the midst of the turbulence and chaos there was order and there was purpose." Bryce paused to see how Mary would respond. "I could see it!"

"How does this dream relate to you?" Mary asked grasping both of his hands and looking into his eyes.

"I think deep down inside we are all conscious that order is continuously fighting chaos. And although our life is filled with trials and tribulations, we instinctually know that without inner conflict we cannot achieve peace within or with others."

"And this came to you in a dream?"

"Yes."

"Are you at peace?"

Bryce said nothing. He thought about his dream and realized that it was the first dream in his life that was reassuring. He thought about his paintings and realized that, after so many years, he'd been able to finish them. He thought about Mary, and for the first time in his life his soul had been able to answer the whisper from another soul. He thought about his life and he was at peace, he had finally emancipated himself from the shackles of this powerless, pathetic and meaningless life. He looked at Mary and finally answered, "My soul has learned to whisper. Thank you."

Bryce sat up on the sofa and reached for his book. He held it tight to his chest and drifted back to sleep.

As she'd done earlier that night, Mary wrapped him in a blanket. She went to the other sofa and fell asleep.

The first thing Mary noticed when she woke up was that the hail had stopped and the storm clouds had blown out. A ray of light burst through the morning fog and shimmered on the calm ocean. She had slept well after the hailstorm, and the fire had kept the room comfortable. She glanced across the coffee table and was pleased to see that Bryce was still sleeping with his book in his arms. It looked like a piece of notepaper had found its way into the book at some point after the hailstorm, but she couldn't be sure. Relieved that his terrible cough had quieted down, she got up very quietly, washed her face, and made some tea. She went outside to gather some wood to put on the fire and very gingerly placed a few logs in the fireplace. When she turned back to the room, she cast an eye at Bryce and felt intuitively that something was wrong. She looked down at him and he looked more peaceful than she'd ever seen him. His book was still pressed against his chest, and he was very still. She put her hand to his cheek and it was cold; she then reached for his hand. It too was cold.

"Bryce? Can you hear me, friend?" She knew the answer to her question, but she asked again.

She lay down next to him and held him with all her might and began to weep. When she finally had cried until there were no more tears, she whispered to his soul, and she felt his soul whisper back one last time.

PART III

The most important decisions in life force us to decide what to hold onto and what to let go.

NINETEEN

A BLACK LINCOLN Town Car sedan pulled onto Gin Lane and turned at *The Love Shack*. The early November morning was crisp, and the barren trees hinted that winter was right around the corner. The car continued down the winding gravel driveway. At the end, a man in a crisp blue-striped dress shirt and grey corduroys got out of the car and rang the doorbell. He could hear the barking of the dog, followed by footsteps.

"Quiet Mr. Wags, shush." Mary opened the door. Her hair was pulled back into a ponytail, silver hoop earnings hung from her ears, she was wearing an oversize thick knit sweater, jeans and a pair of ballet flats.

"Hello, Mason, thank you for coming." She motioned for him to follow her down an open gallery-size hallway to the kitchen. In the corner of the kitchen was a breakfast nook with a cozy fireplace and a stunning view of the ocean through the two-story window. "Please sit; I made some oatmeal and tea for you."

Mason draped his heavy camel overcoat on the back of the chair, placed his briefcase on the floor, and sat down. He wore rounded, horned-rimmed glasses and his wavy brown hair was combed back off his forehead. "This is lovely, thank you, Mary."

"You're welcome. So what have you been able to find out?" Mary asked her estate attorney.

Mason took a deep breath. "Well, I started in Berkeley, California, as you suggested. Bryce's father died when he was in high school, and he had a mother, sister, and a brother. Almost two months ago, his sister, Kate, and his mother, Elizabeth, were killed in a plane crash in South America. His sister was a doctor; she was on a medial mission, and her mother had joined her. We were able to get in touch with his younger brother, Jeff, who said he was estranged from his brother and wanted nothing from the estate. He signed a release and said he never wanted to hear his brother's name again. Bryce was divorced and had no children, so the note he left saying all he had is yours is valid. There are no heirs."

Mary thought about that note she'd found in his book. "He must have known he was dying. But when . . . ?" She didn't finish her sentence. The answer was forever out of her reach. "What else did you find out?"

"That's it, Mary. I focused on determining if he had any living heirs. I'd be happy to delve into other aspects of his life, if you wish."

Mary took a sip of tea and looked out the window. "No, that's not necessary for now."

"So, how exactly did you meet this man?"

Mary looked out at the ocean and smiled a little. "I met him while Mr. Wags and I were walking on the beach. Something pulled me to him, a lost soul with a beautiful gift. Come, I want to show you his paintings." Mary led Mason to a large room filled by five paintings leaning against the walls and propped up by the furniture.

Mason walked around the room, examining each painting. "Mary, these are extraordinary! Technically spectacular. Where did he study?"

"He told me he had no formal training, that his subjects just came to him."

"Have you shown these to anyone?"

Mary shook her head.

"As you know, Preston is an international art dealer, and one of the most respected art experts and historians in the world. I think he should see these. He's back from London and; we're staying at a friend's house in Bridgehampton tonight. We are having dinner at Bobby Van's; why don't you join us?" Preston was Mason's partner of twenty years.

"I can't sell them. Not now."

"No, no, no. Of course not, Mary. I just think Preston would enjoy seeing these. They're stunning."

"I'm not really in the mood to go out. How about if I cook dinner and you both come here tonight? Nothing fancy."

"Okay. I know he'll be excited when I tell him about these paintings. So Mary, aside from these paintings, do you know what else is in Bryce's estate? I couldn't find any savings or brokerage accounts."

"He had very little money, and I got the impression the little he had he kept at home. I have no idea who the home belongs to."

"That's easy enough to check out. Umm, Mary, there's another thing. His body is still unclaimed at the coroner, and they've finished the autopsy. He died of complications from pneumonia. The coroner said a dose of antibiotics might've cured him."

Mary put her face in her hands and began to cry. "It's my fault. I knew he'd been sick for a while, but he refused to see a doctor—said he didn't have the money or the time." Mary's face and body convulsed with sorrow. "And of course he wouldn't let me pay for anything. My God, he was only thirty-nine years old."

Mason hugged her. "Mary there's no one kinder than you in this world. I am so sorry this happened so soon after Art and Peter."

"It's okay. It was meant to be that our paths should cross. I know you probably don't believe in anything like that, but I do. And after Bryce, I'm just certain of it."

"I think there's no one I'd rather cross paths with if I were ever alone in the world. Mary, you are one of the strongest people I know. And I'm not the only person who thinks that."

Mary smiled at him as she brought her handkerchief to her eyes.

After Mary calmed down, Mason gently moved forward onto other matters. "What should we do about claiming the body at the coroner's?"

"Have him cremated. I'll keep him here with me until I sort things out."

"Do you want me to take care of the arrangements?"

Mary nodded

"Now, do you have a few minutes to go over some of your personal affairs? Your financial advisor called me a couple days ago and wanted us to meet to discuss your current situation."

"Do we need to right now? My head is not really in a place to discuss finances."

"Well, I think all we need is a quick overview of things to think about."

"Okay; let's go to the study."

Mary led him to a beautiful paneled study with a picturesque view of the garden. Above the mantel of the fireplace was a picture of Mary, Art, Peter, and Mr. Wags sitting on the beach in jeans and white shirts. Their faces glowed with love and happiness. Mason looked away and took a deep breath, as if the reminder was too much to bear.

Mary confided in him, "This morning it occurred to me that Bryce died exactly one year to the day after Peter and Art."

A look of sorrow spread across Mason's face. "Oh, Mary."

"He strengthened my sense of purpose and destiny. It was not a coincidence. There's comfort in that—a little anyway." Mary motioned for him to sit on a small couch across from her. "How about over here?"

He sat and pulled some papers from his briefcase. "Maybe we should go over this other stuff later."

"No, please. I'm okay."

Mason gave a questioning look.

"Really, dear friend, the revelation has given me peace."

Mason adjusted his glasses and leaned in toward Mary. "Art's partner, Ted, was very generous in buying out Art's share in the firm, but from a cash-flow perspective, this means you need to make adjustments. Over the past five years or so, Art's portion of the business was bringing in an average twenty million dollars a year. Of that, you and Art donated about fifteen million to charities, leaving about three to four million after taxes each year. After the issues with the estate taxes, your estate is now worth substantially less than before. The primary concern right now is that you're still subsidizing the twenty medical clinics you built around the country…to the tune of over three million dollars a year. If you continue, you'll eventually run out of money."

Mary took in what he had to say and looked up at the family picture. "You know, Mason, Art and I were very lucky to have had the success we had. Some people are funny about financial success. Once they attain it, they often forget where they came from. They no longer see or hear those that have less than they do, and when they do, they bask in their sense of superiority. They choose to live in a privileged, cloistered isolated existence of sameness. The truth is many people are just as smart and hard working as they are, and in many cases the dividing line between those that achieve financial success and those that do not is luck. Art and I always believed that we needed to share our luck, and just because he has passed does not mean that I need to change. What's the worst that could happen? I have to sell this house? Somehow, I will survive. Thank you for your concern. I know that you understand what I am saying, because I know that along with being a very smart attorney, you're also a generous and grateful man. That's why we picked you to handle our estate."

"I understand, Mary. Just think about what I've said." Mr. Wags came up and rubbed his nose against Mason, and he bent down and petted him. "Okay then, we'll see you tonight."

Mary brought a tray of after-dinner drinks into the great room. The house's floodlights lit up the sea, revealing a breathtaking view from the large picture window. Preston and Mason were standing in front of Bryce's *Angel of Grief* painting. Preston's arms were folded and his face was ablaze in wonderment.

Mary set the tray down on a large leather ottoman in the center of three couches that faced the fireplace, which was large enough for a man to walk into. "Please come and sit by the fire."

Preston and Mason walked over to join Mary. Preston was a tall, elegant man, who looked a good ten years younger than his sixty years of age. He had been with Mason for twenty years. His dark brown hair had tinges of grey at the temples, and his sharp chiseled face was softened with gentle green eyes. He wore a handsome dress shirt with gold cufflinks and jeans.

"What can I offer you?" Mary asked.

"Cognac please," Mason replied.

"Some port would be great for me, thank you," Preston said.

Mary poured the drinks for them and a glass of port for herself. "So what do you think?"

"Amazed, astonished, speechless. Mary, aside from the great masters, I have never seen works like these in my life. I don't understand; Mason told me he had no formal training. Is that true?"

"That's what Bryce told me."

"Can you review the titles again?" Preston asked.

Mary stood and walked to the paintings scattered throughout the room.

"This one is *The Drowning of Noah*, and this is *The Art of Redemption*; this is *The Judgment Bridge*; this is *The Angel of Grief*, and this is *The Journey of the Soul*."

"How long had he been painting? What do you know about him?" Preston asked.

"Not much. I met him while I was walking on the beach. He never really talked much about his past, and I didn't pry. When I first touched him, it was so odd, I sensed electrifying and confusing signals. Incomprehensible really—as if he was caught in a vortex shifting between redemption and doom. You know me, after sensing his predicament, I couldn't abandon him."

Preston nodded his agreement. "God bless you, Mary, you truly are one of the most altruistic souls I know." Preston focused back on the paintings. "The titles of the paintings and their subject matter certainly reflect a tormented soul. Mary, would you consider letting me take them to my galleries in London and New York? Unless I am very misguided, these are extraordinary pieces of art I feel almost compelled to share at the very least with my colleagues. I understand and respect very much that you don't want to sell them."

"I guess that would be okay. It would be selfish not to share them, I suppose."

"Splendid. Listen this has been a wonderful evening, but if you'll forgive me I'm exhausted. The older I get the more the trips to and from London get to me," Preston said.

Preston and Mason got up and each of them gave Mary a warm hug and left.

Two little girls in bright red coats narrowly missed bumping into Mary as they enthusiastically pointed out the Christmas decorations in the store windows. Mary smiled and continued to walk down the city street. The smell of roasting chestnuts and the sounds of the holiday season always made her happy. When she reached her destination, she knocked and then peered through a tall, modern, glass door at Preston's gallery in Chelsea. She could see a woman facing one of Bryce's paintings and Preston's welcoming gaze when he saw her. He quickly came to the door and unlocked it. "Please, please come in. She's here!"

Mary entered the door and gave Preston a long heartfelt embrace and said, "Dear, dear friend." She was wearing a beautiful, simple, black Armani dress and pearls. The clothes in her Upper West Side apartment tended to be dressier than her clothes at the beach.

"She's looking forward to meeting you. It's the first time she's seen his paintings completed. Very emotional."

The woman turned and Mary thought she looked more like a ballerina than a world-renowned art scholar. She was wearing a black sweater dress, black leggings, and boots. Her hair was pulled straight back into a French twist, and her face was framed by thick silver hoop earrings. Mary quickly approached the woman, and like long lost friends, the two women embraced each other.

Preston broke the silence. "I know you have a lot to discuss, and I have an appointment. I'll leave you two." He gave each woman a quick embrace and left his gallery.

Mary and Becca said nothing. Mary took Becca's hand and they walked around the gallery and viewed each painting.

Finally Mary spoke. "How fortunate that Preston brought us together."

"Yes, we are lucky, aren't we?" Becca replied.

Becca had approached Preston after she'd gone to his gallery to see Bryce's paintings. When she realized that the man she'd known as Calvin Boston was the artist, she'd asked Preston more questions than he could answer. Preston was sure Mary would want to know more about Bryce and his past and thought Becca's questions might be answered if the two women could meet.

"Let's have a seat," Mary suggested, pointing to a small sofa. "Please tell me about how you came to work with Bryce."

Becca gave Mary the background on how Bryce, who'd called himself Calvin Boston, approached her. "He was always an enigma. He never talked about himself, and I had no idea he basically led two lives. I only agreed to tutor him because he was so talented and focused, but occasionally I saw a side of unbridled arrogance that really troubled me. How'd you meet him?"

"When I first saw him, he was on the beach, crying in front of his cottage." Mary continued to share the details about their time together and how painting seemed to both torture and calm him.

"When I was working with him," Becca offered, "Calvin seemed terribly conflicted when he painted, and he was unable to complete any of his paintings except *The Drowning of Noah*. To see the paintings completed gives me such joy. But where, I wonder, is the painting of the woman by the sea? I didn't see it in the collection. It was a masterpiece that was virtually complete last time I saw it, except for the woman's face."

"I never saw it," Mary replied with a perplexed look.

"Hmm, that's odd. It was so important to him. And it was a very large painting."

"Strange," Mary replied. "His cottage was so small, but I will go back and look."

Becca took both of Mary's hands. "The paintings are just spectacular. I'm at a loss for words. Your decision to auction them is right. The world needs to see these paintings, and your idea on how to use the proceeds is beautiful." Becca paused and looked at the floor. "May I ask you, did he find peace?"

Tears welled in Mary's eyes. "Yes."

"Did you come across a book, *Art and Artists*?" Becca asked.

"Bryce died with the book in his hands."

"It served its purpose, then, and helped Calvin find his way out of the prison his soul seemed trapped in."

"I'm confident it did. Look at these majestic paintings. He was never without the book. With a very heavy heart, I took the book from his hands right before the coroner came. Other than pulling out the letter that left these paintings to me, I haven't brought myself to open it. I don't know if I can."

Becca told Mary the story of how the Keeper of the Royal Academy in London had given her the book and what he'd told her. "Mary, it's your turn, you must find a new provisional owner. I'm certain you'll find the right soul. You have the whole world to search for that person as you set up the foundation. However, the Keeper said it's imperative that, until you find a new owner, you mustn't talk about or show the book to anyone. It's a very special book."

Mary understood, and the two women embraced each other for a long while before departing.

TWENTY

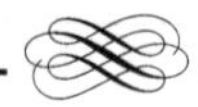

"Mary, are you alright?" Preston asked.

Mary shook her head side-to-side. She was sitting on the couch at her home in the Hamptons. The news broadcast played on the television.

"This is Emily Margaret reporting from Sotheby's Auction House in London," the young, confident woman introduced herself. "The international art world is buzzing with the auction that is to take place for an artist who was unheard of until this past December, just about four months ago.

"Art experts around the word are estimating that the paintings could sell in the range of six to ten million dollars per painting, and many theories abound as to who actually owns the paintings and what will become of the proceeds. Later, we will have Buffi Delahaye report to us from Elliott's hometown of Berkeley, California. From London, this is Emily Margaret, signing off for now."

Mary folded her face in her hands, "What have we done, Preston? What have I done? My God, this is not the Bryce I knew. I never would have wanted his memory to be tarnished by this media circus."

Preston came over and wrapped his arm around Mary's shoulders. "Mary, what we have done is right. Remember, all the proceeds of this auction are going to charity. Think about your plans for these funds and the good it will do for so many lives. They are estimating the sales will exceed fifty million dollars! Fifty million dollars will help so many people."

"Maybe."

"Tell us more about the foundation you are starting," Mason pressed. He had to try to get Mary's attention away from the tawdry details about Bryce's life that continued to dominate the broadcast.

Mary took one last glance at the television and faced Preston and Mason. "We're going to build artist colonies around the world for people trapped in poverty and oppressive situations. The hope is that art will bring voices to those who have none, and it will provide a platform for them to express themselves and for the world to hear their plights. We want to foster the talents of people who have an artistic gift, and help to commercialize their art. So at the end of the day, the art will nourish both their souls and bodies. It will help people to help themselves. The only lasting kind of help there is."

Mason reached for her hand. "Such a beautiful concept and a meaningful tribute to Bryce. Have you decided where to start?"

"I'm searching for the right spot in Appalachia for the first colony in the United States, and our first overseas location will be in Bagan, Myanmar."

"Why?" Preston asked.

"If you think about it, the greatest poverty in the United States is in Appalachia. They have such little hope for a future beyond the grip of poverty for generations to come . . . such a cruel irony that their coalmines supply comfort for so many, when they have no comfort. Everyone has a story to tell; art is the perfect medium… and this will provide some hope for these people, and awareness to others about their plight."

"And Myanmar?" Mason asked.

"Do you remember when Art and I went to Bagan with our friend, Professor Yukio Nishimura of the University of Tokyo, a couple years ago?"

"Yes, Preston and I met him in London. He's very involved with UNESCO mission right? He brought a lot of attention to save all those temples and pagodas that dated to the tenth century, no?"

"He did. It was one of the most spectacular places we'd ever seen. On our first night, we climbed to the top of an ancient temple and watched the sun set over twenty-eight hundred temples and pagodas in a magnificent valley." A broad smile crossed Mary's face. "After we came down, beautiful children greeted us, selling postcards. The first question they asked was my name. I replied, and these lovely children then pointed to me and said in broken English, '*Mary you.*' Then they circled their hands around their faces, and said *'remember'* and then pointed to their hearts and said *'me'*. I still have a hundred postcards to remember each and every one of them!

"The ancient architecture left an indelible mark on us, so did the people. They are beautiful people who have a quiet peace about them despite their poverty and living under the thumb of an extremely brutal military regime. You know the pair of six foot vases in my entry hall?" Mary asked.

"How could I forget them, they're exquisite." Mason replied.

"I bet you didn't know they're lacquer, and the vases were handmade from bamboo. They came from a little shop in Bagan where the family has been making lacquer for generations."

Mason shook his head. "I had no idea."

"And the large piece of art over the fireplace in our apartment—we also brought that back from Bagan," Mary said, referring to a piece of inlaid teak and gold leaf.

"I've always loved that piece; it's so distinctive and has a Zen-like quality to it."

"Anyway, I chose Bagan because it has a concentration of very talented artists and people who have generous and kind spirits despite their terrible predicament. I think that's the perfect combination of elements for an artist colony to thrive."

"Brilliant idea, Mary. Please know Mason and I want to help in any way we can."

"Thank you," Mary replied and turned her attention back to the television.

"From Berkeley, California, this is Buffi Delahaye, reporting," the beautiful and fit young Natalie Wood look-alike began. "The stories and intrigue that keep popping up around Bryce Elliott seem endless."

The reporter's attention shifted to a truck pulling into a driveway. "Oh, just a minute. Here comes Jeff Elliott, Bryce's brother. Perhaps he can give us some insight into this mysterious artist's childhood. Jeff, Jeff, can we please speak with you?" The reporter rushed toward Jeff with the microphone.

Jeff stepped out of his Xerox repair truck and glared at the reporter. "Look, I told you guys I have no comment. Please leave my family in peace." He turned, shut, and locked the door to his truck. As he headed up to his modest old Berkeley bungalow, the reporter ran after him. "Please, Mr. Elliott. You're his only surviving relative. Can you please give us some insight into his childhood?"

Jeff whirled around and faced the reporter. He was still in his uniform that had his name "Jeff" stitched over the pocket of his shirt. He had his mother's soft, blue-green eyes and golden, wavy hair. "What do you want?" he asked in a raised voice.

"Please just a few words. The world is trying to gain some insight into this mysterious man and his art."

Jeff shoved his hands in pockets and looked at the ground. His eyes began to tear and then he looked straight at the camera. "He grew up in the most loving environment in the world. My parents were educated, altruistic, and nurturing. We lived in a commune and shared everything. My father was a gifted poet and an associate professor at Berkeley. My mother was spiritual, benevolent, and a beautiful woman inside and out, and she never gave up on Bryce. She tried everything to resurrect his morally broken soul: music, art and, unconditional love. Nothing worked. All the son-of-a-bitch wanted was to make one hundred million dollars by his fortieth birthday. Nothing else mattered. We hadn't heard from him since my uncle's funeral. My poor mother's only connection with him was in her dreams." Jeff began to cry, and folded his face into his hands. He did not want to share the ending of his family story that he still had not processed in his own mind.

Jeff wiped his tears away. "I have just one more thing to say, and I hope that people will listen. There's a lesson here that possessions, careers and carefully landscaped properties do not bring happiness. It's something that comes from within. The most content person is not the one who has the most, but the one who is happy with what they have. There is poverty, and then there is poverty of the spirit. My brother lived in abject poverty for many years." Jeff turned his back and walked away from the camera and toward the sanctuary of his home.

The reporter seemed to shudder at Jeff's concluding remark. "Thank you, Mr. Elliott." She regained her professional composure and continued.

"The live auction for the paintings will take place in three weeks. Please remember that our network plans to carry the coverage live from London. This is Buffi Delahaye reporting from Berkeley, California."

Mary tossed and turned all night. The stories about Bryce kept replaying in her mind, haunting her—as did the painting that Becca had mentioned. She'd kept meaning to go to the cottage and look for the painting, but how could she return to the place where Bryce had died? She'd been trying her best to go because she knew that was what she had to do. But she felt she just didn't have the emotional strength. She'd even stopped passing by the cottage on her walks—going in other directions instead. Mr. Wags still wasn't used to the new routes and perhaps never would be.

After a fitful night's sleep, she got up at dawn, had a cup of coffee, slipped into a long black cotton dress, and hung her favorite silver dolphin pendant around her neck. Mr. Wags was uncharacteristically anxious and she decided to take him for a walk. In her sleepy state, she failed to securely anchor the leash and Mr. Wags went charging down the beach. In a panic, Mary ran after him. When she finally caught up to him, she saw that he'd stopped at the tideline in front of Bryce's cottage in the exact spot where she was first noticed Bryce.

A sudden windstorm swirled around her, but unlike the gust that has encircled her the night of Bryce's death, it was comforting and warm. An intense light from the horizon momentarily blinded her before unfolding into a vision of a birth.

A mother stilled herself as a sudden, strange gust of wind passed through a windowless maternity room. The wind enveloped the entire room, like a whirling mass of energy that seemed to draw everything toward the lifeless baby.

"Where in the hell did that come from?" someone asked.

"Kamikaze – the wind is divine!" The mother murmured.

Mary could see the wind was not divine. It was dark, a spirit of greed pushing aside a white light of grace that was supposed to embody the mother's precious baby. The dark spirit encircled the lifeless child.

Suddenly there was a faint cry of new life. Doctors and nurses watched in amazement as the baby's blue color slowly transformed into a healthy pink. The baby's cries grew stronger. The doctor's eyes filled with amazement, and he carried the squirming baby boy to the mother, whispering, *"Your gift from God."*

The vision faded and Mary was bewildered by what she had seen. She sat in the sand, and looked out to the sea as the tide rose and fell around her. Broken shells—an unusually high number of them—were scattered all around her, and she wondered if some unusual current had brought them all on shore. She gathered the skirt of her long dress and headed back to the house, determined to find the missing painting. She surveyed the small space for places the painting might have been stashed. She looked under the small rattan sofas and checked the small shed outside the kitchen door. There was nothing.

She then moved into the bedroom, which was barely large enough to accommodate the double bed and two side tables. She opened the small closet, took out Bryce's clothes, and placed them on the bed, thinking that the clothes might hide the painting. She found nothing except comfort and sadness in the scent of Bryce that came from his clothes.

As she was about to leave the room, she glanced at the bed and had a thought. She got down on her hands and knees, peered under the bed, and saw a canvas. Her heart pounding, she slowly and carefully pulled the canvas out. It was difficult; the room was so small she had to move a side table and push the bed against the wall to make more space. After several careful twists and turns, she was able to free the painting and leaned it against the bed.

Breathlessly, she surveyed the work and thought for a moment she might be dreaming. The painting was a perfect image of her standing barefoot in her black dress, facing the sea, wearing her silver dolphin pendant.

Her body convulsed with a chill that ran from her head to her toes. Transfixed, she continued to stare at the oil. In the painting, her long, wavy, light -brown hair blew across part of her face and although she appeared to be the focus at first glance, there was no part of the canvas that was empty and meaningless.

Like a score of music, the painting elicited a range of emotions. On the shore the water gently ebbed back to the sea while in the distance great waves with hues of blues, green and white foam came violently racing towards the shoreline. One of her hands was placed on the crown of a young boy's head. Although his face was clouded in darkness, her hand seemed to channel the rays of light from the sun directly to the boy. The boy looked towards the woman, and he offered her a broken shell in the raised palm of his hand.

Mary was stunned. It was the painting that Becca had mentioned. The one he'd nearly completed before he'd met her! He had started the painting long, before his life changed and he'd lost all of his possessions and fortune.

All at once, it came to her, a sudden intuitive leap of understanding. The past and the present converged. She recalled the first time she touched him and felt a tortured soul torn between salvation and doom. It all made sense now. The spirit of greed wasn't meant to be, and all the events in his life, including her encounter with him, helped shepherd his soul back to the spirit of grace.

Tears welled in her eyes. Bryce had been the little boy wedged in darkness and tortured by the spirit of greed – the demon that brings no peace, happiness, love. Hers had been the hand that helped him to the light. In the end, painting by painting, grace slowly vanquished the unbridled greed, emancipating Bryce from a life he wasn't meant to live.

TWENTY-ONE

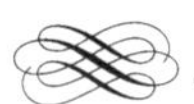

Mary, Preston, and Mason were huddled together around a corner table at the historic Dukes Hotel in the heart of St. James. The bar was small and intimate and unusually quiet.

"Mary, you've come all this way, you must go to the auction tomorrow." Preston said.

As Preston spoke, Mason thought Mary looked stunning in her grey tweed jacket and grey slacks and was thinking about how to convince her to go. "Mary this is a historical event, and you're one of the key players; you need to be there."

Mary took a sip from her drink. "Preston is the frontman for the auction, and no one knows I exist. I want to keep it that way."

"You can easily remain anonymous," Preston said.

"I'm not sure that's possible. I'm afraid my emotions might betray me and I won't be able to keep them in check, especially after deciding not to keep *Epiphany*. I'll be fine watching the broadcast from my room."

Mason reached for her hand, "I understand, no more pressure from us. Subject closed."

Mary had wavered back and forth for several days about keeping the painting, but in the end, she decided that, just as she had done with her husband's and son's ashes, she had to let go. The painting was not hers to keep.

Preston raised his Martini glass, "Here's to Mary, the most kind and benevolent soul we know, and here's to a successful auction tomorrow."

"Here, here!" Mason chimed in and raised his glass to Mary.

"This is Emily Margaret reporting to you, on this day, April 22, from the heart of London's Mayfair district." The tall, thin woman had her blond hair pulled back in a ponytail and was dressed in a simple navy blue dress. She was sitting behind a beautiful antique desk in an elegant room with two older men sitting on each side of her. "We are at Sotheby's auction house, and in just a moment, we will be covering the auction live. As if this story could not get any stranger, just two nights ago another painting, titled *Epiphany*, was added to the lot. So now six paintings will be offered.

"This morning we've invited the renowned religious scholar Huston Smith and the legendary art historian and critic Leo Steinberg to share their thoughts and interpretations of the paintings. Author of more than fifteen books, Huston Smith is one of the preeminent religious studies scholars in the world. His book *The World's Religions* has sold over three million copies and remains a popular introduction to comparative religion. Smith was born in China to Methodist missionaries. As a young man, he turned from traditional Methodist Christianity to mysticism. He is arguably the most important figure in the study of religion over the past five decades. He has been a friend of the Dalai Lama for more than forty years, and he has met and talked with many of the great figures of our century. Prior to his retirement, he was a professor of Religion and Philosophy at MIT and Syracuse University."

The young reporter turned to her left and acknowledged the man sitting next to her. "Few scholars in the field of art history have matched Leo Steinberg's breadth of knowledge. He is one of the most brilliant, influential, and controversial art historians of the last fifty years. He has the ability to tackle the most complex Old Masters and Modern artists alike—from Leonardo, Michelangelo, and Caravaggio to Pablo Picasso, Robert Rauschenberg, and Jasper Johns—always bringing exhilarating discoveries to the table.

"His scrutiny and eye for details have established him as one of the foremost authorities of some of history's most prized paintings and prints, dating back nearly half a millennia. He was born in Moscow eighty years ago and has lived in Berlin and London. After World War II he immigrated to New York. He has taught at the University of Pennsylvania, Harvard, Princeton, Stanford, Berkeley, and the University of Texas, Austin, and is the recipient of numerous awards and honors. Thank you for joining us this morning, gentlemen."

"Thank you," the men replied almost in unison.

"Let me pose the same question to each of you. The interest in this unknown artist is almost unprecedented. Why do you think that is?"

Leo Steinberg was a tall and elegant man. His thinning grey hair was combed straight back, a pointed beard framed his face, and his soft blue eyes were rimmed with oversized glasses. He held an unlit cigarette in his hand and spoke with a soft Russian accent.

"I believe that in art, our deepest human values are at stake, and the extraordinary power of Mr. Elliott's paintings takes us on a journey to those values at a very a raw level. His paintings are both symmetrical and chaotic, just as our own journey in life. On top of that, his technique is on par with the great masters. His paintings are exquisite, elegant, disturbing, and thought-provoking—like nothing I have seen before."

"Thank you, Mr. Steinberg. Mr. Smith, please share your thoughts with us."

Houston Smith was nattily dressed in a tweed sports coat and tie. He was a kind looking man with a neatly trimmed beard and balding hairline.

"Just look at the titles and subject matters of his paintings. Do they not mirror moral struggles and conflicts common to all of us? All the world's religions teach us that our lives here on earth are about transcendence, and that we must learn to exist above and apart from the material world, but in reality, and in the history of the world, how many people are actually able to do this? I would submit very few. Human nature and the soul have always been conflicted. From what I can glean, this man actually found redemption and peace, painting by painting. So perhaps from a religious perspective, people are drawn to his paintings because it gives them hope. If someone like Mr. Elliott can find redemption, perhaps so can they."

"Thank you, gentlemen." The reporter's voice dropped, and there were a series of announcements in the background. "It appears that the auction is about to begin." The camera panned across the large, elegant hall. It was filled with hundreds of people. Men and women, serving as buyers' representatives, were on telephones and computers. Two men dressed in white shirts, grey ties, and black aprons appeared on the stage and unveiled the first painting with their white-gloved hands.

Bill and Liane Holt were huddled in a back corner of the room, conferring with a bidder representing them. "Just to confirm, you understand that we're only interested in the *The Art of Redemption*, and that you're not to bid on any other painting," Bill instructed his proxy.

"Yes, sir, I understand."

"And you understand the maximum amount we would like to pay for the painting?" Bill inquired.

"Yes, sir. If there is nothing else, sir, I should make my way to my seat as the bidding is about to begin."

"Thank you."

Bill and Liane watched the man hurry away into the crowd. Liane turned to her husband and said, "Sweetheart, it's going to work out." She lovingly placed her hand on the side of his face.

The situation with Bryce had taken a terrible toll on Bill. His vengeful retaliation, which he'd rationalized in the name of justice, haunted him, and for months he'd sought redemption for framing Bryce. He spent hours in soup kitchens and homeless shelters, and he gave his time and money to the Madison Square Boys and Girls Club. None of it had helped though—his regret ran too deep. His tall and erect posture, now stooped with shame. And despair pumped through his body with every beat of his heart.

Liane hugged her husband and whispered in his ear. "Everything will be all right. It is time. You must forgive yourself. You have to let the past go and have faith that what happened, happened for a reason."

An elegant man in his late forties stepped on stage dressed in a dapper, conservative suit and walked up to the podium. He spoke in a crisp British accent. "Ladies and gentlemen, on behalf of Sotheby's, I would like to welcome you this morning. We are delighted to have an auction that is historical in so many ways. So without further ado, we will begin. Up first is Lot 1, *The Drowning of Noah*. It is illustrated and described in your catalogs."

The camera turned back to the reporter and her guests seated in the far end of the large room. She turned and adjusted the microphone that was clipped at the top of her dress. "I would like to begin with Mr. Steinberg. From an artistic standpoint, what do you see in this painting?"

Leo Steinberg looked awkwardly into the camera. "Well, Emily, both the theme and technique are reminiscent of the Baroque period, where one finds paintings characterized by great drama, rich, deep color, and intense light and dark shadows. Like the artists of this period, Mr. Elliott chose the most dramatic point, the moment when the action was occurring, to evoke emotion and passion instead of calm rationality."

"And what would be some examples of artists from the Baroque period?" she asked.

"Rembrandt, Rubens, and Vermeer were the most well known."

"Thank you, Mr. Steinberg. Mr. Smith, would you like to weigh in on the religious themes?"

"Yes, of course. First of all, the scene of an angelic little boy taunting a panic-stricken, drowning little boy with a rope is a juxtaposition of good and evil. Why would the boy holding the rope look so angelic? It is a brilliant representation of the idea that the line between good and evil can be as thin as a piece of silk thread. Hidden in the scenery we see angel wings capped in a halo, which symbolizes the fallen angel."

"Thank you." The camera panned back up to the podium.

"We will start the bidding at two million dollars. Thank you, I have two million dollars." The auctioneer pointed to a man on the left. "Thank you sir. We now have two and a half million." He pointed to a member of the British royal family in the middle of the room. "Now going for three million."

A man at the phone banks on the left side raised his hand. "On the phone we now have three and a half million. Four and a half million to the lady in the red dress. On the phone we now have five million. To the gentleman on the right, we have six million."

The man on the phone raised his hand, again. "We now have eight million." The auctioneer looked around the room. "Fair warning at eight million dollars." He glanced one more time around the room and paused for a moment, then hit his gavel. "Sold for eight million dollars to The Getty Foundation."

The attendants appeared back on the stage and removed the painting. Two other men carefully placed the next painting on the easel.

The auctioneer returned to the stage. "Lot 2, *The Judgment Bridge*, is illustrated and described in your catalogs. I will give you a few minutes before we start the bidding."

The camera turned back to the reporter and her guests. "Let's begin with Mr. Smith this time. What do you see in this painting?"

The scholar fidgeted with his glasses and looked back at the reporter. "This is an interesting presentation of the Seven Deadly Sins, sins that are identified in just about every religion known to man. But more interesting is the introduction of The Judgment Bridge, which is a widespread parable in many ancient religions, including Islam, Zoroastrianism, and Buddhism. It is a bridge that separates the world of the living from the world of the dead. All souls must cross the bridge upon death. If a person has been wicked, the bridge would appear narrow and a demon would emerge and drag the soul into a place of eternal punishment and suffering, similar to the concept of hell. However, if a person's good thoughts, words, and deeds in life are many, the bridge would be wide enough to cross, and a spirit representing revelation would appear and lead the soul into heaven."

"Thank you. Mr. Smith. Mr. Steinberg?"

"This is a magnificent and provocative painting. The level of detail in the subjects and their surroundings is extraordinary. As with many of the great artists over time, from the Renaissance period to the Modern Age, the theme focuses on the didactic warning about the perils of life's temptations. However, Mr. Elliott has taken a unique approach by incorporating a diversity of religious beliefs."

The auctioneer tapped into the microphone. "Okay, ladies and gentlemen, we are ready to begin. We will start at two million dollars. Thank you, I have two million dollars. On the phone we now have three million dollars."

The auctioneer pointed to a man with a turban in the front of the room. "Thank you, sir, we now have four million." He pointed to a woman in the back of the room. "Now going for five and a half million."

A man at the phone banks raised his hand. "On the phone we now have seven million." The bidding continued at an even pace until it finally slowed. The auctioneer looked around the sea of bidders, and hit the gavel. "Sold for fourteen million dollars to an anonymous buyer." Following the second sale, the room began to fill with chatter.

The painting was removed and the next one to be auctioned was brought out.

"Up next is Lot 6, *Epiphany*. It is not illustrated in your catalogs as it was added after printing. I hope you have all had time to attend the showing." To avoid losing the momentum of the last bidding session, the auctioneer jumped straight into the bidding, which didn't afford the reporter any time to interview the experts.

"We will start at five million dollars." There were some looks of surprise around the room, and it appeared that few had anticipated the painting to begin at such a high level. "We have five million. We have seven million. We have seven and a half million on the phone. We have nine million from the gentleman on the left. We have ten million on the phone." He pointed to an Indian woman in the back of the room. "Now going for eleven million." A young man with a poker face and two phones to his ears raised his hand. "On the phone we now have twelve million. We have twelve and a half million. On the phone we are up to thirteen million." He pointed back to the Indian woman. "We have fourteen million. On the phone we have fourteen and a half. We have fifteen million. We have fifteen and a half from the man on the left. On the phone we have sixteen million," he nodded to the young man that had a phone in each ear. The auctioneer looked around the room. "Fair warning at sixteen million." He slammed the gavel down. "Sold for sixteen million dollars to the Solomon R. Guggenheim Museum."

The energy in the room began to pick up, and the collective murmur of whispers filled the room. The camera panned back to the reporter.

"Let's use this brief break to get interpretations of the next painting, *The Angel of Grief.* Mr. Steinberg?"

"This painting fascinates me on two fronts. The Angel of Grief, which is the heart of the painting, is modeled after a 1894 sculpture by William Story. He'd made it as a gravestone for his beloved wife after she died. Like Mr. Elliott, Mr. Story went to Harvard Law School, and he graduated in 1840. Like Mr. Elliott, he left the practice of law to become an artist. Coincidentally, I understand a similar headstone marks Mr. Elliott's parents' grave. The technique in this painting is exquisite, and the emotions are strong and dramatic. The strokes come with a sequence and coherence like words in a story. Here is an example of an artist painting as another man writes. This is the only painting where the artist has included an adult self-portrait. If you look carefully at the left bottom corner, there is a man dressed in fine clothes arrogantly stepping over a beggar sprawled out in front of the resplendent door to what is presumably the man's home. The face of both the man and the beggar is clearly Mr. Elliott's. Incidentally, if you look carefully at the side of the stone altar there is a poem by William Story.

'But the gray and the cold are haunted
By a beauty akin to pain, –
By a sense of a something wanted,
That never will come again.'"

Four attendants appeared on stage to remove *The Judgment Bridge* and replace it with the *The Angel of Grief.*

"Thank you, Mr. Steinberg." The camera panned back up to the podium.

The auctioneer appeared back up on the stage. "Lot 3, *The Angel of Grief.* We will start at eight million dollars. Thank you, I have eight." The auctioneer, pointed to a Middle Eastern man on the left. "Thank you, sir, we now have twelve and a half million." He pointed to a woman, wearing a beret, in the middle of the room. "Now going for thirteen million." A man at the phone banks raised his hand. "On the phone we now have fifteen million. Sixteen million from the woman in the beret. On the phone, we now have sixteen and a half. To the gentleman wearing the hat on the right, we have seventeen million." A man at the phone banks on the left side raised his hand, again. "On the phone we have eighteen million." The auctioneer looked around the room. "Fair warning at eighteen million dollars." He glanced one more time around the room and paused for a moment, then hit his gavel. "Sold for eighteen million dollars to an anonymous buyer."

"Wow that is an astonishing increase of ten million dollars since the first painting was auctioned," the reporter exclaimed. "You can feel the energy and anticipation in the room."

The camera panned across the room and captured the emotions of the audience, which ranged from disbelief to wonderment. The camera moved back to the reporter and her two experts.

"Mr. Steinberg, what is your take? The initial estimates were that the paintings would sell in the range of six to ten million dollars per painting."

"It validates that this man had an extraordinary talent, and that there is a very limited number of his works."

"And what are your thoughts on the next painting?" the reporter asked the art expert, as four men returned to the staged to put up *The Journey of the Soul*. In the background, the auctioneer could be seen conferring with several colleagues.

"From a technical standpoint this abstract painting is a dramatic shift from the classical technique employed in his other paintings. It demonstrates the brilliant range of his talent. The symbolic figures, iconography, and complex imagery are genius. There is little doubt that the artist intended for the beholder to experience the unmitigated horror and rapture of the soul's journey."

"Thank you." The reporter turned to Mr. Smith. "What religious symbolism do you see in this painting?"

The scholar rubbed his chin and glanced down at a picture of the painting on the table in front of him. "My goodness, where does one begin with this painting? It has been suggested that this is a representation of the artist's life, a period when he shut out all that is good and kind in this world. An ominous gray figure ascends, but look at the five brilliant little flickers of light that struggle to penetrate the gray pall of the shadowy figure. These five flickers of light, in my opinion, symbolize people in his life who tried to help him find grace and redemption. At the top of the canvas there is a burst of warm light, symbolizing redemption before death."

The auctioneer stepped up to the stage. "If we may begin, ladies and gentlemen, Lot 4, *The Journey of the Soul*, is illustrated and described in your catalogs. We will start the bidding at eight million dollars. Thank you, I have eight million dollars. On the phone, we now have eight and a half million dollars." The auctioneer pointed to a proper-looking English gentleman in the front of the room. "Thank you sir, we now have ten million." He pointed to a young woman in the back of the room. "Now going for twelve million." A man at the phone bank raised his hand. "On the phone we have thirteen million." The bidding continued at a frenzied pace until it finally tapered off. The auctioneer looked around the sea of bidders, and hit the gavel. "Sold for twenty million dollars to the Qatar Museum Authority."

The reporter looked back at the art expert with a perplexed expression on her face.

"As I said before, the exceptionally high prices commanded by a formerly unknown artist validate that this man had an extraordinary talent, and that there will only ever be this number of paintings."

The Journey of the Soul was replaced with *The Art of Redemption*. The audience turned its attention to the massive painting that depicted a tormented man falling from dark, sinister clouds filled with demons into the arms of the archangel Gabriel. Encircling the man were angels representing the four graces of Love, Faith, Hope, and Charity.

"Mr. Smith, it looks like we have a few moments before the final painting is auctioned. Can you please share your thoughts with us?" the reporter asked.

"This is an intriguing painting, indeed. The notion of a person or soul falling, in most literature and religious parables, is universally associated with the concept that the person has 'fallen' to a dark side. Hence, the common expression that *one has fallen from grace*. In this painting, a man falls *to* grace. We know Mr. Elliott painted this before he painted *The Journey of the Soul*. Given this sequence, it is fascinating that he felt he had to fall from grace before he could rise to it. In *The Art of Redemption*, the angels representing the four graces of Love, Faith, Hope, and Charity are at the bottom of the picture, whereas in the *The Journey of the Soul*, they are at the top."

"Very interesting, thank you, Mr. Smith."

The auctioneer appeared back up on the stage. "Lot 5, *The Art of Redemption*. For our final item, we will start the bidding at ten million dollars. Thank you I have ten million dollars." The auctioneer pointed to a man on the right. "Thank you, sir, we now have twelve million." He pointed to the Indian woman in the back of the room. "Now going for thirteen million." A man at the phone banks on the left side raised his hand. "On the phone we have fifteen million. Seventeen million to the gentleman in the front. On the phone, we now have twenty million. To the gentleman with the bow tie on the right, we have twenty-two million." The room went silent and people began to look around the room. A middle-aged fashionably dressed man sitting in the front, on the left side, raised his hand, again. "To the man on the left we now have twenty-four million." The auctioneer looked around the room. "Fair warning at twenty-four million dollars." He glanced one more time around the room and paused for a moment, then hit his gavel. "Sold for twenty-four million dollars to the William Holt Foundation."

Mary sat on the couch in her suite at the Dukes Hotel and watched the end of the auction. She tried to process the stunning success of the auction and its implication. She tallied the numbers four times in her head to make sure that the total was correct. And it was. The paintings had sold for one hundred million dollars—on what would have been Bryce's fortieth birthday.

Epilogue

Mary held the old book, *Art and Artists*, in her hands. Despite many attempts in the past, she had been unable to open the book. And now, two weeks after the auction, the book seemed to open by itself. Perhaps it was a warm spring wind that opened the book, or maybe it was something else, but when she glanced down at the book, she was perplexed to see a copy of Bryce's *The Art of Redemption* painting on one page and a note on the other. Both pages were securely bound in the old book, as if they had been in place for a long time.

On May 15th, my life changed. I changed and the world around me changed. The birth of all things, both good and evil, begins with the common element of change. I have often wondered if the evolution of man's life and mankind, both significant and small, are shaped by man's deeds or a divine, intelligent plan?

As I sit on the precipice of my own life, I look to the horizon of existence for the answer. Was it will or fate that changed my life that day?

Bryce Elliott

Beneath Bryce's passage was a note that was difficult to make out. It seemed to be written in an ancient script. After a careful examination, Mary was able to decipher the message.

But now I know fate is the sum of all the choices we make in our lives. The end will be where the beginning is.

Made in the USA
San Bernardino, CA
17 January 2018